The Girl
with
Emerald Eyes

Also by Debbie Rix:

Daughters of the Silk Road

The Girl
with
Emerald Eyes

DEBBIE RIX

Bookouture

Published by Bookouture
An imprint of StoryFire Ltd.
23 Sussex Road, Ickenham, UB10 8PN
United Kingdom

www.bookouture.com

ISBN: 978-1-909490-83-3
eBook ISBN: 978-1-909490-82-6

In loving memory of my father Norman Rix DFC, FRIBA
an architect, artist, writer and war hero

Thanks:

To Professor Piero Pierotti for so generously sharing
his knowledge about the Tower and medieval Pisa.

Claire Bord
Charlotte Campbell Edwards
Joe Edwards
Victoria Hislop
Rowan Lawton
Vanessa Nicolson
Margaret Rix
Caroline Taylor

My husband Tony
for his constant support; without him
this story would simply never have been written.

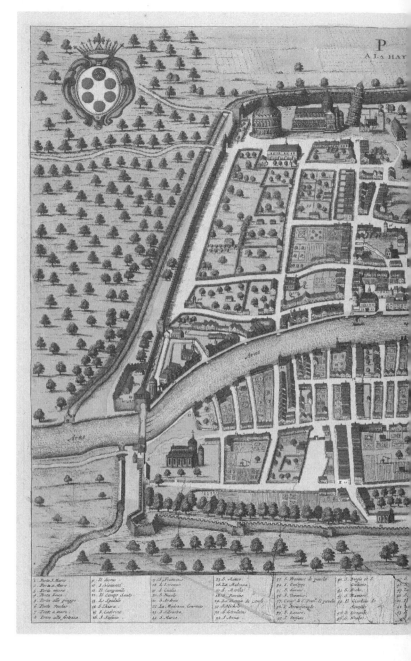

P
A LA HAY

A
ALBENS

I.BLAEU Excludit

12. S. Rocho.
13. S.ta Croce.
14. S. Giovanni euangelista.
15. S. Biria.
16. S.ta Croce.
17. S. Marco.
18. La fortezza.
19. T.Magazino.

67. L.Angelo Rafaelle.
68. S. Giovanni Comento.
69. S. Bernardo Convento.
70. S. Martino.
71. S. Lorenzo.
72. S. Zigulera.
73. S. Bastiano.
74. Il Cerviero.

71. S. Domenico.
72. S. Gilio.
73. S. Bastiano.
74. S.ta Christina.
75. La loggia de' mercanti.
76. La Riviera Grande.
77. La Madalena.
78. S. Cosmo e Damiano.

78. S. Giovanni Spesnato.
80. S. Antonio.
81. S. Lussano.
82. S. Calsiano.
83. S. Benedetto Monte.
84. S.ta Valentina.
85. S. Paulo aragodeno.
86. S. Donino.

87. Il Coppo.
88. Il Baluardo.
89. La Terra.
90. Il Arsenale.
91. Capo Carollo.
92. Bene Grande il Bastione.
93. Strada di Calves.

94. Portale.
95. Pont 8 fa la polvere.
96. S. Barr sopra.
97. La Riviera Compagna.

PROLOGUE

It seemed to the man that he was floating. His hands, he noticed, caught the sunlight, and the almost imperceptible webs between his widely spread fingers glowed bright red shot through by the sun, revealing the complex pattern of veins moving blood around his body. Keeping him alive. The blood pumped harder now, pressing into his skull, restricting the brain until it hurt. Then nothing. A thud. And the birds, free-wheeling high in the sky, looked down on the body spread-eagled and lifeless in the shadow of the tower.

CHAPTER 1

May 1999
Kent

It had been a wonderful spring. The sun shone brightly each day, and the rain fell gently overnight, leaving the lawns vivid green, sparkling in the early morning sun, and the flower beds, freshly washed, bursting with new growth. Each morning, sunlight glinted on the pools of water collecting in the newly unfurled leaves of the alchemilla that lined the path to the front door.

Sam woke early; which was odd, because usually she clung to sleep until the last minute. Most days she was woken by the sensation of a little body climbing into the bed with her. It was a ritual.

'Come on Mummy – I want my brepuss.' The boy could not yet pronounce hard sounds like 'k's' and 't's.'

'In a minute,' she would say, hardly opening her mouth, her eyes still closed, hoping every morning, that he might take pity on her adult longing for sleep and go off to play somewhere quietly by himself. A vain wish. Freddie was not that kind of child.

'Open your eyes, Mummy.'

His hands, clammy, would prod her eyelids. Not painfully, but persistently.

'Now.'

At other times the twins, her darling girls, would arrive with a stereophonic burst of energy, coiling themselves around her like tiny blonde angels, filling the air with chatter and the sweet smell of those newly emerged from babyhood.

But this morning she woke alone.

Early morning light filtered through the closed curtains. She peered at the clock on the bedside table. 6.40 am. She hauled herself out of bed, anxious suddenly for a sight of her children. She padded along the corridor and quietly opened the girls' door. They lay in uncanny symmetry; each one facing the other in almost identical positions, with one arm draped languidly across the bed, the other tucked into their bodies, thumb firmly ensconced in their rose-bud mouths. Blonde curls trailed over matching pillows decorated with pink and purple angels and stars. Their sleigh beds stood on either side of the window that looked out over the garden. Newly, and proudly, acquired as their first 'proper beds.'

Automatically, she bent and scooped up the cast-off clothes that lay on the floor and, closing the girls' door quietly behind her, pushed the grubby tights and T-shirts into the laundry basket that stood on the landing between the children's two rooms.

Quietly, she opened Freddie's door. Toys and clothes were strewn around the floor and the bed. He had been difficult to get off to sleep the night before and she had fallen into her own bed exhausted, without her usual evening sort out. Guiltily, she surveyed the mess. Surrounded by a halo of toy trains and cars with coloured dinosaurs wedged improbably into the driver's seat, the child's angelic face lay upturned, the dark lashes fluttering, mid-dream. His perfect scarlet lips slightly apart. Out of habit, she leant over him, listening for the little wheezing breaths, something she had felt compelled to do since the day she brought him home from hospital. She felt guilty sometimes that she never listened so intently for the girls' breathing. There was something about her first-born child that seemed so vulnerable.

She pulled back from kissing him, grateful for his breathing and intent suddenly on a silent retreat to bed for an unaccustomed listen to the radio.

Desperate now for a cup of tea, she decided to risk the noise of a visit to the kitchen and crept, as silently as possible, downstairs. The kitchen was warm from the Aga and, once the kettle was on, she leant against its comforting girth. The room, painted a pale shade of green that she and Michael had first seen in the restaurant of the Musée D'Orsay in Paris, had a large table in the centre, strewn with the paraphernalia of the previous day's biscuit making – one of the children's favourite activities. Bowls stood unwashed, smeared with butter and raisins. Cookie cutters in all manner of shapes and sizes lay abandoned, squished into the endlessly reshaped dough, that she had finally persuaded the twins was no longer edible. Freddy's dinosaur cutter was making a particularly alarming nose-dive into the leftovers of chocolate mixture. The finished biscuits stood, half-eaten, on a rack to one side. A pang of guilt overwhelmed her as she recalled their unhealthy supper. Biscuits and juice were not really a well-balanced meal, even if they were home-made. She tipped the leftover biscuits into a tin, scooped the remains of the dough into the bin, piled the cutters and spoons into the bowls and put them into the large stone sink, sloshing hot water onto them. The pipes rattled noisily, as the elderly plumbing grumbled its way back to life. Anxious not to wake the children, she hurriedly turned the water off, just as the kettle on the Aga began its early morning salutation – a thin, wheezy whistle that penetrated the silence. Shoving the kettle off the heat, she took a mug off the dresser. Turning the lights off, she retreated once more upstairs, tea in hand, the house still uncharacteristically silent.

Settled once more in her bed, she turned on the radio to hear the familiar tones of James Naughtie. His voice took her back, as it always did, to a time when she was young, before the children, before Michael. She had been a reporter on the Today programme, newly promoted from researcher. She had been in awe of Naughtie and his ilk – the grand old men of radio, as she thought of them then. Bashing stories out on their keyboards at four in the morning, shouting across the newsroom at producers and editors. Demanding, clever. She'd rather liked him.

As she sipped her tea, she listened to a piece on the radio about pollution and environmental damage. It was the kind of story she would have been sent to cover in the old days. Standing in a freezing field at dawn, waiting for a cue in her earpiece from the London producer. The interviewee was a man with a wonderful Norfolk burr who was warning of the absence of birdsong that spring. Naughtie spun the interview out brilliantly: interested, gently chiding, filling the space until he could throw, gratefully, to the weathergirl.

As she described the perfect late spring weather they could all look forward to that day, Sam crawled to the end of her bed and opened the curtains. The sky was a beautiful opalescent shade of palest blue and pink. She could see the sun winking at her through the woods that ran the length of their garden. She looked down onto the newly created flower bed. The early morning light cast sharp shadows and the plants made crisp, clean shapes, their zingy green growth emerging from the freshly dug soil. She and Michael had planned the bed together – he had even helped dig some of the plants in, which had surprised her. His customary attitude to any gardening had always been that it was a nice hobby for her, but not something he needed to bother with. She thought back to that weekend, just a fortnight before. 'Come on,' he'd said suddenly, on Saturday morning, when the children were fractious and squabbling. 'Let's all go outside and put some of those plants Mummy's been collecting at the back door… before they die.' He'd headed off, leaving Sam to find the children's wellies, toy spades and garden implements; to tussle with gloves and little sticky fingers. It had taken her a good half-hour to get them all assembled, by which time Michael had already planted half a dozen new plants, mostly in the wrong place. But she had kept her counsel for once and had surreptitiously moved them to the correct positions when he went in for a coffee.

The sound of little feet padding along the corridor brought an end to her quiet adult thoughts.

'Mummy,' the voice was indignant.

'I was 'sleep and dreaming… 'bout a dragon.'

'Were you darling, how nice.' She was preoccupied.

'Wasn't nice, was nasty.'

'Oh that's lovely, darling.'

'Mummy!' The child shouted, jolting her into alertness.

There was a ringing sound. The phone. Odd, so early in the day.

The child wailed.

She picked up.

'Hello?' her voice uncertain, questioning.

'Mrs Campbell?'

There was an accent. Rather pretty. French, Spanish, Italian.

Michael was in Italy.

'Yes…? Yes, I am Mrs Campbell. What is it?'

The child, her child, began to cry. His ruby lips giving voice to his indignation. His eyes, intelligent, dark, the colour of chestnuts, observed his mother's sharp green eyes. He saw the frown. He knew. It was not going to be a good day.

The phone call was peremptory, brief, curt even.

'It's Michael.'

'Yes?'

At the mention of his name, she felt herself stiffen, tense.

'I'm afraid something's happened.'

'What?'

'He's been taken ill – we're not quite sure what's wrong, but you ought to come out straight away. I'm so sorry...'

Eight hours later, she sat in the business-class lounge at Gatwick. She felt numb, tears etching their way silently down her pale cheeks. She flicked through an album of photos she had grabbed from the kitchen dresser before she left. There were pictures of the children playing in the garden the previous summer: on the slide, pushing each other on the swing, playing in the paddling pool. There was a picture of her, the sun in her hair, as she raised a glass of wine to the anonymous photographer. She was smiling in that picture, wearing her favourite linen dress. Happy. And there were two pictures of Michael. In one he was attempting to slither down the slide, face first, his large frame threatening to overwhelm the flimsy metal chute, as the children lay on the ground helpless with laughter. The final image in the album showed the two of them: Michael's arm around her shoulders, his head resting on top of hers, his lips grazing her hair.

Only the evening before, she had toyed with taking those pictures out of the album; of consigning them to the bin. With the children finally in bed, she had abandoned the messy kitchen and instead retreated to the sitting room where she opened a bottle of wine and brooded on his betrayal. She thought back to their final conversation, before he left for Italy.

'Who is she, Michael?' she had asked, holding up the little photo of the young dark-haired girl that she had found in his jacket pocket earlier that day. 'Who is this girl?'

'Just a friend,' he answered irritably, 'no one important. Stop making such a fuss. Where are my sunglasses?'

'Fuss! I know she's more than a friend, Michael. When did you start carrying pictures of friends around with you? Don't insult my intelligence.'

He had refused to acknowledge the problem – then. He had carried on searching for glasses and notebooks, filling his suitcase ahead of his trip.

Finally, the wall of recalcitrant silence broke, as she knew it would if she pushed hard enough.

'OK… you want to know who she is? Her name is Carrie. She's an assistant producer. I like her. She has an… interesting line in conversation.'

'Conversation!' she spat back. 'Is that what they call it now?'

The conversation comment had stung. The idea of him enjoying another woman's company, her mind, upset her more than the thought of him sleeping with her.

'Am I so dull now, Michael? Is that what you're saying?'

'No, no of course not. Oh God, I don't know. You're just different that's all.'

'Different?'

'From when we first got together.'

'Of course I'm different… I've got three children. I'm here all day making cakes and worrying about taking your bloody jackets to the dry-cleaners and clearing up after people. It's quite hard to maintain an interest in the latest developments in reality television when the only television you actually watch is *Postman Pat*.'

He smiled a little, impressed by her sarcasm. She was always good under fire. She saw the flicker of amusement at the corners of his mouth and she hated him for it. It was as if he was laughing at her. Patronising. She threw the picture of Carrie at him. It floated down onto the bedcover between them. He picked it up and laid it on his bedside table. There was a hooting of a horn; his taxi. He held her to him briefly before he left, murmuring into her hair, 'I'm sorry. We'll talk when I get back. I've got to go.' And he had left, without a backwards look.

Later, she took some small heart from the fact that he had left the picture of Carrie where he'd placed it. She tore it into tiny pieces.

And now, here she was, in the departure lounge, waiting for a plane to take her to him. Her mind a blur of confused emotions and thoughts. Her fingers traced the picture of her and Michael smiling for the camera, as if by doing so she could absorb, and sense again, the happiness she had experienced that sunny day, eight months before. That woman in the linen dress, holding a glass of wine, had thought she was happy. She certainly looked happy. And now...? Had it all been an illusion? Had Carrie been in his life then? Had he been thinking of her small, wiry body as his lips grazed Sam's brown hair? She closed the album and put it into her bag, as they called her flight.

Shuffling forward in the queue, she noted her fellow passengers, mostly tourists getting away for an early summer break, alongside a few Italian businessmen returning to their families on a Friday night. Judging by the number of Gucci briefcases and in-flight suit bags amongst the men in the queue, this was a regular weekly commute for them. As the queue crawled towards the check-in desk, she tripped over a pair of elegant, tanned feet encased in navy suede loafers.

'I'm so sorry,' she blurted out. 'I didn't see you sitting there.'

'*Mi dispiace*, it's my fault,' said the man, rising to his feet. He was tall, around six feet, with dark blue eyes that almost matched his denim shirt. His skin was lightly tanned, his black hair sprinkled with grey.

He smiled sympathetically at her, noticing the pale tear-stained face.

'Are you ok?' he asked.

'Yes, yes of course; I'm sorry.'

She wiped her face self-consciously and attempted a smile, before rejoining the queue.

The flight was without incident. Sam gratefully gulped down a large gin and tonic but she couldn't eat the meal. It lay, unopened and congealing until she asked for it be removed.

On arrival in Pisa she waited near the carousel for her suitcase. The man with the blue loafers stood a few metres away, chatting animatedly on his mobile phone, apparently unaware of her presence. Within minutes, her battered metal case, a remnant of her reporting days, clattered through the rubber doors and fell almost at her feet. Hauling it up, she swung her bag onto her shoulder, and, pulling her case behind her, strode past the customs officers who stood with their backs to the arrivals hall, their attention diverted by a beautiful Italian girl wearing tight white jeans and tiny crop top, her long, dark curls drifting luxuriously down her back.

Smells of pizza and rosemary assailed Sam as she pushed through the gaggle of expectant locals waiting to greet their loved ones. She experienced an almost visceral shot of pain as she witnessed the loving embrace of one young couple newly reunited.

There had been a time when she and Michael met each other at the airport; when one of them had travelled abroad for work. He as a producer of documentaries, she in her role as a news reporter – first for radio and then television. Both often had to be away for weeks at a time, but she always had a sneaking suspicion that he coped much better with her absences than she did. In the days before email he rarely rang when he was away, only occasionally sending a formal telex informing her when he would be returning to Heathrow. As she drove down the M4 towards the airport from the first flat they shared in west London, her heart began to race. She would park the car and take the lift to the arrivals hall, struggling to contain her excitement. She would then pace the floor waiting anxiously for signs that his flight had landed. If he did not appear within five or ten minutes she began to fret. And then he would be there... in jeans and an old sweater, his jacket thrown casually over his shoulders, as he pushed his trolley, tall, handsome, at ease with himself. It was more than she could do to stop herself ducking under the flimsy barrier, rushing into his arms.

It has been a long time since she'd done that. He took a taxi now... it was simpler for both of them, now that they lived so far away. And the children of course, made it difficult. She thought back to Michael's cursory brush of the lips as he had left her this last time for Italy.

At the taxi rank, she was joined by the man in the blue shirt.

'Hello again,' he said kindly. 'Are you feeling better?'

'Yes, yes... I, I've just had a bit of a shock that's all.'

'Oh I'm so sorry,' he said, '... I don't mean to intrude.'

'No, it's fine; it's nice of you. I've had some bad news... About my husband.'

'Oh dear,' he said gently.

'He's been taken ill... here in Italy. He's in hospital.'

'Oh, I'm very sorry; what is the matter?'

'He's had a stroke,' she said flatly.

At that moment, two taxis rolled up and he gestured politely that she should take the first one.

'I do hope your husband gets better soon,' he said and handed her suitcase to the driver, who put it into the boot. 'Where are you going?'

'The Campo Hotel, I think,' she replied.

He gave the address to the driver, before opening the cab door for her.

'Thank you; I'm very grateful,' she mumbled, climbing in.

As he closed the door gently behind her, he pushed his card through the open window. 'If you need anything, anything at all, please do call me. My number is there.'

Their cabs travelled almost in tandem as they left the airport, ploughing through the outskirts of Pisa, past the low apartment buildings and immigrant grocers that encircled the town. They kept pace with one another through several sets of traffic lights, but as they approached the river that snaked its way through the centre of the city, his cab turned right as hers turned left. Looking out of the back window of the taxi, she watched his car as it sped along the busy road, until it was swallowed up in the line of traffic bordering the Arno.

CHAPTER 2

May 1999
Pisa

At her pensione, Sam had been met by a slight, blonde girl, named Mima, who turned out to be Michael's Italian researcher. She was young and spoke reasonable English and, as Sam quickly worked out, was willing to help but anxious to retreat to her happy carefree life. She explained that the hospital was just a short walk across the Piazza and she would meet Sam there once she had unpacked.

The hotel that she had arranged for Sam was a slightly down-at-heel little pensione, right next to the Tower. In contrast to its splendid surroundings, the little hotel had definitely seen better days. The lobby was dark, in spite, or perhaps because of the grimy conservatory that jutted out onto the pavement at the front of the building. Conservatory was a generous term to describe this faded, plastic structure. Elderly cane chairs and sofas were pushed against the walls in an anti-social row, their flowery cushions beaten into submission by the myriads of tourists who had collapsed on them over the years. The lobby itself contained just two small leatherette chairs, between which stood a small, dusty coffee table – its chipped veneer disguised by magazines. Even to the most casual observer, these indicated a clientele drawn from all corners of Europe: *Stern* for the German tourists, *Paris Match* for the French, and an elderly copy of *Hello* in Spanish. The walls were lined, predictably, with images of famous Pisan landmarks – the Tower of course, the Baptistery, the Piazza dei Cavalieri. Early evening sunlight filtered through the dirty windows, reflecting off the haze of dust that hovered in the atmosphere. Sam signed the visitor's book and handed over her passport to the middle-aged man behind the desk. His dark hair conspired to be both oily and wavy, Sam observed; not an attractive look. But he smiled kindly at her, and once he had spirited her passport into the safe, he picked up her suitcase and led her upstairs.

Her room was at the front of the hotel. The long windows looked out onto a tiny street that led to the Campo dei Miracoli. Once she had managed to undo the window catch, which was stiff with lack of use, she was able to lean out and take in the full magnificence of the Piazza. Perfectly positioned in the centre of the frame was the spectacular Duomo, its cupola silhouetted against the setting sun. This remarkable structure had been visible almost continuously on the short drive from the airport; it hovered above the red roofs of the city, a vast, shimmering semi-globe dominating the landscape much as it had done for a thousand years. To find herself living within three hundred metres of it seemed extraordinary. Behind it, she knew, stood the Baptistery, hidden from view by the large cathedral. Looking to the left, the little street on which the pensione stood was unremarkable; tall houses, four or five storeys high, divided into flats, she thought; the odd shop; the awnings of a number of restaurants – their tables and chairs laid out invitingly in the late evening sunshine. Directly below the pensione were three market stalls selling a classic array of Italian market goods: handbags, tourist memorabilia and umbrellas. Noting the darkening turquoise sky spreading with the coral glow of sunset, it seemed impossible to imagine the residents of Pisa would ever need an umbrella.

Sam opened her suitcase and hurriedly hung up the few items she had thrown in before she left England – two pairs of jeans, three T-shirts and some underwear. She wore a third pair of trousers with a leather jacket and ankle boots – her only shoes. Her feet were already rather hot. She would, she realised, have to buy something a little cooler.

She had no computer with her but she noted the internet cable. She would bring Michael's hefty laptop back with her from his hospital room, and plug it in; then at least she could email her mother about the children.

She put her washbag into the tiny bathroom, taking in her reflection in the mirror above the basin. At thirty-six, her face was just developing fine lines across the brow and around her sharp green eyes. 'Don't frown,' Michael used to tell her, 'you'll get lines.' She tried to remember whether Carrie had had any lines. She was certainly younger than Sam. But all she could remember of her rival's appearance was the shiny dark hair. Sam pushed her own pale brown hair behind her ears and splashed her face with water and brushed her teeth.

Moving back to the bedroom, she plugged in her phone charger and attached it to her now dead phone. The battery sparked into life and the message function flashed. Two answerphone messages and four texts awaited her; one from Miracle productions hoping she had arrived safely, and three from her mother. She read them, filled with anxiety that something had happened to the children in her brief absence. But there was no bad news. Just little snippets of information. 'Freddie fine now.' 'The girls are perfect.' 'Can they have cake for pudding?' She texted back hurriedly. 'So glad all well. Yes, cake is fine. Anything. Thank you.'

She emptied her bag of the heavier items she had thrown in at the last minute, including the small photo album. She lay that on the desk. At the bottom of her bag she found a business card. Dario Visalberghi, the man at the airport. She slipped it into the frame of a mirror that hung above the desk.

The hospital of Santa Chiara, where Michael lay, was a short walk away across the Piazza.

He smiled when she burst into his room. A tragic, lopsided sort of smile, but a smile nevertheless. His bed was surrounded by medical staff. *Il Professore* and several of his underlings were discussing her husband's case, gabbling loudly between themselves, apparently paying her husband no heed. It had the feel of an Italian market: busy, bustling, cheerful, argumentative. Mima announced Sam's arrival over the hubbub and led her to the Professor. He took her hand in his and held it for a few moments; his touch was cool, kind. He looked deeply into her eyes and began to explain, in Italian, what was wrong with her husband.

Mima looked on, alarmed, and assumed the role of interpreter.

'He has had a stroke… They are unsure how serious it is… He will need further tests. We will leave you with him now. If you have any questions just ask.'

The group smiled sympathetically and left, taking their noise with them. The researcher retreated too, embarrassed. Sam and Michael were alone.

She sat down, perching awkwardly on the edge of his bed. Automatically, she took hold of his hand and squeezed it. But there was no reciprocal sensation.

'So,' she said. 'Here we are.'

She tried to hold his gaze. Michael's eyes swam; dark brown eyes, made milky with emotion. 'I imagine it's hard to talk.' He blinked in acknowledgement, and a tear trickled down one of his cheeks. It was odd. She had felt such a whirlpool of emotions when she had left home that morning – a bewildering combination of anger, fear, panic and pity, both for herself and for him. But now, what did she feel? Exhaustion certainly. Perhaps it was the shock. The silence was palpable.

He looked old. Before he left for Italy he had grown a beard. Everyone loathed it, Sam, the children, friends. But he was wedded to it. She found herself wondering now, did he grow it for her… the dark-haired girl… Carrie? She fought back tears and leant over to kiss him, grazing his prickly cheek with her lips. Not his mouth. She couldn't kiss the lopsided mouth.

'How did it happen?' Her voice sounded calm, impassive. She had gone into crisis mode, keeping her emotions in check, as she had done when she was a reporter. It was a skill she had developed in order to remain objective in difficult situations. But now, she was using it to protect herself, as if a vast wall of emotion was lying in wait to overwhelm her. If she allowed any chink, any break in that wall, it would lay waste to her. And Michael's eyes were fearful. He needed her to be strong too.

He tried to speak, but no words came.

'Sorry,' she stroked his unresponsive hand, automatically, as if she were visiting some distant relative. 'I forget you can't really talk yet, can you?'

A second tear ran down his cheek and she reached over and wiped it with her thumb, her palm lingering on his neatly clipped beard.

Her eyes filled with tears. She could feel the wall pushing against her throat. She coughed, and wiped her own tears away roughly, almost embarrassed.

'We'll get you well, don't worry,' she said, trying to sound positive. Aware that she sounded more and more like her own cheery mother.

But she could see Michael didn't really believe her. She wasn't really sure she believed herself.

Later that evening, back at the little pensione, she sobbed into her pillow. The wall of emotion had finally collapsed, and she lay exhausted with an amalgamation of grief and a gut-wrenching rage at Michael. Rage at his deception. But pity too, for him, for herself, and for the children. She missed the children terribly, with a real physical pain that was deep inside her, welling up into her throat whenever she thought of them. Her mother had rung her to tell her that all three children were fine, but had let slip that Freddie had stood clinging to the garden gate when she had left, inconsolable, watching the road for two hours after she had gone, waiting for her to come back in the nasty black car. But he was asleep now, her mother cooed, he'd eaten well, watched *Postman Pat* with the twins. It was OK. Maybe, thought Sam.

The next morning she set out across the Piazza. It was a bright sunny day at the end of May, and she stood for a few minutes looking up at the Tower; it gleamed in the early morning sunshine. Not pure white, as it appears in the millions of replicas that sell on market stalls at 10 euros a time, but a myriad of pale shades: cream, beige, grey, palest pink. A mother-of-pearl vision fashioned from marble, gouged out of the ground at Monte Pisano hundreds of years before. It struck Sam that its pretty, intricate carving was somehow at odds with its sturdiness; like a stubby limb, an arm, or leg, covered provocatively by a gauzy undergarment. It was in every sense, feminine, not at all like the intrusive phallic symbols of twentieth-century high-rise architecture. Not a skyscraper in any real sense of the word, and yet, in its day, as much a testament to man's power and strength as the

Eiffel Tower, the Empire State Building or those symbols of twin destruction, the Towers.

Michael had been making a television documentary about the Tower. It was to cover the history of this, the most famous building in the world, from the early twelfth century to the present day. It had stood witness to nearly a thousand years of European history. It had played host to an extraordinary range of visitors, from Galileo to the poets Shelley and Byron. Interestingly, and unusually for that time, the building remained 'anonymous'. It was the norm for architects to sign their buildings, literally to leave their mark, but no one had signed or laid claim to the Tower of Pisa. There were theories, of course, but no one could ever be really certain – and Michael was determined to try to uncover the hidden secrets that lay behind the Tower's extraordinary design. Finally, he would explore the engineering of the building.

Almost from the day the first stone was laid, it had begun to lean. Successive generations had been fascinated by the building's refusal to yield to the silty ground upon which it had been built. Since 1817, architects and engineers had experimented and excavated in an effort to shore it up, almost resulting in its destruction in 1934 when the dictator Mussolini gave orders to fill 361 drill holes in its base with concrete. Miraculously, along with the rest of the buildings on the aptly named Campo dei Miracoli, it had survived bombing in the Second World War, only to once again be nearly destroyed in an effort to shore it up in 1995. Michael had been fascinated by the subject for months, and was now filming the final phase in its rehabilitation, as the vast steel girdle was slung round its middle, holding it in position, after which the engineers, led by Professor John Burland of Imperial College, would excavate down, removing just enough soil from beneath the foundations to cause it to right itself. It would not be completely straight; that would be impossible, and anyway, the good burghers of Pisa, with a keen eye on the tourist dollar, did not want their leading tourist attraction made too perfect. No, it was to be pulled back from the brink of collapse just enough to be safe.

Michael and his crew had been filming in Italy for a few days. He had already got contrasting interviews with the solid British engineer and his colourful Italian counterparts 'in the can'. The engineering aspects would be covered with graphic sequences when he returned to the UK. For the last two days he had been filming the process of erecting the girdle: an extraordinary collection of steel ties encircling the Tower and preventing it from toppling while the 'under-excavation' took place.

What had happened to Michael seemed unclear. Mima, his researcher, knew only that he had been alone, at the top of the Tower, when he collapsed. Found within five or ten minutes by his cameraman returning with equipment, he was fortunate that the old medieval hospital of Santa Chiara was just a short distance away. It had been a struggle to manoeuvre Michael's lifeless body down the winding staircase, but the paramedics were skilled, and emergency treatment was administered swiftly.

A cool breeze brushed Sam's face. She shivered slightly as she wandered around the Campo. The sun was making steady progress behind the Tower, casting a shadow across the bright green grass that lay, incongruously verdant, like a carpet around the buildings. The rotund outline of the Baptistery formed a smoky grey silhouette against the warm apricot sky. The marble paths, pitted by the millions of visitors, led her back to the Duomo. She had no ticket so could not enter, but instead stood gazing up at the twin bronze doors featuring scenes from the Christ's life. To her right stood the Camposanto, the Holy Field – cemetery to the city. Its long, low, marble façade glowing almost pure white in the morning light. The creamy, carved, delicate beauty of the place was without question, and yet it left her untouched; unlike the tourists who gawped and gaped and snapped at these buildings, she felt no emotion, no joy. Glancing up, she took one more look at the cock-eyed crowd-pleaser where her husband had collapsed before she hurried away down the Via Maria, behind the stalls selling tourist models of the building that would change her life forever.

CHAPTER 3

May 1999

After a couple of days in Pisa, Sam settled into a sort of routine. She was relieved to discover that, unlike the centre of many tourist destinations, the heart of Pisa was a living, breathing place where residents mixed with the visitors. And so, ordinary things like soap or newspapers were readily available alongside the tourist knick-knacks being sold at the stalls that lined the Piazza. Within a few hundred yards of her pensione, she found a little chemist, a paper shop which sold cigarettes and postcards – where she could occasionally find an English newspaper – and, on the corner of the main Piazza, a café called Bar Duomo, which stood conveniently across from the entrance to the ancient convent that housed the hospital. Each morning, on her way to visit Michael, she stopped at the café to pick up their breakfast. It was a lively establishment, typical of that part of Italy, filled with businessmen on their way to work who would stand at the polished copper bar, sipping viscous, dark espresso, reading the paper while discussing the stories of the day with the *bariste* behind the counter. Women sat at the tables; noisy and brightly coloured like birds, dressed in spectacular outfits even at nine in the morning, their hair coiffed, their brown legs draped elegantly, chattering and gossiping over cappuccino and pastries.

Throughout the day, people came to the shop to buy exquisite-ly decorated cakes, or tarts, which would be wrapped carefully in white boxes and tied up with pink ribbons by the girls who served at the pastry counter. Sam watched the customers' faces, intense with concentration, as they debated which of the spectacular treats on offer they would take home to share with their families. She wondered, wistfully, what special event they were celebrating that day, what birthday, or anniversary the cake would mark. The purchase of these cakes distressed her a little more each time she witnessed it. There was an intrinsic happiness about it that she found unbearable as she considered the devastation of her own family life – Michael lying half-paralysed in a hospital bed, her beloved children back in England, the discovery of her husband's deception, and the existence of Carrie, the interloper, intruding uninvited into her life. Had anyone, she wondered, told Carrie?

She ordered two cappuccinos *da portare via*, along with a couple of brioches, little croissants covered with sugar, for them to have for their breakfast. Then shoving the brioches into her bag and balancing the two coffees precariously one on top of the other, she walked through the ancient archway, across the cobbled medieval courtyard, the walls of which were painted with peel-ing frescoes, that led to the modern hospital – an example, she thought, of all that was bad about seventies architecture. Each time she arrived at the hospital, she cursed the heavy glass and steel doors, wondering at the lunacy of designers who could make the entrance to a building designed to house sick and frail people so impenetrable. Having navigated the doors while somehow holding tight to her coffees, she was invariably met with '*vietato ingresso*' signs on the lift barring her from using them and requir-ing a long walk up four flights of stairs to Michael's room.

He was sleeping when she entered. She put the coffees and pastries down on the sterile little table next to his bed. She wandered over to the window, gazing out at the jumbled jigsaw of roofs and courtyards below. In those buildings and in those gardens, people were living their lives to the full. Lovers were kissing, children were laughing, mothers were cooking meals for their families.

She, on the other hand, felt as if her life had simply stopped. Like the blood leading to Michael's brain, her future had come to an abrupt end. She had only the present. In this little, stuffy, ugly room.

She tried to open the window to let in some air, but the metal casement was jammed. She turned on the tap at the basin to wash her hands, but there was no hot water. Irritated, she crossed the corridor to the nurses' office. Three women, languid and bored, dressed in shapeless white uniforms, looked up at her with mild surprise as she tried to explain, with a minimal grasp of Italian, about the lack of hot water.

'I would like to give my husband a wash... *lavare* Michael,' she said, frustrated and embarrassed in equal measure by her own inability to speak their language. 'But there is no hot water... *aqua calda.*'

The nurses looked at her impassively. One of them spoke. A dark woman, with golden skin, her hair tinted an unrealistic shade of red, tied up at the back of her head in a loose chignon.

'*Non c'e aqua calda. L'ospedale e in via di rinnovamento...*' her sentence trailed off and she gestured out of the window, where Sam could see groups of workmen labouring in what had been a car park below.

Sighing with frustration, Sam returned to Michael's bedside. He lay unmoving, still sleeping, the two halves of his face somehow at odds with one another - his mouth in a faint smile on one side, whilst the other turned downwards, as if dejected. Both united by the beard, speckled black with red... and, increasingly, grey. She loathed it, as if the beard was in some way responsible for her predicament.

Intent now on shaving if off, she swept back across the corridor, noisily grabbing a large saucepan from beside the ancient cooker where the nurses made their coffee. She found a box of matches, turned on the gas, lit a ring and clanged the pan, full to the brim with water, onto the heat. Then she went in search of towels. There were none in his room so she opened cupboards in the corridor, rifling amongst the linens until she found an old sheet. That would do.

Returning to the kitchen, she walked between the staring, sullen nurses and, using the sheet, picked up the old pan. She walked back into Michael's room and quietly set the pan down on the floor by the basin. She picked up the soap and dipped it into the steaming water. Its heat made her wince. Her hands covered in foam, she sat on the edge of his bed, focused on removing the stubble from his face. As she began to touch his beard with her fingers, his eyes opened and he frowned at her.

'Hello,' she said. 'How are you feeling? I thought I would give you a wash.' Her voice, she was aware, was brisk, efficient. Her emotions checked.

His expression didn't change, but he moved his good hand to touch hers. Then he shook his finger and touched his beard.

'It's all right,' she said, as cheerfully as she could, 'I won't touch the beloved beard.'

Gently, she began to wash his face and neck, lifting his head – so heavy and awkward – from the pillow. She soaped his naked chest and, lifting the sheet that concealed his genitals, she washed that part of him too. All the while, as she soaped, rinsed and dried him with the sheet, he watched her, his eyes filling with tears. At one point, a blonde, plump nurse came to the door. She said nothing, but shrugged and turned away, her lazy shuffling steps audible on the polished lino as she retreated down the corridor. Sam suddenly remembered the coffee she had brought. It was not quite cold, the lids having preserved some of its steaming heat. Carefully lifting Michael's head off the pillow, she held the cup to his mouth. He closed one eye with pleasure, or perhaps concentration, as a dribble of foam escaped from his partially paralysed lips. She picked up the croissant, tearing a small piece from the end. She dipped it into the hot coffee and held it to his lips. He tried to smile and made a little murmuring sound. He opened his mouth just a little, like a reluctant baby tricked by his mother into eating something he does not want. He chewed feebly, finally swallowing the soggy pastry. Then Sam took a piece for herself and they sat like this, silently eating their breakfast, Sam struggling to keep back the tears as she tried to bring some normality to this otherwise quite abnormal situation.

The sullen blonde nurse reappeared at the doorway and seeing the pastry spoke sharply.

'*Signora*... no... no brioche.'

It was Sam's turn to be sullen now. She turned away from the nurse and deliberately inserted another piece of sweetness into her husband's mouth. The nurse sighed and left them alone.

Later that day, as Michael again slept, Sam spoke with the Professor and one of his senior team, who fortunately spoke English.

'It is too soon for us to know how good a recovery Michael might make,' the young doctor said. 'The Professor will have to conduct tests which will take several days before we know anything more. Ultrasound on his head and neck will be required. I am sorry, he says, but there is no more that we can do just yet. We must be patient. But we will do our best to help you in any way we can.'

'Thank you,' she had said, automatically, thinking to herself, it's not his head that we need to be scanning, but his heart.'

CHAPTER 4

May 1999

The washing became something of a ritual for Sam. Day after day she would visit her husband, encroach on the hospitality of the persistently unfriendly staff, sling a pan of water onto the gas, rummage in the cupboard in the corridor for a sheet to dry him with, mystified by the Italians' obstinate refusal to use towels when they bathed, and retreat to his room ready to tend to him.

Every day, as she soaped his limbs, rinsing off the suds as best she could with the warmed water, the repetitive actions took on an almost meditative quality. She could not talk to Michael about the one thing that tormented her – his betrayal, and so she concentrated, instead, on this one task.

But on the fourth day, she could contain herself no longer.

'Michael,' she said, fixing him with her cool green stare, 'we need to talk… about… Carrie.'

He closed his eyes, his head twisting away from her.

'Don't turn away from me!'

She came round to the other side of the bed, feeling the anger welling up in her like a volcano. Tears fell silently from his dark brown eyes, leaving a damp patch on the thin sheet.

'I'm sorry,' she murmured, taken aback. 'I don't mean to up-set you… but I need to know what's going on. Should I be here? Is it serious, I mean… should Carrie be here instead of me?'

He looked up at her, alarm registering on his face; she took hold of his paralysed hand instinctively and squeezed. A small sensation, like a tiny electric shock, pulsed back at her.

'Hey, I felt that she said. 'Did you?'

But he turned his face away once again. She took a tissue from the box on the bedside table and wiped her own nose and eyes, then turning it over to the dry side, she dabbed at Michael's eyes too.

'It's OK,' she said. 'Let's leave it. I'm here. I'm not going anywhere.'

Later that day, as he slept, she took an old notebook out of her bag, a habit that had not left her since her reporter days, and began to write down her thoughts. Frustrated that she could not explore the problems in her marriage with her husband, she found some curious comfort in listing the issues.

'When did Michael meet Carrie?'

'Does he love her?'

'Does he love me still?

'Do I love him?

'Is our marriage worth saving?'

'How would I cope without him?'

At this last question, she looked at the almost lifeless body of her husband in the hospital bed and began to cry.

The following day, she arrived at the hospital, as usual, with their breakfast, and found the Professor talking to her husband.

'Ah *signora*,' he said warmly, as she entered the room. His underling took on the role of interpreter once again.

'Your husband is making good progress. We think that not too much damage has been caused. He has been lucky. He needs to spend a little time each day trying to use his right side. A little conversation would be good for him. See what you can do.'

When they had gone, she sat on his bed and held the coffee to his lips.

He took a few little sips.

'I'm sorry,' he murmured almost inaudibly.

'What? What did you say?'

'I'm sorry,' he said again.

'What for? Having a stroke, or having an affair?' Her voice, she was aware, had taken on a brittle edge.

'Both,' he said with some effort, before sinking back onto the pillow.

'I see,' she said. 'OK, well, that's something, I suppose. I can't blame you for the stroke so you don't need to apologise for that. But the other…'

'You don't understand… it's not what you think,' he said.

'What don't I understand?'

He shook his head slightly, but the effort seemed overwhelming, and he closed his eyes.

'Michael.' She put the coffee back on the bedside table and nudged his arm gently, to check if he was asleep. He opened his eyes once again.

'We're going to have to talk about it sometime you know. We can't just brush it under the carpet. Not that there is a carpet,' she said, ironically, gesturing towards the cheap lino.

He attempted a faint smile.

'We'll park it for now,' she went on, 'and I guess we'd better do as the doctor suggested and perhaps attempt a little conversation? Something neutral.'

His eyelids drooped a little and she could sense the huge effort he was making just to keep awake.

'How are the kids?' he asked, his voice slurring slightly.

'Oh, they're ok… my mother is wonderful – as always. The twins are fine. They're always just happy in one another's company aren't they? And Freddie is up to mischief, as usual.'

Michael smiled a little. 'Good lad,' he murmured.

'I miss them so,' said Sam, her eyes filling with tears.

'Darling...' Michael reached his good hand out to her.

'It's OK,' she said hurriedly, wiping her eyes on her sleeve. 'In some ways, it's best not to think too much about them really. As I have no idea when I'll be home to see them, it's sort of easier – do you understand?'

He nodded sympathetically, and closed his eyes finally.

'How about we talk about the film?' she said a brightly, 'what you've uncovered, what you've found out?'

She noticed his battered briefcase, which lay dusty and forgotten, like a brown leather reminder of the man Michael used to be, beneath his bed in the hospital. Amongst the files, hefty laptop, address book and diary, she found three reference books about the building of the Tower of Pisa.

'Shall we go through your notebooks?'

But Michael's eyes remained closed and a faint snore escaped from his mouth.

Sam thought about what he had said: 'you don't understand'. What had he been trying to tell her? Had she misjudged him about Carrie? Frustrated by her inability to discuss it with him and faced with the prospect of gazing out of the window or going for yet another solitary walk – something that, if she was honest, was becoming more than a little tedious – Sam, in need of distraction, took the reference books over to a table in the corner of the room and laid them out alongside Michael's notebooks. At least, she reasoned, she could get 'up to speed' on the project, ready to discuss it when he awoke. In the old days, before the children, it had been their habit to discuss their work projects. It was one of the things that had drawn them together. One telling the other what they had done that day, exploring the issues, debating the best way of telling a story, writing a commentary. She had acted as an informal editor to her husband, always called in by him when he was cutting a film, her views and analytical mind eagerly explored. He was proud of his wife's journalistic skill. And she of his. He had a vision, a passion for telling a story. He was always keen to look behind the obvious, to seek out truth in the obscure. But those days had gradually lapsed, especially with the birth of the twins. Their life together had become a round of sleepless nights, of just getting through the days. Sam had eventually been forced, or at least had allowed herself to be persuaded, that work and three children under five was incompatible, and she had thrown herself into the business of mothering and home-making. But, whilst she loved the children more than life itself, she knew, in her heart, that it was not enough. Her creativity was frustrated by their very existence.

That was when she had developed a passion for gardening. It provided an outlet for her creativity and afforded her, or so she hoped, a few moments of peace. Alone in the borders, she was able to plan where each new plant should go, to visualise the swathes of colour or form that would grow with each year that passed. But Michael did not really share her passion. He saw it as a curious hobby for his wife. An affectation almost, that was quite outside his own experience. He was still immersed in the business of film making, still travelling to London, meeting fellow producers in trendy cafés and media members-only clubs. When he came home from work, her mind was distracted by the needs of the children and gradually the conversations about work that they had so enjoyed just dwindled. The complexities of finding babysitters precluded meals out alone, when they might have had the opportunity to talk. Their lives instead, were dominated – as were those of most of their married friends – by domestic trivia, anxieties about the children and sheer hard work of managing their combined lives.

As Sam sat at the table, sipping her lukewarm coffee, she realised that this trip to Pisa was the first time she had been alone with Michael since the children had been born. And, in reality, with Michael so unwell and incapacitated, she was effectively alone. Her mind free of domesticity: there were no meals to be cooked, no beds to be made, no children to comfort, no housework to be got through. She missed the children terribly, of course, and rang her mother each evening to make sure they were OK, but she was aware that somewhere, in the midst of her distress, there was an almost tangible sense of peace. Much as she had felt before her marriage, when she had been reporting abroad. Alone in a hotel, researching an idea, making notes, thinking of nothing but the story; there was clarity and calm. Then the crew would arrive and the business of making a film would be frantic and complex and the peace would evaporate.

She laid out the three reference books, and opened Michael's notebook to a clean page. She fished a pen out of his briefcase and wrote in large neat handwriting – Pisa. The first book she opened provided the architectural details of the three buildings that formed the Campo dei Miracoli; the second was more particularly about the Tower itself, detailing its entire history, from the date the first foundation stone was laid to the present day. The third was a large hardback book containing maps, architectural drawings and paintings of Pisa dating back to the fourteenth century. The early images were romanticised drawings of the city that bore no relation to the place in which she now found herself. The town walls were not a square as they were in reality, but were drawn instead in an untidy circle, surrounded by childlike wavy lines representing the sea, upon which galleys rocked and rolled, their oars dipping centipede-like into the waves. Curiously, these drawings rarely featured the city's most famous landmarks – the Tower and Cathedral – but instead portrayed Pisa as a little hilltop town filled with tightly packed tower houses that were such a feature of Pisa at that time. Cheek by jowl with one another, they formed a higgledy-piggledy place, a romantic dream of a city that reminded Sam of an idealised village that she had seen in one of the fairy storybooks of her childhood.

But the image that most intrigued Sam was an early map of Pisa dating back to1625, which provided extraordinarily precise detail of the city as it had been at that time. The city walls were almost a perfect square, drawn with neat crenellations along the top. The neatly labelled Arno Fiume carved its way through the city like a wide blue-green ribbon, decorated with little galleys sailing back and forth. And where it intersected the city walls, the breach was filled with two neat bridges, one on either side. Just one further bridge was marked on the map, quite near the centre of the city, which Sam deduced was now the bridge known as Ponte di Mezzo.

Large houses lined the banks of the Arno, much as they do now, and smaller houses – their roofs painted Tuscan red – fanned out in neat, densely packed rows, almost in a grid system, towards the city walls. And here and there, in between the rows, were small gardens providing areas for people to sit, or to keep a pig, or grow some vegetables. On the outskirts of the town, the houses were less densely packed and the gardens were bigger. Sam could make out neat rows of crops, edged by tiny hedges, large trees providing shade; even the wells where the city's population could collect their water were clearly marked. And all across the city were churches, carefully drawn with spires, and steep greeny-bronze-coloured roofs. All were numbered, their identities recorded in beautiful handwriting in a key at the side. No 13 – the church of S Lorenzo, 14 – S Francesco, 15 – S Antonio and so on. In the top left-hand corner of the map, there was the Campo dei Miracoli, known at that time as the Piazza del

Duomo, with its three famous ecclesiastical buildings including the Tower, already leaning perilously to one side. Next to it stood the hospital where she now sat, the Convent of Santa Chiara, set in a vast garden, presumably growing food to feed the nuns and patients at that time. She thought ruefully of the delicious food they doubtless served up five hundred years ago. She could almost smell the city, so detailed was the map. As Michael slept, she allowed her mind to wander to the little gardens as they were all those years ago, painted a shade of burnt sienna, scorched and dry in the midday heat, cats and dogs seeking shade beneath the arching branches of the carefully painted trees.

Interspersed amongst the maps were portraits of famous Pisans; handsome men with illustrious credentials. Most of the images were from the Renaissance period. But two pictures featured men who had lived at the time the Tower was being built. It fascinated her to think that these men had been witness to the development of that extraordinary building. That they might, perhaps, have been involved in some way. The first was a handsome man with a long straight nose and neat dark beard, wearing a dark red jacket, its sleeves inset with fur – ermine perhaps – the cuffs and collar edged in fine lace. The annotation indicated that he was the Admiral of the Republic between 1242 and 1244, the date he was killed in action. The second was of a man named Lorenzo Calvo. Not as tall as the Admiral, his hair was also longer, his beard not quite so well groomed. He also wore a dark red tunic, with fur at the shoulders and a heavy dark blue cloak held in place with a large jewelled clasp. Beneath the image of Calvo were illustrations of ships at sea and romanticised paintings of what she presumed were far-distant lands that he visited, judging by the pictures of camels and other exotic animals with which they were decorated. There was no date inscribed on the painting itself, but the annotation beneath the image suggested that it was painted around 1165: around the time that the Tower was being planned. Sam spent a lot of time gazing into his hard black-eyed stare as if he might relent eventually and give up his secrets.

She flicked back through Michael's notebooks and read his notes. There were details of the engineering issues of course, exploring what might have caused the Tower to lean. He had met with several key experts and had drawn little sketches showing the Tower slipping into the silty soil beneath, arrows illustrating where stabilising concrete had been injected beneath and rings around the Tower annotated with the words 'steel girdle – John Burland'.

There were notes too, of a meeting he had had with a Professor Moretti, who appeared to be a medieval historian in Pisa. Michael had clearly gone to him for an insight into the lives of the ordinary medieval Pisans. He had made a series of notes beneath the Professor's name: 'no one went out after dark – for fear of robbery and murder.' 'Tower houses standard, one room above another, connected by ladders,' and so on.

On the following page were the words: 'Who designed the Tower?' in black, spidery writing, with extravagant doodles emanating from the letters.

Beneath the first such entry was a list of the possible candidates: Deotisalvi, Gerardo, Pisano and the Hunchback, William of Innsbruck. Each one had a large question mark next to it and lines connecting their name to other buildings they had designed, or, as in the case of Gerardo, worked on. Deotisalvi had designed the Baptistery and the Tower of San Nicola; Gerardo had worked on the Tower of San Nicola, Pisano had been a sculptor and designer of the magnificent haut-relief bronze doors of the Cathedral. The Hunchback had no other architectural credits, and Michael had put a pencil through his name. Buried at the bottom of the page was the word 'Berta', outlined with a carefully drawn rectangle. And next to it, the word Calvo, also outlined in black, followed by the phrase 'follow the money'.

Intrigued, Sam flicked through the rest of Michael's notebook, but could find no further reference to Berta or Calvo. She went again through the book of images, but whilst there was an image of Calvo, there were none of Berta. A scant reading of the book on the history of the Tower made no mention of this woman, nor indeed of any person named Calvo.

Who, then, was Berta?

Packing the books into Michael's briefcase, she wandered over to his bedside. He slept on, his eyelids fluttering mid-dream. She wanted to bend over to kiss him, but held back as the dark-haired vision of Carrie seeped into her mind, shattering the peace.

With Michael's briefcase in hand, she left the hospital and walked out into the sunshine, and across the Piazza towards her pensione. She had a sense of purpose as she strode amongst the tourists gawping at the buildings on the Campo. 'Who was Berta?' she said out loud as she stood gazing at the tower. A Japanese tourist turned and stared at her. 'Sorry,' she blurted, 'just thinking out loud,' before she walked on towards the stalls that lined the little street outside her hotel.

CHAPTER 5

September 1171
Pisa

The afternoon sun glinted on the decorated glass laid out on the long oak table. Berta brushed her fingers across its surface, noting, with irritation, the fine film of dust. She hurried from the dining hall to the top of the stairs that led to the vast kitchens below. The scent of nutmeg and cooking meat filtered up the wide stone steps.

'Maria, send someone up with a cloth… quickly! The table is filthy.'

There was a murmuring from below, and within seconds a young maid ran up the stairs, a linen cloth in one hand and a bowl of water, scented with lemon, in the other.

'There… the table; it is covered in dust.' Her tone was sharp.

'The guests will be arriving in a few hours' time. I don't want to find a speck of dust when I come back down.'

The girl put the bowl of water carefully on the floor and slowly began to remove the valuable items from the table, placing them one by one on a vast serving table that ran the length of the room.

'And make sure you don't break anything when you put the glassware back. Lorenzo found it in Syria and it's irreplaceable.

And don't forget to fill up the ewers,' she pointed at the water bowls in the shape of lions' heads that sat beside each place.

Gathering her skirts around her, she swept up the vast marble staircase to her bedchamber at the top of the tower, calling after herself: 'Send Aurelia to me.'

At the age of thirty-five Berta di Bernardo was a handsome woman, some might even say beautiful, with dark red hair that fell in waves down her back. Her eyes were green, the colour of emeralds. The name she had been given at birth, Berta, was a family name that belonged to her mother and grandmother before her. But it did not suit her. Her father had given her a nickname, Smeralda, or Emerald, to draw attention to the eyes that he said had been a gift from God. He had been convinced that she was born to greatness, and when he had recorded the time, date and year of her birth – 2 o'clock on the 9th August 1136 – on an astrological chart, he was delighted to discover that her destiny was indeed to be one of great wealth and importance.

Once in her room, as Aurelia carried jugs of steaming water to fill up the bath that stood in the centre of the chamber, Berta's husband, Lorenzo, wandered in and out, demanding her attention.

'Berta… what should I wear this evening, do you think? The red robe or the dark blue edged with velvet?'

'The red,' her tone was curt and impatient.

'Really? I rather thought the blue would be better.'

'Fine, the blue then…'

Lorenzo turned to look at her, puzzled at her irritation.

'Cara, why are you so cross this afternoon? It is only a meal for friends and acquaintances; we've had many such parties before. What irks you so?'

He leant over and caressed her ivory-white shoulder, grazing her skin with his lips.

She recoiled almost imperceptibly, pulling the gown around her more tightly.

'It's nothing, Lorenzo, but it is an important party. I have the architect Deotisalvi coming, and I want to talk to him about one of his projects. I have a young mason who needs my help and he'd be perfect for it. I just want everything to go smoothly.'

Lorenzo smiled. 'You and your little protégés. I sometimes think they are like children for you, the way you look after them all.' Turning towards his own chamber, he spoke over his shoulder. 'I will wear the red, if that's what you prefer. I imagine that you rather think it will show you off to better advantage, no?'

Attempting a smile, Berta called after him. 'Thank you, *caro*. Yes, the red would be best.'

As she watched him wander to his room, she was struck by how much he had aged. Whereas she was tall, graceful and slim, her body still firm and youthful, Lorenzo, nineteen years her senior, had developed a large, comfortable belly, and his straggly beard failed to disguise numerous chins.

He had been handsome when they first met: she was just seventeen and living a protected life in her father's house, and Lorenzo Calvo, thirty-six and a successful trader, with an impressive fleet of twelve galleys bringing silks, metalwork, spices and precious stones back to Pisa from his travels to the Orient. At that time, she had thought the older man quite a catch. The daughter of a well-known *capo magister*, a master architect, she had been flattered by the young, thrusting merchant trader when he came calling all those years ago.

Having amassed a considerable fortune, Lorenzo had decided to build a house on the southern bank of the Arno, on the edge of the mercantile district of Chinzica. Pisa at that time was home to some fifty thousand people, who lived in tower houses consisting of one room atop the other, joined by a wooden ladder in the corner of each room. Measuring some thirty-six *braccie,* or an arms length, in height, they were made of an impermeable limestone called *verrucano,* and each one was much the same as its neighbour.

Wishing to demonstrate his considerable wealth to the citizens of Pisa, Calvo had acquired a plot of land, which afforded enough space for both a large house, or *palazzo,* and a *piazzetta* – a little square named after the family, where he could entertain his friends and acquaintances. In search of something unique, he had approached three local architects. Berta's father, Bernardo di Giovanni, had presented a spectacular and radical design, with three towers connected by galleries on each of the floors. A wide staircase, considered avant-garde at that time, was the main feature of the central structure. And at the top of each tower was an open gallery where the merchant could enjoy the evening breeze, watching the activity on the Arno below. At the front of the first floor was a stone loggia, or balcony, from where the family could survey the city, and in return receive the admiring glances of those less fortunate than themselves. At the rear of the house, a large garden was planned, an unusual feature in this overcrowded city, and at the end of the lane would stand Piazzetta Calvo. The design was far and away the most exciting of the plans he had been offered. Berta's father had won the commission and the young Lorenzo, though not classically handsome, had caught his daughter's eye.

The first time they met, she had been sketching in the upstairs sitting room of her father's tower house. Calvo had arrived to discuss the plans for his new *palazzo* to find his architect had been delayed on one of his sites.

As he prepared to leave, promising to return later that day, young Berta put aside her sketch and invited the young merchant to stay and take wine with her.

'Please,' she said invitingly, 'stay and keep me company. My father won't be long and I've heard so much about you. I'd love to know all about your life at sea.'

The young man was flattered by the attention of the ravishing red-haired beauty and set about impressing her with tales of his journeys.

'How large are these vessels you sail?' she asked.

'Well over 80 *braccie*.'

'My…' she said, 'and how many oarsmen do you need to propel such a vast ship?'

'Over 100, and we have mercenaries on board of course, too – ordinary soldiers and officers. We pick them up and take them down to fight the Infidel.'

'And do you row all the way?' she asked innocently, knowing the answer full well.

'No!' he scoffed. 'We set sail once we're safely out at sea. We can get up to 10 knots if the wind is with us.'

'And are your men slaves?'

'Not my men, no. I believe in employing "free men". A man works better if he is free and rewarded for his labour. It's hard work though – I'll accept that. Brutal sometimes. And the food is terrible, of course. It's hard to keep anything fresh for long.'

'So what do you eat?' asked Berta, her fascination mixed with horror.

'Dry biscuits, salted meat – it's a bit monotonous.'

'And how often do you set sail?'

'Twice a year; in spring and autumn. We're usually away for two or three months at a time.'

Their conversation was interrupted by the arrival of old Bernardo, the architect, and Berta politely left the two men to their discussions. But in the days that followed, she made discreet enquiries about the young merchant amongst her friends and contempories. His wealth and ambition were beyond doubt; and what he lacked in formal education was more than made up for by his entrepreneurial knack of recognising the monetary value of art, even if he could not truly value its intrinsic qualities.

'If you want anything rare, beautiful, or collectible,' it was often said in Pisa, 'Calvo is the man to get it for you.'

Lorenzo, it appeared, was the antithesis of her father, who was delicate, intellectual, unworldly, almost ascetic; and therein lay the attraction.

For all his unworldliness, Berta nevertheless adored her father. For the first seventeen years of her life, he had afforded her an extraordinary amount of freedom, encouraging her love of art and architecture, leaving her at liberty to roam the streets of Pisa in search of interesting subjects for her paintings. He took her with him on site visits and used her as his assistant on many occasions. In truth, he saw her more as a protégé than a daughter, a mere chattel who would require nothing more than a dowry in order that she might be safely married off. In fact, the issue of marriage was rarely mentioned as she grew up. It appeared to be of no interest to her father. He preferred, unusually at that time, to ensure that his daughter, an only child, was well-educated, but appeared to give no thought to the practicalities of her future life. He taught her the principles of grammar, rhetoric, dialectic and philosophy, as well as arithmetic, geometry and astronomy; all in addition to encouraging her in the study of painting and drawing. Had she been a boy, she had no doubt that she would have become a *capo magister* herself. But, as a girl, she soon realised this route was closed to her. As she grew into womanhood, the naivety of her father's position became increasingly apparent to her. That he had afforded her freedom and education was without doubt a huge gift, but the only way for her to make use of her education, and truly achieve success – as a patron of the arts and of architecture – was either through entering the church, or as the wife of a rich and successful man.

Not being inclined to spend her life in relative solitude in a convent, young Berta, at just seventeen, took her future into her own hands, and set her cap at the young merchant Calvo, who, she reasoned, would afford her the wealth and position she craved. With her red hair and sparkling green eyes, he was soon ensnared, and before six months were out, they were engaged to be married.

Early on in their courtship, Lorenzo took Berta and her father to the quayside to look round one of the galleys and visit his new warehouse. On board, she was full of questions: Where did the sailors sleep? Where did Lorenzo sleep? Where was the cargo stored? The fleet had recently returned from a trip to the Middle East. On the outward journey, the boats, bearing the Pisan standard of a red cross on a white background, had been filled with Crusaders from France, intent on the liberation of Jerusalem from the Infidel. Once his human cargo had been successfully delivered, Lorenzo had travelled on into Syria in search of objects to delight the increasingly wealthy residents of Pisa. On the return journey, he had stopped in Amalfi and, with his own soldiers, had been part of a small fleet of like-minded Pisans who had looted and torched the town, filling the holds of his boats with stolen artefacts, furniture and fabrics, along with some classical statuary that he had been commissioned to 'liberate' for some of Pisa's more spectacular building projects. He did not discuss this aspect of his work with his future wife, and Berta, young and innocent as she was, either did not care sufficiently to ask about it, or chose not to think how the goods were parted from their rightful owners. She was more interested in the contents of the vast warehouse, filled, as it was, to the roof with fabrics, glass and building materials.

The visit had been arranged, partly, for the benefit of her father who, as architect of Lorenzo's fine new house, was in search of a striking piece of classical statuary to complete one important vista of the building. As he wandered intently between the rows of vast blocks of marble and carved stone, Berta rummaged amongst the trunks filled with valuable bolts of fabric and delicate glassware.

'I have never seen anything like this before, Lorenzo. Where did you get it?'

She held up a saffron-yellow glass vessel, decorated with brightly coloured enamel designs. Even in the dimly lit interior of the warehouse, it sparkled and shone like sunlight.

'The glass comes from Syria; it's extraordinary isn't it?'

'What do you use if for?'

'For drinking from, you goose,' the man laughed and pulled the girl close to him, kissing her neck.

'For drinking! But it's so delicate. Doesn't it break?'

'It will,' he said, taking the glass from her and wrapping it carefully back in its covering, 'but not if you are careful. As you must be with this. I have already sold this collection to the Archbishop.'

'Lorenzo,' she twined herself around him, her father hidden from view by a large Greek statue of a young man. 'When we are married, may we have some yellow glass from Syria?'

'You may have yellow, blue and green glass, *cara* – whatever you desire.'

When the marriage day finally arrived, and the feasting and celebrations were over, the couple retired to their bedchamber, where a bath had been prepared. It was the custom for newly married couples to bathe with one another before they retired to bed. Naturally, it was a young groom's first opportunity to see his new bride naked, and Lorenzo, in spite of his greater maturity and experience, was, excited and delighted at the prospect. Berta, while initially modest, let her long shift drop to the floor and climbed into the steaming water next to her new husband. As he washed her back, she felt her skin tingling with unexpected pleasure. But, turning to face him, she held her hands protectively over her breasts.

Dressed once again in the shift, she lay expectantly in the large marital bed. Her father, naively, had omitted to prepare his only child for what was to come, and the young woman was apprehensive. But Lorenzo was an attentive and kind lover and lingered over his new bride. He held her in his arms and stroked her hair; he gazed at her body as she lay next to him, admiring and caressing her, feeling her heart quicken as he stroked her breasts through the fine fabric. When, finally, he kissed her, probing her mouth with his tongue, after a small pause, she opened her mouth wide to him. As he slid his hands down between her white thighs, he gasped at how wet she felt, as his fingers gently explored her. And when he entered her, shuddering with pleasure after just a few moments, she lay quite still for what seemed to her a polite interval, before asking: 'Lorenzo, can we do that again? I think I must practise as much as possible and get better for you.'

'*Cara*, it's not a lesson to be learnt like geometry or astronomy.'

'No?' she said teasingly, before pulling her shift over her head, revealing her full breasts, their tips hard and firm.

That night they practised… and Berta soon discovered the overwhelming, juddering pleasure that the act of love could bring.

After they were married, the tower house and its adjoining piazzetta, with the beautiful Berta as its mistress, became the centre of Pisan artistic life. Architects, painters and merchants met at the house. Deals were struck, commissions were sought, and all the while Lorenzo's wealth grew and grew like his fleet of galleys that rocked in the wind at the quayside on the Arno.

When they entertained, their table was laid with the exquisite glass Berta had so admired. Her jewellery was kept in caskets made of carved ivory from the Indies; cedar clothing chests overflowed with gowns made from brightly coloured damasks from China, and bedcovers and cushions were fashioned from cut silk velvets in shades of blue and terracotta, their patterns inspired by Islamic art. Berta found herself the leader of fashion and revelled in her elevated position in society. And the more she yearned for what was new or novel, the more her husband was driven to make greater demands on his men.

One afternoon, early in their marriage, Lorenzo arrived back at the *palazzo* after a long journey abroad. Berta heard him arriving, and throwing her book to the floor, rushed down the circular staircase to greet him.

'*Caro, caro*,' she kissed his face and danced around him. 'You are back safely; I am so glad. What did you bring me, Lorenzo, please show me?'

Lorenzo, exhausted but amused, slumped in the large oak chair in the hallway of the central tower.

'Sit here by me, little one, and I will show you what I have brought.'

Feeling into the leather pouch hanging from his belt, he took out a rough-hewn stone, turning it against the candlelight.

'Do you know what this is?'

Berta tried to take the stone, but he pulled away and stood up, holding it above his head.

'No... you must guess,' he teased.

'Oh Lorenzo, you're so mean,' she said, like a little child. 'How am I to know... it looks like nothing, perhaps it is a piece of glass?'

Lorenzo smiled.

'No,' she continued playfully, 'you are more generous than that. Is it a jewel of some kind? It does not look like a jewel, but maybe, is that what it is?'

'How did you get to be so clever?' he asked delightedly. 'You are right... it is a jewel... a very special one, a diamond. It comes from India. It is very valuable and it is for you.'

'Oh,' her tone was disappointed, 'thank you. But what will we do with it? It's not very pretty, Lorenzo.'

'No, *cara*, but wait until the jeweller has cut it and shaped it. Then you will see. It will sparkle like the sun and the moon together. I will set it in gold for you to wear around your neck.'

His wife smiled and, taking the jewel in her hands, held it up to the light.

'After dinner, I shall I tell you the story of how I found it. But first, I need a bath and to bed with my beautiful wife.'

In those early days, during Lorenzo's long sea voyages, Berta created something of a secret life from her husband. Frustrated by the containment that her position afforded her, which required her to stay within her household at all times, unless accompanied by her husband, or a retinue of servants, she found that she missed her young independent life of painting and sketching. And so she had begun to make regular journeys, alone, across the river to the Piazza, in order to watch and sketch the men at work on the new Duomo.

One day, as she sat on a low wall to one side of the building site, her eye was caught by a boy. He had beautiful black curls which fell to his shoulders, and translucent green blue eyes – the colour of the sea on a warm summer's day. The child, who must have been no more than seven or eight years old, was striking a piece of stone with his hammer and chisel, while an old man about fifty years his senior guided his hand. Gently, the man instructed the boy, once narrowly preventing him from chipping off his own thumb.

'Gerardo,' he called out, 'take care,' as he deftly grabbed the hammer just as it was about to injure the boy's hand.

The child, scared by the near miss, dropped the chisel with a clang onto the ground and burst into tears. The old man picked up the boy, cradling him in his arms and soothing him, before placing him back down in front of the stone work and instructing him to take up the chisel again, once more showing him how to hold it with care while tapping gently, the hammer held squarely in the other hand.

Berta, impressed by the older man's gentleness, walked across to the pair and handed the child a little apricot.

'Here,' she said, 'take this. It will take his mind off the pain.'

The old man thanked her, and the child took the soft apricot in his small grubby fingers and pushed it enthusiastically into his mouth. Juice spurted out, and he laughed, before wiping his chin with the bottom of his shirt.

'Say thank you to the lady, Gerardo,' the older man said.

'Yes, grandpa. Thank you, *signora*,' said the boy, with a broad smile revealing several missing teeth.

Over the next ten years, she often saw the boy with the beautiful dark hair and sea-green eyes on her visits to the Duomo. She had fallen into the habit of smiling at him and, on occasion, speaking a few words to him. Dressed as she was, in a simple woollen or linen gown, she did not strike the boy or his grandfather as a wealthy woman but as something of an oddity: a woman who was at liberty to spend her day as she pleased, rather than having to be at home caring for her children or attending to her household. The boy and his grandfather were, of course, too polite to question her, and so she remained something of a mystery.

And now, as she lay in the steaming water, preparing for that evening's dinner party, she thought about young Gerardo. Since she had first spotted him in the Piazza almost a decade before, he had grown into a handsome and accomplished young man… tall and athletic, with golden skin and dark hair curling around his ears. A fine young mason, she was determined to help him. He was, perhaps, the most talented of her 'little protégés', as Lorenzo irritatingly referred to them.

She was jolted out of her musing, as Lorenzo came back into the room. He was wearing the dark red robe, belted tightly across his generous stomach.

He gazed at her as she bathed.

'Still the most beautiful woman in Pisa,' he said, his dark eyes roving back and forth across her white, scented body. The ring he had first given her on their betrothal, an emerald set in gold to match her eyes, hung heavily on her delicate finger. He took the hand in his own big, rough grasp and kissed it. Removing the ring gently, he turned it over, gazing as the stone flashed in the sunlight, and read the inscription that had been engraved all those years before.

'Desire no other,' he spoke the words while watching her sharp beautiful face, waiting for a loving remark, or at least some sign of reassurance.

He was not disappointed. Berta knew how to please him. '*Caro*, I could never desire anyone but you.' And she held out her elegant hand for him to place the ring once again on her finger.

'Now, please Lorenzo, leave me. Aurelia and I have work to do. It is not a simple business preparing for one of these events.'

And Lorenzo, comforted, like a little child, kissed his wife on the forehead and left her to her toilette.

CHAPTER 6

1160

Gerardo di Gerardo was just a baby when his father died from a deadly fever caused by the bad air, or *mal aria,* that floated on the air from the marshes that surrounded the city. This illness, which was both untreatable and often fatal, had spread to that part of Italy hundreds of years before, carried as a parasite within the bodies of soldiers and merchants travelling north from Sicily and North Africa. Pisa, and the marshy plains criss-crossed with canals and rivers that surrounded the city, proved an ideal breeding ground for the mosquito that transmitted the disease, and the illness was endemic. His mother, Carlotta, grieved for her beloved husband and wondered how she would survive with a babe-in-arms to care for. But she was rescued by her widowed father and her father-in-law, who moved into the tower house she occupied on the northern outskirts of the city.

Thanks to the two older men, she did not want for male company, money, or indeed protection – and her child had two father figures to emulate and love. The two men worked hard and provided a reasonable income for the family. Carlotta was even able to employ a couple of servants: a boy to help with the harder chores, and a young maid to work with her in the kitchen. Carlo, Carlotta's father, was away at sea two or three times a year, working for the merchant Lorenzo Calvo, in charge of one of his fleet of ships. He was a trusted employee, a good ten years his master's senior. When he travelled, he would be away from the family for several months at a time, but on his return, he entertained his grandson with tales of life at sea, and helped his daughter around the house. He was a talented joiner and had made several pieces of furniture for the household.

Gerardo the elder, Carlotta's father-in-law, was a master mason, or *lapicida*, on the constantly expanding site that was the Piazza del Duomo. His working life was built around routine and discipline, and did not alter come winter or summer. He would rise before dawn, wash, prepare his tools and leave for work as the rest of the household were just waking. Most of the tradesman were on site early, particularly in the summer months, in order to take advantage of the cooler air. Gerardo would work hard until lunchtime, then eat, rest – sometimes even coming home – before returning to work in the late afternoon. Young Gerardo idolised his older namesake and would often sit and watch him in the early morning as he stood washing at a stone trough near the back door, stripped to the waist. He was fascinated by the older man's hands, which seemed to the little boy so very large. His fingers, long, straight but exceptionally wide, could encompass both of his grandson's tiny hands.

When Carlo was at home, he vied for the child's attention. Tall, darker than his counterpart, his skin burnt and hardened by the sun and wind, he had black eyes that seemed to the child to sparkle as he spoke of his escapades at sea. The little boy loved and admired both his grandfathers, but he was devoted to his mother. His grandfathers made him laugh and shriek with fear and delight as they told their tales, or threw him wildly in the air during games, but he was truly happy and at peace when he lay in his mother's arms, his head resting on her breast, breathing in the faint scent of rosemary or sage from the day's cooking, her sweet floury hands entwined in his own, while Carlo told exciting tales of the strange dark-skinned men he had encountered in foreign lands and of life on the ships where he made his home.

So, little Gerardo was a contented child, for he had everything a child could want: love, attention and food. His mother lay next to him in the big bed on the first floor, and until he was five or six years old, he lay wrapped in her arms feeling her large breasts rise and fall with her breathing. Her face, soft and brown, was the first thing he saw in the morning and last thing he saw at night. During the day, the little child and his mother would bake and cook, or he would sit at her feet when she sewed, embroidered or darned. He would mirror her actions: kneading, stirring, sewing. The men in the household, when they returned from their labours, often chastised her for 'making the child soft, encouraging him in women's work', but his mother took no heed, instead relishing the company of her son, who looked so like the husband she had lost.

'You will spoil the boy,' Gerardo scolded. 'You cannot keep him tied to you forever. Let him come to the Piazza with me. I will school him in the ways of a mason. He will need to learn a trade.'

'Gerardo, he is just a baby, not even seven years old. Besides, who says he should take up your profession? He might prefer a life at sea.'

'That he might; but Carlo cannot take him until he is eight or nine years of age. In the meantime he should learn a skill and spend time with me.'

And so, reluctantly, Carlotta, sent the child off, early one morning, with his grandfather. She fussed and fretted until the older man, normally so understanding and patient, was at the end of his tether.

'Please remember that he has not been away from me before; please don't lose him, Gerardo. And do remember to feed him – he needs meals regularly, little and often. I've packed a picnic for you both... bread and ham and some fruit. Please give him something to drink also. Is there water at the site?'

'Carlotta, we are only going to work... not away to sea for a month,' Gerardo scolded. 'He will be fine. Please stop worrying; there's enough food here to last a week.'

The boy was led away, his tears mirroring his mother's distress. As he reached the end of their road, the tears had become a torrent and he began to sob loudly at the prospect of leaving his mother who, trying to be brave, stood waving at the child, longing to rush to him, gather him up in her arms and bring him back home. But Gerardo picked him up, disappearing into the crowd of men walking towards the Piazza without a backward glance.

Throughout the day, Carlotta struggled to concentrate on her daily tasks. She was short with the maid, causing her to break a dish her father had recently brought back from his travels. Going to the market to buy something special for her son's supper, she forgot her money and was forced to make two journeys to purchase the food. As the time of their homecoming drew near, the meal bubbled over the fire and a flagon of wine stood ready for her father-in-law. She, desperate for a sight of her child, sat anxiously outside the house, distracting herself by shelling a big pile of peas, placing the glistening vegetables into a little bowl on her lap. When she caught sight of her father-in-law, with the child sitting astride his shoulders, she leapt up – the bowl of peas crashing to the ground – and rushed to her son, her arms outstretched in a show of adoration, tears of relief pouring down her soft brown face. The older man lifted the little boy down from his eyrie and handed him to her. She walked back to the house, the child's legs wrapped tightly around her waist, his face nuzzling into her neck as he told her of the adventures that had taken place that day.

Over the next few months, the child grew used to his daily routine and no longer cried when he left the house. He adored his grandfather, and had grown proud of his position as the older man's apprentice. When he returned at dusk, he was very tired, and once he had eaten, his mother would put him into their big bed – and he would often be asleep before she herself lay down to rest for the night. And so that special time when a mother and her child are content to be the other's sole companion had come to an end and the process of separation had begun. Which might explain why neither little Gerardo nor his grandfather noticed that Carlotta had grown pale and thin. It took Carlo, returning at the end of August from a three-month voyage to Syria, to comment on the change in his daughter.

'Gerardo,' Carlo said quietly one night to the older man as they sat drinking wine after dinner. 'My daughter... she looks thin. Does she eat when I am away?'

'Thin... is she really? I had not noticed.' Gerardo was a simple man, a man of few words.

'Yes, thin. And her colour is not good. I am concerned for her.'

'I suspect it is nothing; perhaps she misses the boy. Have you asked her about it?'

'She says she is fine, but Carlotta never thinks of herself. It is not in her nature. She is too stoic. I will be here for another month or so, before I must go back to sea. I shall make it my business to ensure that she rests and eats well.'

Carlo spent his days helping his daughter in the household, carrying in the water, bringing home food from the market on the banks of the Arno, chopping wood for the fire. Sometimes, he would persuade her to rest in the afternoon and would sit with her, stroking her head, as he told her tales of his journeys until she fell asleep, feeling safe and secure as she had done as a little child.

But the time soon came for him to return to sea. Carlotta watched him as he packed his bags, with a sense of sadness and foreboding. He was cheerful, as usual, and as he set off for the docks, he held her tightly, promising to return with some spices and perhaps some new dishes for their table.

'When will *nonno* come home?' little Gerardo had asked after he had gone.

'Soon… in a few months he will be back again.' And Gerardo kissed his mother's face as a large tear rolled down the soft brown cheek.

'Don't cry, *mamma*,' the little boy begged. 'I am here and will look after you.'

And the woman held her child closely – so closely that he finally broke free in alarm.

But Carlo never returned. Three months later, as Carlotta sat sewing one morning, there was a knock on the door.. The maid ushered in a young man – no more than fourteen or fifteen – and showed him upstairs to the sitting room.

'Yes, can I help you?'

'I have come from Lorenzo Calvo.'

'Yes, what is it?'

'It is about your father, Carlo Vaselli. I am sorry to tell you that he has been lost at sea.'

Carlotta could not remember – nor even hear – any more of what the young man said. She fell to the ground and began to wail. The maid, who was only thirteen, stood helplessly by, as the young man, distressed and embarrassed, ran next door to her neighbour Gabriella and asked her to come and take care of

Carlotta, who by now was lying prostrate on the ground of her home, sobbing uncontrollably.

When Gerardo and little Gerardo returned from the Piazza, the day's dust thick on their faces and hands, they found Gabriella, sitting by Carlotta, who lay in the bed she shared with the child, staring at the ceiling and unable to utter a sound.

Explaining what had happened, the neighbour left Gerardo in charge, promising to fetch some chamomile to make Carlotta a calming drink.

There was nothing Gerardo could say or do to salve her pain. She lay in her bed day after day and the older man did his best to manage the house and care for the child while she did so.

One morning, he climbed up the ladder to her bedchamber and, speaking quietly but firmly, said: 'Carlotta... I have something to say. You have been mourning your father for many weeks now. It is right that you mourn, but you have a duty to the child and it is time to put away your pain and get on with your life. I am taking the boy to work now, but when we return tonight it would be good to find some supper waiting for us. The boy is scared by your grief. He needs you.'

Something in what Gerardo said filtered through the blackness and despair that had become Carlotta's mantle, and slowly, as the sun rose and began to glint through the little windows of her house, she climbed wearily out of bed and descended the ladder to the kitchen. Her father's belongings had been returned to the house by one of the seamen a few weeks before, and they lay in a pile in one corner of the room. She took out his clothes and held them to her face, drinking in the familiar scent of sea air they always contained, before setting them aside to wash. She found her father's last journal and placed it carefully in a drawer to read at some later time when she felt a little stronger. At the bottom of the bag, she found a tiny wood carving; her father would often carve pieces of wood on long journeys – and this piece, she saw, was intended for the boy. It was shaped like a camel, an animal that had been newly brought to Pisa by an opportunistic trader, and was often to be seen ferrying goods back and forth across the Arno. She put it on the kitchen table for little Gerardo when he returned home, noting the thick layer of dust covering the table's surface.

Tying her long brown hair on top of her head, she called to the boy to bring fresh water and then set about cleaning the little house with the help of the maid. Leaving the girl to wash the floors, she walked down to the market and bought the ingredients for a special meal. Beef and aubergines, flour and fresh eggs, with figs for their pudding. Then, while the maid cleaned and polished around her, she spent the rest of the afternoon making ravioli with a mixture of the meat and aubergines.

By the time Gerardo returned with his grandson, the house was clean and the kitchen was filled with aromas of the delicious meal. The little boy ran to his mother and kissed her all over her face, until she, laughing, was forced to hide behind her hands to get him to stop. Then, while the older man washed off the day's dust, she showed the child the tiny wooden camel… and together they wept a little for their beloved Carlo, before eating their supper and going more happily to bed.

Over the next few weeks, Carlotta continued to make good progress… until one day she retrieved the journal of her father's last sea voyage. She lay on her bed, alternately weeping and laughing at his tales of life at sea. But the last page of the journal was incomplete.

'Woke early. Before the sunrise. We are in the eye of a big storm and the men are exhausted. I have stomach ache, the water is bad and the food ran out three days ago. We must make port or die. Lorenzo is pushing us too hard; he is determined that we will make Syria. He has promised that wife of his trinkets for her table. I must go up on deck – I hear the bell.'

There were, as Carlotta knew, many bells on board a ship. What had this one signalled? she wondered.

Carlotta began to pace the room, reflecting on the last entry. What, she wondered, could have happened after that bell had sounded? She had been so distressed by the news of her father's death that she had not asked anything about how he died. She remembered only that he had been swept overboard.

Grief enveloped her once again, but instead of the dull gnawing helplessness that she had felt before, she was filled now with desperate longing to know the truth – that, and a growing anger that her father may have died because of Lorenzo's greed.

She re-read the last entry: 'Lorenzo is pushing us too hard.'

Grabbing a shawl, Carlotta jumped down the ladder to the ground floor and, without stopping to tell the maid where she was going, ran out of the house towards the Arno. She went first to the dockside where she knew Lorenzo's galleys were moored. But that made no sense: the fleet was docked now, and there would be no one there – only the guards who slept on board round the clock to protect their master's precious vessels. Remembering that her father had once described the home of Calvo, his master, as being 'the grandest palace on the Arno,' she crossed the bridge over the river, before turning right onto the path that ran along the river's edge. Within ten minutes, she found herself outside the grand and imposing building that she recognised from her father's description – the house of Lorenzo Calvo and Berta di Bernardo.

It was approaching midday – too early for siesta. She thought better of knocking at the grand main entrance, instead walking down the lane at the side of the property, until she found two large wooden gates in the wall surrounding the gardens behind the house. She pushed the gates and one gave way. She pushed a little more, revealing a large, abundant garden. At one end were vegetables and fruit trees laid out in a regular design, overflowing with produce of all kinds. She observed two young men tending the beds with long hoes. Nearer the house, she saw the garden became more formal – geometric beds, edged in dark green box and filled with herbs, were set into a clipped lawn. Paths were laid between the beds, a sundial in the centre indicating the hour. As she walked silently up the path towards the grand house, she saw gillyflowers in shades of pink, purple and red erupting from large pots, and trees – olives and bays – casting short, sharp shadows in the midday sun. A small dog lay beneath a peach tree, snoring quietly. Surprised not to have been challenged, and the two young gardeners seeming not to have noticed her presence, she continued towards the house. She heard voices… and a maid ran up some stairs into the garden from what looked to be the kitchens of the household.

The girl stopped when she saw Carlotta.

'Can I help you?'

'I am here to see your master.'

The girl, thinking it odd that she had not come to the front door, asked, 'Is he expecting you?'

'No,' Carlotta answered, 'tell him that Carlo Vaselli's daughter is here. He will see me.'

Bidding her to wait in the garden, the girl ran back down the kitchen steps.

Some ten minutes later, Lorenzo emerged from the back of the house through imposing doors that led to the terrace.

'You are Carlo's daughter?'

She nodded and he beckoned her to sit near him on a little stone bench in the shade of a large olive tree.

'How may I help you?'

His tone was slow and deliberate. She, nervous, heard the blood roaring in her ears as she struggled to find her voice.

'I need... I need...' the words caught in her throat.

'What do you need... money? I can give you money. Is that what you want?'

She felt the anger rising now and she stood up. 'No! I do not want your money. I did not come here for that. I came because I want to know what happened. What happened to my father? How and why did he die?'

She held out the leather-bound book she had found in Carlo's bag. 'I have his log; there was a storm, he says, and that you were pushing the men too hard. Is that true? I need to know what happened, how did he die? I have to know.'

Bridling as Lorenzo smiled at her, she pulled back from him as he placed his hand on hers in an attempt to comfort her.

'Your father was very brave, very brave. There was a storm, yes. We were trying to make land. The men were hungry. A lad, a young boy on his first trip with us, got panicky. He had not eaten or drunk for a day or so and was hallucinating... it gets some people like that. He wanted water, and in his madness, thought he could drink the sea. He went overboard. Your father went to save him. I'm sorry. That is all I can say. He went over the side and we never saw him again.'

'Did no one try to rescue him?'

'We had lost one hand already, and then Carlo; there was no sense in losing others. The sea was too treacherous and the men too exhausted. The wind dropped a few hours later and we returned to the spot, but there was no sign of him. We were still about ten hours from land; we had to sail on to find food and water, or lose everyone on board. I'm sorry. It was a tragedy. But he died a hero. We all miss him. I miss him; he had been with me for fifteen years.'

As Lorenzo had been speaking, Carlotta had pictured her father attempting to save the boy. It rang true; her father, a hero.

She stood to go.

'I must go. I'm sorry, I ought not to have come. I just had to know.' Then, remembering the log, she added: 'But my father said you pushed the men too hard. Is that true?'

Lorenzo was unrepentant.

'Of course it is true; I expect all of my men to work hard and be brave. We were all exhausted and half-starved, but that is life at sea. It was no different for me or for any other man on board. All rations were shared equally. We were aiming for Syria; we had a shipment to collect and the weather was bad. We had no choice but to keep going. We could not come ashore to get provisions – the sea was too treacherous, there was nowhere for us to stop.'

Carlotta sat down once again, her face flushed, tears smarting in her eyes.

'Look,' said Lorenzo, 'I understand how you must feel. But it was a tragedy that I could do nothing about. Let me help you. You have a child, don't you? Carlo would often talk about him. Let me give you something for the boy. It is the least I can do for Carlo; it would have been his wages for this trip, plus a share of the profits. Take it... please.'

Pulling a bag of coins from his belt, he handed it to Carlotta, who took it, reluctantly.

Guiding her towards the kitchen, he called to the housekeeper: 'Maria, take care of...' and he turned to the young woman.

'Carlotta,' she said.

'Take care of Carlotta. Give her something to drink and send Alfonso back with her.'

That evening, as she served supper to her father-in-law and child, she did not mention her visit to Lorenzo. She placed the money he had given her in the bottom of her clothes chest, think-ing to put it towards some schooling for her son. She hoped he, at least, would never die at sea.

And so it would have stayed, had she not overheard a conver-sation between two women in a queue for vegetables one September evening.

'They say that he had the man thrown overboard.'

'No! Why?'

'For daring to argue with him.'

'Really is that what Marco told you?'

'He did; he is looking for another master. He is fearful that if he keeps on with Lorenzo Calvo the same may happen to him. The man is a monster, he will not be crossed.'

'Well, I suppose you can see his point. You can only have one master on board a ship, can't you?'

'Yes, but the man had been with him a long time. He was just trying to persuade him to go ashore. The men had no water or food and were desperate.'

Carlotta's head began to spin as she listened to the women. She felt nauseous, and her legs buckled beneath her.

As she came to, some moments later, she looked around for the women, but there was no sign of them.

'The women,' she said desperately to the stall-holder, strug-gling to her feet,

'those women in the queue in front of me... where did they go?'

'Oh they've gone. They left, just as you fell. They went that way, I think. But you are so pale, you must stay here.'

But Carlotta pushed him out of the way and, looking wildly in the direction the women had gone, rushed off in search of them.

She returned home, exhausted, two hours later; her father-in-law and son were waiting anxiously for her.

'Where were you, Carlotta?' the old man asked. 'We were worried.'

But she could not answer. She was overcome with grief and rage. Weeping, she cursed the name of Lorenzo Calvo. Her father-in-law, frightened by her hysteria, immediately sent to the apothecary for some healing tisane, and persuaded his daughter-in-law to her bed.

That night, the child slept with his grandfather, but they heard Carlotta shouting and weeping in her sleep. The next day, for the first time in thirty-five years, Gerardo did not go to work, sending the little boy in his stead to explain that he was unavoidably kept at home. During the day, he tried to talk to Carlotta but she simply kept repeating over and over that Lorenzo had destroyed her father. She was burning up with a fever, and he feared that she had contracted some terrible illness – perhaps typhoid or the fever caused by *mal aria*.

Over the next few days, Carlotta's fever subsided… but it was replaced by terrible pains in her right breast. At first, Gerardo thought she was describing a malady of her heart, but when her breast began to ooze a foul liquid from the nipple, he knew that this was no emotional episode. He sent once again for the apothecary.

'Her breast, it seeps,' he said to the woman as she entered the house.

The woman looked at Gerardo and shook her head. 'I will do what I can,' she said.

Four weeks later, Carlotta was dead, and the old man was left to care for a small boy who he loved more than his own life.

CHAPTER 7

March 1171

B erta stood looking up at the small wooden tower house. It was early in the morning and the streets, she was relieved to notice, were eerily quiet. She had left Lorenzo sleeping, and dressed quickly and quietly, anxious not to waken him. Swearing her maid to secrecy, she had roused the housekeeper, Maria, from her bed next to the kitchen. The huge open fireplace had not yet been sparked into life. The ashes from the previous evening lay in drifts in the vast grate. Pots and pans stood soaking in the room next door, ready for one of the kitchen maids to scrub them clean. The room hung heavy with the odour of nutmeg and the hare they had eaten the evening before.

'Maria… wake up,' she shook the older woman's shoulder.

'I'm sorry to disturb you, but I need you to do something for me.'

The housekeeper rubbed her eyes and sat up in bed, pulling her nightgown around her shoulders. 'What is it, lady… it must be early.'

'It is. I am sorry to wake you, but I have to go out now. There is something I must do. If Lorenzo wakes before I am back, please tell him that I have gone for a walk. He is fast asleep. He should not wake for another hour or two, and hopefully I will be back long before then.'

She found the house relatively easily; it was in the old part of the town, on the north side of the river. She knocked nervously at the door. For a moment, no sound came from inside, and Berta, fearing her journey was to be fruitless, turned away with something akin to relief. As she did so, a young girl, no more than thirteen or fourteen, with beautiful blue eyes, opened the door and gestured for her to enter.

The room was furnished simply. Just a table made of local wood – chestnut, Berta thought – and two chairs. A large pot hung over an open fire. The doors of a small cupboard stood ajar, revealing row upon row of glass bottles containing curiously mis-shapen objects and different powders of varying shades. Berta sat and waited, taking in the aromas of herbs and flowers that hung from the wooden beams, drying in rows

A woman, dressed simply in a dark blue woollen gown, climbed down the ladder in a corner of the room. 'Good morn-ing, *signora*... how may I help you?'

'You have been recommended to me,' Berta spoke quietly, 'I have a problem that I am told you can help me with.'

'Please, *signora*, let me take your cloak. Aurelia, take the lady's cloak and bring water for the fire. I can make you an infusion, *signora*... if you would like? To relax you.'

Berta watched the girl as she hung the cloak on a hook on the back of the door, and then, taking a large jug from the floor in both hands, she leant her body against the small wooden door at the back of the room, pushing it open. Berta glimpsed a tiny courtyard garden surrounded by a high wall filled with a patch-work of herbs. Vast bushes of rosemary, as tall as the girl her-self, fought for space with the tall architectural spikes of angelica. Pots tumbled with aromatic basil, tarragon and lavender. Nettles were corralled in a productive corner. Everything had its place. And near the back wall was a pump that the girl now pushed up and down until water gushed from it into the large brown pottery jug.

'We are fortunate to have a well that we share with our neighbours,' said the woman, who had watched Berta's gaze following the girl.

'Tell me a little of your problem,' she said kindly.

Unsteadily, Berta began to explain her predicament.

'I have been married for many years – fifteen, in fact – to a good man. We have everything we could want, except for the one thing he desires more than anything else… a child.'

The woman's gaze never left Berta's face. She smiled a little now.

'I see. And may I ask… are you still intimate with your husband?'

'Of course!' Berta was startled by her indelicacy, 'What do you think I am, a fool? Of course we are intimate, as often as we can, but still, after all this time, I have no child. Maybe it is too late, maybe I am too old… I am thirty-four years of age. The doctors tell me, of course, it is my fault… that there must be something wrong with me, or I have sinned in some way. But I attend Mass, we say prayers to San Nicola… and still no child. A friend told me that you might be able to help me. My husband would not approve of me coming here. He is a modern man. He puts his faith in God and doctors. But I felt I had to come.'

The girl came back into the room and poured water into the large pan that hung over the open fire. She broke some small pieces of firewood in two and pushed them into the flames to provoke them into activity. Steam began to rise up the charred, stone chimney.

'I understand well, *signora*,' said the woman. 'The life of an apothecary has always been shrouded in mystery. Doctors do not agree with our methods, but they can be very effective. The old remedies are still the best way.'

She spoke gently to the girl. 'Aurelia, bring a bowl and some nettles; they are hanging there above the cupboard.'

She turned back to Berta.

'Now, *signora*, there are some things I need to ask you.' The woman took the stiff, drying nettles from the girl and began to pull the leaves carefully off the stems.

'Aurelia, these are no good. Please go into the garden and bring me some fresh nettles. Take the knife.' The girl, glancing uneasily at Berta, went back to the garden.

'You may find these questions embarrassing, *signora*, and I apologise for that, but I do not believe that the fault always lies with the woman. This is heretical talk, I understand well. No doctor would agree with me, but I have helped several women with my methods.'

Berta nodded uneasily.

'Your husband… when you are together, is he hard?'

'Of course!' Berta's tone was once again irritable.

'Forgive me, *signora*, but I need to understand the problem. There are remedies we can try to help you… to strengthen the blood and make you strong, but I need to know everything. Are you satisfied… by your husband? You understand what I mean by satisfied?'

'Yes, everything is as it should be.'

'Because you will not conceive if you are not satisfied.'

'I am satisfied; that cannot be the cause. Might there be some other problem?'

Berta thought of the last time she and Lorenzo had made love. Nearly twenty years her senior, she had to admit she no longer desired him. He had grown fat, his lush dark hair was thin and sparse, and she struggled to remember him as he had been when they first met – strong and virile, able to pick her up and throw her onto the bed, impressing her with his tales of adventure at sea. Then, she had counted the days until her returned from his travels, willing him to come safely back to her, bringing sparkle and noise to the quiet life she led while he was away. But over the ensuing years, she had come to enjoy the periods without him almost more than those times they spent together, bringing as they did the restriction of her freedom, and requiring her to devote her waking hours to making him happy.

Nevertheless, she had always managed to fulfil her wifely duties, and even to enjoy them, as long as the candles had first been extinguished. Then, she would allow her mind to run free, imagining herself with another, younger fantasy lover – perhaps one of the pretty young men she invited to their salons... artists, architects, musicians. For, while she had never actually risked any physical infidelity, her mind was at liberty to fall in and out of love at will. She did not consider this sinful in any way, merely a private expression of her own desire. And, in truth, it enabled her to make Lorenzo happy; to make love to him with the passion she had felt for him when she was young. She still cared for Lorenzo and felt no antagonism to him. He had been generous over the years, encouraging her in her artistic interests and indulging her passion for artistic company, mostly, she suspected, because it leant him an air of sophistication that he did not himself possess. And her marriage to Lorenzo had provided her with financial security and a position in society. But there was no doubt that the first flush of desire she had felt as a girl of seventeen had faded over the years.

The girl came into the room carrying a basket of fresh nettles.

'I shall give you a tisane to drink,' said Violetta, 'sweetened with a little honey. It will strengthen you. Drink it today and ask your maid to make it for you each morning. I will also make you some little biscuits that perhaps your maid could collect for you tomorrow. They will give your husband strength.'

'But my husband doesn't need strength, he is perfectly well,' Berta protested. She had already been assured by her doctor that her predicament was her sole responsibility. No fault could be laid at her husband's door.

'*Signora*, I am sure he is well enough. But his seed may not be strong.'

Berta watched the woman as she soaked the fresh nettles in the boiling water, mixing a small piece of honeycomb to sweeten the drink.

'What sort of biscuits?' she asked after a short pause, curiosity getting the better of her.

'Don't worry, they are delicious, filled with wonderful things – walnuts, pistachio, pine kernels, cinnamon, ginger and cloves. No man can resist them. In fact, he may get a little fat, they are so delicious. But they will strengthen his seed.'

Standing, the apothecary moved to the shelves that lined the walls on either side of the fireplace. She took a turquoise-coloured majolica jar and stood it carefully on the table. Putting her hand deep into the pot, she removed a scaly, desiccated creature.

Berta recoiled involuntarily.

'*Signora*, please don't worry. This,' she said, holding up a dried-up lizard, 'this is the best part. Once it is ground to a fine powder and mixed with the other ingredients he will not notice the taste.'

Then, pulling a vast pestle and mortar towards her, she deftly removed the head and the feet and began to grind the dead creature, while Berta sipped her nettle tea.

When Berta returned home, Lorenzo was looking anxiously out of the window. He turned as she entered the room.

'Berta, there you are; I was worried. Where have you been?'

'Just for a walk, Lorenzo. It was a beautiful morning.'

'A walk, at this time... unaccompanied? Why did you not take the servants with you? You know it is dangerous for you to be alone in the town.' His tone was challenging. His black eyes bored into her, searching her face for signs of guilt.

Berta thought of all the times she had gone unaccompanied into the town, when Lorenzo was away. She would dress in simple clothing – not quite in disguise, but certainly confident that she would not be easily recognised as the wife of wealthy merchant Lorenzo Calvo. These outings were innocent enough, enabling her to visit buildings of interest, or providing inspiration for her sketches, and so she felt no guilt about them. But she knew that when her husband was at home, he expected her to behave as a noble lady should, and that solitary walks were out of the question. She regretted having gone out alone that morning; her desire for privacy had caused him to feel suspicious of her, and in truth there was no need. Anxious to quickly defuse the situation, she began to weep quietly, before sinking dramatically onto the bed.

After a few moments, she recovered herself sufficiently to speak.

'I'm sorry, Lorenzo... I should have told you where I was going, but I thought you might not approve. I went to see an apothecary. To see if she could help me... to have a child.'

His face softened and he sat down on the bed, his arm around his wife's shoulder. 'You are right; I would not have approved. I do not believe in those old women with their magic potions. People in our position do not, and should not, visit apothecaries; we have doctors to help us, Berta. Only the poor still believe their nonsense. Is that why you went alone? Because you wanted to keep it a secret?'

Berta nodded miserably.

'*Cara*,' he said, caressing his wife's shoulder, 'you should have told me. I might have argued with you, but in the end, you know that if you really felt it would help, I would have allowed it. Besides, I have been worried about you.'

'I'm sorry, Lorenzo. Please forgive me?'

'Of course. But next time, please take the servants. Now then, what did she say? Can she help us, this old crone?' he asked gently.

'Lorenzo, she is not an old crone. She is a kind woman called Violetta. Her husband was a painter, sadly now dead. But she is educated, intelligent, and I liked her, Lorenzo. I have faith in her. She is hopeful that she can help me; she says I need to drink a special tisane each day and…' she paused.

'What?'

'Nothing.' The little lizard biscuits, she decided, should remain a secret for the time being. 'It's just that I am to go back to see her in a little while and she may change the tisane for something else. Are you angry with me?'

'No, Berta, I am not angry – perplexed perhaps, and disappointed that you did not feel you could discuss this with me. But you know that a child is the one thing I yearn for – someone to share in our good fortune. And if you feel this woman can help us, then I will not stop you. Maybe you are right, we should try everything.'

Lorenzo stood now. 'But I think we should continue with our prayers to San Nicola, don't you? We might ask the priest to conduct a special Mass for us. We must pray for a son, Berta, a strong son to take on the business. A son who has your beauty and my acumen. He will be the most wonderful child any man has ever had.'

'We might have a daughter,' Berta said teasingly, 'a fine strong girl, with your beauty and my acumen. How would you feel about that?' She attempted a smile.

But Lorenzo said simply: 'It will be God's wish...' and kissing his wife, he left her for the day.

Berta lay back on the bed. She felt drained by her visit to the apothecary. She had found much of what she had seen and heard unsettling – in particular the idea that 'the problem' might not be hers but her husband's. This was radical thinking, not something any doctor she had ever met would approve of. Both the church and the medical profession were united in their belief that a woman's inability to conceive was due to her sin – or at least because of some flaw or fault of hers. Sometimes the remedy was deemed to include more frequent congress and so the man might be encouraged to eat a good diet to give him strength for long nights of passion. But at no time in all the years she had been searching for a remedy for her childlessness had any doctor or priest implied that her husband's seed might be at fault.

She sat at her dressing table, brushing her hair, and considered what it would be like if she did have a child. To have a little person needing her would be a strange experience. At the age of thirty-four, she had become used to her own company – and in truth rather revelled in it. Children would curtail a vital part of her life; the hours that she spent studying art or painting would instead be filled with caring for children. Gone would be the pleasing rhythm of her life, whether Lorenzo was in Pisa or abroad.

When her husband was at home, they would rise together and take breakfast. Then, while he visited the warehouses or clients, she would study alone in her chamber. Normally, he returned at lunchtime, and they would eat together before retiring, as usual, for siesta. In the late afternoon, they would dress – Berta wearing the latest fashions, her hair perfumed, her gowns of finest silks decorated with pearls and jewels. This was when she would come alive, welcoming twenty or thirty visitors to her home, or, taking their retinue with them, she and Lorenzo would meet friends at their private *piazzetta*. Her father's profession of *capo magister* had influenced her greatly, and increasingly she chose to use her new-found wealth and position to nurture young artists and sculptors; she had become a patron, and her husband was proud of her instinctive ability to spot talent.

When Lorenzo travelled, as he still did two or three times a year, Berta would change her routine. Rising early, she would dress simply in a woollen robe, her beautiful red hair covered with a simple linen cap, and walk – usually alone – to the vast building site across the Arno river that was the Piazza del Duomo. Her father had died some years before, shortly after completing the work on her own house; but before his death he had been one of the many *magisters* who had also found employment at the site of the new cathedral. This architectural project would take over 100 years to complete, and as a child, Berta had been brought by her father to visit the site and watch him at work, carving the decorations on columns around a doorway, or sculpting delicate figures from pink marble, beautifying the interior of this extraordinary building.

Berta was familiar with the noises and sights of a building under construction, but she never ceased to be fascinated by the myriads of trades that were plied there. A building such as the Duomo, which was possibly the most complicated and extensive construction in the whole of Italy, required a workforce of literally hundreds of men – masons, gilders, painters, carpenters, even a priest to tend to their spiritual needs. On these early morning visits, Berta would walk around the site, studying the different techniques employed by this stone mason or that sculptor. She marvelled at the noise created by a hundred masons' hammers as they chipped and carved the vast blocks of stone and marble. With the sun rising over the Duomo, they would labour, their backs burnt the colour of hazelnuts as they bent double over their work, the air filled with a choking dust as their tools struck the stone.

Sometimes she would take up position at the edge of the site, sketching the men as they tackled some particularly intricate task, chatting with them, questioning them about a particular technique or method or working. Then, stiff from sitting still, she would get up and stretch, walking around the edge of the site, studying the growing cathedral from all sides, noting how the sun struck the building in the changing light.

On more than one occasion, she had watched, fascinated, as forty or fifty men winched a vast block of marble into position, dragging it hundreds of feet from one of the warehouses that stood on the edge of the Piazza. Carefully chosen for its colour and texture by the master mason, and mined many years before from quarries in Monte Pisano or Elba, each marble block was transported first by boat down the coast, then up the river Arno into Pisa, or placed onto barges and floated down canals that criss-crossed the plains around Pisa, waterways built especially to supply the city with the multitude of goods from Europe and the East to which they had become accustomed – glassware, cloth, gold and spices. The marble was then left to rest or *purifican- teur* in the site warehouse to see how it coped with changes in temperature; for it was vital to first discover how it would react to frost, or snow, or the extreme heat that descended on the flat *campo* in the steamy summer months.

When Berta had been a child, her own father had often travelled great distances in search of the perfect piece of stone for a building. An architect in medieval Italy was required to have many skills, but chief among them was his ability to recognise the perfect stone in its natural state. Many weeks were spent scouring the quarries for the ideal rockface, which had to be both the correct colour and texture for the job – with the right *pell* or skin, almost as if it were a living being. Once chosen, the marble would be split; in winter by pouring water into a crack that had first been made on the surface, allowing the cold weather to do the mason's work, the water expanding as it froze and ultimately splitting the stone. Once cut, the marble would be rolled precariously down the mountain on vast tree trunks, the blocks tied securely to improvised sleighs. Many men were required to control the precious cargo, and few journeys were completed without death or injury. It was a lengthy and exhausting part of the architect's role, but a vital one, and Berta became accustomed to her father disappearing at least once a year on these treacherous journeys. Left at home under the care of a nurse, she could scarcely contain her excitement when her father reappeared after several weeks away. She would rush from her chamber or the schoolroom and throw herself around his neck, filled with relief at his safe return and impatient for tales of his adventures and the inevitable treats that accompanied the stories.

One of her first memories was when she was four or five, and he had sat her on his lap and held out his clenched fists for her to choose – one fist or the other.

'Choose one, Smeralda; see if you can get the prize.'

She, excited by the challenge, keen to show off her skills to her father, jumped off his lap and examined his hands carefully, intelligently pressing his fingers into his palm to see if she could feel any difference between the two hands. Finally, she pointed to the left. Her father unfurled his hand, and there lay a tiny piece of pink marble carved in the shape of a bird.

Berta still had that bird; it sat on her dressing table next to a tiny dolphin made of purest white stone, a memento of a trip her father had made to the far south of Italy when she was eight years of age. He had gone in search of marble to match that chosen by the Duomo's original architect Buscheto. The local quarries had been unable to supply it, and her father had travelled to Sicily by sea to explore the southern quarries. She had loved the tales he brought back from that trip.

'One morning, as we came up on deck, the ship was escorted by hundreds of dolphins, all swimming with us, their bodies rolling with the waves in unison. What do you call a group of dolphins, Smeralda? If you can tell me, I will give you a little present.'

The child thought hard. She had learnt many new words and was sure that she had the answer somewhere in her head, if she could just retrieve it. She paced the room, desperate to remember and to win the gift.

'A flock,' she ventured.

'No, that is birds,' he chided.

'A herd?' she tried, not altogether convinced of her answer.

Her father shook his head.

She thought of the word, dolphins, over and over until, suddenly, the answer came to her clearly.

'A school, Papa, like my school here where I have my lessons.'

And her delighted father took from his pocket the tiny white dolphin that he had carved for her on the return trip, and placed it carefully in the child's palm. It felt as smooth as silk to the little girl.

'Well done, my darling, you are very clever. And now I will tell you what we did on that journey. Would you like that? I found this stone to make the little dolphin at an amazing quarry. I'd been sent to find some snowy-white marble for the great cathedral. It had to match exactly with the stone that Buscheto had chosen. He wanted it to be purest white to reflect the innocence and purity of Santa Maria Assunta to whom the cathedral is dedicated. Well, we found some marble on this trip that was of such purity, I knew it would be perfect. We brought back many large blocks and it was very difficult to get it on board. Can you imagine how we did it? How did we get it from the land onto the boat?'

Once again, the little girl thought hard, and then, fetching a piece of vellum and a pen, father and daughter drew a sketch together: she the marble blocks on one side of the paper, he the galley on the other.

'It was too heavy for you to lift it with your hands, I think.'

'Correct. So what would we use?'

'You would have to tie a rope to it and pull the rope somehow, with lots of men?'

'We did, we did, we lifted the stone like this,' and he drew a picture of a triangular wooden frame, a rope hanging from the centre, tied round the marble block, with the boat floating beneath it.

'We sailed the boat right up onto the shore at low tide so that its bottom touched the sand. Then we dropped the marble onto the boat and waited for the tide to rise... lifting the boat, and setting it free to sail away with its precious cargo.'

Now seated at her dressing table, Berta picked up the tiny pink marble bird that her father had given her all those years before; she rolled it in her hands, feeling its cool softness. She thought back over her childhood. Her mother had died while giving birth to her. Was that why she was so frightened of having a child of her own? The absence of her mother had never distressed her – she had never known her. Her father had been her whole world... and he had been such a wonderful father, teaching her everything he knew. To bear a child of her own, if she survived the birth, would be a wonderful thing. And, she reasoned to herself, it would not necessarily mean the end of her interests... perhaps she could even take a child with her on her visits to the Duomo and Baptistery, as her father had taken her to his own work. But she would need help: a good nurse and a good maid – someone who would support her and care for the child, allowing her the time to do as she wished.

'A child would make Lorenzo so happy,' she said to herself. She knew that for him it was a nagging loss that ran like a thread through their life together. To have a son to carry on his business, to make the name of Calvo great, and found one of the great mercantile families – that was what he truly wanted, and it was her duty to provide it for him.

Berta was brought back from her musing by the sound of her maid, Lucia, entering the room.

She was a large, lumbering, slow-witted girl whom Berta had taken on against her better judgement in order to please Maria the housekeeper. The girl was some relative or other, a niece perhaps, but it had been a mistake. Even her voice irritated her – a slow, deep, nasal drawl, without a trace of energy or enthusiasm.

'*Signora?*'

'Lucia; there you are. I have been back from my walk for hours. Where have you been? I need to get dressed. Get out my green gown and then come here. We need to do something with my hair.'

The girl laboriously removed a green silk gown from one of the large cedar chests that stood under the window of Berta's bedroom and lay it on the bed. As she took up the brush and began to comb through Berta's hair, her mistress yelped in pain and slapped her wrist.

'Stop... now. I have had enough. Please go down to Maria in the kitchen and see what duties she has for you there, and send her up to me... now.'

The girl turned away, apparently unconcerned.

And Berta, twisting her own hair into a neat coil around her head, decided to find herself a new maid.

CHAPTER 8

June 1171

The nettle tea had not worked. And in spite of numerous prayers to San Nicola, the Patron Saint of Infertility, and repeated visits to Violetta the apothecary, Berta remained stubbornly childless. On her last visit, she had even been persuaded to take home a little parcel filled with the lizard biscuits.

'Trust me, *signora*,' Violetta assured her, 'they have never let me down.'

'But how am I to persuade him to eat them?' Berta asked in desperation. 'He will never accept any responsibility for the problem. Besides, he does not like sweet things.'

'Then you must persuade him, *signora*. Please try.'

Reluctantly, Berta had taken the biscuits home, and as she and Lorenzo dressed for dinner that evening, she had the sweetmeats laid out on a majolica dish in the bedchamber.

'Lorenzo, would you like one of these little treats? They go well with the wine.' She poured her husband a cup of wine and handed it to him with the little biscuit.

'Berta, you know I hate such things.' He pushed the biscuits away and drank the wine.

'I was given them today, by a friend, a new friend; her cook made them especially for us. I would so like to be able to tell her that we liked them.'

'Tell her whatever you like,' Lorenzo said irritably as he left the room.

Later that evening, when they returned from meeting friends, she tried again. Lorenzo was a little drunk, and it occurred to Berta he might be a little more malleable.

She undressed in front of him, deliberately letting her shift fall to the floor, revealing her body shimmering in the candlelight.

'Berta, come here to me,' he held out his hand to her. Picking up the plate of biscuits, she walked provocatively towards the bed.

'Lorenzo, darling, eat one of the biscuits first, please. I promised my friend we would try them.'

He smiled at her but shook his head.

'You will have to eat one, if I put it in here…'

And teasingly she bent over and placed the little round biscuit between her legs.

Then, lying on the bed, she murmured in his ear: 'You'd better see if you can find it…'

The following day, she returned to Violetta and recounted her success.

'I have never seen him eat so much,' she said laughing. 'He found the first one and I had to put another and then another there. He ate them all, and this morning demanded more.'

'You see,' Violetta said triumphantly, 'all men adore them… although I have never heard of them being served on such a sweet plate! Let us hope that they do their work. I will send Aurelia round later with some fresh ones.'

As Berta drank yet another steaming concoction, she watched Violetta's daughter, carefully dissecting seed heads with her delicate little fingers, collecting the seeds in little bowls, which she then tipped into a jar to put on the shelves. There was a grace and quietness about the girl, qualities Berta knew were in short supply amongst her present household. A girl like Aurelia would make the perfect maid – discreet and loyal, someone she could trust with a myriad of little confidences. And the girl was clearly intelligent; she would be easy to guide and teach. If Berta was ever to have a child, she would need someone bright and quick-witted to help her; she could never leave a lump of a girl like Lucia with any child of hers. Seizing the moment she said, 'Violetta, I have a proposition for you.'

The older woman looked up from her work, grinding the nuts for Lorenzo's biscuits.

'I would like to offer your daughter Aurelia a position in my household.'

Violetta's face fell; she darted a glance at her daughter. '*Signora*,' she spoke quickly, 'I cannot allow that. Aurelia is all I have in the world; I could not be without her. Since we lost my husband, her father, to the fever three years ago, she has been my only comfort. Besides, who would take care of the house while I did my work. I am sorry, but it is not possible.'

Berta, not to be thwarted, had her argument prepared: 'Violetta, I am not taking her away from you, I am merely offering her a place in my house as my personal maid. She will be well looked after and I will pay her well. Think of the money. She could bring money home to you, to help you, and possibly save something for her dowry.'

Berta caught the eye of the blushing Aurelia.

'Surely it would be better for her to bring money into the household? I have another girl, less delicate than Aurelia, who would be well suited to helping you in the house. If you will let me have Aurelia, I will give you this other girl in return. Aurelia is too refined for this work; she will be happy working for me. I won't make too many demands on her. She will just be required to care for my clothes – nothing that would be too arduous.'

Violetta shook her head. 'No, I am sorry – I would miss her too much; and she would miss me too.'

Aurelia spoke up. '*Mamma*, please… I think I would like to go with the *signora*. It would be an opportunity for me.'

'Aurelia, we will discuss it when the *signora* leaves.' Violetta spoke firmly.

Berta, well schooled in the ways of diplomacy, picked up her parcel of biscuits, along with the recipe for a new tisane, and took her leave of the apothecary.

As she walked away from the house with her page and maid, Aurelia rushed out.

'*Signora, signora*… please, I would like to speak to you.'

Berta stopped and turned.

'If you would still like me to come, I will persuade my mother. You are right, she needs more money and it would be wonderful for me to make a new life for myself. You said you had someone who could help her here.'

'Yes, my personal maid, Lucia.' Berta waved her hand at the hapless girl standing awkwardly some feet away, and lowering her voice said, 'she is not suited to the sort of work I am offering you, but she will be perfectly adequate to help your mother clean the house and bring in water and the like. If you can persuade your mother, I will arrange it. And tell your mother not to worry about the cost; I will continue to pay Lucia's wage, and yours too. Come to my house as soon as you have her agreement, and I will send the cart for your things. You won't need much, I will buy you new clothes. I know you can read, Aurelia. Tell your mother that I will allow you to read each day. I have many manuscripts in my house. Trust me, you will have a fine life with me.'

As Berta reached the corner of the lane, she glanced back and observed Aurelia watching her from the doorway of her mother's house. The girl raised her hand in salutation and smiled. Berta smiled back. She would have her new maid, of that she was certain, and motioning to her retinue went home to the *palazzo*.

CHAPTER 9

June 1999

The morning after Sam had discovered Michael's notebook and research material, she set out for the hospital, his briefcase in hand, with a renewed sense of purpose. She was going to suggest to Michael that whilst he was unwell, she continued his work for him. It would be good for her to have something to occupy her, and besides, she had to admit that she felt just a little excited at the prospect of having a project to sink her teeth into.

Arriving at the hospital, she found him awake, a physiotherapist working on his weaker side.

He smiled weakly when she entered and attempted a feeble 'Hello'.

She put their coffees down on the table and kissed him fleetingly on the forehead.

'Hi – gosh so you're being kept busy then? How are you feeling?'

'A little better,' he whispered.

'Good, good,' she said. 'I'm glad. Look… I've been thinking, Michael. I know we're going to be here for a while yet. The doctors have told me that we won't be able to get you home for a week or two at least and, well, I wondered if you'd mind if I did a little digging on the film… you know… carry on where you left off?'

He frowned a little, and shook his head almost imperceptibly. 'Was that a no?'

He shook his head again.

The physiotherapist looked at her over her black-rimmed glasses, a sense of irritation in her blue eyes.

'Sorry,' Sam said automatically to the woman, 'I'm interrupting. Look, I know you're not feeling great and I don't expect you to help, but it just seems a bit of a shame, me being here and the film languishing and, well, nothing getting done.'

He raised his stronger hand and gestured to her.

She lowered her ear instinctively nearer to his mouth.

'They won't let you... film company.'

'Oh, I see,' she said, straightening up. 'You think they'll have put the project on hold?'

He gave a slight nod.

'And why would they trust a housewife with your project?'

He frowned.

'I was a bloody journalist for ten years, for God's sake.'

The physio stood up: '*Signora... per favore...* no shouting, please.'

'No, no of course not, sorry. I'm sorry, Michael. I just thought I might be of some use, that's all.'

He smiled back at her weakly and waved his hand in what, she felt, was a dismissive gesture.

'Look, I'm off for a walk, I'll be back later when this lady has finished.'

Taking the briefcase, Sam went to the café on the corner of the Piazza. She ordered and paid for a coffee at the bar, before taking a seat at a table in the window. Michael was clearly in no position to fight her corner with the production company. She would have to do that for herself and if she stood any chance of success she would need to get up to speed with the project. She carefully removed the book of maps and portraits from the battered briefcase, and laid it on the table. As the waiter placed her cappuccino on the table, he nodded towards the book – 'Aah, Signor Visalberghi.'

'I'm sorry?' Sam said, a little confused. 'What did you say?'

'The book, *signora*, it was written by Signor Visalberghi. He sells it in his shop just round the corner from here. He comes here for his coffee each morning.'

'Oh, thank you,' she said. 'It's a fascinating book.'

The name seemed familiar to Sam – Visalberghi, but she could not quite grasp why. She drained her coffee, and went to the bar to find the waiter.

'Signor Visalberghi's shop – can you tell me where it is?'

'*Si*. Just down Via Maria, turn left into Via Leopardi and it's just there on the right.'

Sam realised that she must have passed the shop on several occasions, without even noticing its existence.

The woodwork was painted black and the windows were dark, with no lighting, presumably to protect the antique manuscripts and images that were displayed there.

She pushed the door; as it juddered open, an old bell jangled noisily, announcing her arrival.

'*Buongiorno*,' she called out into the gloom. At the back of the shop, an elderly man was stooped over a sheaf of papers laid out on a large wooden desk, a magnifying glass pressed to his eye.

'*Buongiorno, Signor Visalberghi?*'

'*Si, si, signora. Come posso aiutarla?*'

Sam removed the book from her bag and laid it on the old plan chest.

'*Signore... scusi, ma no parlo Italiono bene. E possible assistare mi...* would you help me? *Ho un libro* – I have a book here that I believe came from your shop – your... *negozio.*'

The old man smiled and nodded.

'The images in the book, *le imagine... sono sue*? Do you have the originals here? *Le original....* of people, or maps of the town – *le carte*?'

He nodded once again.

'*Si signora, le originali sono qui.*'

'*Vorrei...* I would like... *un imagine della Torre... quando era construtto...* when it was first built. *O imagini di persone...* images of people living at that time.'

The old man smiled and nodded.

She flipped the book open at Calvo's image, and then to the Admiral.

The old man nodded and went off towards the back of the shop. He pulled open several drawers in the old plan chests that lined the back wall, muttering under his breath as he did so. Sam took the opportunity to study the dimly lit shop.

Every spare inch of wall space was covered with bookcases, filled almost exclusively with leather-bound books. No modern paperback or hardback disturbed the serried uniformity. Little notes had been stuck onto the shelves every few inches, inscribed with perfect italic writing, presumably some kind of referencing system. Down one side of the shop were three large architectural plan chests. These, too, were neatly labelled.

After some minutes, the old man returned with a large piece of vellum. He laid it out before her. It was the image of Calvo.

'The original? *Original*?' asked Sam, incredulously.

'*No – le originali sono nel museo, signora.*'

At that moment, the door juddered open. Sam turned to see a familiar figure entering the shop.

'*Papa... come vai*?' The man, dressed casually in a linen suit, walked across to the old man and embraced him, before noticing that his father was serving a customer.

'*Scusi, signora,*' he said, turning to smile at the woman.

'You're welcome' she said, sensing the warmth of a blush beginning to make its way up her neck.

'Aah,' he said, 'the lady at the airport.'

'Yes. I'm amazed you remembered.' The blush was well and truly established now. Sam could feel her cheeks burning.

'Of course I remembered. I was concerned about you. Your husband... how is he?' His eyes were warm, kind.

'He's not very well, to be honest. But they think he is making a little progress each day. So that's something.'

'Good, I'm glad. So what brings you to my Papa's shop?'

'Oh, of course, I should have realised he's your father. What an amazing coincidence. Well... curiosity really. I have a book that was produced by your father. I was interested to see some of the original images.'

'Oh yes, he's very proud of this book. But it's not the sort of thing tourists are usually interested in.'

'Well, I'm not really a tourist. My husband was making a film about the Tower before he was taken unwell, and he bought the book for research purposes. I'm just doing a little work for him.'

'Ah... *il Torre*. It is a source of endless fascination. And what will your husband find to say that others have failed to say before.'

'You sound rather cynical.'

'I'm a journalist too, so maybe it's not surprising.'

'Oh, I see – for TV or newspapers or...?'

'Newspapers. I'm a foreign correspondent for *La Stampa*. I'm based in Rome really, but I'm spending a couple of weeks back in Pisa... visiting my dear Papa.'

He smiled indulgently at the old man.

'So, what's the angle?' he asked.

'Well, to be honest, I don't really know.'

He looked at her quizzically.

Sam could feel her cheeks burning slightly with embarrass-ment. 'My husband hadn't really told me what the angles were, but I've got his notebooks. I know he was exploring how the Tower would be rescued and so on, but he also seems to have been interested in who designed it. I thought I might follow a few of his leads.'

'Aah... that story. Many have tried and all have failed I fear,' said the man cynically. 'But good luck with it. So, you want to see a few images. I'm sure my father would be delighted... this place is his passion. Pisa is his passion. There is nothing he likes more than showing his treasures to people.'

The man whispered a few words in his father's ear.

'I've asked him to show you some of his special pieces – old maps of the city, as well as some portraits. Would you like that?'

'Oh yes,' Sam said enthusiastically.

'And I'm Dario by the way. Dario Visalberghi, and you are...?'

'Sam, Sam Campbell.'

'Good to meet you at last... Sam.'

Signor Visalberghi shuffled over to one of the plan chests and pulled open a drawer. From amongst the dozens of old manu-scripts and hand-drawn maps, he removed one that bore a close resemblance to the map she had seen in Michael's book and laid it out ceremoniously for her to see. It was at least two feet across and the detail was extraordinary.

'He says this is one of the earliest maps of the city. It is very valuable.'

After a few moments, he covered it with a perspective drawing of the city dated 1730.

'I can't believe,' she said, 'how close to the sea the city used to be. It was basically a coastal town then, wasn't it... and yet now it's almost... what... a mile inland?'

She studied the image, taking in the mountains of Monti Pisani in the distance, the flat plains surrounding the city dotted with trees and fields, a viaduct – presumably carrying water to the city.

'It's beautiful – no?' said Dario. 'Papa wonders if you would like to see one of his real treasures?'

'You mean there's more? Yes, of course, thank you,' said Sam, excitedly.

At the back of the shop was an anteroom that served as office-cum-storeroom. Piles of boxes jostled for space with office equipment. An old desk was piled high with invoices and bills; an ancient typewriter sat incongruously next to a state of the art photocopier. Visalberghi guided them past further book cases packed with leather-bound tomes, towards a metal spiral staircase that led down to the basement. The pungent smell of damp filtered up from the darkness below. The old man flicked an ancient light switch at the bottom of the staircase, revealing a stone-flagged floor, peeling plaster walls and, at the end of the room, a large cupboard with panelled doors, carefully padlocked. Signor Visalberghi reached beneath his crumpled linen jacket and drew out the bunch of keys that jangled from his belt. The key to the padlock was smaller than the rest and silver in colour. He found it quickly, and the padlock snapped apart with a satisfying 'click'. The door creaked open and he withdrew a sheaf of papers interleaved with tissue paper, which he laid delicately on the table nearby.

On top of the pile was a pen-and-ink sketch showing half a dozen spectacular tower houses well spaced out on the shores of the Arno. One in particular struck Sam as especially magnificent; it had towers on either end, and a large balcony across the front of the building.

Signor Visalberghi moved the image carefully to one side, revealing a portrait of a man with a neatly clipped beard, dating from 1250. The subject of the painting stared back at the viewer, his moustache spreading out on either side of his fine-boned face, his neat beard beneath.

'He was an admiral here in Pisa in 1250 – working for Frederico II in Garfagnana,' Dario translated.

'I recognise him,' said Sam, 'this image is in his book.'

Moving the admiral to one side, Signor Visalberghi revealed a portrait of a man and a woman. But unlike the admiral, who was looking directly at the painter, this couple stood in profile, on the loggia of a building, looking almost wistfully out towards the river below. The man was in the foreground. Darker and sturdier than the admiral, he wore a little pointed cap, his dark hair escaping untidily at the sides. He had a small beard that did not quite conceal his slightly jowly appearance, and wore a rich dark red velvet tunic with a silk shirt beneath. Standing just behind him was a woman. Tall and regal-looking, her dark red hair fell in a cascade of curls down her back. It was held in place by a cream cap, decorated with tiny seed pearls. Her dress, also cream, fell in elegant folds over her slender body. The wall behind them was decorated with frescoes – of galleys at sea, their sails unfurled. It was dated 1150, and the name at the bottom was Lorenzo Calvo, *mercante*.

'Lorenzo Calvo!' said Sam. 'You have another image of him in your book. But who is this with him? His daughter? She looks very young.'

Dario quickly translated her question to his father. 'He doesn't know,' he said, 'maybe his wife, maybe his daughter. He doesn't know.'

Sam studied the face of the woman. She was a beauty, but there was a steely quality about her that drew the eye. Situated in the foreground, the man – her husband or father – was obviously intended to dominate the picture, but nevertheless the observer's gaze was drawn to the woman standing behind.

'I'd love to find out more about them both,' said Sam. 'Maybe I could come back sometime and look at the picture again?'

The old man nodded.

'And do you know where the picture was painted...?' asked Sam.

'Judging by the placement of the river and the other buildings visible, it is on the south side of the Arno,' said Dario, 'probably in an area called Chinzica; it was famous as the centre of the mercantile district.'

'How fascinating; do you think the house still exists?' asked Sam.

'Possibly,' said Dario. 'One or two of the houses on the southern bank are from that period; and the open gallery, where they were positioned in the picture, is quite distinctive. Why?'

'Oh, I don't know. I just rather fancied seeing if I could find it. I'm trying to get a sense of people's lives at the time the tower was built. And this man Calvo was alive then, so I guess that's the interest. Thank you, though, both of you, it's been fascinating. I think I ought to be off,' said Sam. 'I've taken up enough of your time already. Thank you both so much.'

As Dario ushered her back up the spiral staircase, she heard Signor Visalberghi carefully putting his treasures back in the locked cupboard before he followed them breathlessly up the staircase and into the shop.

They said their goodbyes to the shopkeeper and once outside on the pavement, Dario said: 'Well, it's nearly lunchtime, and I ought to be getting on. I hope that was useful?'

'Yes, yes very. Thank you... I'm really very grateful.'

'Well, goodbye then,' he said, smiling. He reached down and kissed her lightly on both cheeks.

She blushed slightly, taking in the delicate, lemony smell of his aftershave.

'Well,' she said slightly awkwardly, 'I should go. See you soon I hope.'

'Yes. Look – here's my card. Do give me a call if you need any help with your research. I'm at a bit of a loose end for the next week or so.'

'Thank you,' she said. 'You already gave me one of these at the airport, but I'll take another.' And she slipped the card into her jeans pocket. 'And thank you; I might well get in touch… yes.'

Sam gazed after Dario as he headed towards the Piazza. He had a graceful, loping walk. He took long strides and held his jacket casually over one shoulder. As he reached the end of the street, he turned and looked back at Sam. He raised one hand in salutation and Sam, once again, blushed, embarrassed that he had caught her watching him. She raised her own hand nervously before turning round, in what she hoped was a decisive manner, and striding off in the opposite direction.

Within minutes, she found herself in the Renaissance square known as Piazza dei Cavalieri. From there, the streets became narrower as she walked through the medieval section of the town. She wasn't exactly sure where she was going, but instinctively she headed towards the Arno. The quiet pedestrian streets soon gave way to the main artery that ran alongside the river. The lorries and cars roared past and the sun burned the back of her neck.

Crossing the river, she turned right, gazing at the impressive houses that stood on that southern side. She thought back to the images of large houses on the banks of the Arno that she had just seen in Signor Visalberghi's shop, and wondered if she was actually looking at the original buildings in those illustrations. Walking along, with the river on her right, she could tell that most dated from the fifteenth or sixteenth centuries, but from time to time, wedged between these buildings, the outlines of medieval tower houses were clearly visible, in spite of a later façade. One such building still had the open gallery on top of one of the towers, from where the owners, back in the twelfth century, would have surveyed the city below. Drawn to this large *palazzo* with impressive views of the river and the city, she stood gazing up at the gallery, wondering if this, perhaps, could be the house that featured in the picture of Calvo and his lady. She was about to carry on walking, intending to continue until she reached the Ponte della Cittadella where she would return to the northern side of the city, but she noticed a small path leading down the side of the house. Following her nose, she walked down the path, enjoying the shade, until she came to a pair of huge wooden gates that, she reasoned, presumably led to the garden at the back of the house. Suddenly filled with curiosity, she gently pushed the gate, and was surprised when it gave way under pressure, opening to reveal an extraordinary, overgrown garden. She peeked inside; the house was almost obscured from the garden by a vast fig tree. Hoping this would make her invisible to anyone inside the house, she slipped into the garden and began to explore.

The area at the bottom of the garden, furthest from the house, consisted of an overgrown vegetable garden. Beans, courgettes, peppers and tomatoes jostled for position amidst weeds and stray bits of rubbish that she deduced had been thrown over the garden wall. She bent down and picked a tomato, its skin bursting with juice and sweetness. Sucking the tomato, she turned now to face the back of the house. Four vast olive trees, covered with fruit, were set into a scrappy lawn, like gnarled old sentries standing guard over the house. Beyond them were overgrown box hedges, unkempt and shaggy, surrounding herbs of every description. And there, near the house, stood a vast fig tree, hanging heavy with fruit. Wasps swarmed around it; the air was filled with their buzzing as they hovered near the ripest figs. She reached up and snapped one from the branch, glancing up at the house as she did so. Nervous now that she might be discovered, she retreated through the open gates, pushing them shut behind her, and walked back up towards the Arno. She crossed the road and stood leaning against the wall that lined the river, gazing up at the house, sucking the fig, enjoying its cloying sweetness. The windows were all closed at the front and she could see no sign of life there. But there was a sign in one of the downstairs windows that said '*vendesi*'.

She crossed the road, compelled to try to see inside the house. She rang on the old bell that hung at the side of the door and stood back and waited. No one came, but backing down the steps towards the street, she bumped into a smart young man in a suit, with a leather folio underneath his arm.

'*Buongiorno, signora*,' he said.

'*Buongiorno*,' she replied

'*Che fa? É venuta vedere la casa?*'

'*Mi scusi*, I'm English… *non capisco*,' she said apologetically.

'Oh, I'm sorry. I am here to show the house to a client. It is for sale; I thought it might be you. Signora Capelli?'

Seizing the moment, and anxious not to lose this opportunity to see inside the house, she said: 'Yes that's me. Well, it's not me. I'm not Signora Capelli, but she couldn't come and she asked me to come instead. I hope that's all right?'

Surprised at the little lie she had just told, she wondered if the young man would see through her deception, but he merely shrugged and nodded before taking a large set of keys from his leather case. He unlocked the heavy oak door and ushered Sam into the dark lobby of the house.

He fumbled near the door in the near darkness before finding an ancient light switch. As the hall light came on, it revealed a vast marble hallway with a wide staircase that swept up towards the first floor. He moved confidently into the room at the side of the hall and, brushing away a dense layer of cobwebs and dust, he opened up the shutters that had been clearly closed for some time. Light poured into the vast room. It had been decorated and altered many times. Cornicing had been added – presumably at the same time as the Victorian bookcases has been fitted. Elderly bergère chairs lay dusty and abandoned. A sofa, covered in a white dust sheet, took pride of place in front of a vast marble fireplace. Round the edges of the room were Louis XVI chairs, their tapestries worn thin, threadbare in places, the gilding faded and distressed. It had the air of an abandoned furniture repository rather than a home.

'Would you like to see the kitchen?'

Eagerly, Sam agreed and followed him down the stone steps, worn in the centre by centuries of domestic traffic. In spite of her previous fears, she had begun to enjoy this unofficial tour of one of Pisa's oldest houses. The young man was friendly, he had good English and was fresh-faced and enthusiastic.

The kitchen had the feel of a museum, and reminded Sam of the one she had visited many years before at Chartwell in Kent: everything left exactly as it had been in its heyday.

'How old is the house?' Sam asked.

'Very old… it is one of the oldest houses still standing in Pisa. We think it is around 1150, roughly the same age as the Tower, but a little less crooked of course!' And he smiled and laughed at his own little joke.

At one end of the kitchen was a vast fireplace. A huge wooden table stood in the centre surrounded by chairs. It could have accommodated at least twenty people. A long ceramic sink with a couple of rusty taps was the only indication of modernity – that, and a vast range that had probably been put in some fifty years before. Sam noted a door that led to the garden.

'Can we go out there?'

'Yes of course… if I can find the key.'

He jangled the huge ring of keys and finally found the one he needed.

As he opened the old door, he had to push hard to shift what looked like years of debris that had lain behind it.

They went up the steps into the garden and Sam saw the now familiar fig tree, the ragged box-edged beds, the gnarled olive trees.

'Who lives here?' asked Sam

'No one has lived here for many months. It's owned by a family who live in Switzerland now, the Manocci family. It's been closed up since they left.'

Re-entering by the kitchen steps, they moved up through the house, the agent turning on lights and opening up shutters where necessary. On the second floor were a suite of bedrooms: two with interconnecting doors and a third smaller one that adjoined the first. As Sam walked into the little room, the agent said: 'A dressing room… it could be converted to a bathroom, I think.'

Sam looked round the little room, taking in the small double bed against one wall, the somewhat decrepit wardrobe, the small high window.

'Is there another floor?' she asked. 'Is it possible to get access to the galleries at the front?'

'Yes, there is a wonderful view from the old tower above here. We need to climb up the circular staircase in the East Tower.'

Sam followed the young man up the winding staircase in the tower. At the very top, they came out into a loggia open on three sides, with stone arches framing the view to the north and south. Gazing out first towards the south, Sam surveyed the city stretching away towards the airport in the distance. As she turned to face the river, her eye caught a peeling fresco on one wall – the remains of pale terracotta paint, with a suggestion of blue at the base. The painting had virtually disappeared, but she could just make out the outline of what might have been an oar from a galley dipping into the water, but in truth was just a dark line. She looked out onto the river below, the Leaning Tower and the Duomo in the distance.

'It's a wonderful view. My goodness. It's fabulous up here.' She recalled the picture Signor Visalberghi had showed her of Calvo and his beautiful red-haired companion gazing across the river.

'You say it was built around 1150,' she said, 'do we know who it was built for?'

'I'm afraid I don't know. Maybe the Manoccis have done some research… they may know more than me.'

'Well, thank you,' she said, 'I think I've seen enough.'

The agent led her once again down the steep, winding tower steps and out onto the landing at the top of the marble staircase.

At that moment, the bell to the house rang. Perplexed, the young man ran down the stairs.

Following him quickly behind, Sam was just in time to see an elegant woman standing on the steps and introducing herself as Signora Capelli. The agent turned to remonstrate with Sam, who ducked past him, shouting, '*Grazie mille,*' before jumping down the stone steps and running back along the Arno towards the safety of the bridge.

Once across, she walked along the north bank of the Arno, until she stood opposite the *palazzo*. Her gaze wandered up to the East Tower. Whoever lived there certainly had an extraordinary view of the city. There was no doubt, whether it was Calvo and his lady or no, they had been people of substance.

CHAPTER 10

August 1171

One afternoon in late August, some ten years after she had first noticed young Gerardo and his grandfather, Berta was sitting, as usual, at the edge of the Piazza, sketching the buildings and the men at work. She had shifted her attention from the Duomo – the latest phase of which was nearing completion, with most of the activity now taking place inside the vast grey and marble edifice – to the Baptistery, begun seventeen years earlier and designed by the brilliant *capo magister* Deotisalvi. The Baptistery, which lay to the west of the Duomo, was designed for the rich and influential citizens of Pisa to baptise their children. Deotisalvi was proud of his design, which had echoes of Buscheto's earlier cathedral, with its delicate columns, but was circular in shape in order to prevent it sinking into the silty ground on which it would be built. Without corners, the architect reasoned, the weight of the vast building would be more evenly distributed and therefore less likely to sink or tilt.

Young Gerardo, now seventeen, had been employed as a mason on the Baptistery, and as it rose above ground level, he was developing his skills as a sculptor. Berta caught sight of him standing on the bamboo and raffia scaffolding that surrounded the building. He chatted easily with another young man as they carved and chiselled part of the architrave above the main door. She noted with pleasure how he tossed his head back as he laughed and joked, the shoulder-length dark hair, made wet with sweat, flicking back an arc of water glistening in the bright sunlight. She caught his eye and waved to him, and he, embarrassed, half-raised his hand to return her greeting before turning back to his friend.

He was tall now, taller than his grandfather, his chest and arms revealed well-developed muscles under the smooth skin made golden by the sun.

She lifted her basket, offering him something. Shyly he touched the arm of his friend as a parting gesture, and, jumping down from the scaffolding, came towards her.

He bowed when he reached her, and she patted the low wall next to her.

'Sit, Gerardo. I have some figs today. Would you like one?'

Unable to refuse, he sat down and, wiping the dust from his hands, gratefully took the cool green fruit from her small pale fingers. As their flesh touched, they both felt the shock, the small electric charge of attraction. He took the fig and, delicately peeling off the outer casing, revealed the paler green inner skin. Then, watching her intently, his eyes locked with hers, he sank his mouth into the soft, ripe redness within, sucking and slurping. When he had finished, he grinned a wide happy smile… and she too laughed.

'You must learn to eat them a little more elegantly,' she scolded. 'Try another.' She handed him a fig. But he shook his head.

'I'm sorry, but I must go now. The *lapicida* will notice. We are busy.'

'Of course,' she said, surprised at her disappointment.

Unable to resist the young man, she visited the site as frequently as she could after that. Lorenzo was away on a long trip and Berta intended to make use of his absence. Whenever she and Gerardo met, they would mainly talk about architecture, discussing the work he was involved in, or a particular building or piece of sculpture that he had admired. She found herself impressed by his enthusiasm and knowledge, as well as his desire for self-improvement; and she encouraged and nurtured his ambition. She heard, too, how he had lost his parents – although the boy never went into too much detail, concentrating instead on his gratitude to his grandfather. And while she recognised the differences in their ages – at thirty-five she was twice his age – she felt it was of no importance. There was an easiness about their relationship that allowed her to forget her position: to be simply Berta in the company of a young sculptor.

For his part, Gerardo was amazed and delighted at Berta's knowledge. He had never met a woman who was so well educated, or so interested in the details of his work. She brought her sketchbooks on most days, and he would sit happily looking at her drawings, marvelling at her ability to capture the likeness of a building or a piece of sculpture. He could see, too, that she had imaginative ideas of her own of how a building should be designed. He was aware that his own ambitions were limited by his lack of formal education; he could never become a *capo magister*. But she encouraged him and gave him confidence that he would one day be a fine *lapicida*, like his grandfather. And she was beautiful; there were days when he caught sight of the red hair as a strand escaped from her cap and marvelled at its colour. And although she dressed simply, he knew instinctively that her clothes belied her true position. There was something in her bearing, her confidence, that made it impossible that she was just an ordinary woman of Pisa.

The two of them met often during that late summer. Over time, Berta's feelings for the young man changed, from simple friendship to something deeper. In bed at night, she found her-

self imagining him making love to her. As she sat at her toilette
in the morning, arranging her hair, or putting on a brooch, he
filled her thoughts. And while she knew that there was no hope
for any kind of relationship, she was powerless to put a stop to
her feelings.

When she came to the Piazza, she often brought a picnic,
hoping to tempt him to sit with her. A simple lunch of bread
and ham, or a piece of fruit carefully wrapped in cloth to prevent
bruising. One day, after they had eaten a small tart prepared by
Maria, she searched at the bottom of her basket for some fruit.
Taking a sharp knife she expertly carved a large white peach in
two, offering half to the young man. He bit down on the white
flesh and juice spurted out, running down his chin. As she
moved to dab at his mouth with a cloth, he took her hand in his,
and gently kissed the inside of her wrist. She flushed and instinctively looked anxiously around in case they had been observed.
He, innocent, unknowing, smiled sweetly at her and she found
herself yearning now to kiss his girlish lips. But she held back
and the moment was lost. His friend called him back to work
and he stood up awkwardly and hurried away, disappearing into
the crowd of men at the site.

At the end of August, Lorenzo returned early from his trip,
bringing an end to his wife's site visits. He was tired and irritable; he had developed a bad fever on the outward journey and
had returned home overland, leaving his second in command in
charge of the fleet. He enquired, not quite as delicately as she
would have wished, if, in his absence, she had perhaps found
herself with child. And once again she had to disappoint him,
making light of the revelation that despite her daily tisane there
was, as yet, to be no heir to his great fortune. His annoyance was
palpable, and she found herself struggling to please him. When
he had eaten, and taken her to bed, he retreated, unusually, to his

own room to sleep.   Finding herself not a little relieved, Berta thought longingly of the young man with whom she had such an easy relationship. Curiously, she felt no guilt at this friendship, seeing no real harm in it. And each morning, when she woke, the sound of Lorenzo's snoring drifting through from the room next door, she felt a frisson of excitement as she remembered Gerardo's touch on her hand, the feel of his lips on her wrist. But although she felt no guilt, she was only too aware of the risks she had taken. And so, excited and scared in equal measure, she tried hard to push the young man to the back of her mind, concentrating instead on her wifely duties. She rose late with Lorenzo, and spent the mornings in her chamber studying her books, a habit he, fortunately, had no objection to. If he desired it, she made love with him in the afternoons. She organised parties and dinners that she knew would delight and impress him, while also establishing their household as among the most influential in the city.

But every day she thought of the handsome boy and wondered when she would be able to visit the Piazza.

CHAPTER 11

September 1171

Lorenzo was reluctant to leave the house and seemed keen for Berta to be at his side at all times. He had felt unwell since returning from the Middle East, suffering terrible night sweats, and demanded her constant attention to bring him back to health. Berta, frustrated, railed against this constraint on her freedom.

One morning, she cajoled him to take a little air down in the garden.

'Lorenzo... you have been in this room for several days now, and the air is stale. You need to get outside into the garden and sit in the sunshine. Do that for me, *caro*, will you? It will make you feel so much better.'

Reluctantly, Lorenzo had done her bidding, leaving his wife to her toilette. Finally left alone, she was seized with desire for the young man at the Piazza del Duomo. Her new maid, Aurelia, was dressing her mistress's hair – braiding it and coiling it on top of her head.

'Aurelia,' she tried hard to keep her voice calm as the girl twisted and teased her hair. 'You know how delighted I am that you have come to work for me.'

'Yes, *signora* – thank you, *signora*.'

'You've done my hair so beautifully, thank you... but I need you to run a little errand for me.'

'Yes, *signora*.'

'I would like you to take a message to a young sculptor at the Piazza. Do you think you could do that for me?'

Aurelia nodded, and once she had been furnished with the boy's name and description, and some indication of where she was likely to find him, she left her mistress, only mildly surprised by the errand she was to run, for she was wont to be sent out into the town to invite young artists and sculptors to dine with the household.

She had to walk the mile or so to the Piazza, a route she was not unfamiliar with, as it took her past her mother's house. She had been in Berta's service for just over two months and, true to her word, she was released by her mistress to visit her family one Sunday in four, taking home her wages and a large basket full of produce from the *palazzo*'s gardens. Her mother missed her terribly and was excited to see her beloved daughter and keen to hear about Aurelia's life, and relieved to find her happy and enthusiastic about her new position. Berta had been kind to the girl and, it seemed, was encouraging her to read and even to play a lute. 'Play to me, Aurelia,' the girl mimicked her employer, 'it soothes me.' Her mother had laughed, but also gave her daughter wise counsel: 'Be respectful, Aurelia... she's a good woman. I didn't see it at first, but she has been true to her word. She looks after you well, and the money she pays you makes a big difference.'

Berta had also provided Aurelia with paints and paper, and together they would sit in the garden painting the flowers that grew there, the mistress guiding the hand of the maid as she taught her how to mix pigments to just the right shade. She even allowed the girl to take her pictures home to show her mother.

'Your father would have been proud of you, Aurelia,' her mother told her, 'you have his gift for art.'

Aurelia had grown used to her duties and, in truth, she found it quite enjoyable work. She was required to help her mistress bathe and dress, to take care of her clothes, delivering washing to the maids downstairs, folding gowns neatly and laying them carefully in the chests with lavender and cedar to protect them from moths and other insects. Every few weeks, her mistress would require a bath, or her hair to be washed, and then the girl, along with one of the kitchen maids, would have to carry the pails of water heated in the basement kitchens up the many steps to the top of the tower where her mistress had her chamber. The washing complete, she would comb the long red hair, taking care not to pinch, pull or squeeze. For if she did, her mistress was wont to be short-tempered and even to slap her wrist. But the job was less arduous and boring than helping her mother to run their own household, where she had to tend the fires, collect the water and cook the food while her mother was busy preparing the potions and tonics that brought customers to the house.

When she finally arrived at the Piazza, Aurelia found it teeming with activity. Berta had given her a little money to spend as she chose – a reward for her silence. Being a young girl, little older than a child, she chose to spend it on a honey cake that she had spotted being arranged on a stall next to the hospital of Santa Chiara. To eat one would be a rare pleasure; she handed over the coin eagerly and took possession of the cake, holding it carefully in both hands. As she wandered the vast building site searching for the young man, she ate the cake, luxuriating in its sweetness. Everywhere she looked, men worked – the masons stripped to the waist, sweat glistening on their bodies, mixed with marble dust; painters and gilders hurrying to their work, their tools and brushes in leather bags slung over their shoulders.

The Duomo was nearing completion, but the interior still required decoration. Armies of artists and craftsmen had been drafted in from other towns to complete the work – from Siena and Florence, and even from towns and cities further afield, like Bruges. Living two or three to a room, they spent their nights in little hostelries dotted about the town and their days working from dawn to dusk.

Aurelia wondered how she would recognise the young man amongst so many, and had begun to worry what her mistress would say if she returned empty-handed. She repeated the message over and over again, for fear of forgetting it, alternating the words spoken out loud with little nibbling bites at the cake. She had only enough money for one, and she was anxious to eke it out as long as possible.

As she neared the Baptistery, she stood looking up at the men working from the wooden scaffolding that covered the newly built walls. Raffia 'roofs' had been erected at various levels to provide shade from the late summer sunshine. A young man shouted instructions to a colleague standing below him. Between them was a rope tied around what appeared to be a statue wrapped in sack cloth, which they were attempting to winch into position. The young man with dark curls pulled the rope with great care, and finally brought the statue up to the gallery where he was standing. He shouted acknowledgement to the man below and began to unwrap the statue. As he did so, he sat with his legs dangling over the edge of the wooden platform. He seemed perfectly at ease, some twenty or thirty feet above the ground. At one moment, he leapt to his feet, still holding the statue in one hand, and reached across to place it in position, standing back to admire his work.

Aurelia found herself spellbound by the boy, and gasped as he leant this way and that, terrified that he would fall. The boy, who appeared quite unconcerned, stood back at last, satisfied by his work; he looked down for the first time and caught sight of the watching girl. He smiled at her, a wide happy grin, and made as if to fall from the scaffold. With a whoop, he leapt through the air onto a ladder that connected to the level below. The girl cried out in fear and covered her mouth with her hand as she did so, dropping what was left of her little cake. The boy laughed, pointing to the ground where her cake now lay, the crumbs already being eaten by an opportunistic starling. The girl looked down and began to cry, her hands now flapping madly as she tried to shoo away the bird and rescue what was left of her cake. Within moments, as she stood up, the young man was there with her, helping to gather up the remaining crumbs. He handed them to her and she saw at once that this must be the young man she had been searching for... his eyes the colour of the sea on a warm summer's day.

'That was mean,' she said, sadly. 'The cake was a treat... from my mistress.'

'I am sorry,' he said, smiling. 'I will buy you another.'

She smiled back. 'Can you? Have you the money?'

'Of course,' he said, puffing up his chest just a little. 'I am a mason, and I was paid today. Look.' He pulled a couple of brass coins from a little pouch tied to his belt.

'It's OK,' she said. 'I had nearly finished it anyway.'

Remembering her errand now, she spoke again: 'My mistress sent me here to find you, I think. Are you Gerardo?'

'I am,' he said, curious now. 'Who is your mistress?'

'I may not say, but you know her. She said to say she was the "fig lady".'

He nodded. 'I know her. What does she want?'

'She wants to see you... to meet with you. She asks if you could meet her at the church of Santo Stefano, today at three bells. Can you do that?'

'I could... yes.' He spoke hesitatingly. 'Why does she want to meet me?'

'She says that she will have something for you.'

'Tell her I will be there. Now, let me give you a coin for your trouble so that you can buy another cake.' Reaching into his purse, he took out the money and placed it carefully into the girl's hand, folding her fingers over it.

She smiled at him and he smiled back, drinking in her young golden skin, the fair hair, and her eyes – of the sweetest blue he had ever seen, the colour of ultramarine, the rarest of pigments, used by the painters in the cathedral to decorate the dress of the Madonna.

'What is your name?' he asked, as she turned to go.

'Aurelia,' she said shyly. And Gerardo caught her hand in his and, bringing it to his full lips, kissed it.

When Aurelia returned to Berta shortly before lunch, she found her mistress anxious and short-tempered. Normally she would have been reading in her room before taking lunch with Lorenzo, but that morning she had been forced to deceive him, persuading him that she was unwell with a bad headache. He had offered to stay with her – to soothe her head – but she had refused, finally insisting that he go in order that she could rest. Reluctantly, he had finally left her, announcing that he would take his lunch alone and *siesta* in his own bedchamber that afternoon.

They were due to dine with a business colleague of Lorenzo's later that day, and Berta promised him that, with enough rest, she would be back to her normal self in time for the meeting.

As soon as Aurelia entered her bedchamber, she grabbed the girl's wrist, pulling her onto the little seat that was positioned beneath the window. 'Well ... did you find him?'

Her voice was urgent.

'Yes, *signora*, I did. I gave him your message.'

'And will he meet me today?'

'He will, *signora*, just as you asked.'

Berta smiled now, her shoulders dropping with relief. She stood smoothing down the folds of her dress.

'Good,' she said, 'then we have work to do.'

A little before the allotted time, as her husband and the rest of the household rested, Berta stepped tentatively through the gate in the stone wall that separated their garden from the path that ran up to the banks of the Arno.

As a leading figure of the mercantile community, she was well known in the area, and took care to conceal her true identity that afternoon. Anxious to combine beauty and elegance with discretion, she had been short and terse with her maid, even once slapping the girl's hand when she mistakenly pulled at her hair. Dressed in a gown of dark green silk which brought out the colour of her eyes, her jewellery was simple: just an emerald cross on a gold chain at her neck. This had surprised Aurelia, who had laid out the beautiful pearl and emerald necklace that Lorenzo had given his wife the previous year. But Berta considered it too ostentatious for that afternoon's tryst. She wore a cloak of palest blue wool, the hood covering the red hair that was coiled simply on top of her head, and to shield her face from prying eyes, she was veiled, the lace soaked in sweet-smelling lavender oil, mixed with rosemary. For the river was more than just a conduit of trade, with galleys and fishing vessels under sail and oar. It was also a vital part of the sewage system of the city, and by the middle of the afternoon, the day's heat created a stench that hung in the air. She held the lace veil over her mouth and nose, inhaling the sweet smells of lavender and rosemary oil to ward off the infection that could be carried on the wind, and hurried on.

As she arrived at the church of Santo Stefano, the bells began their simple toll. She looked around for Gerardo and was disquieted to notice her heart beating loudly in her chest. He did not keep her waiting long; in fact he had got there some while earlier, concealing himself in a nearby doorway so that he could watch the street from both ends and spot her arrival.

He had cleaned off the dust of that morning's work as best he could and wore a loose shirt of cream linen. When he saw her, he ducked out of the shadows, noting the green silk which flashed beneath her cloak, surprised at its quality. He had an artist's eye for detail and he understood now, as he saw the silken gown, that she must be a lady of some stature.

When she saw him, she smiled and walked towards him, and he saw for the first time, as she let down the hood of her cloak, her beautiful red hair. She had always been careful to conceal it on their daily meetings at the Piazza. Once or twice he had glimpsed its colour, when a few strands had escaped from beneath their covering. Now, as she stood before him, the bright afternoon sun glinting on her hair, it was like a halo of flames surrounding her smiling face.

'Thank you for coming today.' She spoke calmly, confident in her role as the older woman, in charge of the meeting.

'It is my pleasure, *signora*.' He noticed the emerald ring she wore on the fourth finger of her left hand.

'I thought perhaps it was time to properly introduce myself to you. My name is Berta di Bernardo. I am the wife of Lorenzo Calvo; you may have heard of him?'

The name was familiar to the young man. A flash of pain went through his body, as he remembered his mother weeping at the news that her father had been lost at sea. She had always blamed the owner of the ship for his death, the greedy merchant Lorenzo Calvo. 'He pushed the crew too hard,' she told him more than once, 'he forced them to make too many journeys. The crew were exhausted and my father was worried about it. He tried to stop Calvo, but he wouldn't listen.'

The story lacked detail, or at least Gerardo remembered little more than the bare bones. He had only been a small boy when Carlo died – barely five or six – and this death, significant though it was, was quickly overtaken by the far greater tragedy of his mother's death. He could still remember the cries of pain that filled the small house during those last few agonising weeks.

'How long have we known each other?' she asked.

'Several years,' he said,' I was a boy when we first met… seven or eight years old.'

'And how old are you now?'

'I am seventeen, *signora*.' His tone was wary, no longer the easy sweetness of their earlier meetings, as equals enjoying the pleasure of a fig or a piece of bread dipped in honey. He was unsettled, not understanding what she wanted from him.

Sensing his disquiet, she touched his arm. 'Gerardo, please… let us walk a little way together. I have a proposition for you.'

They walked together, not quite touching; the woman, her hair shining in the sunlight, and the boy, taller by an arm's length. She chose quiet back streets, away from her usual haunts, hoping not to be noticed by anyone of her acquaintance. At that time of day, she was taking a terrible risk of being recognised – abroad in the afternoon, unaccompanied, consorting publicly with a young man.

'Gerardo, I would like to invite you to come to my house tomorrow evening. I have some influential people attending, and it may be useful for you in your work.'

She smiled up at him as they stood now, together, on the banks of the Arno, a mile or more from her house.

The young man looked deeply into her eyes and he bowed in appreciation of this generous offer.

'I am grateful to you, *signora*, but I must decline.'

'Why?' She was startled by his refusal. It was unusual for anyone, save for Lorenzo, to deny her anything.

'I am but a mason. My family is not wealthy. I do not have suitable clothes to wear to such a gathering. I would embarrass you.'

Delighted by his thoughtfulness, she reached out with her fingers and touched his hand. He recoiled almost imperceptibly from her touch. He knew what his mother would have wanted him to do: to walk away and never see this woman again. And yet she was offering him an opportunity that did not come often to a young mason in Pisa at that time. She was also, he thought… as he took in the breasts, the lips, the hair… a great beauty.

The sun began to sink in the west, casting long streaks of golden light across the water below, she reached up and stroked his face with her long fingers, before whispering in his ear: 'Dear Gerardo, that is no problem. I will arrange everything.'

And pulling her hood carefully over her hair, she turned to go. 'Until tomorrow.'

The next morning, the mist hanging heavy over the Arno, Berta woke early. As Lorenzo slept beside her, snoring lightly and turning over in his sleep, she crept from her bed, drawing her gown around her. She withdrew a parcel she had carefully hidden in a chest in the corner of the room. Aurelia, who slept on a little cot in a room off her mistress's bedchamber, sat up, startled, as Berta shook her awake.

'*Signora*, forgive me… I have slept too long.'

'No, Aurelia, don't worry. It is very early – the sun is scarcely awake. I need you to do an errand for me.'

Aurelia climbed out of her bed and pulled her day dress on over her shift. Her mistress noted how the girl had grown since she first brought her to the household. Her breasts had begun to develop, and her face, framed by the golden river of hair, had become more mature.

She handed Aurelia the parcel.

'I want you to take this to Gerardo. But be quick... you will need to hurry if you are to get there before he goes to work this morning.'

She told the girl the address, asking her to repeat it several times until she had committed it to memory.

Then pressing a coin into her hand, she added: 'Buy yourself a little breakfast after you have delivered the parcel, do you understand? And there should be a little money left for you to keep or give to your mother.'

When her mistress had gone, Aurelia, curious, undid its ribbon and carefully folded back the paper. Inside were clothes: a fine linen robe in a deep blue – the most expensive of pigments – with a smooth leather belt. A pair of soft leather shoes completed the outfit, with leather heels and bands of blue to tie the boots at the ankle. These were expensive clothes, she could tell, though not belonging to her master, for he was not such a tall man. Hurriedly, she re-wrapped the parcel, before slipping out of the servants' entrance and running as fast as her coltish legs would carry her to the house of Gerardo.

The city was coming to life with people spilling out of their houses, as Aurelia sped along the lanes and alleys. Pisa at that time was full of incomers. In spite of the constant war that raged with the Holy Land, the the Pisans themselves bore no ill-will to people of any race. Pisan architects introduced Moorish designs to their buildings. Buscheto, the architect of the Duomo, had spent a great deal of time studying the Dome of the Rock in Jerusalem, before bringing many of its influences to bear on his cathedral. In the same way, the prosperous Pisani sought to demonstrate their wealth and sophistication by decorating their homes with furniture and relics from the Holy Land, or by employing a dark-skinned Moor to serve at their table, or act as bookkeeper. Lorenzo and Berta, for example, engaged a notary called Massoud, whom Lorenzo had met in Syria. He had brought the man back with him the year before, and he had been responsible for all their financial and legal affairs ever since. His command of Italian was now excellent, but he kept all of their records in Arabic, a language that Lorenzo struggled to master. There was even a pair of camels which had been brought back under sail from Africa. They were a common sight in Pisa, ferrying goods around the city, crossing the newly built bridge across the Arno.

Aurelia heard the bells of Santa Cecilia toll three times for the morning Angelus, just as she was arriving at Gerardo's home. She knocked on the door, suddenly nervous of seeing the young man again.

An older man opened the door; his hair was grey and thinning. He wore breeches but no shirt, and his arms and chest were dark brown, the muscles hard and strong. The face was gnarled, as if a vice had pressed down hard on his head and chin, pushing the features too closely together. The eyes though were familiar – a shade of green-blue, like the colour of the sea.

'Excuse me… I am looking for Gerardo.'

'I am Gerardo.' The older man looked quizzically at the young girl.

Behind the man's head, she saw the object of her interest hovering behind.

'It's all right, *nonno*. I think it's me she wants to see.'

The older man raised his eyebrows, but left the pair standing in the doorway as he went back inside to resume his preparations. Both men were employed on the Baptistery and needed to be on site soon after the Angelus.

'I have brought something for you, from my mistress.' Aurelia handed the parcel to the young man, who took it from her, squeezing it between finger and thumb as he did so. 'It is clothes,' she gushed, 'they are very beautiful… the most beautiful pair of shoes and a robe of finest linen. I think she must have bought them for you specially.'

He smiled at her and her sweet enthusiasm.

The older man interrupted the two. 'Gerardo, we must go.'

'Of course, *nonno*.'

Gerardo turned and nodded to the man.

'Tell your mistress, thank you,' he said, turning back to Aurelia. And taking her hand in his much larger grip, he brought it up and grazed it with his soft lips.

He watched her walk down the lane, before closing the door and leaning heavily against it. He picked up the parcel that lay on the table, and undid the ribbons revealing the clothes inside. His grandfather, who had been busying himself with preparations for the day's work, glanced at the contents.

'Somebody wants something from you my boy… I hope you can meet their expectations.'

'You are right, *nonno*, as always,' said Gerardo, as he re-tied the parcel, before gathering up his tools for the day.

CHAPTER 12

September 1171

When Aurelia returned from Gerardo's house, she tried hard to concentrate on her duties. She gathered up the clothes in her mistress's bedchamber, hanging them up with care, smoothing the silk and lace, ensuring the sachets of lavender were arranged between each garment. She took the delicate shift and stockings that her mistress had discarded the previous evening to the laundry maid for washing. Her duties completed, she wandered into the large garden that lay at the rear of the house. Here, amongst the rows of sweet red tomatoes and peppers that ripened in the autumn sunshine, she thought about the young man who would be attending the fine dinner that was to be held later that day at the *palazzo*.

She remembered the way he had held her hand, the feel of his lips on her wrist at the Piazza, and again that morning at his lodgings. They had been warm and dry, not wet like the boy who worked in the kitchens at the *palazzo* who had tried to kiss her behind the fig tree a few weeks before. He had been rough and grabbed her from behind as she stood on tiptoes, trying to reach a particularly luscious fig that hung just out of reach. The wasps were circulating, their buzzing, mixed with the cicadas, adding to the sleepy heat of the afternoon. She imagined the rest of the house were resting, but Cosimo was suddenly there, grabbing her roughly, pulling her round and forcing his lips onto hers, his wet mouth dribbling slightly. She had pulled away, fearful of discovery and filled with loathing.

'No!' she had cried, before escaping back to the house, tripping over her skirts, and falling almost headlong into the kitchen, where the cook scolded her for running and tearing her dress.

The boy had followed in after her, laughing slyly behind his hand, and had been given a sweet cake by the cook, who ruffled his hair and pinched his cheek.

Gerardo was different from any boy she had known. He had been gentle and polite and had held her hand to his mouth so sweetly. His eyes, the most beautiful eyes she had ever seen, had held hers with such intensity when she left the clothes with him that morning that she had found it hard to tear herself away. She felt his eyes were boring into her soul, understanding her in a way that no one had ever done before. She began to think about what he would look like in the fine blue-green tunic. She understood well why her mistress had chosen that garment for him. He would look very handsome. She understood, too, why he was to be invited. For while she was still just a girl, she was old enough to understand attraction between a man and a woman – and she had observed the way her mistress became agitated and excited when she talked about the young man.

Aurelia was startled out of her daydreaming by Berta, who had completed her discussions with her head of household, deciding on the menu and plan of the table. Musicians would play at the dinner and she had met with them to discuss suitable music for the evening. She had invited Deotisalvi and several other well-known architects, hoping to introduce her young protégé. There would be twenty guests in all, and the menu had been chosen with care. It would be a sumptuous affair and Berta found herself filled with excitement at the prospect of seeing Gerardo again.

'Aurelia,' she spoke clearly, 'come now; I need to prepare for this evening.'

They went together to her bedchamber, where Aurelia brought jugs of steaming water up from the kitchen, pouring them into the bath that had been set up in the room. The water was perfumed with herbs and essential oils – lavender, chamomile and rose water, made from the dark damask roses that grew in the garden behind the house. To wash her mistress's back, Aurelia took soap from the *cofanetto*, the decorated casket where she kept her toilette treasures. Handmade each summer, it took weeks to produce: plain soap was steeped in rose water in the sun, after which cherry kernels, ground into powder, were added, along with balsam and musk oil. The mixture was then moulded into little balls and wrapped in cotton for storage.

As Berta lay relaxing in the hot water, Lorenzo wandered in and out of the bedchamber demanding his wife's attention. Aurelia noted her mistress's irritation with her husband. Eventually he was soothed and banished... and Berta lay back with a sigh of relief in the soapy water.

Aurelia washed her mistress's hair, pouring the water carefully, making sure not to splash Berta's face. Then, wrapping Berta in a large sheet, she dried her limbs and combed through her hair with the ivory comb that Lorenzo had given her the previous year. It would take several hours to dry, and Berta insisted that it was fanned out across her back before she sat in the window of her room, overlooking the garden, the sun streaming through the open casement, falling onto her hair and making it sparkle like fire while it dried.

While Berta read a little to calm her nerves, Aurelia set out her mistress's gown and jewellery for that evening.

The dress Berta had selected was of pale cream silk, which she knew made her porcelain skin glow with a luminescent quality.

The necklace was of heavy pearls brought back from the East, with a single diamond suspended from the centre, the size of a quail's egg. When her hair was dried, and combed again, it would be coiled onto her head, set off with a silk cap embroidered with pearls and emeralds that would sparkle in the candlelight.

Her shoes were made of silk and were very pointed in the latest fashion. They too were embroidered with pearls, set onto a little heel of leather and wood, to give Berta extra height. As she moved, they would peep out beneath her dress, drawing the eye to her slender feet. The overall effect was magnificent, and Aurelia stood back in admiration when Berta was finally dressed.

'You look very beautiful, *signora*.'

'Thank you, Aurelia,' the older woman smiled, knowing full well the impression she had created. Then, remembering her little maid, she said kindly, 'We must find something pretty for you to wear this evening too. I would like you to be on hand in case I need anything. Just stand at the back of the room and I will call for you. But you cannot wear that,' and she gestured at the simple woollen gown that was Aurelia's everyday wear.

She went to one of the chests in her room and drew out a dress in pale grey silk. She had worn it only once, when attending church with Lorenzo. She had removed it as soon as she returned home, announcing that the colour did nothing for her complexion. Now, she held it up to the girl, declaring it would 'do very well'.

Then, once Aurelia had put it on, Berta combed her hair, holding it in place with a simple linen cap. Rubbing a little rose water onto the girl's neck, she said, 'There. Now go and see if there is anything you can do to help downstairs. I shall be down once the guests arrive.'

Aurelia descended the staircase to the dining hall. She felt very elegant in the new silk dress. She had never worn anything other than a simple woolen or linen gown, and she enjoyed the sensation of the fabric rustling when she moved. She imagined herself the mistress of the house, surveying the vast oak table laid with the finest glass and bowls that the household possessed: Syrian glass decorated with elaborately coloured enamel, ewers in the shape of lions, filled with warm water for guests to wash their fingers at the table, and majolica dishes painted in bright colours filled with *coriandoli* – candied coriander seeds to be thrown by the guests at the end of the banquet like confetti. In the middle of the table stood two gold plates, covered with marzipan *calisconi* – ravioli-like parcels made with almond paste and rose water. Aurelia reached over and took one. She slipped it into her mouth, revelling in the sweetness.

She was interrupted by Maria, who had come into the room with a huge plate of candied fruit. Seeing Aurelia taking the *calisconi*, she said sharply, 'that is for the guests. Get back to your duties,' gesturing up the stairs.

Aurelia stood her ground: '*La Signora* has asked that I remain here for the evening in case she needs anything.'

'Then get to the kitchen and eat something before the guests arrive.'

The girl, taking a last glimpse of the beautiful table, ran downstairs in search of food, her stomach fluttering with excitement. Here every surface was covered by glazed earthenware bowls and beaten copper pots as Maria and the kitchen maids prepared the main dishes - roast quail spiced with cloves and ginger, chicken sweetened with dates, nutmeg and cinnamon, and hare civet – all to be served once the guests had arrived. Taking a bowl of broth she sat at one end of the long table, trying hard not to spill anything on the beautiful silk and wondering if Gerardo would notice her in the new grey dress.

The sound of musicians and laughter outside alerted Aurelia to the guests' arrival. From her position at the back of the dining hall, she observed the men and women, most of them older than her mistress, being greeted and welcomed. As was the custom in Pisa, even the wealthy walked everywhere – the streets being too narrow for carriages. At all times, but most especially on grand occasions, the family were accompanied by a retinue of servants and musicians, all dressed in the costume of their household. As the servants were sent down to the kitchens, their masters were brought upstairs to the grand salon on the first floor of the tower house where Berta and Lorenzo awaited them.

As the guests enjoyed the spectacular views from the loggia looking out over the Arno in the late afternoon sunshine, Berta, her face radiant, her jewels sparkling, laughed and flirted, putting her guests at their ease, guiding the servants with plates of food and ensuring that glasses and cups were filled at all times.

Gerardo, however, had not arrived and both women felt his absence keenly. At one point, Berta excused herself from her guests and hurried across to Aurelia.

'Where is he? Are you sure he understood that he was to come today?'

'Yes, *signora*, I am sure… perhaps he has been delayed.'

'Well, go and find him. All the other guests are here now and we need to take our places at the table. Take the cart… hurry.'

Aurelia, thrilled to be given this task, rushed down to the kitchens in search of Giuseppe, who was in charge of the stables. For, while the family did not use a carriage to get about the city, they had a horse and cart to transport goods and food from their farm outside the city gates. Giuseppe's job was to take care of the horses and make the deliveries once or twice a week, bringing produce for the household. He was eating his supper when

Aurelia found him, and was in no mood to go out again that evening. Reluctantly, he harnessed up one of the horses and soon they set off down the alleys towards Gerardo's house, with Aurelia bouncing around in the back of the cart.

When they arrived, she jumped down and knocked loudly at Gerardo's door, which was opened some minutes later by his grandfather.

'I am here to collect Gerardo; he is expected at my mistress's house this evening.'

The old man gestured behind him and the girl tentatively stepped inside the house. Their table was laid out with a simple supper of bread and some sort of soup. There were two bowls and a flagon of wine. Sitting at the table was the object of her quest.

'What are you doing? You're supposed to be at my mistress's house. You're not even dressed yet.'

The young man looked on rather miserably. 'I'm not coming; I cannot.' He blushed and shifted uneasily in his seat.

'Why? My mistress will be so upset... you must come. What is the matter?'

'Those clothes she gave me, they are too good for me. I don't feel right in them.'

Aurelia laughed now. 'Don't be so silly,' she scolded, 'they are beautiful clothes for a beautiful boy. See, she gave me a beautiful dress too.' And she spun round for the boy to admire her.

Earlier that day, Gerardo had resolved to have nothing to do with the beautiful Berta. Coming back from work, he had held the tiny camel his grandfather Carlo had carved for him on that last fateful trip with Calvo. As he washed the day's dust away, his mind had been filled with thoughts of his mother's sweet face, weeping and raging at her own father's death.

But now, he felt himself weaken, bewitched by Aurelia's sweetness and innocence.

'Please come… for me,' Aurelia said gently. 'We can travel in the cart together, look.' And she gestured out of the door at the waiting vehicle and driver.

Worn down by her pleading, Gerardo reluctantly assented, and climbed up the ladder to the rooms above.

A few minutes later he jumped down and Aurelia clapped her hands with excitement. 'Oh! You look wonderful.' Then seeing the tunic caught awkwardly, she undid the clasp on his belt and, gathering the fabric, correctly fastened it again. Brushing the tunic down over his legs, she stood back and admired her work.

'That's better. Shall we go?'

Bidding his grandfather goodnight, she shepherded the young man outside.

They chatted easily as the cart clattered through the streets. Aurelia, in particular, was full of excitement about what he could expect to eat for dinner. She had the whole menu in her head and chattered away about the sweetmeats and the wine and the quails cooked with spices. All the while, the boy looked on, noticing her hair falling around her shoulders, her soft skin, the pretty full lips and her sweet, sweet blue eyes. As they drew up at Palazzo Calvo, Aurelia made to climb down, but the boy held her hand.

'Thank you for bringing me here this evening… this has been wonderful. You are wonderful,' and jumping down onto the street, he held out his arms to lift her down. Sweeping her to the ground, he held her for a moment, and before she could break away, he kissed her sweetly on the lips.

As Guiseppe drove the cart away, the pair stood together out-side the *palazzo*, their fingers intertwined, gazing up at the great doors. As they opened, she pulled away from him, nervous of being discovered, and once inside, hung back, as a servant escort-ed the young man upstairs to the salon. When Berta caught sight of him, she stood excitedly, too excitedly she realised, knocking a precious glass onto its side. Lorenzo looked up curiously, the sudden movement interrupting his conversation with the merchant on his left, surprised by his wife's clumsiness.

Remembering herself, she smoothed her dress and, making her excuses to her guests, walked over to the young man who now stood in the doorway. Aurelia, she noted, hovered a little way behind him, her cheeks flushed.

'Gerardo... how good it is to see you, and how smart you look. I'm afraid we are already at the table, but come and join us; there are many people I want you to meet.'

Then, gesturing to Aurelia to go and stand at the side of the room, she drew the young man to her side.

During the dinner, the older woman introduced the young man to architects, patrons and artists. Together they listened as the guests discussed their latest projects and, where possible, she encouraged him to make suggestions of how a building might be made safer or more beautiful, demonstrating his knowledge. The big news of the day was that funding was tight on the Baptistery, and Deotisalvi was gloomy about the chances of finishing his project. They would be able to complete the first storey but would not be able to go any further. Gerardo, as a humble mason on the building, had heard nothing of this before and was dumbfounded. Finding his voice eventually, he spoke out: 'What will happen to all the craftsmen working on the building? Where will they find work?'

The *capo magister* spoke: 'They will have to find work elsewhere, of course. What do you think? There is plenty of work in Siena and Florence and there are other projects here in Pisa, if we can get the funding. I myself am starting work soon on the tower at the church of San Nicola; we have yet to recruit a team there.'

The conversation then turned to the plans Deotisalvi had been asked to draw up for another tower, a campanile to be sited on the Piazza del Duomo. To be asked to design two of the three major works at this important site filled his audience with a mixture of admiration and envy. Deotisalvi was without doubt unequalled at the time, the uncrowned king of design in Pisa, and to have been granted this commission was a huge honour. But the old man was characteristically gloomy nevertheless.

'There is always a problem with the money,' he explained. 'First the Baptistery has to stop… and now this; everyone wants the tower, but there is no money to build it, so we must wait and wait. It is very frustrating.'

The guests at the table murmured their agreement, but Berta only had eyes for her young protégé. Seeing the young man's distress at the news about the Baptistery, Berta deftly enquired from the various guests at the table whether any projects might require a master mason and his apprentice. By the time the guests were standing up to leave, she was confident that she could secure some work for Gerardo and his grandfather on Deotisalvi's tower at San Nicola.

As Deotisalvi took his leave that evening, she took his old bony hand in hers. 'I am grateful to you for coming to my house this evening, *signore*. You do me a great honour. And I would like to help you with your exciting *campanile* on the Piazza. Perhaps I can make a deal with you? I will somehow find the money for you to build your tower, if you in turn will employ young Gerardo to be a mason on your next project, the tower at San Nicola.'

The old man pulled away from the woman's soft touch. 'That boy! What experience does he have?'

'He has worked for over ten years on your Baptistery, *signore*. Along with his grandfather who is a *lapicida*, also called Gerardo.

They are a fine team and would make a wonderful contribution, I am sure.'

'Well, maybe. I know old Gerardo; he is a good man. Well, we will see. Tell them to come and see me. And if I do this, you will find me the money for the *campanile,* you say?'

'It might be possible... yes. But I will have to speak with my husband. If he consents, do we have an agreement?'

Deotisalvi called for his household, pulled on his black cloak, and, nodding at his hostess, went out into the night.

With his guests gone, Lorenzo had fallen asleep at his end of the table, his head lolling awkwardly on one side. Gerardo remained, anxiously hovering in the hallway of the house, unsure whether to leave, unsettled by the news about the Baptistery and filled with dread about how to tell his grandfather of their uncertain future.

Berta came back into the hall, and after glancing quickly over at the sleeping Lorenzo, took Gerardo by the hand, and out into the garden. There she pulled him over to a little seat that stood at one side surrounded by lavender.

'Please, sit down, Gerardo. I have some news for you. I could see how distressed you were about the Baptistery, but I have made some enquiries and have secured some employment for you and your grandfather on the tower that Deotisalvi is about to begin at the church of San Nicola. I have suggested your grandfather as *lapicida* with you as his apprentice. I hope you are happy.'

Gerardo was relieved, certainly. 'You are very kind, thank you. My grandfather will be very grateful, if the other work is assured.'

'I am sure of it. Trust me... I will make sure you are well paid and looked after.'

Gerardo found himself confused at the generosity of the beautiful *signora.* All his life he had been brought up to believe in the utter wickedness of Berta di Bernardo and her husband Lorenzo Calvo. But the tale his mother had told him, of how her father was drowned at sea due to the cruelty and greed of Lorenzo and his demanding wife, was at odds with this woman's concern and care for his welfare. He wondered if perhaps his mother had been mistaken.

He was jolted back from his thoughts by a hand brushing his leg.

'I thought you looked very handsome this evening, Gerardo; do you like your new clothes?'

The young man was awkward now, embarrassed by her forwardness. 'The clothes are very fine, too good for me; but Aurelia persuaded me to wear them.'

'Aurelia? What has she to do with anything?' The older woman felt a sharp pang of envy.

The boy, who knew something of jealousy, saw her distress. His future, and that of his grandfather, lay in this woman's hands. It was up to him to protect that future now. Gently, he took Berta's hand in his and kissed it. Then, sensing her desire, he took her face in his hands and gently caressed her closed eyelids with his lips. Berta gave a little gasp at the tenderness of the boy and kissed him then too, opening up her mouth to him with a desperate longing that made her body ache for the young man. He, feeling her softness pressing against him, forgot all thoughts of family feuds, or work, or even of little Aurelia. He could think of nothing but the beautiful, scented, powerful Berta.

Aurelia, who had been watching closely from the door at the back of the kitchen, wept as she saw the boy kissing her mistress and realised that she had lost his love before it had even begun.

CHAPTER 13

June 1999

The house in Chinzica continued to prey on Sam's mind. It was curious, because in truth it probably had nothing to do with the matter in hand, which was to identify the designer of the Tower and discover, if at all possible, the significance of the woman Michael had mentioned in his notebook, the mysterious Berta. And yet something about that house stayed with her throughout the following days. Michael obviously knew, or felt, that Berta and Calvo were connected in some way with the Tower, and the painting she had seen at Signor Visalberghi's shop clearly showed a man named Calvo with a woman standing behind him, who might well prove to be Berta. The painting was done on the loggia of a house that dated back to 1150, and the house she had visited the previous day bore a striking resemblance to it. This was what went through her mind as she jotted down her thoughts in Michael's notebook, next to his spidery instruction: 'follow the money', which he had penned next to Berta's name. What, she wondered now, had he meant by that?

The last time she had tried to discuss the film with him, he had effectively shut her down, and refused to countenance her involvement. But maybe he would be more amenable today...

She arrived at the hospital, as usual, with their breakfast. A physiotherapist was just closing the door behind her as Sam arrived.

'He's very tired,' she said. 'We did a lot of work this morning... and he's exhausted, I think. I'm sure you can see him later.'

Disappointed, Sam nevertheless went into his room and sat for a few moments by his bedside. He slept soundly, snoring lightly, his face with the now familiar lack of symmetry that was the legacy of his stroke. She had hoped he might wake, but he slept on and, reluctantly, she left her husband's coffee on the bedside table, and taking her own, left the hospital, heading for the Piazza.

The sun burned the back of her neck and she realised that she had forgotten to apply any sun cream that morning. Searching around for a shady place to sit, she noticed the museum that stood at one edge of the square. A large stone building with terracotta floors, it looked invitingly cool, and she gratefully paid her entrance fee and wandered in.

On the ground floor was an exhibition of artefacts reflecting the wealth of the Pisan people through the centuries. In the first case were displayed a large collection of housewares from the eleventh and twelfth centuries: spectacular examples of Syrian glassware, in vivid shades of yellow and green; majolica bowls painted brown and turquoise; carved wooden boxes and trunks; and a magnificent set of gold ewers in the shape of lions' heads, where guests of a grand host might be encouraged to wash their hands at the table. The next case contained clothes of the period: two dresses – one of deep red brocade, the other of cream silk, embroidered with seed pearls, reminiscent of the dress worn by the woman in the painting with Calvo. In one case were several pairs of tiny bejewelled shoes which had belonged, incredibly, to adult women of the time. They appeared to be about the same size as the shoes she had recently bought for the twins. Looking down at her own size six feet encased in comfortable flat boots, she found herself wondering how women's feet had ever been quite so small and so forgiving of such uncomfortable footwear. The last case was filled with spectacular examples of medieval and Renaissance jewellery: a pair of gold and amethyst brooches designed, according to the accompanying card, to hold a woman's cloak in place; a small gold crown that had possibly belonged to a member of the Medici family; and, beside it, a large emerald and gold ring, inscribed, according to the description on the card, with the words *'desidereo nessuno'*... desire no other.

Sam looked down at her own fine gold wedding ring. Michael had it inscribed before their wedding with a similar sentiment: 'Love me forever.' The words had worn very thin now and were just a faint representation of their former glory. Rather a metaphor for their marriage, Sam thought ruefully.

She looked again at the emerald ring in the case. It seemed extraordinary that it should have survived at all, but equally remarkable that the engraving was still so clear. Perhaps the lady to whom it had been given didn't wear it very often.

Walking on through the museum, Sam came to a room detailing the history of the three buildings that formed what had become known as the Campo dei Miracoli since the early twentieth century – the Duomo, the Baptistery and the Tower. There was an extensive exhibition on the engineering work that was being executed on the Tower, explaining, in a multitude of languages, exactly how the precarious edifice was to be righted by the English-led team of engineers. She found herself working backwards from the present-day rescue operation to the very beginnings of the Tower, until she came upon a small cabinet containing a brief description of how the famous monument came into being.

'In 1172, a Pisan widow named Berta di Bernardo left sixty coins for the building of the Tower.'

Just that, nothing more.

She felt an involuntary shiver.

So that was what Michael had meant. 'Berta – follow the money.'

Much to her irritation, there was no further mention of 'the widow' in any of the other displays. She went to the bookshop and bought the only books about the Tower that had been written in English. Sitting on a step outside the museum, she flicked through the index at the back, looking for any reference to Berta. There was just one, and it simply repeated the wording in the museum. 'Berta di Bernardo – the widow who left sixty coins for the building of the Tower.' Turning to the relevant page, she was frustrated to find there was no further information, and no image of the lady.

Her mind was now alive with questions. Who was Berta? Why did she leave this money? Was it a lot of money? Clearly it was, if it enabled the Tower to be built. It seemed extraordinary to her that these questions appeared, at least, not to have been answered by historians through the ages. Surely the person who lay behind the building of this Tower which was, after all, the most famous building in the world, deserved to have their contribution properly recognised – and not to be simply a 'footnote' in history. Was this something that her husband had also been intrigued by? Feeling a renewed sense of purpose, and excited that she and Michael could perhaps explore this mystery together, she walked purposefully back towards the hospital, hoping fervently that he would now be awake.

He lay staring out of the window when Sam entered his room.

'Oh darling, good, you're awake,' she said, sitting down on the edge of his bed. 'You were asleep when I came earlier... are you feeling any better?'

He shrugged his shoulders, or at least as near to a shrug as he could manage.

'The physio said you were tired… after your exercises.'

Michael remained silent and stared moodily out of the window.

'It's bound to be a slow process, Michael – I guess we just have to be patient…' Nervously, Sam stood up and began, almost automatically, to tidy Michael's bed, pulling his sheets straight and tucking them in at the bottom, before perching once again on one edge.

'Don't do that,' he sighed irritably. 'Can't move…'

'Oh sorry,' said Sam distractedly, pulling the sheets away from the mattress again so that he could wriggle his good leg.

'You always do that…' he murmured grumpily. 'Don't like it.'

'I know, I'm sorry – it's just an automatic thing I suppose. I do it for the children.'

'Just too bloody tidy,' he said with a faint smile.

'I know. Funny that. I never used to be tidy when we first met, did I? Do you remember? You used to be nagging me all the time about the state of my flat – the kitchen, the bathroom. I can't think why you married me really…'

There was an awkward silence, and after what seemed like a great length of time, Michael reached out and squeezed her hand.

'Sam…' he began.

'I suppose,' she interrupted, prattling on nervously, 'that when you have three children, you have to get tidy or everything starts to fall apart; I think that's what it's about. I can't just think about myself anymore, Michael. I've had to suppress my own personality in order to be a better mother… and a wife.'

'Darling…' he tried to pull himself up from the pillows, but the effort was too much and he collapsed back.

'Don't worry,' she said, conciliatorily, 'I'm not trying to make some sort of point… I brought you a coffee earlier, but I suspect it's gone cold now. Do you want it?'

He nodded and she held the cup to his lips before dipping a piece of brioche into it and offering it to him.

'Michael – there's something I'd like to ask you…'

'Not now,' he said rather miserably.

'You don't even know what I am going to ask you yet…' she said, just a little exasperated. This was something that happened with increasing frequency, even before he came to Italy. He would shut her down, just as she was about to ask or discuss something. She found it both irritating and, if she was honest, rather insulting – as if she were a child that needed to be kept in its place.

'Please don't do that! You have no idea what I'm going to discuss yet. I suppose you think I'm going to challenge you about that girl?!'

'Well aren't you?'

'I wasn't, as it goes, but now you've raised it we might as well have it out, don't you think?'

'I can't face it,' he said dejectedly.

'Well, that's convenient for you. I couldn't really face it either when you left for Italy. I spent the worst few days of my life, if you want to know, wondering if our marriage was over.'

Slight alarm spread over the more mobile side of Michael's face.

'I was considering throwing all the photos of us away,' she continued. 'I had them laid out in the sitting room and seriously thought about chucking them all on the fire. I can't believe what you did, Michael.'

'I'm sorry,' he murmured incredulously, 'Sam you're making something out of nothing. Nothing happened. She's nothing to me – just a friend.'

'And you expect me to believe that?'

'It's the truth.'

'Well... I suppose I can't really argue with that... can I?'

He shrugged his shoulders again. 'Believe what you like... but I know what's true.'

Sam wandered over to the window and gazed out at the roofs below. She fought back tears – more of frustration than misery. Michael had always been impossibly difficult to argue against. In some ways it was one of the things she had a sneaking admiration for, but at that moment, she found his refusal to explore her distress about Carrie deeply unsettling. It implied she was imagining the whole thing. Part of her, naturally, desperately wanted to believe him – that there was nothing in this 'relationship'. But she couldn't quite rid herself of the nagging fear that her first instincts about this girl and the photograph in his pocket had been correct.

She turned and looked at him. He looked so wretched, and lying there in bed, desperately vulnerable; she felt a sudden wave of sympathy for him.

The hospital orderly pushed open the door and enquired if Michael wanted lunch. Sam went to inspect his trolley, lifting the lid on a vast metal vat of pale, greasy broth.

'No! No, *grazie*,' she said firmly. 'Michael, the food here is disgusting. I'll go out and get you something from the town – OK?'

'Thanks,' he said, a hint of surprise in his voice.

She waved the porter away.

'I'll get you some nice salad, or pasta or something. I'll eat with you, if you like.' He smiled, for the first time that day. Could it be that Michael was actually telling the truth about Carrie? He was obviously upset and she shouldn't distress him when he was so ill. Besides, she desperately wanted to get him onside about the film.

'But... before I pop out... there's something else I'd like to raise. It's about the film,' she said hurriedly, hoping to sidestep any intervention on his part. 'I know you said you'd rather I didn't work on it... but I have read your notebooks and I found you had written a note about a woman named Berta, and the name Calvo was next to it, and then "follow the money". I've just been to the museum; I hadn't been there before, which was rather silly of me, but anyway, I found a little display in there with a note that said the widow, Berta, left sixty coins to build the tower. Did you know about that?'

'Sure,' said Michael. 'It's no secret. The weird thing though is that no one seems to know much more about it than that... I guess I was interested to know a bit more – like why she'd done it.'

'I agree,' said Sam excitedly. 'I mean, why would you do something like that?

You would have to be a patron of the arts, or something? Certainly very wealthy? And for a woman, at that time, to be involved in any artistic venture – that must be unusual. I feel sure there's something really interesting there. And who was Calvo?'

'He left her the money... Moretti knows more,' said Michael, his eyelids drooping.

'Oh you're tired, Michael. I'm sorry. I'll go and get that food now. I know this is so hard for you... stuck in here, not feeling well. But the doctors do keep reassuring me that you will make a good recovery; they're very pleased with how things are going. I want you to know that I am with you in that recovery... every step of the way... OK?'

Michael smiled faintly and nodded.

'But... I need you to understand something about me. I'm lonely, Michael, all by myself in that little hotel without you, without the children. I know you're here, but it's not the same. Do you understand?'

He nodded again, but his eyes narrowed a little, querying.

'The thing is, Michael... the thing is... I'd like to carry on researching the film.'

He raised his hand.

'No, don't say anything, please. I know you don't want me to, for some reason – either you don't think I can do it, or you don't want to be bothered, or something... but it would help me, Michael. It would give me something to concentrate on. Please, Michael.'

He closed his eyes and murmured, 'OK.'

CHAPTER 14

September 1171

A few days after the party, Berta sent word requesting a further meeting with Deotisalvi. Somewhat reluctantly, for the old man rather resented her interference, he had agreed to meet her in his elegant home near the Piazza.

After the usual niceties, Deotisalvi came, rather bluntly, to the point. 'So signora, the last time we spoke you persuaded me, probably against my better judgement, to take on your young protégé and his grandfather, in return for some investment.'

'Indeed, and they will turn out to be a good investment, you will see.'

'I hope so. I met with them yesterday and the old man certainly has a great deal of experience. We start in a few weeks, so time will tell. But the point is, *signora*, that I have fulfilled my part of the bargain; now it is time for you to fulfil yours.'

Berta rose from the chair where she had been sitting and walked to the window that overlooked the Piazza.

'Yes, of course, my investment. A campanile that could grace this beautiful Piazza should be the most wonderful campanile that anyone has ever seen. The investment will have to be large and the person who funds it will have to have deep pockets. I feel sure that I can persuade my husband to fund such a project, if I may say so, it is rare that he refuses my requests. Also, he has made some excellent investments over the last few years, and I'm sure he can be persuaded to help us with this,' and then she added, with a smile, 'he is as anxious as anyone to ensure his place in heaven. He has already donated the money to create the great new doors for the Duomo, if you remember.'

Deotisalvi snorted. 'Mmm... those doors; why Bonanno was chosen for that I have no idea.'

'*Signore*,' Berta's tone was playful, almost flirtatious, 'because he is a magnificent sculptor, as well you know. And a great de-signer and a fine *capo magister*. But it is you who the city have approached about the tower, and not him. You have no need for such jealousy.'

'Jealousy!' the old man exploded. 'I am not jealous of that jumped-up little man. It was me the city came to when they wanted a design for the Baptistery. And it was to me that they came about the campanile.'

'Exactly so. But Bonanno has his supporters,' said Berta. 'I hear that there was a contingent who wanted to offer him the campanile. Some say there was a vote.'

'Well, if there was,' shouted the old man, 'it was a vote that I won.'

'True, true... but nevertheless, whoever designs the tower, we are still short of the money to get the job started. Do you agree?'

He nodded.

'So, my family will provide the money. But Lorenzo will in-sist on seeing your initial sketches and workings. It is not his custom to purchase something he has not seen.'

The old man thought long and hard, before calling to his ser-vant to bring a box of drawings from another room. As the oak casket was unlocked, he rummaged amongst the rolled sheets, finally bringing out the largest roll, tied with a dark red ribbon.

The servant was dismissed and the architect untied the ribbon and laid the plan out on the table. It revealed a design, not unlike the campanile he had designed for the Church of San Nicola. As with that campanile and his design for the Baptistery, the base of the tower was dominated by blind arcades. Above, the tower was relatively plain, faced in marble. Supremely elegant, it was a classic piece of Romanesque architecture. It was also a perfect example of mathematical precision.

'It is beautiful,' murmured Berta. 'May I have a copy of the design to take away? I promise it will be safe. I will only show it to Lorenzo.'

Reluctantly, the old man rolled up the plan and handed it to Berta. 'I have others in the strongbox. Take this one. But keep it private. This is not for everyone to see.'

'Of course, *signore*. We will get this tower built, you will see. And it will be the most wonderful campanile the world has ever seen.'

When Berta returned home, she found Aurelia weeping in her room. Since the night of the party, she had observed that her maid was near to tears almost constantly. Berta, by comparison, felt energised; both by her new-found love for her young protégé, and her excitement about the campanile.

'What on earth is the matter, Aurelia?' she asked rather tersely. 'Are you unhappy in your work here?'

Unable to explain her distress, Aurelia said bravely: 'It is nothing, Mistress – I miss my mother.'

'Well,' Berta replied kindly, 'we shall send word to her in the next day or two that she may visit you – would you like that?'

Aurelia smiled meekly and Berta sent her to bed.

The following morning, Aurelia woke to find the bed covered in blood. Filled with fear, she ran from her chamber into that of her mistress, begging her forgiveness at waking her and explaining that she feared she was dying. Once Berta discovered the cause of the girl's distress, she laughed and kindly explained what was happening.

'It is quite natural, Aurelia; it means you are becoming a woman. It will happen each month and is rather a bore, but it is a sign of your fertility.' She was struck by the irony of her words, as she thought of all the bleeding that she had endured with no sign of any child at the end of it.

But, determined to show the girl some kindness, she called down to the housekeeper, Maria, and instructed her to send the laundry maid to take Aurelia's sheets and to provide her with materials to stem the flow.

'You will feel tired today and may have a little pain. We will send to your mother for something to ease it, would you like that? It will only last a couple of days and then you will feel better. You'll see.'

But Aurelia felt overwhelmed with sadness and wept copiously most of the day. Even the arrival of her mother, who Berta had kindly sent for, did not give her any peace. Her mother gave her a tisane of St John's Wort to help with the pain, and then made up a second with Lady's Mantle to regulate her flow, but neither improved her mood and she continued to weep into the evening.

The two older women exchanged glances and smiled to one another in a knowing way about the lot of women and their need to endure pain and sadness, but Aurelia knew that her particular sadness was due to something far more serious than the loss of some blood. Her misery was all to do with the loss of Gerardo, the boy with whom, she now realised, she had fallen hopelessly in love.

Berta, blissfully unaware of her maid's feelings, exacerbated the situation by forcing Aurelia to accompany her on a visit to the Piazza the following day.

Over breakfast with Lorenzo, she raised the possibility of visiting the Baptistery.

'Lorenzo, *caro*, I wonder if you would mind if I took a little walk this morning. I must tell that young mason there is work for him and his grandfather at Deotisalvi's new tower at San Nicola. Do you remember him from the other evening? He was so worried about his future, and yesterday Deotisalvi assured me that he would be delighted to offer him some work.'

'Why do you have to tell him yourself? Send one of the servants.'

'Oh, *caro*, because I would like the pleasure of seeing his face when he realises that he now has a good job to go to. He was so worried that he and old Gerardo would be out of work. But please don't worry; Aurelia and Cosimo will be with me.'

'Well, don't be long,' replied her husband, gruffly.

'Of course, *caro*', she said, kissing the top of his head as she left. 'You feel a little warm Lorenzo – you should take some air in the garden while we are gone.'

Aurelia set off a few steps behind her mistress, with a heavy heart. She dreaded seeing Gerardo again, especially in the company of Berta. Cosimo attempted to chatter with her as they walked, and even tried to wrap his arm around her waist when Berta's attention was elsewhere. But Aurelia had no patience with him and slapped his hand away.

When Berta spotted Gerardo amongst a throng of other young masons, her heart missed a beat and she had to restrain herself from running over to him. Desperate to preserve her dignity, she asked Aurelia and Cosi to wait for her at the edge of the Piazza, while she walked purposefully, and in what she hoped was a dignified fashion, towards the Baptistery. She waved discreetly to Gerardo when he turned round and spotted her. Making his excuses to his workmates, he left the group and came towards her, marvelling at her composure and beauty. Taking her arm, he guided her to the opposite side of the Piazza where they sat together, out of sight of her maid, on a low wall.

'*Caro*,' she murmured, as she discreetly held his hand under the folds of her dress. 'I woke this morning and could think of nothing but you and your mouth on mine.'

He said nothing, but smiled at her, gazing first at her mouth, before allowing his gaze to travel down her body.

'Have you missed me?' she asked playfully.

'Of course, what do you think?' he replied. 'I have scarcely slept since that night for thinking about you.' And he buried his mouth in the nape of her neck, brushing his lips against her fine skin, breathing in the sweet scent of lavender and musk.

She groaned a little, before pulling away slightly.

'Now, I must tell you something – it's good news, Gerardo. Deotisalvi will take you and your grandfather on for the tower of San Nicola – it is all arranged.'

She smiled expectantly. 'Are you pleased?'

'Oh of course... *signora* – of course I am. And grateful... so grateful.' And he lifted her fine pale hands in his own and grazed them with his lips.

His workmates called for him. 'Gerardo! The *capo* says we must get on.'

Instinctively, they moved a few inches apart.

'*Caro* – I am glad you are pleased. I will send Aurelia with a note of where we are to meet. We must be discreet... you understand, I hope. If Lorenzo were to discover this, he would kill you and probably me, too.'

'I understand.' Gerardo stood. But before returning to the gaggle of young men standing waiting for him at the Baptistery, he said: 'I want you to know that I am so grateful.... for everything.'

And then he disappeared into the throng and Berta was left, her heart beating loudly, with a sense of longing that she knew, without a shadow of a doubt, she would have to fulfil. And soon.

She returned to the *palazzo* just before lunchtime. Lorenzo was in a foul mood. The symptoms of fever he had felt a few weeks before had returned. He lay in Berta's bed, hot and damp and angry.

'Where have you been?' he demanded when she returned, flushed, from her errand.

'To the Piazza, *caro*. You know, I told you. I had to give the good news to young Gerardo and his grandfather. They were very pleased.'

'All is well with the world then,' he snapped.

I am so sorry,' she continued, '*Caro* – did the garden air not help you at all?' She felt his head. 'You are very hot, Lorenzo, I will send word to Violetta – she must come back to see us; I'm sure she can help to get this fever down.'

'Ha!' retorted her husband. 'That witch – why not send for a proper doctor?'

'Oh Lorenzo, *caro* – you know how much faith I put in Violetta'.

'I can't think why… I see no sign that her remedies have made any difference to you', Lorenzo snapped back.

'If you are referring to the fact that I am still not with child… then no – the tisane has not yet helped. But it might take time, Lorenzo… we must have a little faith.'

'Do as you will,' he retorted. 'Send for her if you like. But send Maria too, with something for me to drink. I have a terrible thirst.'

For the rest of the day Berta was trapped in her chamber, her husband miserable and demanding. Word was sent to Violetta who arrived before nightfall. After she had examined him, concern was etched on her face.

'*Signora*, I am sorry to tell you, but I fear that your husband has contracted a serious fever. It has all the marks of the fever that took my own husband, caused by *mal aria*. We must observe him carefully. If you will give me a bed here, I will watch over him tonight. I have brought a basket of remedies with me. Would you allow?'

Berta briefly wondered whether the doctor should be sent for. Or the priest.

'What do you think, Violetta? I have more faith in you, as you know, but Lorenzo would prefer to see a doctor. They would bleed him.'

'The doctor's blood letting will do nothing for him, *signora*, and I have the herbs with me that will help him. If he is still bad in the morning, then, if you like, send for the doctor and perhaps even the priest, if you think it will give him comfort. But hopefully this is just a small crisis. We just need to bring his fever down if possible.'

Grateful for Violetta's wisdom and support, and relieved of the burden of caring for her husband herself, Berta made arrangements for the apothecary to share a bedroom with Aurelia. But, concerned as she was for her husband, she could not rid herself of the desire to see Gerardo. She sent for her maid.

'Aurelia, your mother will be staying here tonight, to care for Lorenzo. He has a little fever, but Violetta is confident that it can be brought under control. In the meantime, I need you to do something for me. I want you to go to Gerardo's house and give him a message. I thought the walk would do you good – no? Tell Gerardo that I will meet him tonight, when the moon is high in the sky, near the church of Santa Cecilia. Go now; when you return you may have your supper.'

Aurelia, weakened by the unfamiliar loss of blood and dismayed at being forced to play go-between, meekly agreed. But, reasoning that it would, at least, afford her an opportunity to meet with Gerardo herself, she went first to her room and changed from her simple linen work dress into the pale grey silk that Berta had given her to wear a few nights before. She brushed her hair and splashed water on her cheeks and eyes, in an effort to refresh her tear-stained face, determined to make herself as lovely, and as tempting, as she could. For somewhere in her young, tender heart she still retained a belief that Gerardo might, at last, realise that it was she, Aurelia, that he truly loved. As she left her room, her eyes fell on the bottle of scent that stood on a table by the door in Berta's room. Poking her nose round the door, she noted that Lorenzo was sleeping and the chamber was empty. Her mother, she assumed, must be in the kitchen preparing some tincture or other. Hurriedly, she tipped the bottle onto her fingers and breathed in the sweet scent of lavender and musk before rubbing it onto her neck. Then, grabbing an old cape to conceal her pretty outfit from her mistress's eagle eye, she raced down the stairs, and was away to Gerardo's house before anyone from the household could see her.

She gasped when Gerardo opened the door. He had only just returned from work at the Piazza and his face was covered with marble dust, giving it a strange ghostly appearance.

Seeing her, he felt a childlike joy and, grabbing her hand, pulled him towards him, kissing her sweetly on the cheek.

She brushed the dust off her face with mock seriousness, and scolded him

'Gerardo, you are filthy. Get indoors and wash your face.'

Laughing together, he pulled her into the house with him, before going over to the big marble bowl in the corner of the room and filling it with water from the pitcher on the floor. She sat at the table in the kitchen, watching him as he washed his face, dunking his hair in the water and shaking it out like a dog. He pulled his shirt over his head, dropping it on the floor, and began to wash his chest and arms before turning triumphantly round to see her. She sat, without her cape, resplendent in her silk gown.

'You look beautiful,' he told her honestly.

'As do you,' she replied; and for a few moments they sat in mutual contemplation and admiration, one for the other. She, fair, with golden hair, deep blue eyes and her simple grey silk gown. He, dark-haired, dark-skinned, his green eyes shining like a cat.

He sat at the table and offered her a cup of wine.

She sipped the dark liquid and felt its effects almost immediately, for she had not eaten that day.

'So, my pretty Aurelia, what brings you to me this evening?'

Aurelia remembered her errand: 'My mistress sent me. She has a message for you.'

The young man looked down at the table and, Aurelia noted, flushed a little.

'What does she want?'

'To meet with you, tonight… at the church of Santa Cecilia. Will you meet her?'

'Tell her I will,' and then, as an afterthought, he said, 'Aurelia… it's business, this between me and Berta…just business. Do you understand?'

Aurelia said nothing. She stroked the silk of her dress, the dress Berta had given her. After a little while she said: 'I understand, Gerardo; but if it is just business why did you kiss her that evening in the garden?'

Gerardo flushed once again.

'I know you did; I saw you from the kitchen. I didn't mean to, but I came out for some air and there you were, and you were kissing. I… oh Gerardo… do you love her?'

At that moment, Gerardo's grandfather pushed open the door from the street outside. He took in the scene.

'*Nonno*, you're back.' Aurelia was touched by how genuinely happy Gerardo was to see his grandfather.

'I am,' he replied gruffly, 'but perhaps it is better if I were to leave again.'

Aurelia, ever-sensitive to other people's needs, was quick to respond. 'No, no please, I should go. I need to get back to my mistress.'

Standing, she said more formally to the older man, 'I hope I see you again,' before turning to Gerardo, 'and you too, very much.'

Taking her arm, he guided her to the open door and as he breathed in her scent, said quietly into her ear, 'You smell so sweet, little Aurelia... like a little flower. Will you trust me? I am very fond of you. But this other, it is business... that's all.' And then more loudly, he said, 'Thank you for coming, I hope we meet soon.'

When she had gone, he stood for a moment at the open door, thinking over what had happened, and what he had said. He could not bring himself, he realised, to admit to Aurelia how he really felt about Berta. Why? To protect her feelings, or to avoid a scene. He had flirted with Aurelia, he had encouraged her, and now he saw that he was in danger of hurting her, and that upset him. He was fond of Aurelia; she was innocent, sweet, pretty. He found himself happy whenever he was with her. She made him laugh, and there was something childlike and charming about her. If he had never met Berta, he would almost certainly be courting her. She was the kind of girl he had always thought he might marry. But he had met Berta, and she was not a woman to be shaken off lightly. And more than that, he found her attractive, exciting even. She was forbidden fruit, as ripe as the figs she used to bring him as a boy, and he was intoxicated by her. And yet, Aurelia was someone he could spend the rest of his life with.

'Gerardo.' His grandfather called him back from his musing. 'Shut the door, lad, and come and sit by me. Who was that pretty little miss... your girlfriend?' Old Gerardo was smiling at his grandson.

'No, no,' Gerardo said thoughtfully, 'just a friend. She's just a child really... just a sweet child. I'm coming.'

He turned and went back inside, resolving that he would not hurt Aurelia anymore. If his relationship with Berta was to develop, so be it, but he could not love two women. It was not fair, not right. Somehow he would have to tell her.

CHAPTER 15

September 1171

The brilliance of the full moon cast shadows between the arches that surrounded the church, illuminating the faces of the people gathered there that warm September evening. Berta, anxious to conceal her identity, pulled the hood of her silk cloak up over her hair, partly covering her face. She had rushed to the meeting place, having left home later than she intended. Lorenzo was feverish. Violetta had made a tisane of sweet wormwood, a remedy she had sometimes found to be effective in cases of *mal aria*, followed by another made of Holy Thistle – the cure for fever – but still his head was burning and he drifted in and out of lucidity all evening, at times calling for his wife, grasping at her clothing and clinging tightly to her hand, at others pushing her away, and shouting to be left in peace.

Berta was desperate to leave and yet filled with guilt at doing so.

'Violetta, I'm so sorry but I have to go out. It is a matter of business. Lorenzo knows all about it. But I feel awful. I know I shouldn't leave him. Do you think he'll be all right?'

Violetta, who was engrossed with her charge, scarcely looked up. 'We will be fine, *signora*; please go. I will try to get his fever under control while you are gone.'

But Berta felt guilty nevertheless. Going into Lorenzo's own room next to hers, she felt unable to draw attention to her departure by changing her dress or arranging her hair. But just before she left she dabbed lavender scent onto her brow and her neck, an act that did not go unnoticed by Aurelia.

The walk to the church would not be a long one, but she was uncharacteristically nervous to be out alone so late at night. Once or twice she stopped in her tracks, resolving to return home again. She knew the risks she was taking; for it was not the custom for the wealthy to go abroad much after dark and certainly not alone. The narrow lanes of Pisa were full of thieves and murderers, and twice Berta had to hide in the shadows to avoid being spotted by groups of unruly men. But it was not just the physical danger that she had put herself in. She knew the risk she was taking with her marriage and with her mortal soul. A few moments after she slid out of the garden gate, she stopped and turned around, muttering under her breath, 'I cannot do this.' She thought of Lorenzo lying ill at home and guilt overwhelmed her. But, she reasoned, Violetta was with him. She could do more for him than Berta ever could. Resolving that she would be home in time to stroke his brow, to kiss his forehead, she hurried on, thinking of Gerardo's lips on hers, and the pleasure she would feel in his company. She remembered the kiss they had shared in her garden just a few weeks before, and felt the familiar flutter of excitement, before thoughts of Lorenzo drifting in and out of consciousness shattered the dream. By the time she arrived at the church, she had quite made her mind up to end it there.

Gerardo was nowhere to be seen. She waited in the shadows, anxious to avoid being recognised. The church and its surrounding cloisters were filled with people, much to her consternation. There had been a service to celebrate a saint's day and the congregation dispersed slowly, enjoying the warm evening. As the moon rose high in the sky, she wondered if he might let her down.

And then he was there, walking towards her, his hands in his pockets, his head down. He wore a cape with a hood, pulled over his head. His stride was long and he walked purposefully, carving a path through the people gathered in the little Piazza next to the church.

As he neared her, she was about to call out to him, when his hand shot out of his cape and he swung his arm around her, pulling her into the deep shadows within the cloisters of the church. He pressed his lips to hers; she felt his beard prickly against her skin. His tongue forced its way into her mouth, until she gasped and pulled away, putting her hand onto his chest and pushing him backwards.

'Wait, *caro*, wait. Not here… people might see us.'

Suddenly, he was the young boy she had first met again: 'I'm sorry. I was just so pleased to see you. I didn't think.' And then, looking deeply into her eyes, 'Forgive me… please?'

She took him by the arm and dragged him further away from the church, until they found themselves in a dark alley.

She leant against the wall, still warm from the day's sun and looked up at him.

'Gerardo… I've come to tell you something. I cannot stay for very long, not here tonight. My husband is unwell. I have to go.'

He hung his head, disappointed.

'Of course,' he acquiesced, 'I will take you home now, you shouldn't be alone.'

'Thank you,' she said, her beating heart slowing now with relief, 'I am so sorry; please believe me when I tell you that I am so disappointed. I love being with you, you have brought me such happiness, Gerardo.'

'And you me,' he said, 'I have never met anyone like you, *signora*.'

'Berta please, call me Berta. Gerardo... it is so hard, and you will understand one day... but it is possible to love two people, to care for two people. But I have a duty to my husband and I cannot do this tonight... perhaps not ever. I don't know. I came here tonight determined to tell you that we must end it. Not our friendship, but this other. But now, when I look at you, feel you near to me... I am not so sure.'

She gazed up at him, feeling his breath on her face, his arms still around her waist.

'I understand,' he said, burying his lips into her hair. 'I understand better than you think.'

The churchgoers had moved on, and around them all was quiet, save for the occasional scuttling, as a mouse darted down the narrow lane. In a bedroom high above their heads, a man coughed – a rasping, rattling sound. Gently, Gerardo kissed her closed eyelids. He kissed her cheeks, then her neck until finally he found her mouth. Her lips parted. His hands, slowly, ran down her bodice, under the silk cloak. He felt the soft fabric. His fingers explored the lacing at the back of her dress. Touching the skin beneath the silken ribbons, he let out an involuntary gasp.

With his other hand, he began to pull at her skirts, lifting the layers upwards with his fingers, until his hand touched the soft, velvety skin at the top of her thigh.

She pushed his hand away.

'No, no, Gerardo... not here like this. It is too dangerous. I must go now, but I will send word to you.'

'Let me take you home.'

'No, I will be quite safe. We should part now before anyone sees us together.'

She kissed him fleetingly on the lips, before smoothing her skirts and walking away out of the shadows and into the moonlight.

She did not turn round to look at her lover one last time, and so she did not see him lean against the wall, his head in his hands, before he too turned to walk back towards the Piazza. And as the moon dipped behind a cloud, neither of them saw a young girl, her blonde hair escaping from the hood of her cloak, ducking out of the shadows and running, with tears falling down her pink cheeks, back towards the Arno.

It was a short walk to her home, and when Berta returned, Aurelia, she was irritated to learn, had taken to her bed. But Violetta was on hand and unlaced her gown and sent to the kitchen for hot water to wash her face and hands.

Dressed in her nightgown, Berta went to visit her ailing husband.

'How is he?'

'He is calmer now, *signora*. He suffered a terrible crisis earlier this evening. I have given him something to drive the fever from him. But he is resting now, sleeping.'

Guilt enveloping her, Berta offered to sit with him. 'Leave him with me, Violetta; you go and rest for a while.'

'If you are sure, *signora*, but you must call me if his fever returns.'

Sitting next to her sleeping husband, Berta thought about the young man. As she held Lorenzo's hand in hers, listening to his breathing, she remembered the other's scent, his strength, his passion, and in spite of herself, felt the longing returning, spreading warm and wet between her thighs.

Sometime in the middle of the night, she woke, her dreams filled with thoughts of Gerardo – his eyes, his mouth, his dark curls.

Her neck was stiff, her head having fallen awkwardly against her chest. She stretched and straightened herself. Lorenzo still slept, his breathing heavy. Standing, she went round to the little bed that had been made up for her next to his. She lay down and, with her hand resting lightly against her husband's back, fell into a deep sleep.

She was awoken just after dawn by Violetta.

'*Signora, signora...* you must wake. It is not good. Oh *signora*, I am so sorry. Your husband, he is dead.'

Her mind, fuzzy with sleep, Berta struggled to understand what Violetta was saying. She sat up and leant across to Lorenzo.

'No, Violetta, surely not... he was sleeping just an hour or two ago. You are mistaken. He is sleeping – look.'

She leant over to kiss his cheek and listen for his breathing. But she recoiled at the touch of his icy skin.

She looked into Violetta's kind blue eyes, full of concern for her welfare.

'This is my fault,' said Berta.

'No, *signora* – it is God's will. He was sick. There was nothing we could have done.'

'I should have been here. I betrayed him by... leaving him.'

'But you had important business, *signora*. He would have understood. Please... do not punish yourself. I will give you something now... go and rest next door. I will make him ready.'

'No... leave him with me for a moment.'

The early morning light filtered through the casement windows, illuminating Lorenzo's face. With death had come a smoothing of the weathered lines that had begun to etch their way into his skin.

Berta smoothed the still damp hair away from his forehead. She put her hand over his – now stiff, unresponsive, cold.

The room was eerily silent. The sounds that had been a part of her husband during his life – the gruff voice, the rattly breathing, the snoring, the swearing, the shouting, the laughter – had all come to a sudden halt. In their place she heard the birds singing in the olive trees outside. A distant church sounded the early morn-

ing Angelus. A cart making deliveries clattered by in the lane below. She heard the sounds of her household waking: the rattling
of a grate being cleared somewhere in the bowels of the house; Aurelia and Violetta hovering in the room next door, the murmuring
of concerned voices. She looked up as Massoud silently entered
the room, his dark, intelligent face, etched with tears.

She smiled at him.

'Lady, I am so sorry...

'I know, Massoud. Thank you. Please close the door behind
you.' She heard his heavy footsteps retreating down the staircase.

It seemed impossible that Lorenzo, who had been such major force in her life, had simply ceased. They had been together
for seventeen years and now... it was over. She had loved him;
she also understood his faults, his foibles. His jealousy and occasional rage were the inevitable consequence of his energy and
ambition. Theirs had been a partnership. He had provided her
with power, wealth and position. She had in turn developed
his cultural and business connections, had leant his endeavours
credence and elegance. She had guided his hand on all artistic
matters. And he had been proud of her; she knew that, for he
had told her often. And as for her childlessness... he had never
chastised her, had never laid blame at her door. And yet she
knew a son was the one thing he had desired above all else. And
what would become of her now... a childless widow. Was this
her punishment, perhaps, for loving another?

Berta was in turmoil for the rest of that day and for many days
that followed. The household, too, was in an uproar. The priest
was sent for to pray for the mortal soul of Lorenzo, but Berta was
filled with remorse that she had not requested his presence that last
evening. Her husband's soul was in jeopardy. He had not had a
chance to confess his sins, and in her darker moments Berta feared
that she, too, was now at risk of a life of everlasting torment.

To add to her personal and spiritual distress, troubled business dealings now erupted to the surface. Some months before, Lorenzo had apparently sought a loan from a rival merchant to increase his fleet.

Benedete Zaccaria had been one of the first to visit the *palazzo* within hours of Lorenzo's death, demanding to know when the loan would be repaid. Soon there were others, associates of Lorenzo's, who came to the *palazzo* initially to pay their respects to his widow, but as they left, they produced papers claiming ownership of several of Lorenzo's assets.

Berta was shocked at the speed with which his creditors had descended on her household. She called for Massoud, the notary who kept their accounts.

'Massoud, please… you must help me with these people,' she begged him.

'Lorenzo did not let me into his financial dealings; I had no idea he had borrowed so heavily. We need to establish the validity of their claims. Can I trust you to do this for me?'

'I will do everything, *signora*. Lorenzo was my master; I will not betray him now.'

'Good; you may tell Signor Zaccaria, and any of the others, that we intend to honour any debts, but bring everything to me before any decision is made, or before anything is signed. I will learn how to run the business, it will go on as before. Tell them that.'

Back upstairs, her husband's body had been laid out by the servants. Bathed and dressed in his best velvet tunic, his face was pale and smooth. Around his head, Violetta had placed sweet smelling gillyflowers – carnations and pinks – from the pots that stood along the terrace, and their scent filled the room.

Berta came into the chamber and gasped as she saw him. 'He does not even look ill, Violetta,' she cried, before falling into the apothecary's arms.

Helping her to sit down on the little seat next to her husband's body, Violetta called to her daughter. 'Aurelia, come here and look after your mistress. I must go and make her a tisane… for the shock.'

The girl, who had been lurking in the doorway of the room, came forward reluctantly.

'Sit, girl, here by her side,' her mother instructed sharply, before she hurried down to the kitchens.

Aurelia sat in awkward silence next to Berta, recoiling slightly at the sensation of the older woman's body, as Berta – her head in her hands – sobbed uncontrollably, railing against the fates that had taken 'her Lorenzo' from her.

Disgusted by what she considered a show of fake distress, Aurelia sat unmoved, waiting for her mother to return, which she soon did, bringing a bowl of warming tea and shooing Aurelia back to the kitchen.

'Leave us now, Aurelia; you cannot understand what this lady is suffering. Go and make yourself useful downstairs.'

Down in the kitchens, the staff were all talking together. Word of the line of creditors had spread and they were anxious for their future. Aurelia paid them no heed. Her mind was filled with what she had witnessed the night before – sights and sounds that she was unable to forget. From the big pot over the fire, she helped herself to a bowl of broth, which she ate in silence at the vast kitchen table. Unnoticed, she crept out of the kitchen door and, not quite knowing what she was doing, ran through the garden and out of the big wooden gates, heading for the Arno. The sun was high in the sky when she arrived at the Piazza. Men were still at work, and she paced round the edge of the square looking for Gerardo. Quite what she intended to say to him, or why she had come, was unclear. All she knew was that she was desperate to find him. At one point she thought she saw him amongst a crowd of young men heading towards a small inn, and she raced after them. But as the boy she was following turned around, she realised with a sense of despair that it was not Gerardo. The bells of the Duomo struck three times for the Angelus, before she decided to return to the *palazzo*. Disconsolately, she walked back, past Gerardo's house. There was no sign of him there either. The sun had begun to drop behind the roofs of the city when she returned. Berta had taken to her bed and was sleeping fitfully. But Violetta, returning from sitting with Berta, grabbed her by the arm as she tried to sidle quietly into the little room she shared with her mother.

'Where have you been?'

'I had to get out… for a walk,' the girl retorted.

'You should have said where you were going. Berta had need of you. Fortunately, I was here and able to see to her needs. But you are her maid, Aurelia. I know I was against you coming here at the beginning, but Berta has been good to you, and to me. She pays you well, she also pays the girl to help me out. And she has been very generous and sent many people to see me for advice. For the first time since your father died, I am managing to earn enough money to pay our bills. Do not turn your back on this, Aurelia, we need her too much. Now I suggest that you go and brush your hair and go down to the kitchen and see if there is anything you can do to help. I will stay here with Berta until she wakes, and when she does I will send you to her. She has asked me to remain here until after the funeral and I have agreed, but that does not mean that you can walk away from your duties here, Aurelia. And once I have gone, I will be relying on you to take care of her.'

The older woman went back to Berta's bedside, and her daughter, in no doubt of her duty, and with a heavy heart, went down to the basement kitchen.

CHAPTER 16

June 1999

Sam fingered the business card that she had tucked into the frame of the mirror in her bedroom, tracing the mobile number with her nail, while fidgeting nervously with the flex of the hotel phone. Anxiously, she dialled the number. There was an unintelligible message and the line went dead. She added and subtracted prefixes and local codes, each time getting the same insistent female voice, '*Il numero non esiste…*' At last, some miraculous combination having been arrived at, the phone rang.

'*Pronto.*'

She held her breath.

His voice was deeper than she had remembered; sexy. Say something…

'Hi, Dario… it's me… Sam.'

'Hi Sam, I'm so glad you rang.'

She breathed again.

'Oh… yes, well I'm sorry it's taken me a few days. I've been a bit preoccupied what with one thing and another…'

'I can imagine. How is your husband?'

'Oh, fine. Well, not fine, obviously. Silly thing to say… but getting a little better each day. It's going to be a slow process.'

His voice was kind. 'And how's the research going?'

'Ah, well, that's the thing really. I need your help with something and I just wondered... if we could meet up?'

The appointment was arranged for 2 o'clock. They were to meet at the café on the corner of the Piazza, after Sam had visited Michael. He was asleep when she arrived, and she busied herself tidying his room. There was a tiny wardrobe into which a nurse had placed the clothes he had been wearing the day he had been taken ill. Resolving to take them to the laundry, she removed the shirt and jeans from the hangers and began to fold them. In the back pocket of his jeans, she felt the unmistakable shape of a mobile phone. She took it out and flipped it open. The battery was dead. Looking around the room for the charger, she found it in the small bedside cabinet. Packing it up with the phone, she put the items in her bag to take back to the pensione.

Back in her room, she put the clothes into a plastic bag, ready to take to the laundry round the corner, and plugged Michael's phone and charger into the international plug in her room. She pottered about, waiting for it to charge up, but the battery was completely dead and the phone seemed reluctant to spark into life.

She thought about her meeting with Dario later that day and wondered if she ought to change. The days were getting hotter and her jeans felt increasingly uncomfortable. There was just enough time before the shops shut for their lengthy lunch break to buy something cooler to wear.

She walked towards the commercial district and soon found herself in the busy main road filled with clothes shops of all kinds. Suppressing a small surge of guilt that she should be doing anything as frivolous as shopping, she nevertheless went into a small boutique, next to an expensive shop selling handbags and leather goods. The lady in charge smiled kindly at her as she entered. She rummaged amongst the rails of clothes before finally select-

ing a simple cotton dress in a pale green colour. She held the
dress up to herself and considered her image in the shop's mirror.

'*Bella, signora, molto bella*,' the shop assistant said enthusiastically.

She rifled through the rail until she found the dress in the correct size and pressed it into Sam's hand.

'*La prove, signora... provi.*' She pointed towards a small fitting
room at the back of the shop.

Sam squeezed into the tiny cubicle, and managed to remove
her jeans and top, banging her elbows uncomfortably against the
sides of the changing room. She slipped on the dress. It was cut
quite low over the bust, with a wide neckline that emphasised
her long neck and wide shoulders. It was gathered into the waist
before falling in a bias-cut skirt just below the knee. The colour
set off her pale green eyes, she noted with uncharacteristic satisfaction.

'*Bella... molto bella*,' reiterated the shop assistant.

Sam took out her phrase book. '*Camicetta?*' she asked hopefully pointing to the top half of her body.

'*Si, si*,' the lady said enthusiastically. She went off to the rails
and came back with half a dozen tops: blouses, shirts, T-shirts.
Two or three were typical Italian design, highly decorated with
sequins and illustrations of leopards, or other exotica. But one, a
filmy white peasant top, caught Sam's eye.

She slipped off the dress, and putting her jeans back on, tried
on the top. The edges were decorated with red and blue cross-
stitching, the neckline gathered with a blue ribbon that adjusted
so the blouse just slipped off one shoulder. The shop assistant
brought her a leather belt and cinched in the blouse around
Sam's waist. It suited her.

'*Grazie.*'

'*Le piace?*' the woman asked brightly.

'Si, molto bella... grazie.'

Sam left the shop, shading her eyes against the sun. She carried an elegant shopping bag containing the dress, a pair of shorts and the top and belt. She avoided the expensive handbag shop next door, and went instead into a small shoe shop up a side street. There were summer shoes in all colours arranged outside. She selected a pair of leather sandals tied round the ankle with ribbons in a shade of green that would match the dress. Flat espadrilles in bright stripes also caught her eye and she bought a pair in blue, striped with red and bright green that reminded her of a pair she had bought in a small market in France when she was eighteen and on holiday with a friend.

Back at her hotel, she removed her jeans and tired T-shirt – throwing them into the bag with Michael's clothes ready to take to the laundry. She put on the shorts and peasant blouse along with the espadrilles and studied her reflection in the mirror. Not bad, although her legs, she was mortified to find, were pale and pasty.

At five to two, she was just heading out, when she remembered Michael's phone. It was fully charged and she turned it on. The message function flashed. She opened the text message box. There were more than twenty messages. Most from Miracle Productions. A couple from his Italian researcher Mima with details of meetings and three from a number with no name assigned to it. She opened one up.

'Hey sweetie – how ya doing? Miss ya... Cxxx'

'Hi – just heard what happened – please text me.'

'Mikey – really worried now... Miracle say you're in hospital. I love you, darling – please send word to me.'

Sam closed the phone and sat down heavily on the edge of the bed. She thought about their last conversation, when Michael had flatly denied any 'affair'. In truth these messages did not actually prove an affair, but how many 'good friends' wrote 'love you' in a text message. A combination of anger and disappointment welled up inside her, mixed with a kind of shame that she had allowed herself to be convinced of his innocence.

'God I'm a fool,' she said out loud. She opened the phone again. The dates on the three messages confirmed they were sent after his stroke. There were none before that time. If there had been any, Michael had obviously deleted them as soon as they arrived. There were no replies either; he'd certainly covered his tracks.

She checked the address book. There was no listing for Carrie; he had not saved her number in his phone. Sam sat for some minutes staring into space, reading and re-reading the text messages.

The cathedral bells chimed once for the quarter hour. Sam checked her watch hastily. It was quarter past two. She threw the phone into her bag and rushed out across the Piazza. Dario was sitting outside the café at a table on the corner of Via Maria. He leapt to his feet when he saw her.

'Hi... I was getting worried that perhaps I'd got the wrong place. And I didn't know how to get hold of you.'

'Oh, I'm sorry. I was just caught up in something, and forgot the time.'

He kissed her on both cheeks and guided her into a chair facing the square. He waved discreetly at the waiter.

'What will you have? Coffee?'

'A glass of wine, I think – I need it.'

He smiled and ordered a carafe of local white wine.

'Problems?' he said kindly.

'You could say that... just some bad news that I'd been trying to close my eyes to.'

He looked puzzled.

'It's fine, don't worry about it,' she said, picking up the carafe and pouring them both a large glass.

'Cheers,' she said brightly.

'You look nice,' he said.

'Thank you. I just bought these today. I came out here in such a rush, I didn't really have any suitable clothes with me, and it's getting so hot I needed something a bit cooler.'

'Well, they suit you. And it's good to see you. Now, how can I help you?'

At this, she burst into tears. It was virtually the first time she had cried since she had arrived in Pisa, and his kindness broke her reserve. He looked on, slightly alarmed. He reached across the table and touched her arm.

'I'm sorry; you are obviously very upset about your husband. I understand.'

'I am, yes… but not for the reasons you think.'

Sam rummaged in her bag for a tissue and wiped her nose.

'It's complicated… I'm not even sure if he's going to be my husband in the future.'

Dario looked surprised.

'It's not me… I'm not deserting him when he's ill or anything. But he's… got someone else.'

'Oh… I see?'

'And I didn't know… well not really. Not until just now actually. And I'm not quite sure where I stand. It's a bit of a shock, you see?'

He took in her long fair hair, a couple of sun-bleached strands sticking to the side of her cheek. Her sharp green eyes filled with tears. She had faint freckles across her nose. 'I'm sorry. It must be very hard for you – especially now.'

'Yes, yes it is. I'm not quite sure how to deal with it, if I'm honest.'

'Have you spoken to him about it? It might just be a casual thing. I can't imagine him leaving you. He'd be a silly man to do such a thing…'

'You're very kind. No, I've not really spoken to him about it. He won't discuss it with me. It's all just a bit of a bloody mess, quite honestly.'

She gulped down her wine. Dario refilled her glass.

'Thanks,' she said. 'I don't usually drink during the day – I'll feel dreadful later.'

'Not on this,' he smiled. 'It's local, and has no bad side effects at all. It will do you good.'

'Look, I'm really grateful to you for meeting me. I'm sorry to be in such a state. I was intending to come over here and talk to you about the film. But I just don't know what I'm doing here now really. The whole thing seems rather pointless suddenly. This business with my husband… you understand? I'm so cross with him, but I can't desert him – not now. He's so unwell and it wouldn't be right. But in many ways I feel trapped. To be honest, the only thing that's keeping me sane is this investigation into who built the Tower. It's a sort of reminder of who I used to be – capable, independent. Do you see? Before I had the children.'

'How are the children?' he asked kindly.

'Oh, they're well. My mother is there and is looking after them. They're fine – it's me who misses them really.'

'It must be very hard for you,' he said filling her glass with the last of the wine. Her eyes, he noticed, had filled with tears, which she wiped away roughly with the back of her hand. She attempted a smile as she drained her glass.

'Look, why don't we go for a walk – would you like that?'

'Yes, that would be very nice. Thank you.'

Dario paid the bill and taking her arm, he guided her towards the square. 'Have you seen the Camposanto yet? It's lovely on a hot afternoon…'

'No, no I haven't.'

They walked across the Campo dei Miracoli towards the ticket office. Dario bought two tickets and a guide-book, and they entered the dark, cool confines of the Camposanto – the old cemetery on the northern edge of the Piazza.

'"Built in 1278 on the ruins of an old baptistery and finished in 1464,"' Dario read aloud. 'So, it's later than the Tower and the Duomo.'

'I wonder where they buried people before that?' asked Sam.

'It suggests they just buried people around the cathedral... but they moved them here to "gather them into hallowed ground"... interesting. Apparently they brought fifty-three ship loads of soil from Mount Calvary in Jerusalem to fill the interior courtyard – I suppose that's the bit now covered in grass over there. It has a wonderful sense of peace, don't you think?'

They wandered onto the green lawn that stood at the centre of the cloisters; Sam involuntarily knelt and touched the grass, surprised at her need to make contact with the consecrated soil.

They appeared to be the only people visiting the holy place, and Sam furtively slipped off her espadrilles, feeling the cool smoothness of the marble beneath her feet. The thick walls of the Camposanto were lined with ancient tombs, and she stopped to read who lay in each one. Looking down, she realised the cool marble slabs on which she walked were in fact tombstones too, bearing inscriptions detailing who lay beneath. Some, she was surprised to find, were of people who had only died within the last hundred years. But here and there were older graves, the clarity of their engraving worn down by the thousands of feet that had shuffled across them. Many dated from the fifteenth and sixteenth centuries, but one or two much older stones had survived.

The north wall of the Camposanto was decorated with frescoes – faded a little, but nevertheless beautiful – illustrating life in medieval Pisa. One in particular showed masons standing on bamboo scaffolding surrounding the Duomo – chiselling, chipping, carving. Boys working with men, stripped to the waist, hauling huge pieces of stone onto the scaffold with simple pulleys and weights.

'It's extraordinary isn't it,' she said, 'to think of all those young men – some of them no more than children, creating these remarkable buildings. It seems almost impossible.'

Her feet were feeling chilly and she dropped her espadrilles onto the floor to put them back on. Looking down, she realised she was standing on yet another gravestone. The writing was worn so as to be virtually invisible. But she could make out a couple of the letters of what might have been a name: L.O.E. Then a gap, a 'C' and an 'L'. L.O.E... C.L. Her crossword-trained brain began to fill in the missing letters excitedly. She skipped ahead to the dates, surprised by how fast her heart was beating... MCLXXI – 1171.

'My God,' she said out loud, as a tiny nun walked past her on her way to prayer in the chapel. She nodded her head in approval at the kneeling woman, and scurried away.

'Dario – look... I think this might be the grave of that man Lorenzo Calvo – do you remember... in your father's book?'

'Oh yes... maybe,' he said. 'Is it important?'

'Well... not in itself. But there was something I was going to tell you – about Calvo and the Tower. All this business with my husband rather got in the way and... I forgot!' They emerged, blinking, into the bright sunlight of the Campo. Sam put on her sunglasses and they walked towards the Tower, their fingers just touching.

'So, what did you want to tell me?' asked Dario.

'I went to the museum the other afternoon and I found out who Calvo was... and, more importantly, who Berta was. She was the widow who left the money for the Tower to be built. They had a tiny little notice in one of the glass cases there. They didn't actually mention Calvo, but my husband had obviously also discovered there was a link between them – I found a couple of references to them in his notebooks. Berta was Calvo's heiress apparently – so presumably his wife, or maybe his daughter.'

'Oh, of course,' said Dario, ' I should have realised. I did know about the widow who left the money, but I didn't know she was called Berta.'

'Well, it seems we are not alone in being ignorant about her – remarkably little has been written about her.'

They arrived at the base of the Tower, encircled by barriers to protect the building works from the visiting tourists. As they stood gazing up at the building, Dario tentatively put his arm around her shoulder. She felt herself leaning in towards him.

'The other thing I don't understand, Dario, is why no one signed the building? I understand that all buildings at that time were signed by their architects – but not this one. The masons did carve things above the main entrance – the two galleys there, for instance, which I suppose signify Pisa's marine success. But there is no indication of who designed the building. It just doesn't make any sense. And if it was Deotisalvi who built it, which is the current theory, I gather, then that makes even less sense. He signed the Baptistery over there, and also the other Tower of San Nicola. He always signed his buildings. So why not this one?'

'I don't know,' said Dario, 'we should find out...'

'I agree. My husband has a contact here in Pisa – a Professor Moretti. He's the Professor of Medieval History at the university and is the resident expert, from what I can gather. Surely he would know more about her? I've looked him up in the phone book and I've got his number, but I'm nervous of calling him. My Italian is just not very good.'

'Do you want me to call him for you? We could go and meet him if you like…'

'Oh would you? Do you have the time?'

'I told you… I'm here for two weeks kicking my heels. Sure. Let's do it now.'

Half an hour later, they were walking towards the Professor's apartment, through the spectacular Piazza dei Cavalieri and on into the old medieval part of the town, until they came to a tiny little square near the church of San Frediano.

Dario stopped outside a tall tower house. He rang one of the six bells that were set beside the large wooden door. The buzzer sounded and Professor Moretti's voice filtered through the intercom. *'Vi entrare.'*

They pushed the heavy door open and stepped into a dark tiled hall.

'He's on the fifth floor, I think. There's no lift by the look of it. Ready to walk?'

They arrived a few minutes later, slightly out of breath, and were greeted by the Professor, beaming from ear to ear.

'*Benvenuto,*' he said warmly.

The apartment was tiny, consisting of one room which obviously served as both sitting room and office, an unseen bedroom, a small bathroom and tiny galley kitchen. After the formalities of greeting, the Professor brought in coffee and a little plate of almond biscuits for his visitors. Sam was invited to sit on the elderly sofa, and gratefully accepted the coffee. Dario sat on an old leather armchair, ready to translate.

'Now,' the Professor said, when they were all settled, 'how can I help you?'

'Professor,' began Sam, 'I am so grateful to you for seeing me today at such short notice, and for taking time out of your busy life. I think you may already know my husband Michael, a television producer from England making a film about the Tower. I think he may have written to you? I'm not quite sure... but I don't think he had a chance to meet with you yet – unfortunately he was taken ill a couple of weeks ago here in Pisa, and I...' she faltered slightly, 'have taken over this project whilst he is in hospital.'

She waited while Dario translated.

'He says he had been looking forward to meeting Michael and is very sorry to hear that he is unwell, and hopes that he makes a speedy recovery.'

'Thank you... *grazie. E molto importante per me...* to meet you today. I need to find out as much as I can about the Tower from you... the world's greatest expert.'

The Professor smiled graciously.

'It is his pleasure to be of help,' Dario translated.

'There are so many details I need to know about the Tower. I have read quite a lot about it, of course, and know that it took several hundred years to complete. I know, too, that there is some question mark over who designed it. I am eager to understand as much as possible about its history; who built it, why it began to lean, and so on.'

'Well,' began the Professor, leaning back in his chair, as Dario began to translate: 'It is important that you first understand that Pisa was, at that time, one of the most powerful city states in Italy. There was much rivalry with Genoa, Venice, and later with Florence. Wars were fought and so on. The elite of this city were desperate to demonstrate their wealth and power to the rest of Italy. But most significant of all was their need to demonstrate their supremacy over the Muslim world. Pisa was central to the shipment of crusaders to the Middle East. Merchants in this city made fortunes trafficking men south – to rape and pillage and conquer. On the way back they filled their ships with plunder and goods of all kinds. It made them rich, and the people of Pisa were determined to show their superiority by building something which would honour their Christian God. And so began the development of what we now call the Campo dei Miracoli. First, the Duomo, designed by Buscheto, a great architect, begun in 1064 and not finished for three hundred years. Then the Baptistery, designed by Deotisalvi, another great architect, the first stones laid in 1153. Then, finally, the ultimate architectural glory... the Tower. Now, of course, there were hundreds of towers built in Italy at that time. But this tower, with its magnificent bells, was to be the best of all. It was positioned at the end of Via Santa Maria, the main artery through the town at that time. A showstopper, something to take the breath away. And those who were lucky enough to be allowed to climb up it would get a fantastic view of their Piazza, the city and the sea beyond, where all the galleys that brought goods to Pisa were moored. And the bells at its summit would, of course, call the faithful to prayer.'

'Are there good written records of how it was built and so on?' asked Sam.

'Some, yes. But there are not as many as you may imagine. It was a long time ago – when written records were not so common.'

'And who designed it?' Sam asked, scribbling in her notebook. 'I understand there is some doubt about that.'

The Professor stood up and wandered absent-mindedly over to his desk, piled high with papers and books.

'Well, that is a bit of a mystery,' he said.

'Mystery? Why?'

'Well, frankly, we do not really know who designed it. We are clear on the other buildings at the Campo. Architects at that time signed their buildings and so it is quite straightforward. But with the Tower...' he turned away and gazed out of the window.

'So we have no idea?' asked Sam.

'Oh, we have ideas...' he said, 'many people believe it to have been a sculptor at that time... Bonanno Pisano. But in my view that is mistaken. He was an excellent artist, but no architect. No...'

'Anyone else?' asked Sam.

'The Hunchback,' said Moretti, smiling.

'The Hunchback; yes, I've read about him. His real name was William of Innsbruck, wasn't it?'

'Yes. That's right. The story goes that this hunchback built the tower out of alignment in retaliation for his own terrible predicament. Madness of course; it's quite impossible that it was him. Then there is Gerardo... he was a builder... a master mason. A talented man, but in my opinion not talented enough to have created this extraordinary building. He worked on it though... that we do know.'

'And Deotisalvi?'

'Yes indeed... the great Deotisalvi. He is the man. The building has the same delicate touch as he used on the Baptistery. He was the only one with the skills for the job at that time.'

'But he didn't sign it...'

'No, that he did not.'

'Because?'

'That, my dear, is a mystery... impossible to solve.'

'So you don't know it was him,' said Sam, 'you are just making an educated guess.'

The Professor turned to look carefully at the young woman.

'I am... and it's a good educated guess.'

'I'm sorry, I don't mean to be rude. I just want to understand. There is another name associated with the Tower, but I can't seem to find out anything much about her. The lady named Berta; can you tell me anything about her?'

'Ah... the widow.' The Professor smiled. 'Now she too is a mystery.'

'Why, who is she?'

'Well, the woman who left the money to build the Tower, of course...'

'I know... but why did she do that?'

'Here... I have something that might interest you.'

He handed Sam a piece of paper.

'I can't read it... It's in Latin.' She looked helplessly at Dario.

'It's her last will and testament,' declared Moretti dramatically, 'I have an Italian translation somewhere.' He rummaged around on his vast desk, moving books to one side, until he finally retrieved an old photocopy. 'Ah, here it is.' He handed it to Dario to translate.

'In the name of our Lord Jesus Christ, Eternal God,' read Dario, 'in the year from his birth 1172, 9th January. I am Berta, heiress of Calvo and daughter of Bernardo. I give and dispose of my assets in the following manner. I declare that the Uguccio family owes me fourteen and a half pounds and no more, and from this sum I donate sixty soldi for the stonework of the Santa Maria bell tower.'

'The Leaning Tower,' interrupted Moretti.

Dario continued: 'I leave this matter in the hands of Lord Archbishop Villani and Lords Guido and Benetto and Magister Marignani. I have requested Signor Ugoni, the notary of his Lordship Emperor Frederico, to draw up my will, which is hereby signed at the North gate of Pisa, near the house of the Santa Maria site where the said Berta lives. Signed by the hand of the said Berta who asked for this document to be prepared. Witnessed by the Signori Ugo Belacto, Guido Sardi, Phillippo Corso, and Gerardo, Magister of the Santa Maria site.'

Dario and Sam looked at each other.

'So, heiress of Calvo... what does that mean? Was she his ward?'

'No, no they were married,' the Professor said casually.

'Professor, I've found an image of Calvo – this man mentioned in the will – with a woman. Could it be Berta, his wife? The image is in Dario's father's bookshop... Signor Visalberghi's.'

The Professor shrugged his shoulders. 'I don't know, but I'd be happy to look at it for you.'

'But don't you think that's extraordinary? That she left this money? Might she have been more significant than just the donor of the money?'

'No!' he exclaimed. 'She was just a woman. She was a widow... she left the money. That's it.'

'But without it, the Tower would not have been built.'

'Hmm yes, that may be true. But she was just a woman, just a widow.'

'But why did she do it?' persisted Sam.

'An act of piety?' said the Professor, peering at Sam over his spectacles.

'But what about the people who witnessed her will – they sound very important... the notary of the Emporer... who was it?'

'Frederico,' said the Professor airily, sitting once again at his desk and beginning to write in one of his notebooks.

'She was obviously important... to know such important people...?' Sam persisted.

Dario nodded at Sam. 'I think it might be time for us to leave,' he said, gesturing towards the Professor who appeared utterly engrossed in a manuscript on his desk.

They rose in unison, and as Dario gathered up their notebooks and papers, Sam walked across to the Professor at his desk.

'Professor, I am so grateful to you for your time. Might I call on you again?'

He nodded benignly, without looking up, murmuring, '*Si, si...*'

'I am very keen to understand more about this lady... Berta. I feel that she must be more important than you suggest.'

Dario hesitated before translating her words, but did so nevertheless.

Moretti, looked hard at Sam, peering at her over his glasses. 'You must understand, young lady... this woman was of no importance. None at all. You must look to Deotisalvi for the answer to your mystery.'

And with that he turned once more to his desk and began to write, waving his visitors away with an absent-minded hand.

CHAPTER 17

September 1171

Aurelia awoke very early the day after Lorenzo's funeral. The body had been taken for a burial service to the Duomo. Although not yet completed, the great cathedral was nevertheless open for business. Lorenzo had been a generous donor to the church over the years, bringing back spectacular ancient monuments from his trips abroad, which had been used to decorate both the interior and exterior. Only that year, he had provided a large donation earmarked for the creation of a pair of magnificent doors celebrating the life of San Ranieri, the recently sanctified patron saint of Pisa who had died in 1160. It was intended that the celebrated architect and sculptor Bonanno Pisano would design the doors – but that was only made possible because of Lorenzo's bequest. As such, he was afforded the honour of a burial service in the Cathedral, and the Archbishop himself presided over the funeral. The great and the good of Pisa turned out for the event, which, as was the custom, was more of a celebration than a wake. Berta, magnificent in a scarlet silk gown, attended the coffin, walking through the streets of Pisa on its final journey to the Duomo, accompanied by musicians and her entire household. After the service, the body was laid to rest in a magnificent sarcophagus in the graveyard next to the cathedral. The business of the burial complete, Berta returned to the *palazzo* with one or two close friends, but retired to bed early, claiming a headache.

Violetta, who had stayed on at in the *palazzo* in order to provide both emotional and medicinal comfort to Berta, slept deeply on one side of Aurelia's narrow bed. Early the next morning, the girl rose silently, sliding out past her mother so as not to disturb her. She heard the bells of the nearby church of San Paolo toll for the morning Angelus, hoping they would not wake the household. Pulling on her dress as quietly as possible, she slipped out of the room, checking that Berta was not already awake. Her mother had provided a tisane for the headache and to help her sleep; judging by her gentle snoring, it appeared to have done its work.

She ran down the central staircase and unlocked the front door, praying with each turn of the key that she would not wake one of the servants. She set off at high speed – not running, but at a brisk walk.

When she arrived at Gerardo's house, she hung back, filled with remorse at her recklessness. With her heart racing, her stomach lurching with nausea, she paced up and down in the little lane opposite his house, checking the door every few moments and debating whether she should leave and go back to the *palazzo*. Within minutes, the old wooden door opened, and Gerardo, accompanied by his grandfather, came out. The two chatted companionably, and headed towards the Piazza.

Aurelia felt a surge of relief that she had found him, followed by the now familiar feelings of anger and despair. Unable to confront Gerardo in front of the older man, she resolved to follow them. From time to time she had to duck into a doorway when one or other stopped for some reason – to tie the leather bindings on their shoes, or to speak to a friend in the road. Once they arrived at the Piazza, the two separated. She watched the young man hug his grandfather, and for a moment, her anger and jealousy melted, as she saw the intense affection he had for the old man. As soon as Gerardo was on his own, she quickened her pace. Following hard on his heels, just as he arrived at the Baptistery, she tapped him on his shoulder.

He swung round and broke into a broad smile when he saw her.

'Little flower... how wonderful to see you,' and he leant down and kissed her on her cheek.

She pulled away from him, her eyes filling with tears.

'Don't talk to me like that. I'm not your little flower; I know that's just a lie... she is.' She spat the words out and turned to walk away from him.

'What do you mean?' he asked, grabbing her by the arm and turning her to face him.

'You know what I mean... I saw you with her... near the church... the night Lorenzo died. I saw what you did. I hate you, Gerardo, do you understand, I hate you. And I hate her too.'

With tears running down her face, she wrenched her arm away from his grasp and began to run across the Piazza.

Gerardo's workmates called to him: 'Gerardo, the *capo* wants us.'

But Gerardo ignored them, rushing across the Piazza after Aurelia, and caught up with her in a lane that ran south to the river.

'Aurelia, please you must listen to me.'

'There's nothing to listen to. You love her and not me, that's clear. You were just playing with me. Because I am young and I am her maid... you think I am stupid. But I'm not. You can't treat me like that, Gerardo. I loved you, but now I hate you; you disgust me.'

Gerardo hung his head. 'I'm sorry. I didn't mean to hurt you. I hate seeing you so upset, Aurelia. I... maybe it's best if we don't

see each other anymore. It's hard to explain. I can't expect you
to understand. I'm sorry.'

He turned and walked slowly back towards the Piazza.

Aurelia, who had gone to the Piazza filled with anger, found
herself bereft at his answer. She had expected an argument. Or
an explanation. At best, she had hoped for a declaration of love.
At worst, that he felt nothing for her. But she had received neither. He had simply walked away, provoked, she now saw, by her
own impetuous anger. Deflated and sad, she walked slowly back
to the *palazzo*.

Berta was awake when she returned.

'Aurelia, where have you been... I have been in need of you.'
Her tone was sharp. But she looked tired, exhausted, her eyes
red-rimmed. 'I woke early and you were not here. There is so
much to do, Aurelia. I am meeting with Massoud this morning.
Lay out my clothes. Bring some hot water from the kitchen; I
must bathe. Be quick, girl.'

Within an hour, Berta, suitably dressed in dark blue brocade, her hair covered with a simple linen cap, was seated with
Massoud at the big table downstairs, studying the *protocolli*, the
books recording all the transactions that had taken place in the
business over the last twenty years. Every item that had been
transported, purchased or sold, was detailed in these hefty tomes,
and Berta was determined to understand what had gone on in
her husband's business.

'Signor Goro Dati, the silk merchant... he is threatening
an action against us for non-payment. You must show me,
Massoud... where are the relevant entries? Where are his
goods? Why has he not been paid? I need to see an inven-
tory for the warehouse. Did Lorenzo have other places he
kept goods? Presumably much of what he transported was
bartered or sold abroad. It is a huge task, Massoud, but if

we are to save the business and Lorenzo's reputation I must master it.'

The notary brought out the records and talked Berta through all the figures. Her education stood her in good stead. She understood the Arabic numbering that he used, and proved a more able student than her husband had ever been. But there were times during the day when she felt close to tears: tears of grief for her lost husband, mixed with a kind of rage that he could have left her with such terrible financial problems.

As the sun sank over the Arno that evening, she closed one of the vast books and sat gazing out at the ships that sailed up and down the river.

'Massoud, it seems that Lorenzo has been a little reckless over the years. We will continue with our work tomorrow, but I have seen enough to realise that, while not a dishonest man, he has tried to make his investments go too far. There are debts and they must be paid. I need to know how much our goods are worth. I would like you to work out the value of what we have, what we are owed, and what we owe to others. Once we understand the full extent of the problem, we can make a decision about what we do next.'

Massoud bowed and left, taking the vast leather books with him.

Berta called to the kitchen for some supper. Once she had eaten, she sent for her maid.

'Aurelia, I need you to do something for me. Please go to Gerardo, I need to see him… to discuss a project,' she added after a moment.

The girl, horrified at the thought of seeing Gerardo again, begged leave of her mistress. 'Signora, I am not well. Please do not ask me to go. I have a fever, a sickness, please, *signora.*'

Irritated, Berta acquiesced. 'Very well. I will send Giuseppe. Thank goodness your mother has not yet left us. Ask her to give you something. Oh, and Aurelia, you had better go to bed. You look exhausted.'

An hour later, the driver returned. Gerardo was not with him.

'Where is he?' she asked impatiently.

'He was unable to come, he said he was ill.'

Aurelia, who had been listening at the top of the stairs, felt only a surge of relief and retreated silently to her bed.

Berta, forced to spend the evening alone, sent for a jug of wine. As it began to numb her anger and loneliness, she called for vellum, quill and ink.

Berta went to the large oak casket in the hall and brought out the roll of drawings she had borrowed from Deotisalvi some days before.   She had not had a chance to show them to Lorenzo before he died, and after her day of reckoning with Massoud, she wondered if she would ever be able to fulfill the promise she had made the *capo magister* to fund the building of the new tower. She laid the plans out on the large oak table, holding down the corners with the majolica dishes that decorated the long dresser running the length of the room.

His tower was elegant, it was true. The ground floor in particular was very pretty, consisting of sixty graceful arches, decorated with columns. But there was little of interest until the top storeys, where Deotisalvi had repeated a feature of the Baptistery by placing a concentric ring of blind arches, topped off by a bell chamber. The building was graceful, charming even. But there was nothing extraordinary about it.

Berta took a fresh sheet of vellum and began to draw the bottom storey.   Her draughtsmanship was good.   She sat for some minutes, maybe as much as an hour, quietly sipping wine, considering the building. Her mind wandered to Gerardo. She yearned to see him, and yet she knew she must be careful. It was probably better he had not come that evening.   He might even be trying to protect her reputation. She smiled as she thought of his hands travelling up her white thighs, touching the stockings, her soft flesh. She remembered his fingers pulling on the lacing at the back of her gown.

She looked again at the original plan. It was not right. It was too plain, too austere, too masculine. She began to draw another layer of arches above the first. She took great care to ensure each column was expertly drawn. They were smaller than the ground floor but, as she worked out the relative heights, tall enough for a man or woman to stand and look out over the city and its spectacular Piazza. Each column measured ten Roman feet. This tower, were it ever to be built, needed to be novel, different, to properly reflect the power of the city of Pisa. On top of the second storey, she drew another layer of arches, then another, in fact five more layers of arches were added before she judged it had the right proportions. With the bell chamber, she calculated that the tower would measure 100 *braccie*.

The candles sputtered their last, and the sky glowed violet through to pink as the sun began its journey across the sky. A cart rumbled noisily past, its wheels clattering, crashing into the quiet of the early dawn, drowning out the birds as they began their early morning ritual. She had worked at the table all night, and was looking at a revolutionary vision of a tower which soared out of the ground like a delicate woven column.

'Like a piece of Venetian lace,' she murmured as she rolled the vellum and placed it carefully in the big oak chest.

And blowing out the candles, she took herself, finally, to bed.

CHAPTER 18

June 1999

Pisa was approaching midsummer. It was June 15th and the
weather was hot. Even in the early hours of the morning,
Sam's cramped pensione bedroom was stifling. She lay on top
of the bed, her sheet thrown off some hours before, a faint layer
of perspiration on her forehead. The phone rang – an insistent
noise that woke her from a dreamless sleep. She fumbled with
the receiver.

'Good morning, darling… and how are you today?' Her
mother's chirpy voice bounced loudly from the earpiece.

Sam groaned.

'Sorry, did I wake you? I just wanted to catch you before you
went off to see Michael; I know you like to have breakfast with
him.'

'Yes,' Sam mumbled, 'but not at seven in the morning. What
are you doing up so early anyway?'

'Have you forgotten what children are like, darling? It's six
here, but we've all been up since five. I've already done breakfast,
put on the washing, emptied the dishwasher and started to make
a cake with the twins. If they weren't due to go to nursery in two
hours' time, I think I might have a nervous breakdown!'

Sam sat up in bed and took a deep breath. 'Mum, I'm sorry.
You are such a star; and you know how grateful I am to you, don't

you? I haven't the faintest idea what I'd have done without you these last few weeks. Are the children driving you mad? I know they can be hard work.' Sam tried to sound apologetic.

'They're adorable, and just as they should be,' said her mother matter-of-factly.'

'Can I speak to them?' asked Sam.

'Oh darling, I'm not sure that's a good idea… we don't want them unsettled.'

'Mum… please I miss them so much – do you have any idea what it's like?'

'Oh, all right then, I suppose it will be OK.'

She heard her mother calling to Freddie. Distant strains of Radio Three filled the silence until she became aware of a familiar, faint breathiness at the other end of the phone.

'Freddie darling…?'

'Mummy!' His voice was indignant, cross. 'Where are you? Want you here.'

'And I want to be there, darling – but I've got to stay here with Daddy for a bit longer.'

She could feel the familiar nagging pain in her heart.

'Why?' he asked logically.

'Because he's poorly, darling, and he needs me to look after him.'

'But I need you to look after *me*. I'm poorly – I've got a sore finger…'

She heard her mother snatching the phone and muttering, 'Don't be silly, Freddie, there's nothing wrong with your finger. Darling… they're all fine.'

'Really – what's wrong with his finger? Are the girls OK?'

'Darling, there's nothing wrong with it… the cat scratched him that's all. And the girls are making a cake at the moment, so it's probably better not to disturb them.'

'Oh, OK... if you think it's best,' Sam's disappointment was palpable.

'I do, darling – it just unsettles them really. Now that's not why I'm ringing. I wanted to talk to you about arrangements for getting Michael home. I've been chatting to the insurance company that you put me onto... who work with Miracle Productions, and they are going to cover all the costs of getting you back to the UK. They are also seeing if they can get you both onto a plane, possibly at the beginning of next week. But you will need to go and discuss all this with the Prof and see if it's medically possible.'

Sam was stunned. She sat for some moments, trying to take in what her mother had said. Light poured through the chink in the shabby brown curtains and, holding the phone in one hand, she stretched the cable across the room and opened the curtains. Immediately, the room was flooded with light. Dropping the phone on the bed, she stood up and pushed open the casement window; hot air enveloped her.

'Are you there?' her mother shouted.

'Yes, yes... I'm here, Mum,' she replied, before picking up the phone, as tears rolled gently down her face. Taking a deep breath, she sank back onto the bed, propping herself up on a couple of pillows.

'I'm here; I'm just a bit overwhelmed that's all.'

'Well stop being overwhelmed and get over to the hospital and get organised. There's a lot to do. Now I've got to go. I think Freddie's just emptied cake mix on his sisters' heads, and that's not going to be easy to wash out, I can assure you.'

'Oh Mum, thank you.'

Her mother hung up; Sam tried to imagine the scene in her kitchen back home. Chocolate mixture dribbling down the girls' little golden faces. Freddie laughing like a naughty little gnome, gleefully smearing cake mix onto their faces and then greedily licking his fingers.

She looked at the clock. It was ten past seven. Already hot, she decided to take a cool shower. Then, dressed in shorts and a T-shirt, she went out into the heat of the Piazza. As she crossed the square, she felt the sun's familiar burn on her neck. She stopped at the chemist on the corner and bought some sun block, which she applied to her neck, arms and legs in the shade of the shop's awning.

She made her usual stop at the coffee shop. Hot coffee seemed ridiculous in such heat, so she ordered two ice-cold *frappés* and carried them out through the hot soupy air to the hospital. Given the messages she had found on his phone the day before, it struck her that she was behaving rather well towards her husband. Had he not been so ill, would she have bought him a coffee? Would she be visiting him at all?

Michael was sleeping deeply as she entered his room, the thin white sheet thrown off during the night, his long limbs sprawled elegantly along the length of the small hospital bed. In repose, he looked quite well; just a man at rest, no hint of the illness that had brought his world to a full stop. For a moment, watching him sleeping, she almost forgot her rage at his deception, and considered lying next to him, longing now to feel his body next to hers once again: to inhale the familiar scent of his skin, the warmth of his chest against her cheek. But his angular six foot three frame dominated the entire length and width of the bed and there was no room. So, instead, she perched on the plastic hospital chair, made tacky in the heat, the backs of her thighs sticking uncomfortably to its jagged fraying edge, sipping her icy coffee and eating her brioche. Her mind was whirring with a complex mix of emotions. Looking at him now, peaceful, beautiful, she felt the familiar surge of love. A bad dose of flu had forced him to bed the year before and she had experienced the same emotion then, as she sat at his bedside one afternoon, his fever having at last broken and he lay finally, peacefully asleep.

A lot had happened since then, of course. Michael's affair had soured everything: she had no doubt about that. It was as if the jigsaw puzzle that had been her life had been thrown in the air and now several vital pieces were missing. The picture could never be put back together again. She could no longer conceive of a life in which her fulfillment was provided solely by caring for her family. The prospect of seeing her children again was, of course, exciting, thrilling almost, but her new-found sense of purpose in working on the film had complicated things. It was as if some fundamental part of her being had been anaesthetised for a long time – asleep almost – but had now woken, rested and vigorous.

And then there was Dario. He was attractive of course, there was no doubt about that. Sophisticated, charming, well read. And sensitive and attentive to her. When she first met Michael, they enjoyed long conversations – discussing work, their ambitions, their views on everything. He listened to her then, respected her opinions. Somewhere along the line, he had begun to... what? Ignore her? Surely not. Tune her out? Not exactly. But there was certainly no listening any more Was that perhaps when he had met Carrie?

Dario did listen. He was calm, attentive. His dark brown eyes full of laughter, concern, interest. Since their visit to Moretti, he had been much in her thoughts. She had even dreamt about him, her subconscious taking her to a place and a situation that on waking had made her blush as she emerged from the half sleep, feeling his hands on her body, his lips on hers.

Michael opened his eyes and smiled weakly at her. She stared back at him, resentment bubbling beneath the surface, accompanied by a little wave of nausea. His phone, a palpable reminder of his betrayal, pulsed provocatively in her pocket. She stood abruptly and wandered over to the window.

'Hi,' he said weakly. 'How's it going?'

'OK,' she said tersely.

He frowned a little.

'I found your phone, Michael.'

He said nothing.

'There were three text messages on there, and I think you can probably guess who they were from.'

He closed his eyes.

'Don't shut me out on this, Michael. We have to talk about it. You owe me that.'

He opened his eyes once more, fixing her with an anxious stare.

'Do you love her?'

He grimaced a little.

'Because she loves you… at least if her texts are to be believed. Do you want me to read them to you?'

He shook his head.

'So, what am I to make of it all then? Yesterday you told me that I was imagining things – that there was nothing to it. You almost had me believing you – do you know that? I was so nearly taken in. I really began to think that maybe I'd misjudged you. I cannot believe you could lie so spectacularly about this. After all we've been through – your stroke, the kids and all that. How could you treat me with such disrespect? And why lie now? That's what upsets me. Was it because you were hoping to keep the relationship going when you got back? Keep seeing your… bit on the side? Did you just hope to hide it from me and carry on behind my back? Is that it?'

He turned his face away.

'Don't do that!' Anger was welling up inside her.

'I'm tired of this; of you ignoring me, of ignoring this situation. I have no idea what you think I should do about this. And, quite honestly, part of me doesn't really care anymore. After the way you've treated me, Michael, I'm not actually sure I can forgive this. I think, maybe you've pushed me just too far. Here I am, away from the children, missing them desperately – oh and they're fine, by the way, just in case you were wondering. Here I am, alone and miserable and here you are getting text messages from some bimbo in London and lying, lying through your teeth about it to me.'

She walked over to the window, grabbing her coffee as she went.

'I brought you a coffee – it's on the side table, but you can bloody well drink it yourself. She gulped her own coffee down. 'Oh and your production company are talking about getting you out of here in the next week or so, which I suppose should make us both rather happy. But in fact, Michael, it just feels like an enormous problem as far as I'm concerned, since I'm the one who will have to work out the bloody logistics.

The only thing that is giving me any pleasure at all at the moment is the fact that I'm working on your film. I emailed the production company a couple of days ago and mentioned that I was carrying on with your research. They seemed delighted, once they knew what experience I have had as a reporter, and have given me the green light to proceed. So that's what I'm doing. And I'm rather enjoying it. It's about the only thing I am enjoying at the moment.'

He raised his eyebrows slightly.

'What… still don't think I'm up to it?'

He shook his head. 'No, of course not. Not that. I'm glad.' His voice was weak.

'Well that's very big of you. Look, I've got to go and speak to the doctors in charge of your case about when they might let you out of here. I'll come in and see you later.'

He forced a weak smile and raised his stronger hand out towards her.

Reluctantly, she reached over and took his hand in hers. Tears stung her eyes.

'I'm so, so sorry,' he said, 'I've been a fool, selfish. I don't know what I was thinking. It just didn't seem important. You must believe that, Sam… she wasn't… isn't important. Not like you. Not anything like you.'

She let his hand drop onto the hospital sheet.

'Well that, at least, sounds like the truth at last. The problem is how can I ever believe you about anything again?'

He looked up at her, with fear in his eyes. 'God… you must hate me.'

'I don't hate you, Michael. But you've spoiled everything… do you see?'

'I'm sorry,' he repeated again, as he blinked back the tears.

'So am I,' she replied.

Back out on the Piazza, she took out Michael's mobile phone. The messages were still there and she considered deleting them, but something stayed her hand. Instead, she took out Dario's card and dialled his number.

'*Pronto.*' His voice was reassuring.

'Dario, it's me, Sam.'

'Hey… it's good to hear your voice. How are you?'

'Not great if I'm honest, but it's OK. I wondered if we could meet today.'

'Sure. I'm spending the evening with my father… part of the holiday preparations, but I could meet you beforehand.'

'What holiday?' asked Sam.

'The Festival of San Ranieri; it's an annual two-day affair. Ranieri is the patron saint of Pisa and every year there is a wonderful celebration of his life,' Dario said enthusiastically. 'Tomorrow night the whole of the river is lit up by about seventy-five thousand candles; the next day there is a boat race, a bit like your famous Oxford and Cambridge race, but the participants wear medieval dress, and there is a parade with hundreds of people dressed up in medieval costume. It's great fun.'

'It sounds amazing.'

'It is, but it's also chaos and the whole city comes to a standstill, as I'm sure you can imagine.'

There was an awkward silence.

'Look, what are your plans for the next few days?' he asked. 'You ought to see the festival; especially the city all candlelit tomorrow… it's a fantastic sight. I've been invited to a party, hosted by an old friend of mine called Adriana. She has a lovely little apartment down on the Arno. We'll watch the whole thing from there. The lights, the firework display at midnight; it's a spectacular view. There will be a little supper, nothing too elaborate. Perhaps, if you don't think it's too forward of me, would you like to come with me?'

It didn't take Sam long to make up her mind.

'I'd love to. Thank you Dario.'

Plans finalised for the following evening, they arranged to meet that afternoon to discuss the film.

Dario arrived, slightly breathless, at the café on the corner of the Piazza.

'Hi, it's so good to see you. Look, I've got something rather exciting to tell you.'

'Well, sit down and get a coffee and calm down,' Sam said brightly.

'I've just been to see my father to make arrangements for this evening; you remember I told you he and I are having supper together?'

Sam nodded.

'Well, he has just been sent a large package filled with documents from the big house you went to visit the other day.'

'The one owned by the Manoccis?'

Yes,' he said, 'it seems that some builders had been employed to do some work to get the house into a more saleable condition, fixing dry rot and so on. They were removing some damaged panelling in the East Tower and they came across some very old documents. They gave them to the agent of course, who then told the owners, who are based in Switzerland. They asked for them to be sent round to my father for him to look at. He says there are some extraordinary things there... I thought you might like to see them.'

They drained their coffee cups and rushed over to the bookshop.

It was approaching one o'clock, and once they had arrived, the old man turned the shop sign to closed and pulled down the dark blinds.

He took them to the back of the shop and began to lay out the items: various letters, and several sheets in Arabic script, of what appeared, at first glance, to be accounts.

'But this is the most remarkable thing though.'

Dario moved the smaller items to one side as his father delicately unrolled a large piece of vellum, on which was a detailed drawing of the Tower of Pisa.

'The tower,' Sam said with surprise. 'What was that doing there? It's so beautiful. Is it very old?'

'My father says it will have to be sent to the university for accurate carbon-dating – he doesn't have the right equipment here – but judging by the paper, he believes it dates from the middle of the twelfth century... when the tower was first started.'

'OK, so what are we saying here?' asked Sam. 'That this item, this image of the tower, has been in the Manoccis house for...

what… hundreds of years? Hidden away behind some panelling. Why would it be there?'

'Well, the obvious conclusion is that someone hid it there. The items were kept in a kind of secret strongbox, set into the panelling. It was only when the builders started pulling it to pieces that it was discovered.'

'So the Manoccis had no idea it was there?'

'No, apparently not. They've owned the house for seventy or eighty years, but didn't know of its existence until the builders found it.'

'May I take a closer look?'

'Of course,' Dario said.

'There are some initials at the bottom; can you see that?' Sam leant intently over the picture.

Signor Visalberghi handed them a strong magnifying glass.

'What does that say?' asked Sam. 'BP? Bonanno Pisano maybe?'

'Maybe,' said Dario, 'or is it BB?'

'BB… you mean Berta… what was her other name? Calvo. So, that would be BC – Berta Calvo.'

'No,' said Dario, 'wives took their fathers' names in that time; he was Bernardo; do you remember the will? Heiress of Calvo, and daughter of Bernardo. She would have been BB.'

The two looked at each other in amazement.

'Well, what does that tell us?' said Sam eventually.

'I'm not sure,' said Dario. 'That she put her name to a drawing of the tower. That the drawing was found in that house, and maybe… that was her house. I'm not sure we can deduce much more than that from it… do you? It's not possible to verify anything really.'

'Do you think Moretti could help us?' asked Sam.

'Maybe,' said Dario.

'Could you set up a meeting?'

'Sure,' agreed Dario.

They said their goodbyes to Signor Visalberghi. Sam was touched by the warmth with which Dario embraced his father.

'Ciao babbo – a domani'.

The old man hugged his son closely before waving them off and retreating into his shop, closing the door behind him.

'Something has been bothering me,' said Sam, as they wandered back towards the Piazza, '… about the possibility of Berta living in that house on the Arno.'

'Go on,' said Dario.

'The will… you remember. It said something like: *In the house of the Opera Sancta Maria where the said Berta lives.* Well that's not the house on the Arno, is it?'

'No… no it's not.'

'So did she ever live in that house on the Arno, or did she move perhaps? And if she did… how can we prove it?'

'We could check to see if the *operaio*'s office has records of her living there…' said Dario.

'Could we?' said Sam excitedly. 'Would they keep records that far back?'

'To be honest, I don't know… but we can ask. I'll make a couple of calls and see what I can arrange. But I doubt anyone will be around till after the holiday, if I'm honest. The whole town stops work over the next couple of days.'

'Oh!' said Sam, a little disappointed.

'Don't worry; as soon as the holiday is over we'll get on with it. And in the meantime, maybe you need to try to relax and enjoy the festivities…' said Dario with a smile.

The following day, June 16th, was another blisteringly hot day. Sam woke early, bathed in sweat. Her window had been shut by the maid and Sam had forgotten to open it before she went to bed. She threw back the sheets, simultaneously ripping off the old T-shirt of Michael's she had taken to sleeping in. She had bought it for him on their honeymoon in France. It was striped blue and white and, in truth, was really too small for him now. The business lunches and foreign travel had begun to take their toll on his waistline. She had been touched that he continued to pack it whenever he travelled abroad - like a talisman, or a way of keeping her close to him, or so she had thought. She took some heart that he had brought it on this trip. And now... it was just a small piece of him that represented what had been good between them and she was unable to part with it.

She yanked open the curtains and pushed up the window. A cool breeze blew in off the Campo. She stood for a few seconds, enjoying the sensation, before she remembered that she was naked and visible to anyone on or near the Piazza. Quickly, she grabbed a curtain and pulled it around her body.

The hawkers and traders who ran three stalls just below the pensione were just setting up for the day – the man selling imitation designer handbags, the Egyptian guy selling an unlikely combination of tea towels and umbrellas, and the old man who struck up a conversation with every passer-by, whose stall was littered with the ubiquitous models of the Tower. All three looked up at Sam's window and waved to her. Embarrassed, and clutching her curtain tightly to her, she waved back at them before retreating out of sight.

Sam lay back on her bed, luxuriating in the cool breeze blowing across her naked body, and thought about her discovery of the previous day. It seemed almost too extraordinary to take in.

That she and Dario had uncovered something quite new in the story of the Tower. When they were first together, both working, before the children came along... before Carrie... the first person she would have shared something so exciting with would have been Michael. In the old days, they would have pored over all the details together, examining the facts. But how could she tell him about it now – after all that had happened between them the day before? It seemed pointless. Would he have even cared?

Following their meeting with Signor Visalberghi, Dario had rung Professor Moretti to arrange to show him the find, but he had gone off to his villa in the mountains for the duration of the holiday. He would not be back until after the weekend, so things would just have to wait. But Sam was excited. She was onto something. Her journalist instincts were acute and she could 'feel' it.

She looked at the clock on the bedside table. It was ten o'clock. She had a curious rush of guilt that she had slept so long and Michael had not yet had his breakfast. 'Although why I should care whether he has bloody breakfast or not, I really don't know', she muttered to herself as she brushed her teeth. She showered and dressed quickly and walked through the large crowds of holiday-makers already gathered on the Campo. Preparations were in hand for the celebrations later that day and she could see officials setting out candles on the ledges of the Tower's galleries. She had a sudden frisson of excitement that she would be spending the evening with Dario. As she bought her two coffees and brioche, she tried to analyse her feelings. She didn't need to look too deeply. She knew what was happening: she liked him, he liked her. There was a mutual respect. And... he was very attractive.

Michael was awake when she arrived.

'Thank God you're here. I'm hot... couldn't sleep.'

His room was like a furnace. Not for the first time, Sam struggled to force open the metal casement window. It would not budge. Sweat began to trickle uncomfortably down her back. Finally, it gave way, and the room flooded with cool air.

'So...' she said at last. 'I imagine you had a bad night – with it being so hot.' Their conversation of the previous day lay like an unnavigable chasm between them.

'Yeah,' he said desultorily. 'Sam, I'm so sorry,' he mumbled at last.

'I know – you said... yesterday.'

'But I am, really.'

'OK,' she said, uncertain how to respond.

'Please talk to me, Sam...'

'It's just so difficult, Michael. I know we need to talk, but I don't want to say anything that I'll regret later. I think we both have a lot of thinking to do. And maybe we need to just be a bit kind to each other today... you know?'

He slumped acquiescently back into the bed.

The rest of the day dragged by. Many of the staff had taken a couple of days' holiday, so there was no physiotherapy to break up the monotony of Michael's day. Sam did some of his exercises with him, but her heart was not in it and early in the afternoon, when Michael finally fell into a deep sleep, she left the hospital and went onto the Campo.

She had intended to go back to her pensione but found herself walking instead towards the Arno. Her route took her past Signor Visalberghi's shop and she stopped outside, gazing at the books in the window, thinking about the pile of documents he had discovered. She realised that she and Dario had not studied the letters or accounts that had been found with the drawing of the Tower. Frustratingly, there was a blind pulled down over the glass door and the sign clearly read 'chiuso' – closed. Just as she was about to leave, irritated with herself for not retrieving the documents the day before, the door juddered open and Signor Visalberghi emerged, blinking, into the bright light.

'Ah, *signora*,' he smiled and held out his hand in greeting.

'Signor Visalberghi... how lovely.'

Somehow, with a few words of Italian and lots of sign language, Sam explained that she would love to be given access to the package of letters they had seen the day before. He took her inside and retrieved the documents from his safe. Once again, she asked, in her faltering Italian, whether it would be possible to obtain photocopies of the originals in order to get them translated.

'*Sì, sì*,' he said obligingly. The photocopier blinked into action.

After much '*grazie*,' '*prego*,' nodding and smiling, she left the shop clutching the papers, and retraced her steps to Michael's room, stopping at the little ice cream stall in Via Santa Maria.

It was four o'clock, and the sun was reaching its trajectory across the sky, creating lengthening shadows across the square.

Michael was awake when she returned. She fed him a few spoonfuls of lemon sorbet – his favourite.

'I thought I would pop out and get you something to eat this evening. I know how you hate the food here.'

'OK,' he replied. 'Will you eat with me?'

It was the first time he had asked this of her since she had arrived.

'You think that's a good idea?'

'Yes... Sam I meant it – about being sorry.'

'So we have a quick supper and it's all forgiven, is that it?'

He began to protest.

'Well, I can't, as it happens.'

'Why, got a better offer?' he said, smiling at his own joke.

'Yes,' she replied starkly.

'Oh!' he looked a little surprised.

'Yes, someone who's helping me with my research. He's a journalist here in Italy. He's invited me to see the celebrations this evening.'

'What celebrations, what journalist?'

'It's the Feast of San Ranieri today, the patron saint of Pisa; and there will be fireworks, candles all over the town and so on. It sounds rather magical and I thought I'd like to see it.'

Michael turned his face towards the open window and slumped down into his bed, his voice muffled by the sheet.

'Who is he? This journalist? How do you know him?'

'He's someone I met here... at the airport actually. He's a journalist for *La Stampa*. He's visiting his father who owns the shop where you bought that amazing book... Signor Visalberghi. It was just a coincidence that we met, but he's been so helpful. He's in Pisa for a couple of weeks' holiday, so he's at a loose end at the moment. Really, I'm so lucky that's he's been available to help. He can translate when I meet Moretti, his father is obviously rather useful, so it's all a bit of luck. And he's being rather supportive. It's been good to have someone to talk to while I'm here.'

Michael turned over in bed and looked at his wife. 'I bet he has. Supportive, hmph.'

'Well, Michael... you should know.' Her voice, she was aware, was a little harsh.

Michael looked at her. 'So you're getting your own back; is that it?'

He blushed a little as she snapped back: 'No, Michael, that's not it. I've not slept with him, if that's what you're asking. Which I'd like to point out puts me in a slightly more elevated moral position to your good self. I'm sorry that I won't be around to have supper with you, but I want to see the celebrations and that's that. I don't think you really can have any objection, do you?'

'No, of course not, I'm sorry.'

It gave her no pleasure to see her husband so deflated. 'Michael, there's nothing going on here. I just need a night off, that's all. Do you understand?'

'Yes,' he said, 'you go. Have fun. You deserve it.'

Sam left Michael's hospital room racked with a complex combination of emotions. A sense of self-righteous anger pervaded all that she did since his admission of the affair, but there was an undercurrent of pity for her husband, tinged, if she was honest, with just a small portion of guilt that she was about to go out to a party with a man she hardly knew, leaving her husband unwell in a hospital room.

In the old part of the town she found a charming little health food shop and bought a picnic supper of quiche and tomato salad – something she knew Michael adored. When she returned to the hospital she sat on the edge of his bed and fed him mouthfuls of supper. When he had finished eating, the two sat in silence for some moments. Michael stared sullenly at the wall. Anxious that they should part on good terms that evening, she tried to make conversation:

'The children are well...'

'Are they? Good.'

'Freddie got ten out of ten for a spelling test, Mum told me. Can you believe that?'

'Did he? Good lad.'

'Mmm... and the girls went to a party – fancy dress I think. Poor Mum had to make them a costume each. She is a star'.

'Sam!' Michael interjected. 'I am interested in the kids, of course, but is this what we ought to be discussing?'

'Maybe not, but I can't think what else to talk about. Everything else seems to be so upsetting… I'm making good progress with the film.'

'Oh,' he said. His lack of interest was palpable.

'Or is that something else you'd rather not discuss?'

'No… no', he said more magnanimously, 'Go on'.

'We've found a new piece of evidence. It's rather remarkable actually and I'm going to show it to Professor Moretti next week hopefully.'

Michael continued to stare miserably out of the window.

'I've found some interesting letters – I've got them with me, as it happens… I wondered if you'd like to take a look at them.'

He remained resolutely silent.

'I'd really appreciate your thoughts, Michael', she cajoled, 'your judgement… you know?'

He turned, at last, to face her.

'My judgement!' he almost laughed. 'I think I've demonstrated a woeful lack of that recently – don't you?'

'Well, that's honest at least. But it doesn't mean you've suddenly become a terrible journalist. Please, Michael – just take a look at them. Here they are… some builders found them whilst doing some work on a very old house on the Arno – we think Lorenzo Calvo and Berta may have lived there…'

She laid the photocopies down on the bed.

Michael listlessly picked one of them up.

'They're in Italian – but an old dialect,' he said desultorily. 'Can't see what this has to do with the tower anyway.'

'Well, neither can I just at the moment, but… I wondered if you might be able to translate them for me.'

He stared at her: 'Me?'

'Well you speak good Italian… I just thought.'

He picked one up and screwed his eyes up with the effort of concentrating.

'Difficult, it says something about the *Operaio*... thanking him, I think. I don't know...' he muttered impassively, 'I can't make it out.'

'Michael, aren't you interested in anything that I'm doing?' Sam asked exasperatedly.

'Not really, no,' he said harshly. 'The film... all that... means nothing to me now.'

'And me? Do I mean anything?'

'Yes, of course. You're my wife. Don't be silly.'

'Silly... I'm silly.' She rose from the bed.

'Sam, I didn't mean...'

'What! What didn't you mean? Michael, I think you need to do some serious thinking. I don't know what you want from me any more. I have been faithful and loyal to you for years and look where it's got me. You have a girlfriend, you have no respect for me, you think I'm just... what... the mother of your children and that's it?'

'She's not a girlfriend,' he replied.

'Oh really? Tell *her* that.' And she threw his phone down onto the bed. 'Here, ring her. Or shall I?'

She picked up the phone and flicked through the text messages until she found the ones from Carrie. She dialled the number. It rang.

Michael made a clumsy lunge for the phone, but Sam evaded his hand easily.

'Michael? Thank God.' Carrie's voice was higher, lighter than Sam had expected.

'Michael... is that you? Are you OK? I've been so worried, darling.'

'No,' interjected Sam curtly, 'this is not Michael. This is his wife, Sam. I've got Michael for you…'

And she chucked the phone at her husband before turning on her heel and leaving the room.

But halfway down the corridor she stopped. She walked quickly back to the door of his room and stood silently, breathing heavily, trying to hear what Michael was saying.

'No,' he said.

'I'm OK.'

'I can't talk now, Carrie.'

'Maybe… I'm not sure.'

'Carrie – please. I just don't know.'

Sam's mind was a whirr of conflicting emotions and questions: What didn't he know? Maybe… what?

She regretted giving him the phone; it was a childish thing to do. He'd had a stroke. She was supposed to keep him calm. She stood for a few moments, uncertain whether she should go back into his room and apologise. Then, of course, he would know that she had been listening. And after what he had just said, or not said, why should she say sorry? It was he who should apologise to her. He was the one at fault here, not her. Conflicted and confused, she wandered slowly down the corridor and out of the hospital. In the courtyard, she turned on her heel intending, once again, to go back and apologise. But she stopped at the door to the hospital, resolving… finally… to let it lie. He'd be asleep soon, she told herself. And they could talk about it the following day.

CHAPTER 19

October 1171

Resolving Lorenzo's complex financial affairs was a lengthy business. Day after day, Berta sat with the notary, poring over ledgers containing details of goods in and out, monies paid and owed. A large loan had been acquired from the Uguccio family. Benedete Uguccio owned an alum mine in Phoenicia and had a monopoly on importing this vital dye into Italy, where he processed and exported it to the cloth industry. He had become fabulously wealthy and, like Lorenzo, was one of the few merchants at that time to possess his own fleet of galleys. But he carried no debt and owned his fleet outright. Lorenzo, having overextended himself with his latest addition to his fleet, had been forced to seek a loan from his rival. Had Lorenzo lived, Uguccio would have been content to wait for his money, but with his death, he was anxious to clear the loan.

Massoud was dispatched to ask for more time to pay the debt. But Uguccio had refused and insisted on a meeting with Berta herself.

And so, ten days after the death of her husband, Berta, dressed elegantly in dark green brocade, sat across the table from Benedete Uguccio.

'I need to understand, *signora*, how you are to clear this debt of your husband's. It is a considerable sum that he owes me.'

'I am sure you will appreciate,' the widow said, 'that there are many dealings, none as significant as yours I hasten to add, that require my attention. I am working very hard to understand what has gone on in my husband's business and am committed to clearing any outstanding debts as soon as at all possible.'

'I am glad to hear it, *signora*. There is one easy way in which the debt can be discharged. If you were to cede the galley to me, I would walk away.'

'I can see, from your point of view, that that would be a simple and expedient way, to resolve the matter. But I see from our records that Lorenzo had already paid off part of the loan to you… so, even with compound interest that is due, the value of the galley would far exceed the monies owed.'

Realising the widow was no fool, Benedete smiled and nodded.

'I have another proposition for you, *signore*,' Berta continued. 'I am in need of an amount of money for a personal project. Sixty florins to be precise. I will sign the ship over to you in return for such a sum. If there is any imbalance, I would happily include part of our latest cargo of pepper, brought back only a month ago by Lorenzo from his last trip. It is the freshest cargo in Pisa, I understand, and would fetch a good price. Massoud can help to work out how much would be needed to make up the debt.'

'Why would you sell the galley now?' the merchant enquired.

'Because my husband is dead. And I am no longer sure I will be able to manage the business as he chose to do, extending the fleet, making more and more journeys in search of imports and exports. I have my own interests, and they do not extend to the sea, at least not at this stage. But I want it understood that this is not a loan. The galley and the cargo of pepper will discharge the debt. Do we have an agreement?'

The merchant did not keep her waiting long. 'You drive a hard bargain, *signora*, but we do. I will send my notary to deal with yours, and the monies shall be paid over directly, as soon as the papers are signed.'

'Thank you, *signore*, I will leave Massoud to make the arrangements.'

Berta rose and went upstairs to her chamber. Aurelia was busying herself tidying the room, folding clothes, placing her mistress's gowns back in the oak chests.

'Aurelia, I would like you to lay out the grey silk gown for me.'

'*Signora*, the grey? You mean the one you gave to me.'

'I mean the grey silk that I *lent* to you, yes, Aurelia. Please fetch it.'

The girl went to her own room and took the dress from behind the door, where it had hung since she last wore it.

'Help me to change, please.'

'But *signora*, I thought you said the colour did not suit you?.'

'Well, I have changed my mind. Now help me please.'

The girl unlaced the gown and laid it on the bed before helping her mistress step into the grey silk.

Seated at her dressing table, Berta considered her maid. There was something in her manner that had changed. She was older, of course... more mature. But there was something else, a slight defiance, which surprised her.

Looking at her reflection in the glass, Berta thought back to the evening Gerardo had come to the *palazzo*. Aurelia, dressed in the grey silk, her pale skin flushed as she entered the dining hall with the young man. What was it that he had said that evening? Aurelia had persuaded him to come. She had dismissed it that night as an idle remark, but now she wondered if it had more significance.

'I think the colour suits me well, don't you, Aurelia?'

'Yes, *signora.*'

'I had thought to give you the dress, but on reflection, I think I will keep it for myself. There are days when pale grey like this is the perfect colour. It suits my mood: neither dark, not colourful, but quiet, sombre, elegant. Don't you agree?'

'I do, *signora*... it is very pleasing.' Aurelia's tone was muted.

'I think, on reflection, it is a little too elegant for you. We will find another... something to match your eyes perhaps? Made of linen, or wool, I think, not silk. It is a little too refined for someone in your position.'

Aurelia attempted a smile, but the spite of this last remark had stung. She was just a maid, but somehow, until this day, Berta had always contrived to make her feel just a little more important than a mere servant. It was an unusually cruel observation.

'Please dress my hair, Aurelia. Something simple away from my neck. Then cover it with a cap, just that plain linen one.'

The girl brushed, twisted and coiled the beautiful red hair, fighting the inclination to pull it just a little too hard, while Berta stroked lavender water on her neck. She watched the girl as she worked, noting the pursed lips pinched together. She was a pretty girl, but not a beauty. It seemed impossible that Gerardo might prefer her – young and sweet though she was. She touched her fingers in the pot of cochineal on her table, dabbing them onto her lips to give them a little colour. Pinching her cheeks to drive away the pallor of the last few days, she stood at last and sent for three members of her household to accompany her to the Piazza.

Leaving her retinue on the edge of the square, she walked around the buildings studying the progress of the work. Although funding was short, a smaller core workforce remained, finishing off certain jobs at both the Baptistery and the Duomo. Gerardo, she knew, was amongst them.

Several storeys up, Gerardo saw a figure in a familiar grey dress. His heart missed a beat. He swung down from the scaffolding and made his excuses to the *lapicida*. Once on the ground, he ran his hands through his hair and wiped the dust off his face with the edge of his shirt. He followed the dress round the Piazza, before finally coming up behind her; inhaling the scent of lavender, he tapped her shoulder.

'So you came back, my little flower.'

Berta swung round and Gerardo, confused, gasped before saying quickly, '*Cara*, I am glad to see you.'

'And I you; but you seem surprised.'

'No, no,' he said hurriedly, hiding his disappointment that it was not Aurelia standing before him.   'It was just that I did not think to see you for a while longer. I heard about Lorenzo; I am so sorry. I did not send word, it did not seem right. Are you all right?'

'Yes,' she smiled at him, 'I am well. It was a shock, you know, and there is so much to arrange; but I will survive. He was a good man, and I cared for him but... well you know... things were not what they were. The business is in such a mess and I have been very busy trying to unravel it all.' And then, touching his arm, she said, 'I have missed you... so much.'

He smiled and she took his arm. They walked to the edge of the Piazza.

'What did you mean? I came back.'

'Nothing, only that... well it's been some time since we last met. I merely meant that it I was glad to see you.'

Berta studied his face, intently. 'My little flower... is that how you think of me?'

'No, yes. Well... of course. Except that you are so much more than that; you are a field of flowers, all sweetly scented, waving in the wind; like a field of poppies, with your beautiful red hair.'

And at this he stroked her cheek, leaning in to kiss her.

She ducked and pulled him by the hand down a quiet side street.

'Pretty words, Gerardo. But listen to me, I have things I need to discuss with you. We need to find somewhere where we can meet. I cannot invite you to the house yet, it would not be seemly. In time, perhaps, but not yet, and I would so like to see you, Gerardo.'

She slipped her hand inside his open linen shirt and stroked his chest. 'I have been thinking of you so much.'

'And I you.' With Berta standing before him, regal, beautiful, enticing, all thoughts of little Aurelia disappeared from his mind.

'I will take a small house… on this side of the river and we can meet there. I will send word with the address as soon as it is arranged. I could send Aurelia with it. Would you like that?'

Gerardo flushed. Desperate to conceal his feelings for Aurelia from Berta, his thoughts were now filled with the vision of Aurelia's tear-stained face when they had last met: 'I hate you, Gerardo, do you understand,' she had said 'I hate you. And I hate her too.'

'I see that you would. Is she your little flower, Gerardo?'

'*Cara*, Berta… no. She is nothing to me… just a child. It is you that I want.'

'Good, I am glad to hear it.' Her tone was crisp, businesslike suddenly.

'And Gerardo, do not forget the work at the Tower of San Nicola. Deotisalvi will be starting that project soon, and your place and that of your grandfather is secure. I have made sure of that. Your talent will soon be recognized, *caro*, believe me.'

She pulled him towards her and, in the lengthening shadow of the building, she kissed him, secure in the knowledge that whatever his feelings for Aurelia, he would at last be hers.

The house that Berta final chose was on a very quiet street in the north-east of the city, near the church of San Francesco. It belonged to old friends who agreed to lend her the property in return for past favours.

'I need to get away – the *palazzo* is so full of memories of Lorenzo. Just for a few weeks,' she assured them, 'possibly less.'

When she first visited the house, she had been struck by the quality of the light that poured into the upper rooms. She was also thrilled by how isolated it was, sitting, as it did, away from other houses, and within a large garden of its own.

The property had been uninhabited for some time, and she instructed Massoud to arrange for some simple furnishings to be installed.

'I shall need a table and some chairs, and a couple of tapestries; please bring some from the big house. And a bed of course, in case I need to rest, or even stay the night from time to time. I need the house as a refuge, Massoud,' she added, 'somewhere I can go to work on my designs and think. This house is filled with too many memories of Lorenzo and our time together.'

Massoud made the arrangements and, within a week, Berta sent word to Gerardo to meet her there. She despatched Giuseppe, who fortunately could not read, with a note for her lover, rather than entrusting the information to Aurelia. She understood now that her maid and her lover shared an attraction. Perhaps Aurelia even believed herself in love with Gerardo, and the location of her love nest, for the moment, must remain secret.

He was to meet her after dark, to avoid attracting too much attention. And Berta, who had never been required to cater or manage her own household, threw herself into the arrangements.

Informing staff at the *palazzo* that she would be going away for a day or two, she packed a small bag with one change of clothing, and a few household items such as dishes and cups. Her belongings were piled onto the small handcart and Berta, accompanied by Giuseppe and Massoud, walked in bright sunshine to the house. With her belongings deposited and farewells said to Massoud, Berta went into the town to purchase food and wine, arranging for it to be delivered later that day. She explored the large garden and was delighted to find that vegetables had been grown by a previous occupant. There were herbs of all kinds, with sorrel and wild garlic growing on the edges of the garden. She picked a large basket of leaves and set about preparing a dish of greens for their supper. As soon as the food arrived, she lit the fire in the kitchen and prepared a stew of fresh rabbit with herbs and wine. It was a dish that she remembered eating as a child, and while no expert cook, she understood what was needed to make a good dish.

Massoud had arranged for the house to be expertly cleaned, and sheets had been delivered along with the furnishings, but the bed itself was not made up. Berta had never performed this task before, but soon mastered the art, and stood back triumphantly, once the job was done. She draped a tapestry that she had brought from the *palazzo* over the top and lay down on the bed, delighted to find it was comfortable. From there, she had a wonderful view of the Piazza in the distance and she could clearly see the Duomo and behind it the Baptistery. When her preparations were complete, she collected water in a bowl from the well in the garden and took it upstairs and washed. The clear water was cold, fresh and reviving. She had brought few clothes with her – just a pale lilac silk gown – and this she changed into, adding a pearl necklace and earrings, leaving her hair down around her shoulders.

Pouring wine into a majolica cup, she waited for Gerardo to arrive.

Aurelia had spent the day in a state of panic. Berta had not taken her into her confidence, but she had observed the hushed conversations with Massoud. She heard her mistress rise early that morning. Normally, Berta would have called for her the moment she awoke, but that morning no call came. Eventually, Aurelia crept out of bed and opened the door into her mistress's chamber. She saw Berta's lilac dress laid out on the bed and heard her humming softly to herself. Silently, she watched as Berta took a small leather bag from the chest in her room, folded the dress carefully and put it inside. She saw Berta leave the room and go downstairs, soon returning, clutching two cups and two plates, which she wrapped carefully in fabric before placing them, too, into the bag on her bed. Aurelia observed her removing her comb and some jewellery – a simple string of pearls and two pairs of earrings – from her dressing box and slipping them deftly into the little pouch she wore at her waist.

'Massoud,' shouted Berta, as she quickly left the room.

It was unusual for Berta not to call on Aurelia before she left home. In fact Aurelia could not recall any day when she had not been asked to find a dress, or a piece of jewellery, or arrange her mistress's hair. Clearly, whatever Berta intended to do that day was to be a secret. She could think of no subject her mistress had ever kept from her. She had shared her rage about her husband's financial difficulties, had expressed grief on his death, and had gossiped about friends, servants and relations. Through her mother, she was even aware of Berta's sadness about her lack of children. There was only one topic she and Berta had never discussed…Gerardo. Aurelia began to think back over their recent exchanges. The day she had taken back the grey dress. Why had she done that? Was it simply to hurt Aurelia? That had been her initial understanding. A way of putting Aurelia back into her place. Had she become too bold perhaps? Expecting a beautiful silk dress as a gift. She was after all just a servant in this household. And yet... Berta had shown her great kindness in the months since she had lived in her house and it seemed out of character of her to take the dress away. Was it perhaps because she was jealous of her young maid... that the dress gave her a beauty and a sophistication which the older woman did not like? Was it because she understood that Gerardo might, in some way, care for Aurelia...?

Desperate now for some sort of clarification, Aurelia went downstairs to the kitchen, and saw Maria. 'Where is *la signora* going?' she asked her.

'She has had to leave for a few days; she has urgent business elsewhere,' replied the housekeeper. 'Now get on with your duties, Aurelia. You should take the opportunity to clean her room and make it tidy for her return.'

Back in Berta's room, Aurelia searched for clues for where Berta might have gone. She was certain that she had left to be with Gerardo, and while she knew in her heart that there was nothing she could do to prevent it, the jealousy and pain were so acute that she was unable to think of anything else.

Before lunch, she went down to the stables to look for the carriage driver.

'Giuseppe, how are you?' she asked sweetly. 'I have brought you some cider from the kitchen.'

Giuseppe, who was unused to such kindness, took the jug and drank it down in one draught. It was a hot morning and he had been cleaning the horses' hooves.

'Thank you, Aurelia; and what brings you to me this lovely day?'

'Oh nothing really, but with the mistress away I have some time on my hands. Where did she go, by the way?' she asked innocently.

'Oh, the top of the town. Massoud says she's taken a house there.'

'Oh, I see. When you say the top of the town, what do you mean? Near the Duomo?'

'What's it to you, little miss nosy,' Giuseppe said with a smile.

'Oh, I just wondered, in case she needed me to take her anything, it would be useful to know where she was.'

'If she'd wanted you to know, she'd have told you, wouldn't she? Now be off. I've got work to do. Thanks for the cider.'

Aurelia went dispiritedly back to Berta's room. But as the afternoon wore on, she was unable to contain her curiosity. She would go to Gerardo's house. If Berta was intending to meet him, he would be sure to go home first. As the bells of San Sepolcro tolled for the evening Angelus, she crept down the *palazzo*'s grand staircase and opened the front door as quietly as possible. She ran as fast as she could to Gerardo's house. It took her only a short time and she was out of breath as she positioned herself in the little lane opposite his doorway. The house was made of verrucano – the local stone. A traditional tower house, the lintel over the wooden front door provided a clue as to the occupations of its residents, for old Gerardo had carved, in intricate detail, a galley in full sail and, beside it, a mason swinging his axe down onto a piece of stone. She did not have to wait long before the object of her desire returned from work, sauntering down the lane with his grandfather. The two chatted amicably and Aurelia felt a kind of helpless fury at the young man's cheeriness, while she felt nothing but misery and distress.

As they entered their house, Aurelia kept out of sight, certain that young Gerardo would soon emerge and she would be able to follow him. She was unsure what she might achieve by doing so, but was powerless to leave. However, the long wait began to exhaust her. As the sun dipped down over the roofs and the moon began its rise, tears were falling down her pale cheeks. Still there was no sign of Gerardo. Her legs aching, she slumped down onto the ground, hoping the earth would not mark her dress. She was hungry and beginning to regret coming. At the other end of the lane, she had noticed a stall that sold tempting little onion and vegetable tarts. She could smell the onions being cooked; her mouth watered, and her stomach began to rumble. She felt in her pocket; she had a couple of coins that Berta had given her for an errand the previous day – just enough to buy something to eat. But still she stood watch, waiting and hoping that Gerardo would emerge.

Finally, unable to bear the hunger any more, she ran up the lane to where the merchant had laid out his stall.

'An onion tart please, and please be quick, I am in a hurry.'

'All right! I'm being as quick as I can,' he replied, handing over the tart. It was hot and buttery and it burned her hands as she ran back to her post on the corner of the lane. She devoured the tart in moments, relishing the sweetness of the onions and the sour-tasting cheese on top.

Darkness came and the city began to glow with candlelight. Aurelia, realising her vigil had been pointless, struggled to her feet ready to leave. Perhaps, she thought hopefully, Berta and Gerardo were not intending to meet after all. But as she stood in the middle of the road outside his house, brushing the crumbs off her dress, the door opened and he emerged – so handsome and freshly washed, she thought. She, by contrast, was ashen and tired. Her mouth and chin covered with crumbs and grease from the tart. Her dress was dusty and dirty and her eyes were red from crying.

She turned to run away as soon as she saw him, but he caught her by the arm and pulled her towards him.

'Little flower, what are you doing here? I am so happy to see you.'

'Are you, Gerardo… really?' she gazed hopefully into his eyes.

'Of course; I thought perhaps you did not want to see me anymore,' and he kissed her softly on the cheek. The kiss was affectionate, but chaste – as a brother might kiss a sister. He knew that Aurelia loved him, and he cared for her too, but his entanglement with Berta meant that he must now conceal his true feelings from Aurelia.

She, encouraged by the kiss, kissed him back and their lips met. His touch was soft and gentle. He held her very tightly and, when he had stopped kissing her, buried his face in her hair and kissed her ears, her cheek.

'Oh Gerardo, I have missed you so.'

'And I you, little one.'

'I have been so upset, about you and her. Oh Gerardo, please tell me that you don't love her?'

'Aurelia, please don't ask me about her. It is difficult. I cannot explain to you.'

'Yes,' she shouted, 'you can… you can explain. You either love her or me. It is simple.'

'Aurelia, you will understand one day, but, please, now you must trust me. I do care for you, very much. But I care for her too. She has been kind to me and she wants to help me… to become a *lapicida*. Can't you see how important that is for me? I am just a mason, Aurelia, but she is offering me the chance to be someone; to make my mother proud of me.'

'And would your mother be proud of how you are doing it— by giving yourself to her? Can't you see that she is using you, Gerardo?'

Stung by this last remark, Gerardo sought to calm the situation: 'Aurelia, you must go now, back home. You should not be out so late at night on your own. I will take you. Come, let us go together.'

'Aren't you supposed to be seeing her? You don't want to upset her do you?' Aurelia snapped.

Gerardo said nothing, but pulled her towards him. Together they walked towards the river, and Aurelia slowly relaxed into his body, relishing the warmth of his arms around her.

When they got to the *palazzo*, he suddenly pulled her into a side street and firmly but tenderly kissed her, exploring her mouth with his own, stroking her cheek, her hair.

'I care for you very much, Aurelia. Please know that. I can imagine that one day we might be together. But it cannot be now. I wanted to tell you before, to explain things. But it is so hard. Please try to trust me. Will you do that?'

Aurelia, overwhelmed by his passion and her own love for him, could only smile mutely and nod as she walked unsteadily back into the *palazzo*. Inside, she was angrily confronted by Maria, the housekeeper, who shouted at her for being late, and took the birch to her hand. But Aurelia felt no pain, only love.

When Berta woke early the next morning, Gerardo was already up. The sun lay low in the morning sky, winking through the small panes of glass in her window of her *cassetta*.

'Gerardo, you're leaving so early? It's not even light yet. Please don't go, *caro*, please stay with me?'

She lay across the bed, stroking his back, as he sat on the edge pulling his shirt over his head.

'I must go; I'm sorry. I'll be late and I don't want to get a reputation for being unreliable. And I need to collect *nonno*…

he's getting on. He doesn't like to admit it, but he needs me to help him carry his tools to the site.'

'Well I'm sure that's very laudable, and I'm sure I'm very impressed by your sense of duty, but what about your duty to me?' And she coiled herself around him, kissing his stomach before laying her head in his lap.

'I could come back later if you would like?'

'Yes of course, I would like it very much. Please do.... can you stay again? I can cook another meal. Did you like the rabbit I cooked last night? It would have been better, but you were so late. Why were you so late? I never asked.'

Gerardo wandered over to the window, tying his belt around his waist.

'I told you, I had to go to a meeting with Deotisalvi; we lay the foundations for the new Tower of San Nicola today.'

Gerardo had a momentary frisson of guilt as he remembered kissing Aurelia the evening before. He was uncomfortable with having to lie, it was not in his nature. But he had set himself on a course and was powerless to walk away now. He went on with the deceit, to protect his lover's feelings, to protect Aurelia from Berta's inevitable rage if they were discovered, to protect himself.

'I'm sure you understand I couldn't let him down, it's our first week. And he is a difficult man to please; I need to show him what I can do. But I'm sorry if I spoiled your meal, which was delicious by the way. I had no idea you could cook.'

Berta smiled and uncoiled herself, lying back down against the pillows.

'Neither did I, truth be told. But I don't think cooking's as hard as people make out. I'm glad you are so enthusiastic about the tower. Deotisalvi is a great man, and we are fortunate that he has agreed to take you on; not that you don't deserve it. He is impressed by your grandfather. He has great respect for him. So, you will come back tonight? And I will cook you another meal and we will spend another wonderful night together. Would you like that?'

He leant down and kissed her, pushing thoughts of Aurelia out of his mind.

'Of course, you know I would. Now, I must go.'

Kneeling on the bed, she watched him leave. He walked fast towards the Piazza, turning and waving just as he got to the corner. She waved back, feeling excitement and love in equal measure. She had never felt this way before. She had cared for Lorenzo and she had imagined at the time that she loved him, but she knew now that she had never loved anyone the way she loved Gerardo.

Once he was out of sight of the house, Gerardo leant back against the wall of the nearest building and breathed deeply. He had promised himself it would 'just be once'. Just one night, then, perhaps he could find a way to explain to Berta how he felt. But how did he feel? He cared for Berta, yes. But he cared for Aurelia too. His head spun as he wrestled with his feelings. Easier to put it to one side. At least for today.

Gerardo hurried back towards the house he shared with his grandfather. The sun was just rising and the wooden tower houses, recently built along the lanes in the north-east part of the town, cast long shadows. In the early morning light, the roof of the Duomo glinted in the sunshine. There was a chill in the air and Gerardo quickened his pace. He arrived home just as his grandfather was opening the front door.

'Aah, good you're here,' his grandfather smiled.

'I'm sorry, *nonno*. I had to go out early. I'll be quick. I just need to collect some tools.'

'Out early… or back late?' the old man winked, and slapped the young man on the back as he rushed past him.

They arrived at the new site in good time. Gerardo carried his grandfather's tool bag and laid it carefully down. Deotisalvi was waiting for them.

'Good, you've arrived. Gerardo the elder, I need to discuss the stonework with you. Young Gerardo, you organise the rest of the team. We need to make a start on the foundations today. The air is turning cold and we need to make progress before the ground gets too hard.'

The day went well. Young Gerardo, excited to be in charge of the building team, worked tirelessly. First, he explained the plans to the team of men who had been hired to lay the foundations. Then he marked out the ground plan using wooden stakes linked with ropes. The building was to be octagonal in shape, so the angles had to be carefully calculated. The ground was soft and marshy, much like the ground beneath the Duomo and Baptistery, so digging out the foundations would be relatively easy work. But the trenches would have to be deep – twice the height of a man – which would then be filled in with rocks brought on wooden carts from sites around the city. Gerardo organised the men into relays – one crew digging and the second taking away the spoil.

'First team… keep digging until it reaches about here on my thigh,' he called out, and taking a pickaxe, he swung it hard into the earth.

'He works hard,' Deotisalvi growled to Gerardo. 'Your boy… he works hard.'

'He does, *Capo Magister*. You won't find a better mason in Pisa. Some day he will make a fine *lapicida*,' said old Gerardo proudly.

Deotisalvi grunted a reply, before turning his attention to some samples of marble lying on the ground. Quarried from marble works all over Italy, each one was a subtly different shade of cream.

'We need to find the perfect stone to decorate the face of the tower. The building should reflect the evening light. I want something with a warm pink tone, a contrast to the works at the Piazza with their grey and white.'

As the two debated the superiority of the marble quarries at Monte Pisano over Elba, young Gerardo dug. He tried hard to concentrate on his work. It was the first time he had been put in charge of a team and he relished the challenge.

'Can we stop for a break?' one of the young labourers asked.

'Not yet; not till we've broken through that bit of hard ground down there. Keep working. If we all work hard, we can stop in a while and have a break.'

The rest of the day went by with few major problems, apart from uncovering an underground stream which they had to find a way of diverting. Gerardo was decisive and intelligent, expertly directing his men to fashion a neat stone culvert for the water to escape down. As the distant church bells struck the six o'clock Angelus, the team wrapped up their tools. Gerardo felt a huge sense of achievement.

'You did well today, Gerardo,' his grandfather said, as they walked home together. 'I was proud of you. We have been fortunate to be offered this job, just as work ceases on the Baptistery. I suspect we have a friend of yours to thank for this, no?'

'A friend, maybe. Yes. She put us up for the job, but Deotisalvi chose you, *nonno*. He had heard of your work on the Duomo and the Baptistery, and he wanted you as his *lapicida.*'

'Well, you be sure to thank *la signora* for me, won't you? '

'I will. In fact,' he paused, 'she has asked to see me later. Would you mind if I went to see her?'

'To the *palazzo*? No, not at all. I'm tired, Gerardo; I'm not so young. I shall eat some supper and go to bed. I'll see you tomorrow.'

His grandfather now settled, Gerardo washed carefully and, dressed in the blue tunic Berta had given him some months before, set off with a certain unease for the little house on the north-east of the town. He found Berta slightly flushed, her hair tied casually at the back of her head.

'*Caro*, you are here… how wonderful. Sit here… let me give you something to rest your feet on. I have made us some supper; it cooks away there on the fire. I found a wonderful fowl in the market, but I had to ask them to dissect it for me. I have never cut up a chicken before. The butcher was very nice to me and showed me how it was done. He must have thought me a very strange housewife, don't you think, not to understand such things.'

Gerardo listened to his lover with a growing sense of anxiety. That she loved him was not in question. And he was fond of her too; she was beautiful and powerful and he had her to thank for his new job. But he found this new aspect of her personality, domesticated and intimate, unsettling. He did not see her as a wife but as an exciting companion, someone he could please, a woman of the world, who could give and receive pleasure in equal measure. Their first night together had been exciting, enchanting even. She had been a little shy, insisting on wearing a shift, but had soon allowed him to remove it, and as she lay bathed in the moonlight, he had marvelled at the beauty of her white body, at the hair tumbling around her like a fiery pillow. But he knew that fate had played a part in their relationship. If Lorenzo had not died, he was in no doubt that they would never have consummated the affair. Perhaps, over time, her passion would have cooled, he would have worked with Deotisalvi, his career would have progressed, they would have stayed friends, but he would have been free to pursue his own life, away from his powerful mistress. A life that might have included Aurelia, who, for all her youth and inexperience, he now realised he loved with a sweetness and purity he did not feel for Berta. But now he and the beautiful Berta were lovers, he could not imagine how he would ever be able to extricate himself. He knew her personality well enough – had seen her tempers, had heard her denounce others – to know that she would not let him go without a struggle.

'Berta,' he interrupted her in full flow.

'Yes, *caro*, what is it?' She looked up from stirring the pot over the fire. Her face glowed faintly with perspiration, and strands of her long red hair clung to her brow.

'Berta, we need to talk about something.'

'Anything, *caro*. What is troubling you?'

'Berta, you know that I love being with you… at least I hope you do?'

'I know that, yes.' She noted he refrained from saying 'I love you.' But she was not a child. She did not need words. He was here, with her, at last. She left the pot, brushing the hair from her face with the back of her hand. She came over to Gerardo, and sat on his lap, burying her head in his shoulder. She inhaled his scent, warm and fresh, like the smell of the chestnut woods on the low hills around Pisa.

'I just want us to understand one another, to understand what you…' His voice trailed off. He could not complete the sentence. Berta had begun to kiss him. He kissed her back.

'We understand one another very well,' said Berta. 'We love each other, that's all we need to know for now. I am in no position to marry you, not yet anyway. It would not be seemly, so shortly after Lorenzo died. But we can go on meeting here from time to time. Isn't that enough for now?'

He could think of nothing to say, and when she served up their delicious 'fowl', he struggled to eat.

'*Caro*, don't you like my chicken? I went to such trouble.'

'It is wonderful, Berta, I'm sorry. I must be tired, I think. It was hard work today.'

'Of course, you must tell me all about it. Come and sit here by me.'

Reluctantly, he walked around the table and sat on the bench by her side.

She tried to feed little mouthfuls of food to him as they chatted, but he wasn't interested. Finally, and a little tersely, she enquired if he would be 'quite so reluctant to make love to her'.

He took her to bed, but his mind was filled with images of Aurelia, laughing sweetly and kissing him shyly on the cheek. As his lips kissed Berta, his heart kissed Aurelia. As he cupped her breasts in his hand, it was Aurelia's that he stroked. And when he came inside her and she cried out in ecstasy, it was Aurelia's face that he saw.

They lay entwined, as lovers do, for a short while. But Gerardo was anxious to leave.

'I ought to go Berta – I need to get home and prepare for work tomorrow,' and he deftly removed his arm from beneath Berta's head.

'Please don't go yet; we have so little time together,' she pleaded. 'Tomorrow, I must return home. I have meetings with people about Lorenzo's business, and cannot risk remaining here too much longer. The staff will begin to wonder at my absences. Please stay a little longer; it may be a while before I can escape here again.'

Gerardo did as she asked, but as they lay, her head resting on his shoulder, her arm draped over his stomach, he could not sleep. Just before dawn, he gently moved her onto the pillow beside him. And while she slept, he rose quickly and dressed. Kissing Berta chastely on the forehead, he left.

As Gerardo opened the door of his house, he heard a woman's voice from upstairs. 'Please try to rest. I'm sure he will be home soon.'

'Hello,' he called out, 'who is there? *Nonno*... are you ok?'

Aurelia's face appeared on the floor above and she slid down the ladder to join him and threw herself into his arms.

'Oh Gerardo, thank God you are here. We have been looking for you everywhere.'

'*Nonno*, where is he?'

'He's all right... well, he's not well. But he's alive, Gerardo. Oh Gerardo, he was taken ill last night, and your neighbor, Gabriella, came to find you. He thought you were at the *palazzo* with Berta, but we couldn't find you. She was not at home either. I was upstairs tidying the *signora's* room, and I heard the noise in the hall. I came out and saw this woman crying and saying how ill your grandfather was. So I asked Maria, the housekeeper, if I could come and look after him until you returned home. Oh Gerardo, where were you?'

Gerardo did not answer, but clambered up the ladder to his grandfather's room. The old man lay very still in the little cot bed that he had slept in for so many years. He was pale, his skin had turned a curious shade of grey. Gerardo sat in silence next to the old man and gently stroked his head, tears streaming down his face.

Old Gerardo opened his eyes.

'Ah my boy, there you are. I am glad.'

'Oh *nonno,* I'm so sorry. I should have been here... I'm so sorry.'

And he wept like a small boy.

Aurelia, who was standing nearby, came over and touched his hair. He reached up and held her hand, pulling her down to sit by him. Together they sat, both weeping, as the old man lay almost forgotten at their side.

'What happened, *nonno*?' he asked.

'I don't really remember,' said the old man, 'I was cutting some bread to eat for supper and I began to feel ill – you know, light in the head. I had a pain in my arm and it got worse and worse. I knew it wasn't right so I called next door to Gabriella and asked her to go and find you. I lay down, I knew that was best, and waited for you to come. But this little angel came instead.'

Aurelia smiled at the old man; she reached across and held his hand.

'I've sent for my mother; she's an apothecary,' she said. 'I don't know exactly what she can do, but she will come with her remedies.'

There was a knock on the door and Aurelia leapt up. 'That will be her now, I hope.'

Violetta came upstairs and the two young people made way for her to sit down next to old Gerardo. She carefully examined the old man, asking him where the pain was, how long he had felt unwell, whether he felt breathless, and so on. Finally, she inspected his eyes, tongue, and pallor.

Satisfied with her diagnosis, she rose and beckoned young Gerardo to follow her down the ladder to the kitchen below.

'It is his heart, I believe. He is short of breath and cannot sit up. He must rest. I will make him something to help him sleep.'

'*Signora*,' young Gerardo spoke softly, 'I am grateful to you for your help, you must let me pay you for your trouble.'

'Please,' said Violetta, 'I do not expect payment. Aurelia has explained how important you and your grandfather are to her; maybe you can render me a favour sometime in return. Now, please would you go and heat some water – the fire needs tending. And Aurelia, take these herbs and strip the leaves off the stems as you used to do.'

The two young people suitably occupied, Violetta climbed back up to the bedroom and plumped the old man's pillow, pulling his blanket around his chin and tucking it into the side of his bed, before settling herself onto a small nursing chair that stood in the corner of his bedchamber.

'I will not leave you; you will be safe with me,' she said kindly.

'*Signora*, I am grateful,' whispered the old man, struggling to speak, 'but I am not a fool. I know that what has happened to me cannot be cured with a tisane. You are very kind, but I need you to prepare young Gerardo, in case I do not survive. I am all he has in the world, apart from your lovely daughter. Look after him for me. He is a good boy... and strong and ambitious.'

'We will love him like one of our own,' Violetta promised. 'Now lie still and let me tidy this bed.'

CHAPTER 20

October 1171

Massoud put down his pens and slammed shut the huge Calvo ledgers with their columns of figures. He stood gazing out of the window of his office, which overlooked the lane at the side of the *palazzo*. Before Berta had left for her sojourn at her *casetta*, she had arranged with him to send Giuseppe with the cart at noon to bring her back home.

Massoud heard the wheels clattering in the lane below and rushed to the main door. Berta was standing on the steps outside, looking tired but happy.

'Forgive me, *signora*, for making you wait. I did not hear you knock.'

'You are forgiven, of course, Massoud. It's good to see you.'

'I will send the staff to collect your baggage from the cart.'

'Oh, there is not much... just a few clothes. I left most of my things at the *casetta*, for when I return. Is Aurelia upstairs? I must get changed ready for our meeting later today with the silk merchant... er, what's his name?'

'Goro Dati, *signora*. We also have a meeting with the wine merchant Bartolomeo di Michele del Corazza. And yes, *signora*, Aurelia is upstairs.'

Massoud thought it advisable not to mention that Aurelia had only just returned home from her visit to Gerardo's grandfather.

Berta reached her room and looked around for her maid. She was nowhere to be seen. She opened the door to the girl's bedroom, and there she was, fast asleep on her little bed.

'Aurelia,' she shook her awake. 'Aurelia, what are you doing asleep in the day? Get up now and help me please. If this is what you get up to when I leave town for a few days, in future I shall have to ensure that Maria keeps you fully employed while I'm away. Now wake up and find my dark grey damask dress.'

Aurelia had not slept all night, having kept vigil at old Gerardo's bedside. She began to protest self-righteously, but registered the annoyance on Berta's face.

'I am sorry, *signora,* I merely laid myself down for a moment, and must have drifted off to sleep. Please forgive me.'

Aurelia found the dress Berta wanted, and helped her into it. She brushed out her mistress's hair, and then coiled and plaited it. For her meeting with creditors, Berta preferred to adopt a demure style of dress, covering her hair with a plain linen cap, and wearing a simple gold and pearl cross on a gold chain.

'Now Aurelia, please fetch me a little food. I will eat here in my chamber. I have some papers to read through before Massoud and I go for our meeting.'

The girl brought a bowl of broth, some bread and fruit and a little jug of wine, arranging them neatly for her mistress on a small table near the window.

'Thank you, Aurelia; you may go.'

The girl, exhausted from the previous night, went downstairs to the kitchens and out into the garden. The wind had changed. It was blowing from the north, a sure sign that autumn was coming. But the sun was shining, and Aurelia headed for a little stone bench she knew would be a warm spot by the wall. She sat down and before long had nodded off, her head lolling against her chest.

Meanwhile, Berta had retrieved her sketches of the tower from the oak chest in the dining hall, and had been working on them for several hours. When at last she was satisfied, she called for her notary. 'Massoud, please bring me the business accounts to study before our meeting with Signor Dati. While I am studying them I would like you to take a message for me. I am sorry to ask you, but I need someone I can trust. Will you go to Signor Vernacci, the *Operaio* and tell him that I would like to arrange a meeting with him as soon as possible – to discuss the new *campanile* at the Piazza del Duomo. Will you do that for me, please?'

Massoud bowed deeply. 'It will be my pleasure, *signora*. I will come for you in two hours for our meeting with Signor Dati; we are meeting at his offices.'

'Very good, Massoud.'

The notary brought the ledgers and laid them out on a large oak table in Berta's room. She sat for more than an hour, going over the figures, making a note of goods that had yet to be sold, and monies owed. Finally, her neck and shoulders aching, she rose from her ornate chestnut *sedile*, slumping exhausted onto the luxurious bed she had shared for so many years with her husband Lorenzo. She reflected on the years they had shared… of his sadness at not having children, but his joy at the beautiful house they had built together. It had been a strange marriage in many ways, and yet they had created something extraordinary – or so she had thought. Throughout their many years together, she had imagined that their wealth was secure… that she was free to pursue her interests in art and architecture, unburdened by any anxieties about money. And she herself had been generous with that money over the years, being an illustrious and steadfast patron to many young artists. But their wealth, it now seemed, had been an illusion. Her study of the ledgers that afternoon had revealed the full extent of their debts. Lorenzo had left her with a string of irate creditors; and her hopes of an enduring personal legacy, of leaving her mark on the city that she loved, were disappearing fast.

She got up and walked across to a large oak cupboard that stood next to the bronze bust that Lorenzo had commissioned of his beautiful new wife, Berta, daughter of Bernado, on the occasion of their marriage seventeen years before. It had been sculpted by a young man who had gone on to make quite a name for himself, Bonanno Pisano. The girl she had once been, so sure and strong and optimistic, smiled at her. Her hair loose around her shoulders, Bonanno had depicted her wearing a string of huge pearls, with the large multi-faceted diamond pendant that Lorenzo had brought back for her from India.

She took the little clinking collection of keys she wore hanging from a chain at her waist, and unlocked the cupboard. She took out the clothes and damask throws that were stored inside and laid them on the bed. Using a small hunting knife that lay on the floor of the cupboard, she prized open a section at the back, revealing the oak panelling that covered the walls of her chamber. She inserted the blade of the knife into the edge of one piece of the paneling; it came away in her hand, exposing a deep cavity in the thick wall of the house. Inside the cavity were numerous papers and a small metal box which she removed. She took a second key and unlocked it, tipping the contents onto the bed. Jewels of many colours clattered onto the silk throw: the diamond egg, another cut from the largest emerald ever found, the emerald ring that Lorenzo had given her for their betrothal, rubies and pearls set into combs to wear in her hair. And finally, carefully stowed away in a stout linen bag, were the sixty coins that Benedete Zaccaria had given her as payment for the galley. She picked up the pieces one by one, holding them to the light, before putting them carefully back in the metal box and concealing them, once again, in their hiding place. She placed the drawings of the tower in the cavity too, before replacing the panel and the back of the cupboard. She hung cloaks on the pegs to conceal the secret entrance, and piled up the folded the clothes and damask throws, before finally locking the door.

When Massoud returned, she was ready. He had good news: the *Operaio* would meet her later that day. Checking her reflection one last time in the glass, she set off for the apartment of the silk merchant – Dati, the first of many such meetings to unravel the life she had created with her husband.

Aurelia woke, stiff and a little cold, on her stone seat by the garden wall. The sun had gone behind a cloud and her hands felt icy as she rubbed them together. She came in from the garden and discovered her mistress had already left.

'How long will she be gone?' she asked Maria, as casually as she could.

'Quite a while I think,' Massoud said, 'they won't be back till later this evening.'

Aurelia, desperate to see Gerardo again and to find out how his grandfather was, decided to risk a small lie.

'This morning, *la signora* asked me to take a message for her. I really must go now; I may be a couple of hours.'

Maria looked up from rolling out pastry on the long chestnut table and pushed a strand of hair that had escaped from her cap away from her face with the back of her floury hands.

'Well, mind you're back in time for her return; you don't want to upset her now, do you?'

Aurelia took a warm cape from her cupboard and began the walk to Gerardo's house – first heading north across the new bridge over the Arno, then branching east along its banks, before turning into Via San Cecilia, past the church of the same name, where she turned, diving north into the jumble of narrow streets in Pisa's oldest quarter. As she passed the church, its huge bronze bell tolled the evening Angelus. Gerardo would be leaving work now, she thought, and be home shortly – unless he had decided to take the day off and spend it with his grandfather.

When she arrived at his house, he was not there. She called upstairs; there was no answer. The servants – the maid and the boy – were nowhere to be found. As quietly as she could, she climbed the ladder to the upper floor where old Gerardo lay very still in his bed.

Even from across the room, Aurelia could see that all was not well. Terrified, she crept towards him, dropping to her knees at his bedside. The skin was grey, the lips blue. She put out her hand and touched him. He was cold. She pulled back her hand, recoiling from the sensation of his smooth, icy skin. Like marble, she thought.

A few moments later, she heard voices below. It was her mother... and Gerardo. She heard the ladder creak as he climbed to his grandfather's bedroom. He said nothing as he entered, and appeared not even to notice Aurelia. He walked tentatively over to his grandfather, and touched him, feeling his cold hand; he lay down next to the old man, wrapping him in his arms, and weeping.

Aurelia, unable to bear the sight of the man she loved in such distress, backed away and retreated to the kitchen with her mother.

Violetta was breaking wood onto the fire, beneath a large copper pot filled with water. She put her arms out to Aurelia who broke into floods of tears.

'There now, Aurelia, just cry, darling – it's sometimes better to cry.'

After a few moments, the girl's sobs subsided.

'*Cara,*' her mother said kindly, 'help me to make a little food for Gerardo, will you? I know how distressed he will be, but he must eat, Aurelia.'

They found onions and garlic in an earthenware pot near the fire and began to chop them on the big kitchen table.

'I feel so bad that the old man died alone,' Violetta said as she peeled the onions. 'I persuaded young Gerardo to go to the site this morning after you had left. I knew that the job was important, old Gerardo told me that last night. He made me promise that I would not let him stay here with the old man. "This job could be the making of him; this is his opportunity to change his life," old Gerardo said. And so I persuaded him to go. But I felt bad about it. I knew that there was a risk he could pass away at any time. He was so very ill. And then, this afternoon, I had just come down here to collect a little broth that I had made for him, and I heard him shout. A strange noise, then a sort of gurgling sound. I rushed up there, but he had gone. It was so quick, Aurelia. There was nothing I could do. But I feel that I have failed him.'

Tears fell down her face.

Aurelia got up from the kitchen table and held her mother. '*Mamma*, there was nothing you could do... you said so. Gerardo will understand.'

'I do,' said a man's voice suddenly. The two women looked up. Gerardo was standing at the bottom of the ladder.

'I know there was nothing more you could do for him, Violetta,' Gerardo said gently. '*Nonno* has been getting weaker for a while now. I knew he was not well. He has had such a hard life and his heart was not strong. I am just sorry I was not here; I would have liked to have been holding his hand. It does not seem right that he should have died all alone.'

He went over to the two women, and together they stood and held one another.

Gerardo sat silently at the kitchen table, as Violetta and Aurelia quietly prepared a simple meal of soup. If they asked him a question – 'where are the vegetables, Gerardo,' or 'where do you keep the plates?' – he responded. But otherwise he sat quite still, mute, unable to take in what had happened. Once the meal was prepared, Violetta ladled some of the soup into a bowl and set it before the young man. But he did not pick up his spoon; he merely sat staring ahead of him. She touched his arm gently.

'Gerardo, here is a little soup for you. Eat it… it will be good for you.'

He obediently took up the spoon and took a couple of mouthfuls before thanking her and replacing the spoon on the table.

Aurelia, distressed at the sight of him so changed and unhappy, could think of nothing comforting to say. As her mother busied herself with washing some utensils, she said finally, 'I ought to go, Gerardo. *La signora* will be very unhappy if I am not there when she returns.'

At the mention of Berta, Gerardo was jolted out of his silence. He wanted to say to Aurelia that he was sure Berta would understand, but he knew that was not so. Torn between his affection for Aurelia and his loyalty to his lover, he merely said, 'Go then, but maybe we can meet tomorrow or the next day? Would you be able to come to me here?'

Aurelia, understanding why he would be reluctant to meet her at the *palazzo*, simply nodded. She kissed him tenderly on the cheek, opened the front door, and hurried down the now darkening streets.

The servants were eating dinner when she got back to the *palazzo*. Refusing supper, she went upstairs and prepared her mistress's room ready for her return. The bed was turned down, her brushes were laid out on the dressing table, and a bowl of scented water stood nearby. But exhausted by her sleepless night and the emotional turmoil of the previous day and night, she lay down on her bed.

She was woken by her mistress's excited voice. 'Aurelia, Aurelia... where are you? I need you to help me.'

The girl dragged herself out of a deep sleep and struggled to her feet.

'My goodness, you are asleep again!' shouted Berta. 'Whatever can be the matter with you, girl? Well, I can't worry about that now. Help me to get undressed and then you can go back to your beloved bed.'

'You seem cheerful, *signora*,' said Aurelia, as she unpinned the long red hair.

'I am! I have just had a very exciting meeting... with the *Operaio*. I have some wonderful plans, Aurelia. Everything is going to work out. Now brush out my hair, girl, and then you may go.'

Waiting until Aurelia was safely in bed, Berta went again to the oak cupboard, and once more retrieved the strongbox from its secret hiding place. She laid the box carefully beneath the pillow on her bed, rested her head on it, and went to sleep.

The following morning, Berta woke early. Checking that her maid was still asleep, she took the strongbox down to Massoud's office. He was already at work, preparing for further meetings later that day.

'Massoud, I have something I need you to do for me. Inside this box is some precious jewellery; I would like you to get it valued please. But we will need to be discreet. I do not want word of this spreading about. Take the jewels to Bonaccorsi

Pitti. He can be trusted. Tell him we will pay him well for his silence.'

Gerardo had also woken early. The house was still in darkness as he threw off the covers. He lit a candle from the embers of the fire in the kitchens and sat at the table, fingering the tiny carved camel his grandfather Carlo had made for him all those years before. To be drowned at sea – that would be a terrible way to die. At least his dear old Gerardo had died peacefully in his bed. He thought too of his mother's last days. He could remember the sounds she made at the end; terrible sobbing. And the awful smell of her dying… that too had stayed with him. But, as time went on, her sweet face became a blurred memory, as if it were reflected in a pool of water.

He had arranged for his grandfather to be buried in the same graveyard as his mother. It was sad that Carlo could not lie there too.

The funeral service was due to take place the following day. Old Gerardo still lay in his bed upstairs. The young man was reluctant to leave his grandfather's body alone in the house. He packed up his tools, but before leaving for work, rushed upstairs to his grandfather's room, and hugged the cold, lifeless body, kissing it tenderly on the forehead.

'Goodbye, *nonno*; I'm off now. But I'll be thinking of you, and I promise… I won't let you down.'

He approached the building site with trepidation. He dreaded telling Deotisalvi about his grandfather's death. He knew well that the great architect had respected his grandfather, but had made no secret of his impatience with the grandson. The architect had not yet arrived at the site, so Gerardo organised the men and began work.

'Where is my *lapicida*?' Deotisalvi shouted impatiently as soon as he arrived.

'*Capo Magister*, I have some bad news. Last night my grand-father passed away.'

Gerardo hung his head.

Deotisalvi sighed. 'Well that leaves me in a pretty fix. I am sorry for your loss, Gerardo. Your grandfather was a fine *lapicida* and a good man. But this presents us with a problem. The foundations have been started, and we cannot wait too long; we must get that part of the job finished and make better progress with the build before the winter comes.'

'I understand,' said Gerardo. 'I will do anything I can to help. You can rely on me.'

Deotisalvi paced around the site, stroking his straggly beard, before speaking again. 'Gerardo…. I have a proposition for you. Your grandfather had great faith in you. He said he thought you would be a fine *lapicida* one day. I imagine you learned a lot from him. Do you have the skills to take over from your grandfather? I will need to find a new master mason, but that should not be a major problem. But a *lapicida*… it is a difficult job. It is not just a matter of running the site and managing the men – you are doing much of that job already. But there is the choosing of the stone and so on. I had discussed this at length with your grandfather and we were shortly due to make a visit to Monte Pisano to start our search. '

'*Signore*, are you asking me to become your *lapicida*?' Gerardo asked, incredulously.

'What do you think I'm asking you? Well… do you want the job?'

'Of course! *Capo Magister*, it would be an honour.'

'Then it is done. We shall leave for the mountains the day after tomorrow. We will be gone several weeks.'

'But *Signore*, that is the day I bury my grandfather. I cannot go so soon.'

'The following day then… Friday. And if I may, I shall come to the funeral and pay my respects to your grandfather. A fine man and a fine *lapicida*. Now, you had better explain the situation to the men and get those foundations sorted out.'

When Aurelia woke, she found her mistress gone, so she spent the day catching up on simple jobs: rinsing out Berta's undergarments and hanging them in the big laundry room off the kitchen, mending the hem of a velvet cloak, and dusting and tidying her mistress's room. As Berta was out, Maria kept Aurelia busy collecting ripe tomatoes and pears from the kitchen garden and bringing them to her for preserving and bottling. But Aurelia struggled to keep her mind on her job, overwhelmed by thoughts of how she could get to see Gerardo that evening.

When Berta arrived home, she went upstairs, calling out for Aurelia.

The girl ran up the two flights to her mistress's bedchamber and found Berta seated at her dressing table, having already taken off her own gown. Wearing just her corset and underskirt, she was pulling out the combs and pins that held her hair in place.

'Ah good, Aurelia; we have work to do. I have to go out in a little while… something very important. Please get out my cream silk dress.'

'Very good, *signora.*'

The girl went to the largest of Berta's caskets – the one made of tooled leather – and took out the gown. As with most of Berta's dresses, it had sleeves hanging almost to the ground. It was traditional for the wearer's hands to poke out half way down the sleeve, leaving a long train of fabric hanging to the floor, but this dress was of the latest fashion and the sleeves were gathered on the forearm so that the hands passed through the opening at the end.

'Will you wear it with the emerald and pearl necklace, *signora?*'

'No!' Berta replied a little sharply. 'No, no jewellery – just a cross, I think. I don't want to look too ostentatious. I have a meeting with Bonanno Pisano, the sculptor. Now hurry, girl.'

Aurelia was delighted by this news; if her mistress was going out for the evening, it would give her the opportunity to see Gerardo. Humming quietly to herself, Aurelia laid out the gown and jewellery, along with some long cream leather gloves. She took special care with Berta's hair, combing it thoroughly, before weaving it into two long plaits, which she decorated with ribbons. When she had finished, she stood back and admired her work.

'Well done, Aurelia, that is very good. It would appear that you are finally becoming an excellent maid. Now, tighten this corset for me will you, and then help me into the dress. Have you my velvet cloak?'

'Yes, *signora*,' answered the girl, 'it is here; I mended the hem for you this afternoon.'

'Excellent,' said Berta delightedly. 'I shall be gone for several hours, so you will have a little time on your hands. Perhaps you might visit your mother?'

As soon as Berta had left the *palazzo*, Aurelia threw on her cloak, and ran all the way to Gerardo's house. She arrived out of breath, and found him sitting at the table in the kitchen, while Fabricia, the maid, was preparing his supper.

'Aurelia, how wonderful. Come in. Grandfather's body has not long been taken to be made ready for the funeral. I still cannot really believe he has gone. But I am glad to see you... will you stay and share my supper?'

Fabricia was a sturdy girl with mousy brown hair and pale skin. She was not a skilled cook, Aurelia thought, as she observed her clumsily rolling out sheets of pasta.

'What are you making, Fabricia?' she asked the girl.

'Ravioli,' Fabricia replied, a worried look on her face.

'Here, let me help you,' said Aurelia kindly.

While the maid cooked up the filling of chopped rabbit and hard cheese, Aurelia expertly rolled out the pasta before creating the ravioli.

Gerardo sat and watched her fascinated by her skill.

'I had no idea you could cook, Aurelia' he said delightedly.

'My mother taught me,' she said shyly, 'but I don't get much chance to practise at the *palazzo* – Maria does everything.'

Her task complete, she left Fabricia boiling the ravioli in the pot over the fire, while she and Gerardo went upstairs to the sitting room.

'It was kind of you to come,' said Gerardo. 'Will you take a glass of wine with me?'

Together they sat companionably while Gerardo told her his news.

'Deotisalvi has made me *lapicida* on the tower at San Nicola. I am to travel with him to find marble for the face of the building. We leave on Friday for the quarries at Monti Pisani.'

'That's wonderful news, Gerardo. Your grandfather would have been very proud of you.'

'I hope so… yes. He had faith in me, I know. It just seems a tragedy that my elevation has happened because he…'

Tears welled up in his eyes.

'Oh Gerardo, don't cry. Your grandfather was a wonderful man – and he had a good life and a long life.'

'I know. You're right. It's just that he has been my only family for so many years. And now I am alone.'

'You're not alone, Gerardo... you have me.'

Gerardo took Aurelia's face in his large hands and kissed her tenderly on her closed eyelids, her cheeks, her forehead.

'Thank you, Aurelia. Now, I must think about *nonno's* funeral the day after tomorrow. You will come to the funeral, won't you?' he asked earnestly. 'He would have wanted you to be there. And your mother too, of course. Please ask her to come.'

'We will both come, Gerardo. I will tell *mamma* on my way back to the *palazzo.*'

'Why don't we tell her together? After we've had our supper we can go to her house via the site of the new church I'm working on. I'd like you to see it. Then once we've visited your mother I'll take you home. I must keep you safe, my little flower.'

Fabricia called up to them that supper was ready. As they got to the top of the ladder leading downstairs, Gerardo touched Aurelia's arm.

'Thank you for all that you did for my grandfather. You are such a good person. I want us to be together always. But we have time, little flower. You are young and so am I. Now let us eat, I am keen to taste your delicious-looking ravioli.'

CHAPTER 21

October 1171

Bonanno Pisano lived in an impressive tower house in the heart of the city on the north side of the Arno. Part of the new vanguard of Pisan artists, he was a gifted sculptor specialising in bronze. Although three decades younger than Deotisalvi, he was nevertheless considered, along with the great man himself, to be one of the most significant talents of his generation.

His house, as was the custom amongst the wealthy elite in Pisa, consisted of three tower houses joined together by galleries. It had a rambling, chaotic quality and, when Berta arrived, was filled with the sound of children's laughter. Pisano's wife, a beautiful dark-haired woman named Alfreda, was trying to control four young children, who were giggling and chasing one another along the main gallery. Laughing, Pisano shooed the children away and took Berta into his studio on the first floor.

'Come in here. The children are not allowed, so we will have peace and quiet.'

Berta was delighted to be invited into his studio. It was not unlike that of her own father. Large and airy with natural light from the north, the walls were covered with sketches and designs for pieces of statuary and intricate drawings in preparation for his detailed sculptures.

Berta had met him once before. He had been commissioned to sculpt her as a new bride, and while she did not consider herself a close friend, she had an easy relationship with him.

He poured her a glass of wine and together near the window, overlooking the city.

'So Berta, how are you? I am so sorry to hear about your husband's death. That must have come as a great shock.'

'I thank you, *signore*; it was indeed a shock. He had been unwell for a little while, but we had not realised, until it was too late, just how seriously. It has left a great hole in my life. But I still have my interests in art and architecture, and that is a great comfort.'

'Ah yes. How are your little group of artists? The last time I saw you, you were encouraging a young mason... what was his name?'

'Oh, you mean Gerardo di Gerardo. He is well, thank you. He is working on the new San Nicola tower for Deotisalvi. It is an interesting project and I understand he is doing very well there. He and his grandfather, who is a very experienced mason are working as *lapicida* and assistant; it is going well I believe.'

'Good, good. I had been meaning to thank you for the bequest your husband made before his death for the new doors on the Duomo. I am so grateful. I have started work on the designs already. Would you like to see them?'

'Yes. Thank you, I would like that very much.'

Bonanno took a thick roll of paper, tied with ribbon, from a large chest that stood beneath the window of his studio and smoothed it out on the table.

'The drawings are not finished yet, you understand; they are just ideas at this stage, but I am quite pleased with them. I think they are coming together.'

Drawn in exquisite detail were twelve scenes from the Life of Christ; the three kings on their way to visit the holy child;

the angels of the Lord visiting the shepherds and telling them of Christ's birth. The infant Jesus laying in a manger – each square panel following the life of Christ from birth to his crucifixion.

'They are charming, Bonanno... I may call you Bonanno, I hope? Really quite charming. They have an almost childlike quality about them, as if you are explaining the life of Our Lord to your own wonderful children.'

'Thank you, *signora*. I trust I might take that as a compliment.'

'Of course, Bonanno. They are full of poetry and drama, really most thought-provoking. I know Lorenzo would have loved them. Now, if I may, I have something I would like to show you.'

'Please,' he said, 'I am intrigued'

Berta opened a soft leather bag and took out a roll of cream vellum. She untied the ribbon and laid it flat on the table.

Bonanno whistled quietly through his teeth.

'So,' said Berta, 'what do you think?'

The sculptor looked long and hard at the belltower. Layers of arches, one upon the other... delicate... unlike anything he had ever seen.

'I think it is extraordinary and very beautiful. Who designed it?'

'Ah... well that has to remain a secret for now. But you like it?'

'I do. It is very grand, very bold... although the engineering will be quite a challenge. Is it a design for the new belltower for the Piazza del Duomo?'

'It is. And interestingly, the engineering is precisely what I wanted to discuss with you. I wondered if you could do me a favour.'

'Of course,' he replied.

'I want you to tell me if the design is feasible; I need proper mathematical calculations. Can you do that for me?'

'*Signora*, I am flattered that you should ask this of me. But in all honesty I do not have the skills for such an adventurous design. I can take it to a colleague, someone at the School of Architecture here in Pisa. It will be a most interesting project. But first let me ask you something. I understood that it was Deotisalvi who had won the commission for the new *campanile* on the Piazza. Surely, a work of such genius must be his? If so, why has he not done the calculations himself?'

'Bonanno, can I trust you with a secret?'

'You can, *signora*.'

'Deotisalvi did win the commission, yes, but I think his initial design can be improved upon. I am an architect's daughter, as you know, and I will try and persuade him the design I have shown you is better. He is a wonderful architect, please do not misunderstand me, but I believe that Pisa deserves to have the most wonderful campanile the world has ever seen. I have commissioned this design from a young, untried architect. But I need to know that it is sound, that the calculations are correct, before I present it to the great man. And although the *Operaio* will no doubt appreciate the revolutionary nature of the building, he will not be pleased if it falls down!'

Bonanno laughed. 'Of course, that is vital. Well, it will take me a little time, *signora*. I will speak to my friend and get the information to you as soon as I have it. I will need to keep these drawings.'

'Of course, but please, please, impress on your friend that this must be kept a secret. Do not show them to anyone other than him. Can I trust you?'

'You can, *signora*.'

As Berta left the sculptor's study, his children came running along the gallery towards him. He swooped the two youngest into his arms and turned the smallest child upside down, causing him to squeal with laughter. Putting the children down, he took Berta's hand and walked her to the front door. When she got to the end of road, she turned round to see the family waving from the loggia. She could still hear the sound of children's laughter as she reached the corner.

Two days later, young Gerardo and his little household led the procession to the Church of San Sepolcro, on the south bank of the Arno, for the funeral of old Gerardo. Masons, carpenters and gilders filled the church to pay their respects to a man they had worked with for over sixty years. Built by Deotisalvi at the start of his career, this hexagonal church was commissioned by the Jerusalem Knights of St John. The site was significant because it was the point from which pilgrims would embark for the Holy Land.

Deotisalvi was touched that his *lapicida* had chosen this church for his beloved grandfather's funeral, and when he arrived for the service, he nodded at the young man and patted his shoulder.

Berta, who had been shocked to hear of the death of old Gerardo, attended with Aurelia and Violetta – Aurelia, dressed for the occasion in a new gown of fine pale blue wool, and Berta resplendent in dark purple brocade.

At the end of the service, Gerardo briefly acknowledged both women. He spoke formally to each one in turn, studiously avoiding any kind of intimacy with either.

But before he left, he stole back to speak to Berta, pulling her away from the crowd by her elbow.

'Thank you for coming, Berta.'

'*Caro,* of course I came. I was so distressed to hear of your grandfather's death. I am just sorry I could not have been with you sooner. I had business with Bonnano that evening and had no idea what had happened. You are being very brave,' she said, holding his hand.

'Thank you; yes it was a terrible shock. But *nonno* was an old man. And I am grateful that it was not a lingering death, like my mother's.'

She squeezed his hand tenderly.

'Berta, I wanted to speak to you on another matter. I must leave Pisa tomorrow. I am to be *lapicida* on the Tower of San Nicola, and it is you I have to thank for that. The *magister* and I are to visit Monti Pisani in search of suitable stone, and I have no idea how long I will be away; a few weeks certainly.'

'I am pleased for you, *caro*, you deserve this success. Your grandfather would be very proud of you. I will miss you, and will be here waiting for you when you return.'

Violetta bid her daughter farewell at the church and left Berta and Aurelia to walk back to the *palazzo*. Aurelia was keen to discover what her mistress had been discussing, so intimately, with Gerardo.

'The service… it went well,' she began.

'It did,' agreed Berta dreamily. 'It was very beautiful indeed. It was good to see so many people represented there. Gerardo must be very proud.'

'Indeed, *signora*. And how did he feel it went… when he spoke to you?'

'Oh very well. Very well.'

'Was that all that he said?'

'You are very curious, Aurelia,' Berta spoke sharply, 'about a private conversation; but if you must know, he was telling me that he would be leaving tomorrow. He is to travel with Deotisalvi to Monti Pisani in search of suitable stone for the tower of San Nicola. He has been asked to take his grandfather's position as *lapicida*; it is a great honour for him. He wanted merely to thank me, as I made the introduction to Deotisalvi for him. Now let us hurry. I have many things to do this afternoon.'

Aurelia wanted desperately to snap back at her mistress: 'I know that. I was with him the night his grandfather died. He told me about his promotion before he told you. He wants us to be together always.' But instead, she had to hold her counsel, and walked in sullen silence back to the *palazzo*. Just a few days before, Gerardo had led her to believe that she was vital to him, but here, in public, he had practically ignored her. She felt humiliated, and sulked all the way home. She could barely look Berta in the eye as she attended to her that afternoon.

Her behaviour did not go unnoticed by her mistress, who now understood now that Aurelia was hopelessly in love with Gerardo. She felt sure that he cared for the girl too – in his own way. But for now, she felt secure in the knowledge that she and the young *lapicida* had a bond – both physical and emotional. In truth, perhaps her vanity precluded her from believing that any man could care for a young maidservant as intensely as he cared for her. Berta calmly ate her lunch and, dressed in a simple gown, went downstairs to spend the afternoon with Massoud.

Miserably, Aurelia put Berta's clothes away and tidied her room. The afternoon dragged on into the evening and she became desperate to see Gerardo before he left the city, to prove to herself, if nothing else, that he did truly care for her. But Berta returned to her room after supper and began to read. Aurelia, trapped by the presence of her mistress, was unable to escape to her beloved's house.

Aurelia woke very early the next morning. She pulled her dress on over her shift, grabbed a cloak to keep out the autumn chill, and ran down the stairs and out into the street to Gerardo's house. She arrived, panting, and knocked hard on the door.

Antonio, the page, opened up, rubbing sleep from his eyes.

'Gerardo… is he at home?' Aurelia asked

'No. He left very early this morning… for Monte Pisano. He will be gone for some weeks.'

Aurelia felt the tears filling her eyes, and embarrassed and exhausted, she mumbled her thanks and apologies; she began the walk home.

The boy came after her.

'Are you Aurelia?'

'Yes, yes I am.'

'Signor Gerardo left a message for you, before he left. He said to tell you that he will back soon… and that he will miss you.'

Aurelia clapped her hands with joy and hugged the boy.

'Thank you, thank you so much,' she said, before running through the city streets back to the *palazzo*.

While Gerardo was away, Berta was kept busy. Massoud had calculated that the debts of Lorenzo's company were too big to be covered by the sale of her jewellery and the remainder of the fleet. That would go part of the way, but the house, her beloved *palazzo*, would have to be sold.

Massoud wept as he revealed the full extent of the problem.

'*Signora*, I am so sorry. My heart is full of sorrow to have to tell you these things.'

But Berta was brisk. 'Massoud, please do not weep for me. I have had an exciting life and achieved many things. Between us, Lorenzo and I helped to create many wonderful works of art, this house amongst them. So, it's now time for me to leave. I will survive. The important thing is that we find a place for all the household. I will be able to keep some of the staff, of course. Your good self, if you will come with me, Maria too, and Aurelia.

Perhaps Giuseppe, but it depends where we end up. So, first, let us take care of the staff and then let it be known that the Palazzo of Lorenzo Calvi and Berta di Bernardo is for sale.'

The weeks that followed were full of activity. A buyer was swiftly found for the *palazzo* and Berta's goods were either sold, or packed up and made ready for the move to the house she had shared so briefly with her lover. But as the cases and trunks filled with china and glass were stacked up in the dining hall at the *palazzo*, Berta had a change of heart.

'The *casetta* was fine for those few days, Massoud, but is not really suitable for me to live in permanently. I would prefer to be somewhere nearer to the Piazza that I have loved all my life.'

But that was not the only reason why the little house at the top of the town would not be suitable. It would not, Berta believed, be large enough to accommodate her household, especially as she was now quite certain that she was to have a child.

The day of old Gerardo's funeral fell on the day Berta would normally expect to start her monthly bleed. But it did not come that day, nor the next. At first, she thought little of it, but as the days went by, she began to wonder at the cause. Two weeks after young Gerardo had left, and still there was no sign. But her belly had a distinct swelling. She could feel it beneath her hands as she lay in bed at night.

She sent for Violetta.

'I believe,' she said when the apothecary arrived, 'that these years of waiting might finally be at an end. I think I am with child.'

Violetta, who knew nothing of Berta's relationship with Gerardo, asked, 'How many weeks is it since your husband died?'

'Eight weeks.'

'By the swelling, you must be more than two months pregnant; I would estimate nearer four. Have you bled in that time?'

'Yes,' answered Berta, 'twice... but not this last time.'

'Well, that can happen sometimes. I am happy for you, *signora*; it is a gift from God, and may go some way to make up for your loss.'

After Violetta left, Berta thought back over the last months she had spent with Lorenzo. He had been unwell for some weeks before his death, and they had not made love in that time. It was possible that the baby was his, but there was another contender as father for this child: her absent lover, Gerardo.

Monte Pisano was some fifty miles from Pisa, a journey that would take several weeks to complete, initially by sea, and then on horseback. The group consisted of Deotisalvi, Gerardo and some twenty men who had worked with the old architect for many years, who were not only skilled masons but also experienced sailors and horsemen. They were to travel north up the coast on a small galley to the small port of Forte dei Marmi. From there, they would go on horseback across the plain and up into mountains. Gerardo was surprised to note that he felt no sea-sickness on the day-long sail. He thought of his grandfather Carlo, and wondered if he had, perhaps, inherited the old sailor's sea legs. But the journey on horseback was not so straightforward. The days were long and hard and the pace set by the elderly architect, Deotisalvi, was impressive. The party set off at first light, and rarely stopped before the sun had set. If their journey took them near a village, they spent the night at an inn, or billeted amongst the local people. But if, as often happened, they found themselves deep in the woods, they would make camp, erecting tents, cooking over an open fire. The men, all of whom Deotisalvi had worked with before, were experienced travellers. They rode well, pitched tents with ease, and hunted their supper with skill. But their real value lay in their ability to manoeuvre and transport vast pieces of marble down from the mountain to the coast and thence to Pisa.

Gerardo, however, although young and fit, was no horseman, and at the end of the first day, as they set up their tents in the foot hills of the mountains, his legs and back ached more than he had ever thought possible. When he was finally able to lay himself down at nightfall in front of the fire, the pain burned in his thighs.

'Not used to horseback, I see,' Deotisalvi smiled ruefully, poking a stick in the fire.

'No, *capo magister*… I have not ridden much.'

'Not at all by the look of it. Never seen such terrible horsemanship. You could ride in the cart if you'd prefer?'

Tempted as he was by the offer, Gerardo was determined to prove himself to the old man. 'No thank you; I'll learn. It's good to learn new skills.'

'Well,' said Deotisalvi, 'learn to use your knees. You need to grip the horse more between your legs; he needs to know who's boss. The ride will get harder tomorrow; from now on it's all uphill and he'll shake you off if you don't grip him hard.'

'Thank you, *capo magister*… that's helpful advice.'

'Ha! Well, if you weren't a rider before this trip, you will be by the end of it.'

And the old man threw the stick in the fire and took himself off to his tent, adding as an afterthought, 'I'd get to sleep if I were you; we'll be off at first light tomorrow.'

Gerardo lay looking at the embers of the fire, thinking of how his life had changed in the last few months. He wondered what his grandfather Gerardo would make of his promotion. He hoped he would be proud. Something about the bright flames evoked a memory of his mother teaching him, when he was a little boy, to hang the pot over the fire in the kitchen without burning his arm. His memories of her were fading, and he wondered if they had been supplanted by stories his grandfather had told him. The three people who had meant most to him in his life had gone, and he was completely alone but for the two women who had come to mean so much to him, Aurelia and Berta. He saw now, as he gazed into the dying embers of the fire, that he loved them both, but in different ways. His love for Aurelia felt gentle and natural. There was an inevitability about it, as if she was his destiny. She was young, and naive at times, it was true, but she was also loyal and loving, with a streak of impetuousness that amused him. And there was Berta, a woman who could be bewitching as well as infuriating. There were times when he found her intoxicating, and that was part of her attraction, but it was also daunting. He knew in his heart that he could not, would not, choose to spend his life with her, but equally he was powerless to leave her.

One hundred miles to the south, while her lover went in search of the perfect vein of marble for the new tower at San Nicola, Berta, anxious to secure her future, had arranged another appointment with the *Operaio*, Benetto Vernacci.

She arrived with her notary, Massoud, just before lunch, and was shown into a quiet sitting room in Vernacci's sumptuous apartments in his official rooms next to the Duomo. She sat in a high-backed leather chair opposite the *Operaio*'s desk, with Massoud standing behind.

'*Cara signora…* how good it is to see you here. I note you have made yourself comfortable, excellent. What can I get for you – a glass of wine?' Vernacci beckoned to a steward who was standing in the corner of the room.

Berta shook her head. 'Thank you, no – nothing.'

The *Operaio* waved the boy away. 'Very well, now what would you like to discuss?'

'Signor Vernacci, you know that I have always been a faithful servant of Pisa and its people.'

The *Operaio* nodded.

'That is never in any doubt, *signora*; you and your husband have always been most generous patrons of this great city.'

'As you may know, since the death of my dear husband Lorenzo, I have had a change in circumstances. Various debts have accrued that we have had to deal with.'

'I am distressed to hear of this, *signora*.'

Berta smiled serenely and nodding towards Massoud, she continued. 'With the help of my trusted friend here, the debts have all been dealt with. Massoud has been most loyal and inventive and we will be in a good position once the fleet my husband built up has been sold. That, and our house, of course – for the *palazzo* must be sold too. Then I shall be in a position to move forward with my life and dedicate myself to the one thing that has been my life-long passion – our great city of Pisa.'

'Your house! But *signora*, the *palazzo* of Lorenzo Calvo and Berta di Bernardi is legendary – it is one of the most beautiful houses in the city.'

'Indeed, Signor Vernacci. It is a beautiful house – an elegant building that gave us great pleasure… and now it will give pleasure to others. That is the nature of buildings, is that not true?'

The *Operaio* nodded as Berta continued:

'The important thing is that the members of my household will be secure. Massoud once again has excelled himself and everyone has been found another position – many with my friends and relations. I will maintain a small retinue of course; Massoud here has generously agreed to stay with me, for his counsel is invaluable. So I will not be abandoned. And there will be enough money, I am glad to say, to pay for a house or apartment – and that, *signore*, is partly what has prompted me to come here today. I would like to ask you, as head of the Opera del Duomo, if it would be possible to rent one of the Opera's apartments here on the Piazza; I know that granting such a request would be within your gift, and I would take it as a huge kindness were you to afford me the opportunity to live in the confines of the Piazza del Duomo. It would be such a comfort to know that although I have lost my husband and my home, I could wake up every day within sight of the most beautiful cathedral and baptistery in the whole of Italy.'

Berta paused, waiting for the *Operaio* to respond. But he said nothing, his face impassive, his long fingers fiddling with the leather box that sat on the table in front of him.

She dropped her voice: 'I have something else to discuss too, before you decide on my request about the apartment.'

Berta felt beneath her cloak, and untied a small linen bag from the girdle that she wore round her waist. It chinked slightly as she lay it on the table in front of the *Operaio*.

'I would like to make you a donation. There are sixty florins here, a sizeable sum. I am offering this gift to you now, on the understanding that it is to be used to buy the foundation stones for the beautiful campanile that I know we both want built here.'

The *Operaio* bowed his head in acknowledgement, and his elegant fingers reached out to touch the bag of coins.

'*Gentile signora*, that is a very generous gift and one which I will need to discuss with my colleagues here. But can I say that, as far as I am concerned, it is an offer that I would be minded to accept. As you know, our finances have been severely stretched by the war with our neighbours over the last decade. And if we are to do God's work and see the new campanile completed, we will need a miracle!' He laughed. 'Perhaps, *signora* - you are that miracle?'

Berta, who had been sitting tense and erect in her chair, relaxed a little.

'But more importantly,' the *Operaio* continued, 'I am distressed to hear of your change in circumstances. This must be a very difficult time for you and, once again, if my colleagues agree, I would be very happy to offer you a home here within the Opera Santa Maria. I know that we have two apartments that are currently vacant; they should provide adequate lodging for you and your household.'

Berta smiled with relief and thanked the *Operaio*. 'I am very grateful to you. There is one other thing that I would like to raise with you. The plans for the tower, the ones Deotisalvi has drawn up. You know I think Deotisalvi is a genius and we are all in awe of his wonderful work. Please do not misunderstand me when I say this – but his design for the tower seems to me to be not quite as spectacular as we might have hoped. You may recall that I think I alluded to this the last time we met; and I also mentioned that I had taken the liberty of exploring one or two design alterations. I have the sketches with me here… if you would like to look at them?'

The *Operaio* motioned towards the table and Massoud laid out the plans for the campanile.

Berta and the Vernacci stood up to admire the drawings. He walked around the table so as better to study them, peering intently at the design. Slowly, a smile spread across his face.

'It is a beautiful building, *signora*; a work of great creativity. Who has designed it? And more importantly, can it work? It looks so delicate; will it stand up?'

'The designer should perhaps remain a secret for now; suffice it to say that it is the work of a new talent in our great city, someone who admires the work of the master Deotisalvi, but has taken pleasure in developing his ideas a little. As for whether it will work… I can assure you that it can and it will, *signore*. I have taken the liberty of asking two experts at the University to check the figures. The workings are all here.'

She motioned to Massoud, who unrolled two sheets of calculations on top of the drawings.

'But Deotisalvi, has he seen all this?'

'Well, *signore*, here we come to the heart of the matter. I thought that if you were minded to assist, we might go together and show him the plans. If you felt that the design was an improvement on the original, I'm sure you would be able to persuade the *Capo Magister* to consider these alterations?'

Berta let her cloak slip off her shoulders onto the chair behind her. She wore a dark red damask dress that showed off her slim waist and white skin. Playing with a long ringlet of her hair, she smiled at the *Operaio*.

'It is, as you have seen, still substantially Deotisalvi's original design. It is round, not square, and still features his idea of the ring of blind arcades at the base and again at the top. This new design simply echoes his original.'

The *Operaio* stroked his long beard and glanced at the widow. She was, he thought to himself, a remarkably beautiful woman.

'It will still be Deotisalvi's commission though?'

Berta smiled and nodded, 'Naturally,' she said.

'And when all is said and done,' Vernacci continued, 'it is he who will be paid – and substantially – for it.'

Berta fingered the bag of coins that lay between them on the table, causing them to clink delicately.

'Well, *gentile signora*,' the *Operaio* said eventually, 'I think some wine is called for,' and he motioned to the page in the corner of the room.

Berta smiled graciously and touched his arm with her fine long fingers: 'I'm sure it is the right decision, *Operaio*.'

Pouring Berta a glass of wine, took her hand and kissed it.

'*Signora*, we will go and see him. Together we will create a fitting monument to the city, to the people of Pisa, and to God.'

CHAPTER 22

June 1999

The Arno glittered, reflecting the thousands of candles decorating the houses on both the north and south banks of the river. Set into tiny glass jars surrounding the windows, outlining the doors, roof lines and balconies, the shape of each house was delineated as if with strings of fairy lights. As Sam gazed out of Adriana's top floor window at the scene below, she thought they sparkled like stars reflected in the river that snaked between them, doubling the effect. Starlight squared, she thought to herself. Far below, on the roads running either side of the river, all traffic had been banned. In its place a constantly flowing tide of people meandered aimlessly back and forth. Families, friends, colleagues all promenading, meeting one another, shouting, laughing, queuing to buy sweet pancakes, burgers, candy floss – sold from brightly coloured stalls, lit up as if at a funfair. Children ran around wearing flashing bunny ears or waving electric wands. Somewhere in the distance a band played, but to Sam, high up on the sixth floor in Adriana's apartment, it was the insistent beat of a bass drum that filtered up over the noise of thousands of revellers on the streets below.

From her vantage point, Sam could see that almost every window on the opposite side of the river was lit up and filled with people having private parties – luxuriating in a sense of superior-

ity over their fellow man. Up here, where the air was clear, free
from the overwhelming scent of cheap sweets and melted sugar
below, Prosecco was being poured into glasses, little dishes of antipasti were being handed round. There was laughter and earnest
discussion. Below, the townsfolk of Pisa walked aimlessly back
and forth calling for their missing children, jostling for position,
sitting on the wide sturdy walls on either side of the river, their
plastic glasses filled with beer and wine.

As Sam looked down onto the crowds, a line of young people
– students at the university perhaps – snaked in a conga through
the crowds.

Dario tapped her shoulder and proffered a bottle Prosecco. 'A
little more, Sam?'

'Mmm… yes please, it's delicious. Thank you, Dario.'

'Having fun?' he asked.

'Absolutely,' she said. 'I've never seen anything like it; it's so
beautiful… the lights reflected on the river, I mean.'

'It is…. glad you came?' he asked her kindly.

'Oh yes – I needed to get away,' she said, thinking momentarily of Michael's one-sided telephone call with Carrie.

Dario had collected Sam at exactly 8.30 from the lobby
of the hotel. She had washed her hair, and put on the new
green dress. She had even tipped her bag out onto the bed and
thrown away the debris of three weeks of living… receipts for
twenty-two breakfasts, pharmacy bills for painkillers, bottles of
sun block, the receipt for her new dress… it all went into the
waste bin. She had shaken the now empty bag over the bath in
a messy cloud of dust and sluiced it down the plughole. And
with a few minutes to spare before she was due to meet Dario,
she had sat quietly on her bed, collecting her thoughts. She
did not know what was going to happen to her marriage. She
felt in a state of almost suspended animation about it. But

she was clear about one thing; she felt no guilt about having a night out.

Once outside the hotel, Dario had taken her arm and guided her through the Piazza. 'There's no point in taking a taxi; the whole town is turned into a... how do you say, pedestrian...?'

'Precinct... pedestrian precinct.'

'Exactly so,' he said. 'I thought we could walk through the Piazza on our way. They sometimes put candles in the windows of the buildings there, so it's worth us looking at that on the way down to Adriana's flat.'

On the Campo, the last halo of the setting sun glowed, blood red on the horizon.

'It's not dark enough to be able to see the candlelight yet – why don't we stop here at Bar Duomo and have a glass of wine?'

He guided her to an empty table outside the bar. 'No,' he said, 'champagne, it must be champagne tonight.'

As they chinked their glasses, the last rays of the sun faded from the evening sky and the white marble of the Duomo glowed softly as the cool pale moon rose above the Piazza. The Tower, by contrast, stood in darkness.

'Normally they would set candles at regular intervals on each level of the Tower – it looks very beautiful. But because of the building work, it has not been possible I suppose.'

'It looks a little spooky,' Sam whispered.

'You think there's a ghost up there?' Dario asked with a smile.

'Who knows... but it's certainly not a happy place.'

'You think? Well that could be because of the work they are having to do to stop it from falling. That huge steel girdle does give it a strange appearance.'

Their champagne finished, they carried on towards the Arno. Down the Via Santa Maria, through the noisy market that had been specially set up for the two-day holiday. There were the usual stalls selling cheap shoes, plastic toys and hideous china. Sam wondered at the Italian's love of tat.

'Dario, for such a stylish people, I don't understand how you can put up with all this rubbish.'

He laughed. 'The Italians are a people of conflicting characteristics. We love children, but increasingly people only have one child per family. We are incredibly good at designing cars and furniture, but most Italians own a clapped out Fiat or a moped and fill their homes with cheap tat. On a personal level, the people are the most straightforward and honest you could hope to meet, and yet our country is riddled with bribery and corruption at the highest level. Welcome to Italy.'

Nearer to the river, the crowds intensified, and as they got onto the Lungarno, the main road beside the Arno, Sam gripped Dario's arm tightly for fear of losing him in the crowd.

'Don't worry,' he said, 'I won't let you go.' He put his arm round her shoulder and pulled her towards him. They battled their way through the revellers, and across the Ponte di Mezzo, where, incongruously, amidst the partygoers, a group of burly men were setting up a small boxing ring, ready for a match the following day. Sound systems, riggers, all casually getting on with their jobs, while around them people pushed and shoved, eating, drinking, laughing.

Once finally across the Arno, Dario swiftly led the way to Adriana's flat. The main door to the house had been left slightly ajar to save the hostess answering the buzzer to her guests throughout the evening.

So Italian, thought Sam.

The guests at the party were just as Sam had imagined – colleagues of Adriana's from the university, and a sprinkling of journalists and other professionals. Sam soon found herself deep in conversation with a fascinating woman in her mid-fifties. The woman was fascinating.   In her mid-fifties, elegant, wearing a loose white shirt with narrow black pants, she was the epitome of Italian chic.   Her dark wavy hair was tied into an elegant but messy chignon, and on her wedding finger she wore a huge silver ring set with a jet black stone

'My name is Benedetta Gasparello – I lecture in English at the University of Florence. And you?'

Sam, enjoying the moment, chose not to complicate things so early on in the acquaintance by mentioning her sick husband. She said merely: 'I'm Sam. I'm English and here... just visiting Pisa. I came with Dario.'

'How clever of Dario to finally find a suitable woman at last. He's been hopeless, you know... for years. We'd all just about given up hope of him ever finding anyone. He's had the most disastrous love affairs.'

'Oh no,' said Sam hurriedly, 'he's not my boyfriend – we're just friends.'

'Oh,' said the woman, 'just as well for you then, he really is the most frightful mess emotionally.'

'Really?' said Sam, her curiosity aroused. 'Do tell me about them.'

The litany of mad, sad, or crazy women unfolded.

'The problem is', said the woman, conspiriatorily, 'that he is just too kind, too understanding. No one else's problems are ever too much for him. So he's just a sitting duck – is that what you say... sitting duck? – for all these mad women. They are always beautiful though, I'll say that for him. He has great taste.'

The woman smiled at Sam. 'I love your dress by the way... very pretty. Did you get it here?'

Dario moved towards them, holding a bottle high above the guests' heads.

'Now Benedetta, what are you saying to my new friend? I don't like the way you two have had your heads together for so long. Sam, you must not believe anything Benedetta says to you. She is a witch and tells lies and is not to be trusted.'

Benedetta, laughing, kissed him on the cheek and moved away through the crowd.

'So tell me, what was she telling you?' Dario asked, refilling Sam's glass.

'Oh you know, just boring stuff, like everyone you've been out with for the last twenty years. It's quite a list, Dario,' she said teasingly.

'Mmm,' he replied, 'I know, it's nothing to be proud of. But I've just never managed to meet the right person. I always go into each new relationship feeling hopeful – that this time I've found someone perfect. But then the bad stuff starts: they get hysterical if I have to work late, or they turn out to be emotional wrecks, and the whole thing falls apart.'

'Oh my god,' said Sam, suddenly worried, 'that sounds like me… I think I might be a bit of an emotional wreck.'

'Well, yes and no,' Dario was gently reassuring. 'Because first, you are not an emotional wreck at all, you are just in the middle of a difficult emotional time that, really, is not actually of your own making. And secondly, we are not going out together… are we?'

He looked deeply into her eyes.

'Aren't we?' Sam asked, faintly surprised at her own candour.

The question hung in the silence, unanswered, until Adriana arrived with Benedetta, clutching a bottle.

'Come on you two', she said, filling their glasses once again, 'stop gazing into each other's eyes and come and meet some new people.'

The couple were parted; Benedetta steered Dario towards a doctor from Milan, while Adriana introduced Sam to a couple who both worked at the local TV station, but spoke little English.

'*Caro*,' Adriana said expansively, taking the man's arm and handing him the bottle of Prosecco, 'meet Sam, she's Dario's new girlfriend and knows no one.'

The couple smiled and shook her hand. Sam, embarrassed at the introduction, did not have a sufficient grasp of Italian to correct the mythology that had developed around her relationship with Dario. So she smiled back, and together they stumbled their way through a stilted conversation about their mutual experience of the TV industry, while her Italian companion replenished Sam's glass at every inevitable pause in their conversation. Sam began to feel a little woozy and started to look around desperately for a plate of antipasto, realising that she had drunk far more than was good for her.

She was rescued by Adriana arriving with a bowl of pistachio nuts which she handed to her guests. Sam took a large handful. '*Venite, venite, tutti,*' Adriana announced loudly over the hubbub in the crowded room, '*i fuochi cominciano!*'

Dario worked his way back to Sam. 'Fireworks, they're starting now, it's midnight.' He whispered in her ear, 'There won't be room for everyone here to see them properly. Adriana's windows are not that big. Let's go down onto the street.'

And he pulled her towards the door.

'Shouldn't we say goodbye?' Sam asked.

'No, it's fine. Adriana won't even notice we've gone. Come on.'

Down on the street, there was an air of expectation amongst the crowd. Within thirty seconds of them arriving at ground level, the first firework ripped through the sky and exploded into thousands of scarlet stars. As wave upon wave of fireworks erupted, Sam stood close to Dario, her arm linked through his.

Occasionally, as a huge firework exploded with a bang, she hid her face in his sleeve. As the display crescendoed, with a spectacular three-minute finale of silver stars, the crowd whooped and cheered.

And then it was over. The crowd began to move almost immediately, heading home for the night. A huge wave of people surged towards the Ponte di Mezzo, heading north across the Arno. Caught up in the melée, Sam lost her grip on Dario's arm and he was pulled further and further away from her across the bridge. She saw him turning round to look for her, but he was unable to fight his way back. She pushed forward determinedly but lost sight of him and found herself heading up towards Piazza dei Cavalieri. The grandiose Renaissance square was filled with yet more market stalls selling yet more tat – anything from Indian kaftans to cheap men's shoes. Disappointed to have lost Dario, she distracted herself by idly rifling through the multicoloured outfits in front of her. As she fingered a delicately embroidered turquoise kaftan, she heard a familiar voice.

'That would suit you very well.'

'Dario!' she turned and saw his smiling face and excitedly threw her arms round his neck.

'I thought I'd lost you forever.'

'No, never forever. Just for a few moments.'

And there, in the square, he kissed her.

CHAPTER 23

November 1171

Berta's move to the apartment within the confines of the Opera Santa Maria went without a hitch. Most of her staff had already moved on to other positions, so it was a small group of people who walked out of the front door of the *palazzo for* the last time. Giuseppe had gone on ahead with the cart, making several trips back and forth with the household items that his mistress was moving to the new house. Her bed, and the chests in which she kept her precious clothes and other personal items, were all to be taken – as was the glassware that Lorenzo had brought back from Syria, along with pots, pans and her collection of majolica dishes. The long serving table from the dining hall was too large to transport, and so had been sold with the house. But the tapestries, bedcovers and wall hangings were carefully packed and moved across the river to decorate the new apartment.

Massoud stopped when the party was halfway across the Arno and stood gazing at the *palazzo*.

'Don't look back, Massoud… never look back,' said Berta. 'We are going forward… I cannot wait to get to our new home.'

It took several days to arrange the apartment to Berta's satisfaction. Massoud was dispatched to buy a new smaller table and chairs for the dining hall. The chests, and other smaller pieces of furniture that she had brought with her from the *palazzo* were all moved from room to room until Berta was happy with their final position. The room she had chosen for her bedchamber was on the top floor, from which she had a spectacular view of the Piazza del Duomo.

'I shall be able to fall asleep each night gazing at the buildings I have spent my whole life studying,' she said to Massoud.

The previous inhabitant of the apartment had been a solitary man who had done little entertaining. The kitchens were consequently sparsely furnished. The first time Maria lit the fire in the big kitchen fireplace, the room filled with acrid smoke. After much prodding and rodding of the chimney, an old bird's nest was finally dislodged, bringing down decades' worth of dust and debris. Once swept, the fire drew well and Maria organised the kitchen, arranging the utensils and pots on shelving on either side of the fireplace. With no kitchen staff at her disposal, she needed everything to be easily to hand. When finally the new kitchen was cleaned and tidy, she sent out for supplies – fresh white bread, a tray of fresh vegetables and two plump chickens that she plucked and boned at the kitchen table.

Berta was delighted with her new home. Her bedroom had an outdoor loggia that provided a perfect vantage point for observing progress on the Piazza del Duomo and she spent many hours each day, wrapped in a fur blanket, sketching and reading, enjoying the sensation of the winter sun on her face. The slight swelling in her abdomen grew almost imperceptibly each week. On her first night at the new house, she lay in bed, gazing at the Duomo in the moonlight, her hands resting on her stomach, and thought of the child that she was carrying, aware of a tiny fluttering sensation beneath her fingers.

There had been no word from Gerardo, but learned that the *Operaio* had received a letter from Deotisalvi telling him he would be returning to Pisa with his young assistant at the end of the week.

Berta sent Giuseppe to Gerardo's house with a note inviting him to visit her in her new apartment on the day he returned. That evening, she dressed in the pale lilac gown that she had last worn for their assignation at the little *cassetta*. Berta had asked Maria to prepare an intimate supper for two – *limonia*, a delicate dish of chicken cooked with lemon and almonds – and had a table set up in the corner of her bedchamber so they could dine admiring the fine view of the Duomo. She sat on the loggia, wrapped in her blanket and waited for him to come, but he did not appear.   Disappointed, she sent the chicken back to the kitchen and took herself miserably to bed.

She woke the following morning very early. The sun was just rising over the Duomo when she called for her maid.

Aurelia, who slept in a room down the corridor, was deeply asleep and dreaming of Gerardo when she heard Berta call. Pulling on her dress over her shift, she ran into her mistress's room.

'What do you need, *signora?*'

'Some breakfast – bring it up to me here, would you please. And lay out my green damask dress. I have to go out this morning.'

As the Duomo struck the morning Angelus, Berta, wrapped in a warm velvet cloak, walked briskly to the building site at the tower of San Nicola. Gerardo was there, organising the men, who by now had now finished the foundations. They were laying out samples of marble on the ground to allow it to weather over the winter.

'Gerardo,' she called out as cheerfully and casually as she could, 'you have returned.'

As he looked up, she thought she detected a faint air of irritation in his manner. But he swiftly finished his conversation with one of the masons and came over to Berta.

'I am so sorry; I got your message very late last night. The *magister* and I returned well after nightfall, but it was too late to visit you then. How are you, *signora*?'

Berta took his arm and guided him to a quiet corner of the building site.

'Such formality, *caro*. I am well. But there is so much to tell you, so much has happened since you went away. As I wrote in my note to you last night, I have sold the *palazzo*, and moved to a wonderful apartment owned by the Opera Santa Maria on the Piazza del Duomo. It is perfect, and I can watch how the Duomo and Baptistery progress from my balcony.'

A little nervous, she found herself prattling. 'I cannot think why Lorenzo and I did not build our house there at the start. And I have dismantled the business. I am free of it at last, free to pursue my own ambitions. Oh, and there are one or two other bits of news, but they can wait until we are alone. I have missed you, Gerardo, we have missed you.'

'And I have missed you too. May I visit you this evening?'

'Of course. Come as soon as you have finished here. Will you dine with me? There is so much to talk about.'

'It will be my pleasure,' and he kissed her hand, before returning to his work.

When Berta returned, Aurelia was filled with curiosity as to her mistress's early morning appointment.

'Did you have a good walk, *signora*?' Aurelia asked as she took Berta's cloak.

'I did, Aurelia, thank you.'

'Where did you go?' Aurelia asked innocently, as she removed Berta's linen cap.

'It is none of your business, but if you must know, I went to the church of San Nicola. Gerardo has returned from his travels with Deotisalvi.'

At the mention of his name, Aurelia dropped the linen cap on the floor.

'Pick it up, Aurelia… it will mark if you are not careful.'

'Sorry, *signora*.'

As she put away clothes and tidied the bedchamber, Aurelia wondered how she too might be able to visit Gerardo. The solution soon presented itself.

'It has been a while since you saw your mother, Aurelia. Why don't you go and see her this evening. If you like, you may stay with her tonight. I am sure she'd enjoy your company.'

Aurelia was delighted. 'Thank you, *signora*. I am so grateful.'

For the rest of the day, Berta sat, as usual, on the loggia, sketching and reading. Aurelia helped Maria in the kitchen, who taught her how to pluck a pair of little quails that she was preparing for Berta's supper. As the Duomo struck three bells, Berta asked Aurelia to lay out the lilac gown and bring some water to her chamber so that she could bathe. Excited at the thought that she might see Gerardo later that evening, Aurelia went happily about her work, washing her mistress's hair, laying out her clothes and jewellery.

'You are cheerful this afternoon, Aurelia…' Berta said, as she lay languorously in her bath.

'I am, *signora*… I am excited to be seeing my mother,' said Aurelia hurriedly.

'I'm delighted to see such devotion. She is a fine woman and deserves your love. You blush, Aurelia… are you sure it is just your mother that excites you so?'

'Of course, *signora*,' Aurelia said quickly. 'Should you not get out of the bath now, *signora?* The air is turning cool and you might catch a chill.'

By early evening, Berta was dressed and sat once again on the loggia.

'Thank you Aurelia, You may go now. I hope you have a pleasant time with your mother this evening.'

Aurelia nodded and made to leave.

'Oh, and Aurelia… I have a note here that I would like you to take to your mother; would that you do that for me? Perhaps you will bring back her answer when you return tomorrow?'

The girl took the note reluctantly, slipping it into the sleeve of her dress.

'Be sure to bring back your mother's reply, won't you?'

Berta, convinced that Aurelia intended to meet with Gerardo herself that evening, was determined that she should visit no one but her mother. Gerardo would be sharing supper with her on her loggia soon, and her little maid would be safely ensconced in her mother's kitchen. But it aggravated her that she should have to stoop so low. She had never concerned herself with rivals before. But this girl, she knew, mattered to Gerardo, and that, if she was honest, disturbed her a little.

Aurelia, went to her room. She took the note from her sleeve, intending to read it, but Berta had sealed it carefully. Frustrated, she put it on the table next to her bed and changed into the blue dress, recently purchased for her by Berta. Aurelia knew that she should have been grateful to her mistress for this generosity. The dress was a beautiful colour, similar to that of a duck's egg, and made of the softest wool. And yet she could not feel genuine gratitude, for she knew that the dress was merely a reminder of her true position. She was Berta's maid; she must look clean and tidy, nothing more. No silk, or brocade for her. Nevertheless it was the best dress she owned and she would wear it to visit Gerardo that evening.

She brushed her hair and tied it up into two coils at the side of her head. Taking her cloak from the hook on the door, she left the apartment, forgetting the note intended for her mother. For she did not, of course, go to her mother's house, but went straight to visit Gerardo. Standing anxiously in the lane outside his house, she was relieved when the page Antonio opened the door.

'Is Gerardo here?'

The boy showed her inside. Gerardo was standing at the old stone sink at the back of the kitchen, his shirt discarded on a chair, washing the dust from his face and hands.

'Little flower, here you are.' He wiped his hands and face with a towel and pulled his shirt over his head before drawing her towards him and kissing her on both cheeks.

She looked a little pale, he thought, as he held her face in his hands. He sensed her waiting, wanting him to kiss her as she gazed up at him. But knowing he would be seeing Berta later that evening, he resisted the temptation.

'Let us go upstairs,' he said.

The sitting room of the house was sparsely decorated. Scarecely used, the furnishings were neither luxurious nor especially comfortable. Three high-backed chairs, their seats embroidered many years before by Gerardo's mother, stood in an awkward line with a table set in front of them. The only illumination came from two narrow windows. The fire had been lit earlier in the evening by the page, and the flames cast a warm glow on the otherwise inhospitable room. Gerardo beckoned to Aurelia to sit on the chair nearest to the fireplace. He turned his chair round to face her. Aurelia's gold hair shone in the firelight and her eyes sparkled with anticipation.

'Are you well?' Gerardo asked.

'Yes, yes, I am well. And you?' she replied.

'Yes.'

'And your trip... was it a success?'

'Oh yes,' he replied with enthusiasm. 'Deotisalvi is very pleased. We found the perfect stone for the tower, and I am rather proud to say that it was I who located it; so I have gone up in his estimation.'

Gerardo recounted the tale of their long, arduous journey, and of the conversations he had shared with the celebrated *Capo Magister.*

'The great man was a bit reticent at first, reluctant to talk to me. But as the days went on, he began to trust me, I believe, and to respect my opinion a little more. I am so happy, Aurelia; this is the best thing that could have happened to me. It is what my grandfather wanted for me; and I have Berta to thank for that.'

As soon as the words were out of his mouth, he regretted them. He saw Aurelia's face fall.

'I am pleased for you.' she said curtly. Distressed and disappointed at the mention of her rival, she stood up. 'I ought to leave, Gerardo. I expect you have things to do.'

'Yes, I have an appointment this evening, it is true,' he admitted. 'But Aurelia, my dearest Aurelia,' he stood and took her hands in his, 'I want you to know that nothing has changed. I still feel the same way about you, but I need you to understand that Berta is my patron and I owe a duty to her. You do understand, don't you?'

Guilt began to bubble to the surface, and the happiness and sense of satisfaction he had felt about the success of his visit to Monte Pisano began to evaporate. What was the point of being a professional success when he was trapped in such a duplicitous personal situation? He had never meant to hurt Aurelia, but he could see that the more he tried to tell her that he cared for her, the more confused she became. He yearned to be able to tell her that he loved her, that he would never see Berta again. And yet he knew well that Berta held the key to his future and, much as he hated to admit it, he also found her fascinating, bewitching even.

Aurelia could feel tears welling up in her eyes. She blinked them away. She had hoped Gerardo would feel as she did: that he would be willing to give Berta up. Humiliated and feeling slightly foolish, she pulled her hands away from him and walked quickly to the ladder leading downstairs.

'I must go now, Gerardo; I must visit my mother. I wish you well. I am sure you will be a great success.'

And before he could remonstrate with her, she was gone.

She ran all the way to her mother's house. Alarmed by the violent knocking, Violetta was surprised to see her daughter sobbing wildly when she opened the door.

'Darling child, what is the matter?'

She brought Aurelia indoors and sat her down near the fire. She took her cloak and hung it behind the door. Gently, she placed a little rug around her shoulders and gave her a cup of chamomile tea to drink. Finally, as the girl calmed herself, she told her mother about her secret love for Gerardo.

'*Cara*, I don't know what to say,' her mother stroked Aurelia's tear-stained cheek. 'It is such a difficult situation. Let us consider it calmly. You love Gerardo and you believe him when he says that he loves you. But Berta loves him too and you know that he spends time with her. Do you not think it possible that they are actually lovers?' Aurelia's face went pale. 'And remember, my darling, how alone in the world he must feel. He lost his parents as a child – and now his own dear grandfather, to whom I made a solemn promise to look after his Gerardo. So, perhaps the best way for me, and for you, to help keep that promise is to allow your Gerardo to spend at least some time with Berta. It's surely what his grandfather would have wished, at least for the sake of the boy's career.'

'I know, you're probably right,' wailed Aurelia, pacing angrily across her mother's kitchen. 'But *mamma*, it is not fair. I love him, he loves me and we want to be together. And she is so old, *mamma*, too old for him,' she pleaded. 'He can't really love her; I think he believes he owes her something – for helping him with the job at San Nicola. Why can't he tell her that he really loves me? She'd be upset, but she'd get over it.'

Violetta grabbed her daughter firmly by the shoulders. 'Don't you know Berta at all, child? She is not the kind of person who would let go of someone so easily.' She paused, uncertain whether to continue, 'and there is something else you should know, Aurelia. You may not want to hear it, but it's important.'

Aurelia studied her mother's face anxiously.

'My darling… Berta is with child, and if what you say about their relationship is true, the child may well be Gerardo's.'

Aurelia fell to her knees on the stone floor of the kitchen, screaming and tearing at her clothes. Her mother helped the sobbing child to her feet, and half carried her to a little bed in the corner of the room. She covered her with the blanket made of rabbit fur, which Aurelia had slept under as a little child, and held a tisane of chamomile to the girl's lips.

'There, there, darling… just drink this. We'll work out what to do – you'll see.'

Her mother's soothing words, the hot drink, the feel of the fur beneath her fingers, calmed the girl, and within a few moments she was asleep.

Distressed by Aurelia's sudden departure, Gerardo sat for over an hour staring into the fire. The maid came upstairs and asked if he wanted supper, but he waved her away. He realised, perhaps for the first time, how much Aurelia loved him. He had been stupid… blind to her feelings… and he cared for her too… very much. He remembered the way she had helped him when his grandfather had died. Her selflessness then had impressed him so much. Perhaps, this evening, he should make a bad situation better and tell Berta that their relationship must come to an end. The idea of such an exchange filled him with anxiety. It wasn't so much for the harm it might do him professionally, which was less of a worry now that Deotisalvi had seen him at work and appeared to be convinced, at last, of his worthiness to be his new *lapicida*. No, it was more a sense of unease about the emotional turmoil that would ensue if he deserted Berta now. She would be angry – he knew her well enough now to know that was inevitable. Furious, in a jealous rage even. There would also, of course, be despair. For he knew, in his heart, that she loved him desperately. She had told him as much when they had spent those long nights together.

'I have never known such love as I have with you. You have made my life complete,' she had said.

Wretched with indecision, Gerardo changed out of his work clothes, put on a clean tunic and cloak, and headed along the narrow streets to the Piazza. The sun had set, and a new moon was making its slow climb across the sky as he arrived at Berta's apartment. He had spotted her as he entered the square, standing on the loggia outside her bedchamber, gazing at the Duomo, wearing a velvet cape edged with fur. As he was shown into her bedchamber, she came towards him, her hands outstretched.

'Gerardo – you are here at last. How wonderful to see you.'

She kissed him on both cheeks, and held his face in her long elegant fingers.

'What do you think of my new apartment? Isn't it beautiful?'

He smiled and nodded. 'It is certainly... and what a view.'

Gerardo stood on the loggia and admired the Duomo and Baptistery. Berta joined him, slipping her arm through his.

'These are your buildings, Gerardo; they belong to you and all the other talented men who have helped to create them. They look wonderful from up here, don't they? We must go in and eat.'

Berta shepherded him to the table. 'Now, come and sit down here and have a little wine. I have some news for you.'

Obediently, he sat on a low seat set into the embrasure of the window, with Berta by his side. She placed his hand in hers.

'Gerardo, something wonderful has happened while you have been away on your travels. You know that I have never had children. It was a great sadness to me and Lorenzo, something that we hoped might happen for many years. I tried many remedies over the years: I saw doctors, I prayed to San Nicola for his intervention, and latterly I sought help from Violetta, the apothecary, but nothing seemed to work.'

Gerardo had a creeping sense of unease.

'But now, darling, something remarkable has happened. I am to have a child.'

Berta placed his hand on her belly. 'Here, feel it swelling, growing, beneath your hand... can you feel it?'

Gerardo took a deep breath. 'Berta, that is remarkable. You must be very pleased. It is a gift from God – and of course from your husband before he died.'

'A gift from God... yes... that is what Violetta said too. But not perhaps from Lorenzo. It is very possible, Gerardo, that this is your child, darling, our child.'

Gerardo pulled his hand away.

'You are displeased?'

'No, no, not at all. I am just surprised. It is so unexpected, you know?'

Any thought he might have had of telling her that their relationship must cease... evaporated. He felt a rising sense of panic;

he stood up, awkwardly, and went out onto the loggia, staring out at the Duomo. Berta followed him.

'What is it that you would like me to do for you, Berta?' he asked hesitantly.

'There is nothing that I want from you, Gerardo, nothing at all. Except for your love.'

'Are you sure?' he asked. 'Nothing else?'

'What should I want?' she asked kindly.

'I thought... perhaps... you might want to marry?' he asked nervously.

'I do not think that is necessary, do you? As you say, the child may well be Lorenzo's. I am a widow, with a husband not yet cold in his grave, and I am to have a child. There is no shame in that. But to have your love, Gerardo, that is all I seek, that and your companionship. And then, if we decide to marry, it will be because we wish to... because you wish to marry me.'

And Gerardo, turning back from the Duomo, took her in his arms and kissed her with a passion that had more to do with gratitude and a sense of relief than love.

CHAPTER 24

November 1171

In the weeks that followed Berta's revelation of her pregnancy to Gerardo, she was more content than at any other time in her life. Her new apartment was beautiful and comfortable. Her household was manageable and affordable. There were still debts to be dealt with, but Massoud proved an able negotiator, managing to dispose of cargo, goods and vessels – getting high prices which more than covered the outstanding losses. She spent her days organising her new home, and her evenings sketching and designing. When he had time, Gerardo would come to her, and they made love without guilt or complications. She asked little of him and he grew to love her for it. But above all else, the years of longing for a child were finally over; and whilst she felt a little trepidation at what might lie ahead, she began to understand the overwhelming sense of satisfaction that bringing a child into the world could provide. It was, she realised, the ultimate creation – and as her belly grew, so too did her sense of purpose.

For Aurelia the situation was almost intolerable. She found herself hiding in her room whenever Gerardo visited, often lying on her bed, her hands covering her ears, for fear of what she might hear coming from Berta's private chamber. Her mistress's pregnancy was a visible sign of Gerardo and Berta's relationship, and it was as much as she could do to perform her duties, laying out Berta's clothes, styling her hair, tidying her chamber. She began to spend more and more time helping Maria in the kitchen. The old housekeeper was grateful for her help, being without kitchen maids in the new apartment, but she was mindful too of the young girl's distress.

'Roll this dough for me, Aurelia – there's a good girl. You have lovely cool hands and you're getting quite a talent in the kitchen. You'll make some young man a happy groom one day, you mark my words.' But her kind encouragement only served to aggravate Aurelia's despair and, often as not, she ended up with the young girl sobbing over her duties in the basement kitchen.

Berta chose not to notice nor even acknowledge Aurelia's distress. She was truly happy for perhaps the first time in her life, and refused to let her maid's jealousy spoil her joy. In ignorance of Gerardo's true feelings for her maid, she had no reason to fear that his loyalty was divided, for he, of course, never told her of his love for Aurelia. His sense of duty to Berta had won the day, and believing himself the possible father of her child, he was unable to shatter her illusion that he loved her truly and completely. Instead he had resolved, however much it might hurt Aurelia, to throw himself completely into his relationship with Berta. He was deeply conflicted about this of course, and felt guilty when he caught sight of Aurelia at Berta's apartment. In fact, the time came when he began to hope that she might be out when he arrived, or in the kitchens helping Maria and consequently out of earshot. He left the apartment each morning very early to travel to the site at San Nicola, and thus avoided any encounter, but in the evenings, when he arrived to have supper with Berta, he often caught sight of her tear-stained face disappearing into her room, and this caused him terrible distress. His love for Aurelia had not evaporated – rather it had been suppressed, like an underground spring, that he had to deal with at the site. He knew it could be diverted but then it would bubble up a few feet away. And his feelings for Aurelia were no different. They might be repressed now, but when and where they would reappear was a question for which he had, as yet, no answer.

Berta for her part relished his company, free of any guilt about Lorenzo. As the days shortened and the weather grew colder, in the evenings Berta would sit on the loggia gazing at the Piazza, wrapped in a fur blanket… until Maria or Massoud urged her indoors, for the sake of the child and her health.

But one day, towards the end of November, Berta began to bleed – a small patch of blood soaking into her skirt. She called for Aurelia, who, running into her room, was shocked to see Berta trying to lift her dress over her head, her underskirt covered in blood. Berta, endeavouring to remain calm, lay on her bed and asked Aurelia to fetch her mother. When Violetta arrived, she was alarmed to find the bed soaked in blood and Berta faint and weak. Sheets were changed and the patient was made comfortable, but she had a nagging pain in her lower abdomen. Violetta felt Berta's stomach.

'*Signora*, I fear this is not a job for me. You should be seen by a doctor.'

'But surely we should send for a midwife? A doctor won't come out to a pregnant woman.'

'It is your choice, *signora*, but I think a doctor would be best.'

The doctor arrived later that evening. He was a tall, laconic man – bearded, with grey hair and a greyer face. He was shown into Berta's bedchamber while Massoud and Violetta stood anxiously outside waiting to hear the news. The doctor emerged at last, wiping his hands on a piece of linen cloth.

'I fear the lady has a growth. There has clearly been some disturbance or damage to her uterus… that is the usual reason. I understand she believes herself to be pregnant. I fear that is most unlikely. From what I can see there is no child.'

Visibly shocked, Massoud asked, 'What is to be done?'

'Very little I fear. Your friend here – you are an apothecary, I believe – can administer a poultice two or three times a day to relieve the pain, but the outcome is not at question. In my opinion, your mistress will die... probably within a few weeks, or months at most.'

And proffering no words of comfort, he collected his cloak, and was gone.

Berta lay propped up on pillows. The bleeding had slowed a little, but she was very pale, her skin almost translucent in the candlelight. Violetta busied herself making a tisane of chaste berries, a traditional remedy for menstrual conditions.

'Violetta... the doctor... he spoke to you?'

'Yes, *signora*.'

'Well... tell me... what did he say? He was such a horrid little man, I could not get a word out of him.'

'He fears you may have lost the child, *signora*.'

Berta looked out of the window. 'Is that what he said?'

'Well he said that you were not with child.'

'I see.'

Berta lay still. 'So why is my belly so swollen, Violetta. Please... tell me that. Did he say? I need to know.'

'You have a growth, lady. It is causing the bleeding, I think.'

'A growth. So there is no child then?'

Berta smiled – a wry, small smile.

'No, *signora*... no child.'

She sank back on her pillows, her fingers resting lightly on her belly. It was a position she had often adopted in the previous weeks, as if her hands could in some way touch the child that lay sleeping inside.

'I must have sinned terribly, don't you think... for God to punish me so.'

'Oh *signora*, do not say such a thing.'

'Well, it is God's will if a woman is to carry a child. Isn't that what they say? And if she cannot, that is God's will too, surely? And why would he not allow me to have a child, Violetta? I can only think it is because I have sinned, in my heart.'

A tear began to snake its way down her pale cheek.

'It is not God's will. I do not believe that,' said Violetta firmly.

'And will I die, did he think?'

At this, Violetta's eyes filled with tears.

'I see that I will. Will it be soon?'

'I do not know, *signora*. It is impossible to say.'

'I see, well then I am no different from any other woman.' Berta's voice began to break, 'I shall die, and we do not know when.'

Finally, her composure gave way and she wept. 'Oh Violetta, is there nothing to be done? No treatment he can give me?'

'Nothing, *signora*. But I will be here, and will help you all I can.'

Berta wiped her eyes on the edge of her nightgown's sleeve, and held out her hand to Violetta.

'You have been a good friend to me, Violetta. You have given me so much and I have taken so much from you.'

'No, *signora,* you have given so much to me. You gave Aurelia work in your home, you have recommended friends to seek counsel with me. I am grateful to you for all that you have done.'

'Good, good. Well I am glad. But there is something else that I need you to do for me. Please send word to Gerardo... that I need to see him.'

The bells were tolling the evening Angelus when Massoud knocked on Gerardo's door. It was opened by the page, Antonio.

'Is your master at home?' Massoud asked.

'He is upstairs, *signore.*'

Massoud found Gerardo sitting quietly by the fire, a jug of wine on the table at his side. He was reading by the light of a solitary candle but leapt to his feet as the Moor appeared.

'Massoud, how good to see you. May I offer you some wine?'

'No, no thank you, *signore*. I come with bad news.'

Gerardo gestured to Massoud to sit.

'It is my mistress…' Unable to complete the sentence, he broke down, sobbing like a small child.

Gerardo came to his side. He put his arm around the Arab's heaving shoulders. 'Massoud, Massoud what is the matter? What is wrong?'

'She bleeds, *signore*. The child is gone. She has a sickness; the doctor says it is very bad… that she will not survive.'

'I will go to her,' Gerardo said.

Together the two men ran through the streets towards the Piazza. Arriving out of breath, Gerardo ran up the stairs to Berta's bedchamber. She looked tiny and frail, he thought, lying on the large bed. A lone candle flickered next to her, illuminating her hair, which fell like a red river around her shoulders. Her green eyes sparkled in her pale face.

'Gerardo, *carissimo*, you have come. I am so glad.'

Gerardo knelt beside Berta's bed and took her hands in his. 'Of course I have come. Massoud told me; what is to be done, Berta?'

'Nothing is to be done, darling; there is nothing to do. I am unwell, there is no child, perhaps there never was any child. And at some point I will die. That is all.'

'All! What do you mean that is all? How can you be so calm? Surely there is some treatment that can help you?'

'There is no cure, I believe… But do not weep, Gerardo.'

He lay his head on her breast inhaling the scent of lavender.

'I am not yet finished, Gerardo,' she said, stroking his dark hair. 'Look at me, darling – please. There is still something very important that I want to do before I die… something that matters to me more than anything else, more even than my love for you, my darling. I have a dream… that the people of Pisa will have a beautiful campanile built on the Piazza. I have some money kept safely aside that I have offered to the *Operaio*, to get the tower started. As you probably know, Deotisalvi has won the design contract for the tower, and I would hope that you will be asked to assist him. To have you working with him on so prestigious a building, Gerardo, would make me very happy. We may not have had a child together, but to share in the creation of a tower would be the most wonderful legacy, do you not think? Maybe better even than a child? To leave to the world the most beautiful campanile that was ever built.'

'It would indeed be a wonderful thing,' he said, swallowing back his tears.

'Good,' replied Berta,' we are agreed then.'

The household had been in disarray since the discovery of Berta's illness. Massoud sat inconsolably at the kitchen table, as Maria tried to encourage him to eat her simple supper of roast partridge.

'You must eat, Massoud – you starving yourself to death won't help her now.'

'I cannot eat,' he declared wretchedly. 'I cannot imagine life without *la signora.*'

'Well, you know her – she's strong. Don't despair just yet.'

Aurelia also sat at the table, watching her mother prepare fresh herbs for her mistress. She had seen Gerardo arrive with with Massoud not an hour before and had been upset by his obvious distress. She knew, of course, that he and Berta were lovers, but such tangible evidence of his affection for her had been painful... a shock even.

'Aurelia,' said her mother as she ground herbs in a pestle and mortar, 'I think we should go for a walk in the Piazza.'

'I don't want to walk,' said her daughter.

Violetta shot an anxious glance at Maria.

'Go with your mother,' she said, 'we'll still be here when you come back – and your mistress has no need of you at the moment.'

Wrapped tightly in their woollen cloaks, mother and daughter walked around the Piazza, the Duomo shimmering in the moonlight.

'Aurelia darling,' she said, taking her daughter's arm, 'there is something I need to discuss with you. Berta is not well... you know that. I am sorry to say that she will not survive. It is very sad, of course, but it will be very hard for you, seeing Gerardo with her every day, for he is a loyal friend to her and he will not desert her. Do you think you can bear to see him so often, knowing that he is with her?'

'No. I don't think I could bear it,' she said, dejectedly. 'But what else is to be done?'

'Well,' said her mother, sitting down on a stone bench outside the Baptistery, 'if you will allow, I will speak to Berta about it.'

Aurelia began to protest, '*Mamma*, you can't. She doesn't know about me and Gerardo.'

'I know, perhaps not – although she is more perceptive than you might give her credit for, Aurelia. Let me try at least. If she will agree, I will send you to stay with my sister, Lucia, in Siena. I shall remain here with Berta; she will need me now.'

'But *mamma*... how will you live...? Without all your patients?'

'Berta will take care of us, Aurelia – I'm sure of that.'

The following morning, as Violetta tended to Berta's pain, she raised the matter: 'Mistress, I have a small favour to ask you. I believe that you will need me here to help you over the coming months.'

'I will,' said Berta, 'and am grateful for it. I know it will mean you will have to forgo your other patients, but I hope you know I will be generous. You will not be out of pocket.'

'That is of no importance, but I am grateful to you. No... there is another matter I would like to discuss with you.'

'Ah Violetta – you mean Aurelia.'

Violetta nodded

'Yes,' said Berta, 'I too have been thinking about your daughter. I am not ignorant of the.... feelings that she has for Gerardo, although I do not believe they are reciprocated. I know you all think I am blind to other people's feelings... selfish even.'

'No, *signora*, not selfish ever... no.'

'It's quite understandable. I am, and have always been, strong-willed. And I have become used to getting my own way. Gerardo and I are very close. I love him, Violetta, and it would be better, I believe, for all concerned if Aurelia were sent away.'

'I am grateful to you for your understanding.'

'It is not generosity on my part, Violetta. I need to feel free to love Gerardo without restraint, and having Aurelia here would, I believe, complicate matters. Do you understand?'

'I do, *signora*.'

'Where could she go?'

'To my sister... Lucia. She has a farm just outside Siena.'

'We will send Giuseppe with her.'

Lucia lived on the farm where she and Violetta had been raised. After the death of their parents, Lucia and her husband Guido had taken it over and now earned their living producing pecorino – a sheep cheese, and red wine from the grapes that grew on south-facing slopes surrounding the house. On the ground floor of the old stone farmhouse, below their living quarters, they kept domestic animals: a cow, a pair of goats and four pigs, which wandered inside and out, warming the house above in the long, cold winter months. Outside, sheep grazed in fields on the north side of the farm and dozens of chickens, kept for eggs and the pot, chased around the farm yard, scattering noisily as the children ran amongst them throwing their corn to the ground.

Aunt Lucia and Guido had five children. The eldest girl, Alessandra, was a year older than Aurelia; the youngest, Madelena, was just two years of age. In between were three boys – Paolo, Rafaello and little Fabio.

Aurelia missed her mother, and thought often of Gerardo, but she was distracted by the large family and was relieved to be away from the apartment in Pisa with its ever-present scent of death, and the constant pain of seeing the man she loved caring for another.

She spent most of her days looking after her younger cousins, and, much to the delight of her aunt, even taught the two youngest children to read. When she was not working in the house, she helped on the farm. There was not a lot to do in the winter months, but the vineyards needed pruning – and the hillsides were filled with the smoke from a hundred bonfires. She and Alessandra tended the fires, gathering armfuls of old vines and sweeping them up in tidy piles.

Aurelia grew to love the gentle rolling hillsides, dotted with pale cream stone farm buildings. When she thought back to Pisa, with its tall houses and dark streets, she wondered if she could ever bear to return. She relished her country life, running with her cousins through the chestnut woods or helping her aunt milk the cow stabled under the house. She enjoyed the sensation of the cow's teats between her fingers, and the sight of the frothy milk squirting into the bowl. Lucia taught her how to make cheese and she spent happy hours wandering around the creamery, smelling the curds as they matured in large bowls. She became quite expert at kneading the curds once they had drained through the muslins, pressing them with the cheese 'stone' that had been in Lucia's's family for many generations.

'You have the knack, Aurelia,' her aunt said delightedly.

When the cheese was just twenty days old, it was sent to market and sold as 'fresh' Pecorino Toscana. But a proportion of the cheeses were left to age for four months on the shelves at the back of the creamery, developing a dark yellow flesh and distinctive flavour. Once a week, her uncle brought their produce to the markets of Siena and its smaller neighbour San Gimignano. Aurelia relished these visits as they offered her the chance to help on the stall, and, if sales were slow, to wander the wide streets, studying the buildings and sculptures in the churches, before returning home to the farm, bouncing happily on the back of her uncle's cart, in the wintry setting sun.

Her mother wrote to her as often as her duties allowed. But the letters lacked vital information. She appeared to be deliberately skirting any mention of either Berta or Gerardo, and instead concentrated on idle chatter from the apartment's kitchens: 'Maria's brace of partridge was stolen by the *Operaio*'s dog.' Or 'Giuseppe's horse was lame.' Even when the story related directly to Berta, she avoided mention of her mistress: 'Yesterday we had a visit from the Archbishop. The house was in turmoil, with Maria frantically cooking a vast meal for the assembled company. The Archbishop was accompanied by the *Operaio* and several members of the household of the Emperor Lord Frederico. It was a very splendid affair...' But she made no mention of the lady at the centre of the splendid meal nor, more importantly, of Gerardo.

Aurelia replied to these letters, and her mother was encouraged to hear of the healthy life that she was living. Having been brought up on the farm herself, she could well imagine the wintry picnics in the woods that her daughter shared with her cousins, or the visits to Siena market. She was relieved that her daughter appeared to have taken to country life and, in her heart, hoped fervently that Aurelia had begun to forget the young *lapicida*.

But Aurelia could neither forget, nor completely excise all thoughts of Gerardo and Berta. Late at night, as she lay in her little bed in the eaves of the farmhouse, she imagined Gerardo lying in the arms of her mistress, and wept. And in the darkness just before the morning, if she awoke to the sound of the cockerel in the yard outside, she would wish with all her heart that Berta di Bernardo was dead.

CHAPTER 25

December 1171

With Aurelia gone, Berta was at liberty to love Gerardo, free of any impediment, save the knowledge that their love would inevitably be cut short.

Gerardo was also relieved that little Aurelia had been sent away. For whilst he cared deeply for her, her departure spared him the torment of seeing her hurt and resentful face each time he visited Berta. And visit her he did. Each evening he washed and changed and walked over to her apartment to have supper with his lover. There were times when he left her in the morning, when she would wince in pain, and he would beg her to let him stay with her during the day to care for her.

But Berta insisted that Gerardo continue with his work at the tower of San Nicola.

'I will be fine. It's better that you go, so I can rest. I love to see you each evening. This is such precious time that we can have together, but you must work hard on the tower. I want Deotisalvi to see what a wonderful *lapicida* he has in you.'

Gerardo worked tirelessly at San Nicola, and by the middle of December, they had completed the first storey and were well advanced with the walls of the main part of the tower. Deotisalvi, though permanently bad-tempered, developed a grudging respect for his young *lapicida*.

Berta resolved that until Deotisalvi had agreed to her new designs for the campanile, she would keep her part in them a secret from her lover. If there were to be an argument between herself and the architect about the design of the tower, it would be awkward if Gerardo was caught in the middle, forced to choose between his lover and his employer. It would be hard enough persuading the architect to offer Gerardo the position as his assistant. The new campanile was considered the most prestigious architectural project since the Baptistery, and she had heard from the *Operaio* that Deotisalvi had insisted on total autonomy about the choice of his new team. He was concerned that the tower of San Nicola might suffer if both *magister* and *lapicida* moved on so soon to another job.

Berta, desperate both to persuade the old man to accept her design and also her lover as *lapicida,* requested a meeting with the *Operaio.* Before he arrived, she asked Maria to prepare her a bath. The water was scented with her favourite lavender and she smiled as the old woman poured water through her long hair.

'It has been weeks, since I washed my hair – it feels so good, Maria.'

'I'm not sure we should wash your hair, *signora...* with you being so ill.'

'I must look my best for the *Operaio*,' Berta said as she struggled to get out of the bath. She had lost a lot of weight in the last weeks and when Maria washed her back she could feel her ribs protruding through her pale skin.

Dressed in a dark red damask gown, she sat on one of a pair of high-backed leather chairs that had been placed by the window in her bedchamber.

'Benetto,' she said, as the *Operaio* kissed her hand and sat down opposite her. 'You know that I intend to donate the money for the building of the new tower. But privately, you also know that it is with certain conditions. I want Deotisalvi to make the changes that I have suggested to the design.'

The *Operaio* nodded graciously.

'Now, Bonanno has had them checked with a colleague of his at the school of architecture, and they are confident that the design will be feasible from the point of view of stability. The tower can withstand the unusual forces involved in my drawings. And, from an aesthetic point of view, you agree, I hope, that the new design is more impressive than Deotisalvi's original.'

The *Operaio* nodded once more.

'So if you, the *Operaio*, believe mine to be the better design, and there is no problem with its stability, the *Magister* must be persuaded to accept it.' She was firm, but cajoling.

The *Operaio* shifted a little uneasily in his seat, imagining the impending confrontation with the great man. 'Er, of course, *signora*. It may be difficult, but I will…'

'I also want you to do something else,' Berta interrupted, 'something almost as dear to my heart as the tower itself. I want you to persuade Deotisalvi to take on Gerardo di Gerardo as his *lapicida*. As you probably know, Deotisalvi already thinks well of him. The old man can easily find someone to replace Gerardo on the San Nicola job, but I insist Gerardo is transferred to work on the campanile.'

Berta, who had struggled to find the strength for the meeting, sank back into her chair, and theatrically wiped a tear from her eye with the back of her hand.

'*Gentile signora*, please do not distress yourself. I am sure we can arrange things to everyone's satisfaction. If I may, I shall arrange a meeting with the *Capo Magister* and, if you allow, explain the situation to him in a way that he will understand. Now you must rest, *signora*; you look tired.'

And kissing her once more on the hand, he took his leave and sent word to Deotisalvi that he required a meeting the following day.

When the old man walked into the *Operaio*'s office, he was surprised to find several members of the Opera present, and with them, Bonanno Pisano.

'What is *he* doing here?' he asked rudely.

'Maestro Deotisalvi, it is good to see you', said the *Operaio* soothingly. Signor Bonanno is here as a trusted friend and supporter of the work of the Opera. Do please sit down.'

The room contained six chairs arranged around a central table. Before Deotisalvi took his seat, he studied the plans that had been laid out; he bristled with irritation.

'What is this? These are not my plans for the campanile. What upstart has dared to meddle with my design?'

The group was silent.

'Was it him?' He pointed at Bonanno.

'He has been involved, yes.'

'How and why?'

'This will be the most important structure our city has built since the construction of your Baptistery, an architectural jewel admired by all,' cooed the *Operaio*. 'But, regarding the *campanile*... on reflection... the committee...' he was beginning to hesitate now, 'the committee no longer feels that your original design, although of a supreme elegance and graceful simplicity, quite reflects the glory of our great city, the glory that we wish should shine forth from this, our third and final masterpiece on the Piazza del Duomo. We have therefore conceived another design which is a slight emendation of your brilliant original concept of a galleried tower, but which simply adds further open galleries extending up the whole building. It's a practical issue, *Maestro*, and thus no adverse reflection on your design. The committee felt we should have as many vantage points as possible for the notables of our great city to witness the grand civic spectacles we intend to mount in the Piazza, as well of course as to admire the beauty of its buildings, including your own masterpiece, the Baptistery.'

'And you did this without consulting me!' The *Magister* was not to be placated so easily. 'And who did the new drawings, I'd like to know. Who has prepared the calculations?'

The group looked towards Bonanno Pisano.

'What him, the sculptor! The bronze foundry man!   You trusted him with this work?'

'No, well not exactly,' said the *Operaio* apologetically. 'The design was the inspiration of several people, people who care desperately that it should be the crowning glory of our wonderful Piazza del Duomo. Maestro Bonanno was responsible for ensuring that the calculations were satisfactory.   He has been working closely with the staff at the school of architecture here in Pisa.'

'He did not see fit to come to me with these calculations then?'

'Well, we felt it was important to ensure that the workings were correct before we spoke with you. Signor Deotisalvi, I realise that this is a little unorthodox, but I want to make something clear. This is the design that the City would like to proceed with. But it is you that we would like to employ to build the tower; you who will receive the glory and the very handsome fee that the city is able to offer. In that context, you should be aware that we have been made the recipients of a very generous bequest which has enabled us to get started on the project. But the bequest has been made on the condition that we proceed with this particular design.'

The room went silent.

'I will not do it,' Deotisalvi erupted. 'I will not pass off someone else's work as my own. It is not my design. Get Bonanno here to build it for you.'

He stood to leave.

'*Maestro*, listen,' pleaded Vernacci. 'Are you telling us that you would pass up the opportunity to build the most spectacular tower that has ever been created for the sake of wounded pride?'

Deotisalvi considered. He sat down. Then he stood, and studied the drawings once again. 'Where are the calculations?'

Bonanno hesitantly handed him several sheaves of paper, covered in figures.

'These are not correct. I see several errors already. I shall work on them.   Good God – why did you not come to me before wasting time with this? I shall prepare the calculations; and there may be one or two alterations. Design is not just a matter of drawing pretty pictures, you know; it is a deeply complex business of mathematics. And unless the calculations are perfect, the building cannot succeed.'

The *Operaio* bowed to the old man. 'Signor Deotisalvi... we are once again in your debt.'

Later that evening, Vernacci visited Berta. She was seated in the high-backed chair, her back to the window, framed by a stunning vista of the Piazza. On the small table next to her lay the bag of coins that she had promised the Operaio.

'Deotisalvi has agreed to the design, *signora*; he will make some adjustments to the calculations, but essentially it will be the design you have put forward.'

Berta reached across the table and pushed the bag of coins towards the Operaio..

'*Gentile signora*... we are all most grateful, and are in your debt'.

'What about Gerardo?' Berta asked anxiously. 'What did the old man say of him?'

'One thing at a time, *signora*, one thing at a time. You must trust me in this.'

In the weeks that followed, the design was finalised, the calculations perfected and Deotisalvi, as is the way with some men, began to believe the design was in fact his own. But Berta fretted about Gerardo's involvement. She had raised the subject with the *Operaio* on two occasions, but each time he had prevaricated. Deotisalvi, it seemed, had plans of his own. She tried to keep the issue a secret from her young lover when he came to her each evening, but one night, when pain had tormented her throughout the day, she broke down.

'I cannot get that old man to agree to you working on the campanile. It is not fair. I have made it possible. It is my money they will be using. I have insisted. But he is stubborn. I hate that old man.'

Gerardo tried to soothe her. 'Berta, you have done so much for me already, but perhaps you cannot make this happen. And maybe it is better that you cannot do so. I must win the position on my own merit, and not because you will it so. I hear Deotisalvi is asking for *lapicida* to present themselves to him and the *Operaio*. I shall apply with the others, and let us see if I can win this job for myself.'

Over the next few weeks, Berta helped Gerardo put his ideas together for the interview. He was amazed at the immense knowledge of architecture she displayed. Under her tutelage, he studied designs of other towers, and those of Deotisalvi's Baptistery. She challenged him about technical issues to do with the build, quizzing him about foundations, soil structure, stonework and construction techniques. Finally, she was confident that he was as well prepared as he could ever be.

When the day came for him to meet with Deotisalvi and Vernacci, he left her bed, kissing her lightly on her forehead, and was gone before she woke.

She was out of bed when he returned that evening, sitting by the fire.

'Well?' she asked when he arrived.

'I do not know. I think it went well enough, but they are seeing many others before making up their minds. I must just wait.'

The days of waiting turned into weeks, and still no word came from the Opera committee. Berta, weakened by her illness, could contain her anxiety no longer. She sent for the *Operaio*.

'You must tell me Benetto... is Gerardo di Gerardo to be *lapicida* on the tower. I am ill, I may die at any time, and I must know.'

'*Signora*, we have two more *lapicida* to meet tomorrow, and then we shall make our decision. I promise, we shall send word as soon as we have a final decision. It will not be long.'

Two days later, Gerardo returned home from work to wash and change. As he opened the door, the maid Fabricia motioned upstairs.

'There is a gentleman waiting to see you.'

Fearful that it might be bad news of Berta, Gerardo bounded up the ladder.

Sitting in a chair by the window was Benetto Vernacci. He stood as Gerardo entered, smiling and holding his arms out to the young man.

'My dear Gerardo,' he said, embracing him, 'I have some excellent news for you. You have been chosen, from amongst fifty highly qualified candidates, to be the *lapicida* and assistant to Deotisalvi on the new campanile. Congratulations.'

Before he left home that evening to visit Berta, Gerardo took down a box of jewellery that his mother had left to him. He took from the box a small ring his father had given her. It was made of pearls and rubies and she had worn it only on special occasions, fearful that she might lose a stone from the setting.

He bounded up the stairs to Berta's bedchamber. She was sleeping when he entered. Violetta was seated next to her and she quickly stood up, putting her finger to her lips as he approached her.

'Shhh… she is sleeping. She has been in terrible pain today, Gerardo. I will leave you with her, but please do not upset her.'

He sat next to Berta's bed, holding her hand in his, and as she slept, he slipped the ring onto her finger. Watching her sleep, he was struck by how pale and thin she had become; her collarbone protruded sharply beneath the fine, translucent skin at her neck, the small gold cross nestling in the little hollow at the centre. He followed the rise and fall of her chest as she breathed. He sat in silence for what seemed an age. Finally she woke, her eyelashes fluttering as she focussed on the face of the man by her bed.

'*Caro*, you are here.'

'I am, *cara*. I am here, and I have good news. You are looking at the new *lapicida* on the campanile at the Piazza del Duomo.'

Laughing, she pulled him towards her with her thin arms and hugged him.

'I am so proud of you, so proud. You have made me so happy.'

'Marry me, Berta, marry me?' And Gerardo kissed the ruby ring that he had placed on her finger.

Seeing the ring, she held her hand out and let it sparkle in the evening light.

'How pretty, is it for me?'

'It was my mother's. My father gave it to her before he died.'

'And now you give it to me before I die,' she said.

'Don't say that, Berta, please. Marry me.'

'No, Gerardo. We are not destined to be man and wife. I am not your destiny. There is someone else who will have that pleasure when I am gone. I have everything I want with me now. I need nothing else. You will be a wonderful *lapicida*, Gerardo; you will be written about in the history books. And you will marry… to someone young who will give you children and make you happy… Aurelia perhaps?'

Gerardo blushed.

'Ahh, so you do still care for her. That is good. For I am sure that she still cares for you. You have been so good to me, Gerardo, and I do not like to think of you left alone when I am gone. You may not love Aurelia as you love me, but I feel sure that with time you will love her with all your heart. You have such a great capacity for love Gerardo, and I know Aurelia will return that love. Give the ring to her, Gerardo. It is a ring for a wife, from a husband. I have had rings and have no need for them anymore.'

And kissing the ring, she handed it back to Gerardo, who closed his fingers tightly around it.

'Now,' she said, 'there is something very important that needs to be done. I must make a will. Please send for Massoud. And Gerardo, stay with me. I would like you to be a witness.'

And so Massoud was sent for and dispatched to bring back three further witnesses, along with Benetto Vernacci, the *Operaio*, and the Lord Archbishop Villani. He arrived within the hour, bringing with him the notary of the Emperor Frederico, a man named Ugoni.

'*Signora*, I hope you will allow that I have brought Ugo Belacto with me. He is an excellent man and I would like this important moment witnessed by someone who we might all consider impartial. I trust that is to your satisfaction.'

Berta nodded, and Massoud bowed deeply and showed Ugoni to the desk in the window. Parchment and a pen were laid out ready for him, a candle flickering nearby, for the hour was late and the light was already fading. And there, in the gathering darkness, the light from the solitary candle falling on the assembled group in Berta's bedchamber, she dictated her last will and testament:

'In the name of our Lord Jesus Christ, Eternal God, in the year from his birth 1172, 9th January. I am Berta, heiress of Calvo and daughter of Bernardo. I give and dispose of my things in the following manner.........'

The will was witnessed and signed by all those present, and the important work over, Massoud, Ugo and the rest took their leave. But Gerardo remained. He lay with the lady that night, and every night until her death, holding her closely, thinking of the love she had shown him, cradling her in his arms and inhaling the scent of lavender on her skin. Until, one morning in early March, her pain having been relieved the previous night by Violetta's tender work, he woke to find her skin cold and pale, her hair spread out on the pillow like fire... and he wept for the woman he had loved and lost.

CHAPTER 26

June 1999

Sam woke early riddled with guilt. It had only been a kiss. But it had been a long, passionate kiss.

Sharp light glinted through the crack in the curtains and she fumbled for the glass of water by her bed. Draining it in one gulp, she mentally totted up how many glasses of champagne and Prosecco she had drunk the evening before. She had been overtaken by a devil-may-care attitude after the first glass in the Bar Duomo, knocking each one back with something akin to abandon – to blot out, she realised, the memory of Michael's phone call with Carrie.

'What was I thinking?' she muttered out loud, as she staggered to the bathroom.

There, sitting on the edge of the bath, her throbbing head in her hands, she stopped counting when she had got to thirteen glasses. She tried to recall if she had eaten anything; a couple of antipasti and a handful of pistachio nuts were all she could remember. She began to piece the evening together, and blushed with embarrassment when she remembered an excruciating conversation she had had with the Italian couple who worked in TV. Unable to speak each other's language, the conversation was pretty stilted, but it took a turn for the worse when she realised they believed she was Dario's girlfriend. Unable to deny it satisfactorily she'd spent the rest of the evening looking round wildly for Dario to come and rescue her. Hardly surprising that she grabbed every glass of wine offered to her.

She had a vague memory of a mishap on the stairs. She re-ran the whole episode, recalling having drunkenly tripped over, nearly falling down one entire flight, saved only by Dario. He was walking down ahead of her and had heard her gasp of surprise as she slipped. As he caught her, he had held her in his arms; she had been laughing, with a combination of fear and embarrassment, grateful to be saved. As he checked she was unhurt, he had stroked her hair and face; it was sweet… touching even… but, she realised now, a precursor to something else.

'Stupid girl,' she said out loud to herself in the bathroom mirror. Dark rings circled her bloodshot eyes. She splashed water on her face and brushed her teeth.

She slowly replayed the kiss in the Piazza dei Cavalieri. She had to admit she had enjoyed it. It was romantic, exciting even. They had walked slowly back to the pensione, his arm wrapped round her shoulders, her head tucked neatly against him. He stopped a couple of times and kissed her again, at one point leaning her up against a wall in a narrow lane. There was a faint stench of rotting food and debris, the lane was dank and dark, but all she was really aware of was the gentle lemony scent of his aftershave and the sensation of his mouth on hers.

At the door to the pensione, he made to come inside with her.

'No, Dario – I can't… not yet.'

'No, of course. I'm sorry. It's been lovely,' he said, kissing her gently on both cheeks.

'It's just a bit soon, and well – you understand, what with my husband and…'

'It's fine. I totally understand. Can I see you tomorrow? We could go to the boat race together.'

'Yes, that would be great – thank you.'

She showered, standing for a good ten minutes under the hot water, switching the control from hot to cold to 'shock' her system awake. Wrapped in a towel, she applied some tinted moisturiser to cover up the dark circles and gulped down six glasses of water. She dressed in shorts and a T-shirt, and headed out of the hotel across the Piazza, picking up her usual two coffees and brioches at the Bar Duomo.

Michael smiled his familiar lop-sided smile when she walked in and held his hand out to her.

'Darling, thank God.'

As she kissed his prickly face, she noticed tears in his eyes. Putting the coffees down on the side table, she sat down on the edge of his bed.

'I'm sorry I'm so late… I had a bit of a lie-in.'

'Was it fun?' he asked.

'Oh, it was fine. The lights were very twinkly, the fireworks were noisy, you know, firework-like! The party was OK; there were some interesting people there, I met a couple who work for Italian TV; but it was all quite hard work because my Italian is not great, as you know.'

Michael pulled her hand to his mouth and kissed it.

'I'm so sorry, darling. I hope you know that. It's over… the thing with Carrie. I told her last night. It's finished. I know that now. It's you I want.'

She smiled ruefully, an image of Dario floating into her mind. 'Oh, good.'

'You don't sound very pleased.'

'Of course I am, Michael, of course. But it's not that simple, you know. You don't just go "sorry" and it's all done and dusted. You slept with her. It's not nothing.'

'I know. But it was a fling. You must understand. Men do that sort of thing sometimes. You know that. It didn't mean anything.'

'Does she know that?' Sam asked as she crossed over to the window. She could just see the Arno glittering in the sunshine.

'Yes, I told her yesterday – on the phone.'

'How did she take that?'

'Not well... obviously, but she'll get over it.'

'Nice,' Sam said.

'Darling...' Michael stretched his hand towards hers, but she pulled back.

'I've got to go out now, Michael. I'm going to look at the boat race. They do it in medieval costume and it might be useful research for the film.'

'I thought you'd be pleased,' he said.

'What? That you've dumped the girlfriend? And you think that everything's OK now – is that it? Good old Sam will forgive you and everything will go back to normal? It doesn't work like that, Michael. I'll see you later,' she said from the doorway.

She had arranged to meet Dario at the café on the Piazza. They were going to walk down to the river together. As she wandered through the medieval courtyard that led from the hospital to Via Maria, she almost collided with a young dark-haired girl, rushing determinedly in the other direction.

'*Permesso*,' said Sam politely.

But the girl said nothing, and rushed on.

As Sam mused on this uncharacteristic Italian's rudeness, she realised that the girl was familiar. The picture of a face framed with short dark hair floating down onto the bed the day Michael left home for Italy, filtered into her mind... It was Carrie.

Sam, momentarily disbelieving, turned on her heel and raced after her. An Italian family were just leaving the hospital, filling the entrance hall with their chatter. She pushed past them, just in time to see the lift doors closing. She ran up the stairs – taking two at a time – and along the corridor; Carrie was visible at the other end, just entering Michael's room. She was leaning over Michael's bed and embracing him when Sam arrived, breathless.

'I don't believe it...' said Sam.

Carrie turned round, tears streaming down her face. Michael looked from one to the other, his face registering sheer panic.

'Sam... I didn't ask her to come,' he said at once.

'Right. So what's she doing here then?' asked Sam.

'I don't know, Sam! Carrie, I told you yesterday, it's over. I can't do this.'

'Did you Michael – really?' Sam challenged.

'Yes I promise, Sam. Carrie – tell her please.'

Carrie looked down at her feet, all the while refusing to relinquish her grip on Michael's hand, who was attempting to remove it from her grasp. But she had hold of the hand on his weaker side and he simply did not have the strength. It was almost laughable, and Sam suppressed an ironic smile.

'Well?' she asked Carrie.

'No... he didn't know I was coming – but I know he's glad to see me.'

For the first time since he admitted the affair, Sam actually felt sorry for him.

'Carrie – you have to understand this,' Michael interjected desperately. 'I am not pleased to see you. I'm sorry if you're upset. But it's over – OK? Finished. This was a terrible mistake.'

Carrie dropped his hand and stared at him, stunned.

'OK, young lady… I think you heard him', said Sam, grabbing the girl by the arm. 'Out. Now.'

'No,' said Carrie wildly. 'I love him. I'm not leaving; he doesn't know what he's saying.'

'Oh, I think you'll find that he does, and you are most definitely leaving – now.' Sam pulled the younger woman away from Michael's bedside. But she fought back and slapped Sam squarely across the face.

Sam reeled– more in surprise than pain.

'If you don't leave the hospital this minute, I will have you escorted off the premises.' Sam's voice was firm.

'But… I know he loves me,' Carrie insisted passionately.

'I don't think so,' Sam turned to Michael for confirmation, who fiercely shook his head. 'Good,' she continued, 'so if I were you, I'd get back to the airport and get the first plane out of here.'

The girl looked imploringly at Michael. But he turned his face away from her.

'Just go, Carrie. This was all a terrible mistake,' he said impassively.

Sam guided her out of Michael's room and down the corridor. Once outside in the Piazza, she turned Carrie to face her, holding both her arms firmly. 'Listen to me; this is not a game. He's had a stroke. He's very unwell. He's told me all about you, and as far as he's concerned, it's over. It was a mistake. He's sorry. OK – understand? Now, get in a cab and get back to the airport. I'm sure there's a flight going back to England sometime soon. And don't even think about coming back here. I mean it. I won't be so kind next time.'

Once the girl was out of sight, Sam went back to Michael's room. He looked so terribly distressed, she thought, as she lay down on the narrow hospital bed and put her arms around him.

'It's OK... she's gone. Oh darling, you are a silly boy.'

'I'm so sorry, Sam,' he murmured through tears.

'I know.'

It was five o'clock before Sam got back to the Piazza. She was amazed to see Dario still sitting at the café.

'My God,' she said, 'I'm so, so sorry. Something happened... with my husband, and I couldn't get away. I should have rung you, but... things just got a bit out of hand.'

'It's OK. I hope it's not serious,' Dario said.

'Not really. Just a bit time-consuming. How was the boat race?'

'Much as last year and the year before that. I'm sorry you missed it. It's a lovely sight. Do you want a drink?

'Thank you, just an orange juice. I think I had a bit too much last night.'

'Ah... so it was the booze...' he said, smiling.

'Not exactly, Dario. Oh God... this is so complicated. I think you're lovely. I hope you know that. But it's so difficult with my husband. He's had a fling with some girl, he's now dumped her and thinks everything will go back to normal. But... now there's you.'

'Is there?' he asked.

'Well yes. I mean, I don't go around kissing strange men all the time, you know. I really like you, Dario – you're lovely.'

He took her hand across the café table. 'I think you're lovely too,' he said.

'But my husband has just had a stroke, and whatever else he's done, I owe it to him, to our children, to try to keep it together. To get him home, help him get well. Do you understand?'

'Unfortunately for me, yes I do. I completely understand…
he's a lucky man.'

'Mmm, well I'm not quite sure he'd agree with you about
that.'

They finished their drinks and walked together across the Piazza to her hotel, their hands just touching.

'Can we meet up tomorrow?' she asked. 'There is so much still
to do. We need to get someone to look at those documents that
turned up with the drawing. They appear to be in an old dialect.
Do you understand them?'

'No. They're not Italian, but what looks like a medieval vari-
ant of Latin. I can make out the odd word, but nothing more.
Let me get in touch with the *Operaio*'s office – they're bound to
have an archivist there. Or we could speak to the curator of the
museum. But the *Operaio* would be best.'

'OK, and I really want to meet up with the Professor again
and show him your father's incredible find.'

'Yes, of course; I'll call them both in the morning. You're
right; there's a lot to do, and I have to get back to work at the end
of this week… back to Rome.'

Sam was surprised by her own disappointment. 'Oh, of
course,' she said, 'somehow I just imagined you always being
here.'

He smiled at her. 'Hold that thought,' he said before kissing
her, just once, on her mouth.

'See you tomorrow.'

The archivist for the *Operaio* worked in a set of offices that adjoined the hospital of Santa Chiara, on the edge of the Piazza.
The building formed a quadrangle, with the hospital on one
side and open loggias running the length of the pale terracotta

buildings on the other. Sam and Dario entered the quadrangle through a large archway from Via Santa Maria.

Dappled sunlight filtered onto the open loggia, highlighting the peeling plasterwork and the worn tiled floor. 'This used to be part of the hospital, I believe,' he said. It's where the whole thing started. There is a chapel down here too; the hospital was originally a convent, and the nuns took in patients as part of their Christian work.'

Dario turned left off the loggia into a narrow alley that intersected one side of the quad. Bright sunlight beckoned at the other end, but he stopped halfway along and knocked at an old wooden door, before pushing it open and motioning Sam to follow.

She found herself in a small square room painted entirely in white, with a dark chestnut floor. In spite of the white walls, the room was dark – with just one small window onto the loggia. At the far end stood a simple table, decorated with an old majolica vase, filled with dried flowers. That's certainly seen better days, thought Sam. A crucifix hung above the table, and against the third wall were two simple wooden chairs. After a few minutes, an elegant woman, with dark brown hair, appeared at a doorway in the corner.

'*Buongiorno*,' she said warmly, 'you must be Dario Visalberghi. Please come through to my office. My name is Gina Balzarelli. How may I help you?'

Gina's office was as dark as the anteroom, but much larger. There was an elegant mahogany desk, two guest chairs, and hundreds of leather-bound volumes packed into sturdy dark wooden bookcases which lined the walls from floor to ceiling.

She gestured to them both to sit down.

'Welcome,' she said warmly.

'Oh good,' said Sam, 'you speak English.'

'Yes,' said Gina, 'I worked in London for a while – at the British Library. Now, Dario has told me a little of your interests in our city and its history. He says you are making a film here?'

'Yes,' said Sam, 'that's right. I am making a film about the rescue of the Tower, but we are also interested in exploring more information about "the widow", Berta di Bernardo, who left the money for the tower to be built. I have spoken to Professor Moretti, who has been most helpful to me. He is of the opinion that she was a simple patron of the arts, but I am struggling to find out more about her. A few days ago, some builders found a collection of letters and documents, hidden behind some panelling in an old house on the Arno, which might have been where the lady herself lived. We are not sure. These letters, however, contain reference to the *Operaio*... and Dario and I wondered if you might be interested in them, and whether you had any more information in your records about "the widow".'

'Our records do not go such a long way back, I'm afraid – nothing much beyond the eighteenth century in fact. Record-keeping was not such an exact science before that time. So I am fascinated to see your documents... may I?'

Dario handed over the sheaf of papers and Gina took each photocopy out in turn and studied it.

'They appear to be in some kind of dialect,' said Dario, 'I couldn't quite work out what they were saying.'

'Yes... they are. Which is interesting in itself. Italian as we know it now was not in use before the thirteenth or fourteenth century. These appear to have been written in a Tuscan dialect – based essentially on Latin – that was in use no later than the twelfth century – so that certainly puts them squarely in the time of the widow. She died in...?'

'Around 1172,' said Sam, 'or at least that's when she wrote her will. I have a copy of that too – it's been translated into modern Italian fortunately. I have it here if you'd like to see it.'

'Thank you. I have seen it before of course. Now let's look at these other pieces. They are photocopies. Where are the originals?'

'With my father, Lino Visalberghi, but they are being sent to the university for carbon-dating and restoration.'

'Good. I can see that they must have been very damaged by... what... damp? But some words are still visible fortunately.'

'Yes could read the word "*Operaio*," but we couldn't make out anything else,' said Sam.

'You're right... this is a letter from the *Operaio*. From what is legible, he appears to be offering Berta sanctuary here... in the confines of the Opera.'

'Yes,' agreed Sam, 'we know from her will that she was living in the "house of the Opera Sancta Maria" when she died. What are the other documents?'

'There seem to be some accounts here. There is something that looks like a promissory note. It says: 'I agree to pay sixty soldi paid to the widow.of Lorenzo Calvo'. The signature says Benedette Ugoccio.'

'She left sixty soldi for the tower to be built,' said Sam excitedly. 'Might that be where it came from? It does look as if Berta lived in that house on the Arno. I mean, why else would her letters and documents be found there?'

'That does seem a reasonable deduction,' said Gina, 'but we'd need a real expert to examine these more closely. This last document is quite different from the others. It appears to be a letter. It's quite hard to read.'

'The original was very badly damaged by damp and mould – the ink had almost disappeared,' interjected Sam. 'Dario's father did his best with the photocopy, but I know it's not very clear. Can you make anything out at all?'

'Not much, but this last page has a few words that are intact.'

Gina rummaged in her office drawer for a large magnifying glass and peered intently at the letter, shining her desk light on it. 'I will translate. *More grateful than you could ever know.* I cannot read the next bit... ah, this is clearer... *adore you... pray for you each day. Gerardo.*'

CHAPTER 27

March 1172

The chestnut woods that surrounded Lucia's farm were just coming into bud on the day Aurelia received a letter from her mother telling her that Berta had died, and they would be sending Giuseppe with the cart to collect her and bring her back to Pisa. The days were getting longer, and she relished the feel of the spring sunshine as it warmed her face... and the scent of the apple blossom in the orchards. Aurelia was sad to leave her new family. She had come to love the company of her cousins, and felt a real connection with the countryside around Siena.

'Thank you, Lucia,' she said, as Giuseppe piled her belongings into the cart for the return journey. 'You have been so kind to me, I won't forget you all. One day, I hope, I shall return.'

Back home, Aurelia moved into her mother's house. It felt as if the years spent with Berta had been a dream. She and her mother slipped back into their old routine – her mother prescribing teas and herbal medicines to an increasingly wide circle of customers, Aurelia helping to clean and tidy the house, fetching water from the well in the garden, and collecting herbs to dry over the fire.

A few days after she returned, Violetta handed Aurelia a letter Berta had left for her. She took it into the little garden behind the house and sat on the bench against the wall, near the well, enjoying the spring sunshine. As she broke the seal on the letter, she smelt a strong scent of lavender, and in her mind's eye she saw Berta lying in her bath, her hair fanned out behind her. Inside was a small ring decorated with rubies and pearls.

My dear Aurelia, she read, *when you read this note, I shall be dead. I wish you happiness and success in your life. You are a beautiful girl, and a good one. Be content, for you are about to embark on the most thrilling journey of your life. Gerardo loves you – be assured of that. I know that you love him. Thank you for allowing me to share his love – it has meant more than you can ever know. Take him now, bear his children, and give him the life he was destined to have. Take this ring also, it belonged to his mother and he lent it to me to cheer me before I died. But it belongs to you as of right.*

God bless you. Berta.

Aurelia read and re-read the letter. The gentleness of Berta's tone surprised her, as did her intuitive understanding of the love Aurelia had for Gerardo. But what she found most disconcerting was Berta's insistence that Gerardo returned that love. She had left Pisa four months earlier, convinced that Gerardo truly loved her mistress. To discover now that he had actually loved her all along seemed almost incredible.

Wrapped in a small red velvet bag, nestling in the fold of the letter, was the ring. She removed it and tentatively slipped it on her finger – before quickly removing it again. She took it inside, placing it carefully in the little carved box her father had given her as a small child. Her mother waited for Aurelia to tell her what was in the letter, but the girl hid the note and refused to discuss it. Aurelia appeared cheerful, and over time, her mother wondered if, perhaps, she was beginning to forget Gerardo. But alone at night, Aurelia would take out Berta's letter and read and re-read the words, 'Gerardo loves you', wondering if Berta had perhaps mistaken her lover's feelings. For Gerardo did not come. Each morning, when Aurelia woke, she wondered if today would be the day that he would turn up at her mother's house and declare his love. But each day she was disappointed, and slowly, over time, she began to believe that he did not care for her. She put the ring and the letter back in the box and placed it deep in the bottom of a trunk beneath some winter clothes.   Weeks turned to months and still there was no sign of him.

But twelve months, almost to the day, after her mistress had died, Gerardo came to call on Aurelia. Her mother opened the door, showing him through to the garden behind the house. Aurelia was sitting on a little bench by the well, wearing a warm woollen cloak, catching the last rays of the evening light. She had grown, he realised. No longer the innocent girl, but a beautiful woman. She looked up from her book, her pale face registered shock and surprise, but she nevertheless stood and held out her hand to him – polite, formal.

'Gerardo, how good to see you.'

'And you, Aurelia.'

They sat, silently, next to each other, neither quite sure how to start.

'You are well?' he asked.

'Yes, yes… very well. And you?'

'Yes, I am well.'

'And you are busy? I hear you are to be congratulated on being made *lapicida* on the new tower. You must be very pleased.'

'Yes, it is a great honour. I am delighted. But there is a lot of work to be done on the other tower, at San Nicola, before I can

hand the job over to a new mason – we have found a replace-
ment, a good man, who worked on the Duomo, so I am confident all will be well.'

'Good.'

'And you?'

'Well, not so busy. I am helping my mother of course. But I
have no other occupation, as yet.'

'Aurelia?'

'Yes.'

'Aurelia, I came to you today because I wanted to tell you that
I still care for you.'

'Do you?'

'Yes I do. And I know you must have been very hurt by my
relationship with Berta.'

Aurelia was silent.

'But I could not leave her when she was in trouble. I hope
you understand?'

'I suppose so. But it has been hard, Gerardo.'

'Aurelia... do you think you could care for me again?'

'I have had to learn to live without you. Especially when you
were with her at the end, before she died. It was unbearable.
That was why my mother sent me away. It was the only way I
could cope. Before that, I used to run and hide when I heard you
arriving in the evenings. I only got through it because I knew
she was going to die. It sounds awful to say that now, but I was
happy when she died.'

'I'm so sorry.' Gerardo stared disconsolately at his feet, 'I did
not realise how much I had hurt you.'

'Gerardo, I was in love with you. How did you think I would
feel?'

'Was? So you do not love me anymore?'

'Gerardo, I don't know. I thought after she died that you would come here for me. I've waited over a year, Gerardo. I began to believe you did not love me at all. I didn't know what to think. And now I don't know what I feel anymore.' She stood up and began to pace the garden, the light now fading.

Gerardo followed her, took hold of her arms in his strong hands and turned her towards him.

'Through all the time I was with Berta, I never stopped loving you. You know why I stayed with her at the end. She was dying, and I could not leave her. I cared for her very much, but I did not love her in the way I loved you. Never. I know you cannot understand that, but it is true, Aurelia. And I did not come to you before now because it would have been wrong. Things have happened so fast and I needed time to think it through. Now, I know what I want, and it is you, Aurelia, if you will have me. I would like to think that we could now have the relationship that we should have had from the start.'

'I don't know. I feel so... broken by it all. You broke my heart, Gerardo.'

'Then let me mend it again... marry me, Aurelia.'

She did not give him her answer straight away. Their love, she felt, needed to be tested a little first.

Gerardo began to court her, visiting her at her mother's house each evening after work. Gradually, as she realised his affection was genuine, she began to look forward to his visits, helping her mother prepare special meals for him. Together they walked the narrow lanes near her mother's house, and over time she let him kiss her, feeling herself falling in love with him once again. One evening, as they walked to the tower of San Nicola, she handed him the ruby ring.

'This is for you,' she said.

'How did you get it?' he asked

'Berta gave it to me – she left it to me before she died. You gave it to *her*, Gerardo. I do not feel it's right that I should have it.'

'She meant it kindly,' he said, 'giving it to you. She felt it was a ring for a wife… and she wanted you to be that wife.'

'I know,' said Aurelia, 'but I do not need the ring. I have you now.'

CHAPTER 28

August 1173

Early in the morning of August 9th 1173, Gerardo di Gerardo set off for the newly laid out groundworks of the Tower, just as the sun began to rise. He had woken early, his bedchamber illuminated only by moonlight, filled with a mixture of excitement and trepidation at the task that lay ahead. He walked the now familiar route from his home to the Piazza, pausing to take in the breathtaking sight of the massive Duomo which stood proudly on the Piazza's north boundary. Consecrated some sixty years earlier, but still unfinished, it had been designed by the master architect, Buscheto di Giovanni Giudice, a local man who had a solid architectural reputation for church design. The Duomo, however, was the most ambitious project he had ever undertaken. It was to be unlike any building that he, or any other architect, had ever built. For this was not just a monument to God, it was also a testament to the power of the Pisan people and their well-deserved reputation as a seafaring power. Funded by the shipload of treasure brought back from an expedition to Sicily in 1063, during which they had successfully plundered and defeated Palermo, the Muslim Capital of Sicily, the Duomo was designed to represent the supremacy of Pisa over Italy and that of Christianity over the Saracen world.

Gerardo stood, as he often did, admiring the spectacular marble façade of the church. As a *lapicida*, he was well versed in the myriad techniques of construction and decoration that had been employed in its creation, and he knew well how much extraordinary effort had gone into creating this revolutionary building. The layers of pure white marble interleaved with grey, extracted from the quarries at Monte Pisano, a nod to the traditional Roman style of decoration. The monumental proportions of these vast slabs of marble, chosen with care by the architect and his masons, provided an exciting juxtaposition with the delicate and intricate carvings that decorated its surface. Buscheto was relentless in his search for the perfect raw material. No stone had been left unturned, almost literally: white marble was quarried in Monte Pisano, tufa was transported by ship from Livorno, and limestone brought down the river from Veruca. Even the long-abandoned quarries of Elba were reopened to provide Buscheto with the stone he required – almost all of it transported by sea and brought up the Arno River into the heart of Pisa. Classical monuments plundered from Elba and Sardinia, were shipped back and forth on board galleys ferrying goods and human cargo between Pisa and the southern states of Italy. Re-sited in the Duomo, they added layers of exotic texture to the building.

Buscheto had died many years before, and a succession of *magisters* had taken over the ambitious project. While it was nearing its conclusion, an army of craftsmen continued their work – carving, gilding, and painting. Each time Gerardo visited the cathedral, he saw something new to excite his imagination. The building was one of the first of what would later be referred to as the Romanesque style of architecture – bringing influences from classical Rome, together with those from the Byzantine and Lombard eras, mixed in with Islamic influences. In many ways, the Cathedral was the physical manifestation of Pisan socciety at that time – a melting pot of cultures and peoples. While Gerardo could not perhaps understand the significance of the architectural forces at work in this building, he certainly recognised it as a supreme example of the latest in modern architecture, and was impressed by both the scale and the detail.

He stopped, as he often did, to study a pair of magnificent pillars delicately carved with animals of all kinds, sculpted by the celebrated artist of the day, *Magister* Bonanno Pisano. He found the naive quality of the carvings touching; it was as if Bonanno was telling a story to a child through his work. Entering the Duomo, he admired the work of his own grandfather, old Gerardo. He thought of him, stripped to the waist in the summer months, sweat pouring down his back as he worked. His large hands remarkably deft as they carved and chiseled the stone so delicately. He had been such an important influence on the younger man. He hoped he would be proud of his young grandson today.

Venturing further into the cavernous building, he stood and watched the gilders and painters hard at work in the dimly lit interior. Here and there, he admired the simplicity of the columns plundered from classical sites on Elba and Sardinia many years before. It thrilled him to think of these pieces, perhaps more than a thousand years old, still fulfilling their purpose – but instead of decorating a Roman monument, they were now supporting this most modern and exciting of buildings; a building which was designed to demonstrate the supremacy of Pisa amongst all the city states of Italy. He was reminded of his other grandfather Carlo Vaselli, lost at sea on a trip to The Holy Land with the merchant Lorenzo. Had these columns been part of that ill-fated cargo?

Gerardo emerged from the gloom of the Duomo's interior and blinked as the bright sunlight bounced off the white marble steps outside. Glancing up at the sun as it made its steady climb across the Piazza, he hurried on. Deotisalvi had called his team together for an early meeting and Gerardo was anxious not to be late. Having been chosen for the position of *lapicida* from more than fifty stonemasons, he was well aware of the honour the great man had done him. He also knew that Deotisalivi, now entering his eightieth year, was a difficult man to please.

The old *Capo Magister* stalked impatiently back and forth over the bare earth where the new building would be sited, east of both the Duomo and of his other 'work in progress', the Baptistery. Begun some twenty years earlier, the Baptistery along with the Duomo and the Campanile were to form the extraordinary architectural vision of the Pisan people for their cathedral square. Sixty years older than his new chief stonemason, Deotisalvi was at the peak of his powers, entrusted by the good burghers of Pisa with two of their most prestigious new buildings, and this August morning, as the sun soared over the Duomo's roof, he felt confident and full of excitement.

'You are late,' Deotisalvi spoke roughly without looking up at Gerardo.

The mason bowed low, using the old man's full title. 'Forgive me, *Capo Magister.*'

Vernacci, the *Operaio* came forward and took him by the arm. 'Welcome Gerardo; this is an auspicious day. We are pleased to see you and delighted that you have accepted the position of *lapicida.*'

The old man scowled, and led the group to an exquisitely detailed model placed on the dusty ground.

Gerardo had been *lapicida* on Deotisalvi's other campanile, at the church of San Nicola, just a short walk from the Piazza. Here the *magister* had decorated the circular upper storey of the octagonal tower with a ring of Pisan arches. He had made great use of the Pisan arch at the Baptistery too, a building Gerardo was well acquainted with. But with both these buildings, the arches formed mere decoration on the surface, the weight of the building being supported on a solid marble base.

The new campanile was quite different. In spite of the fact that it would support the weight of seven vast bronze bells to call the faithful of Pisa to prayer, the tower consisted of six layers of open galleries, each one supporting the next. On every level were thirty columns supporting the signature Pisan arches. The effect it created was of the galleries floating one on top of the other. It was almost lacy in appearance, not unlike a piece of woman's clothing – a stocking or a lace veil – and of a delicacy which defied the builder's logical mind.

Gerardo studied the calculations on the geometric drawing that lay next to the model. The columns measured ten Roman feet in height and the tower was a hundred feet in circumference. In total, the tower measured 100 *braccie*, or 'arms'. Gerardo stood up and stroked his neat beard. He looked at the older man who was watching his face intently.

'Well,' said the *Operaio*, 'what do you think?'

Gerardo fingered the soft stubble of his beard. 'I am not employed to think,' he said guardedly, 'I am here to build and do the *magister*'s bidding.'

A faint smile flickered across the architect's face.

'I know that,' said the *Operaio*, 'but is it not beautiful?'

'It is indeed the most beautiful campanile that I have ever seen,' pronounced the younger man.

'And we can build it, do you think?'

'If the *Capo Magister* believes it can be built, then we will build it.' Gerardo was determined not to be drawn.

'Good, good,' said the *Operaio*, 'then let us proceed with the oath.'

All those involved in the creation of any new building – the master masons, labourers, painters, even the *capo magister* himself – were required to take an oath of loyalty to the project.

Gerardo stood erect, one arm across his chest, his hand feeling the quickening heart beneath his linen shirt.

'I, Gerardo di Gerardo,' he declared, 'pledge to be solicitous and attentive in the building of the campanile of the cathedral, in accordance with the means of the Opera.'

The two older men embraced him. It was now the *Operaio's* turn to speak: 'I, Benetto Vernacci, declare this site open and ask for God's blessing on this campanile on this, the Lord's day of August 9th 1173.'

Six days later, on *Ferragosto*, the Feast of the Assumption, Gerardo and Aurelia were married in the Duomo.

CHAPTER 29

August 1173

For Aurelia, her marriage to Gerardo was both the beginning and the end. It was the end of her life in service and of her years of longing and waiting for Gerardo to give her his love. It was the beginning of a new chapter: as wife to a *lapicida*, a respected member of the city, and of her elevation to the ranks of the elite of Pisa.

Once they were married, Aurelia and her mother took charge of Gerardo's tower house. The family acquired the property next door to make the living arrangements more comfortable for the household. The maid Fabricia and page Antonio were not considered sufficient for the new extended family, and Aurelia made discreet enquiries amongst some of Berta's past employees. Massoud had found a good position with the Archbishop of Pisa, but Berta's housekeeper Maria was unhappy with the family who had taken her on after Berta died. Hearing of her troubles, Aurelia offered her the job and Maria quickly accepted.

'There is no better housekeeper in Pisa than you, Maria,' Aurelia said generously.

'Well that is true,' Maria said proudly, 'but I shall have to remember who you are now; not the little maid anymore, *signora*, but the mistress.'

Gerardo was happier than at any other time in his life. For, while he had adored Berta and found her exciting and stimulating, his love for Aurelia was more complete. It had a gentleness and naturalness about it. It felt right. When she fell pregnant six months after their marriage, he believed himself the most fortunate man alive. And so it remained until the Feast of the Assumption on the 15th August, one year to the day after they were married.

The first evening of the fiesta, they, along with every other family in Pisa, had taken part in the Festival of Light. Thousands of people carrying candles processed through the town from the Arno to the Duomo for a celebratory Mass. All along the route, houses were decorated with candles, placed in the windows to shine out in the darkness.

The following day dawned bright and sunny. Aurelia and Gerardo spent a quiet morning at home and then, after lunch, she suggested that they walk down to the Arno to watch the regatta. Aurelia tired easily and Gerardo was concerned that she should not have to rush, or battle with crowds.

'*Carissima*, do you think that is wise? It will be so busy down there, and you are already tired.'

'Oh Gerardo, stop fussing. It will be fun. It's our wedding anniversary. Are we to spend the entire day indoors? Besides, it's a beautiful day, I'd like some fresh air.'

The banks of the Arno were busy. The fine weather had brought out the crowds and they stood four or five deep on either side of the river to watch the regatta that took place each year between the four quarters of the city.

Finding a small gap some two or three hundred yards from the Ponte di Mezzo, Gerardo manoeuvred his way between two large ladies who were cheering excitedly, and found a space for Aurelia to stand.

All the bridges were marked with flags indicating which lane each team should start in. The crowd waited. As the bells of the city struck three times, the race began. The four boats, beautifully decorated, each bearing the standard of their area of the city, charged off through the water. One boat quickly took the lead, and headed straight for the left hand side of the river to steal the advantage As it crossed the finish line, one of the rowers boarded a boat anchored nearby and climbed one of the four cables leading to the top of a mast. Grabbing a blue banner attached to the top, he cried out in triumph and the crowd went wild. As the second boat arrived, one of their rowers climbed the mast, claiming the white banner, the third one claimed the red and so on. As the last crew crossed the finish, they hung dispiritedly over their oars. When they finally climbed back onto dry land, they were presented with a pair of goslings, the traditional reward for the last boat.

The race over, *la grande processione* began. Hundreds of people marched down the banks of the Arno, playing drums and horns – some on horseback, others walking.

Aurelia, hot and uncomfortable between the two fat ladies, began to feel a little faint, and looked around for Gerardo to help her. But he was nowhere to be seen. With difficulty, she extracted herself from between the two women and made to cross the road. A large grey horse, a young man in the saddle, and a boy, no more than eleven or twelve, leading the horse by a bridle, trotted towards her. The horse, made skittish by the noise and the crowds, reared up as Aurelia rushed in front of it. It stumbled sideways, crushing Aurelia against a wall. She felt nothing, just pressure. No pain. Then blackness. Until she heard Gerardo's voice. 'Aurelia, Aurelia.'

She woke up to find herself at home in bed, Gerardo lying next to her. She was in terrible pain. She felt down and touched her skirt. It was wet. She looked at her hand. It was covered in blood. Later that night she gave birth to a tiny stillborn girl.

The months that followed were difficult for them both. Nothing her mother nor Gerardo could say could comfort Aurelia. She felt the loss of her beautiful baby daughter, and guilt at her recklessness in attending the regatta. 'Why did I go? Gerardo told me not to.' She could not forgive herself, and sat in her room rocking back and forth holding the tiny dress that she had been making for the baby. Her mother was unable to comfort her. Nothing in her apothecary's armoury had prepared her for such torment. She could only sit with her daughter and try to convince her that she would have another child, that Gerardo had forgiven her, that all that mattered was that she, Aurelia, was safe and well.

Gerardo too was wracked with guilt that he had not protected his wife, and grieved for the child they had lost. But the pain they each experienced could not be shared. And being unable to provide comfort for one another, they suffered in separate agony, a deep divide opening up between them.

Over the next few months Gerardo lost himself in hard work. The foundations for the new tower had been laid the previous year through the summer and autumn of 1173. In fact, work had begun on the very day he had taken his oath of fealty. Measuring more than three *braccie* and filled with a concrete mix of crushed quartzite stone, the foundations had been left to settle and harden in the soft, alluvial soil over the winter. But the site was never idle. The masons and sculptors were already hard at work carving the columns and corbels of the building, which would later be pieced together, like a vast jigsaw puzzle.

In the spring of 1174, the build began. First, a base wall measuring thirteen feet thick – according to their calculations, strong enough to support the weight of the seven upper storeys and the seven bronze bells that would one day adorn the top of the tower. Above the base, they began to construct the open galleries, from which visitors would be able to stand and admire the city, and half columns: Gerardo building the first one and the masons then copying his work exactly – there being no detailed plans or working drawings, merely the example set by the *lapicida* on the build.

All through the summer and autumn of that year they worked tirelessly, building as they went the wide marble staircase. Never before had a tower been built that contained such a revolutionary design, wide enough to allow illustrious visitors to ascend it in pairs, or, it was even said, to take a man on horseback. On the exterior of the tower, individual masons created bizarre and strange figures, symbols and inscriptions. On either side of the main door, wild beasts gave chase to a winged serpent. Nearby, Gerardo himself carved two galleys entering the port of Pisa with its harbour towers – a reference both to its nautical and architectural heritage, and a personal tribute to his grandfather, Carlo. Deotisalvi, of course, took it as a tribute to himself – a reference to the sea towers that he had built at the entrance to the harbour. What no one else recognised was that it was also a symbol of his love and respect for Berta, the person whose generous legacy had made the tower possible, and the trading ships that had provided her wealth.

In the Spring of 1175, Gerardo visited the marble works at Monte Pisano with Deotisalvi, searching for the white and grey marble with which to face the Campanile.

He was reluctant to leave Aurelia, but could delay the trip no longer. Aurelia, who had now been grieving for many months for her lost child, found herself distraught at the departure of her husband. By day she fretted about him, imagining all manner of harm befalling him; by night she had recurrent nightmares in which Gerardo was killed – devoured by strange monsters... or crushed and broken after falling from a great height to the ground.

Gerardo returned to Pisa at the beginning of June, and for a few days, the relief that she felt at his return made her genuinely happy once again. But her joy was short-lived. Within days it was clear that he had contracted a terrible malady, and he began to suffer from raging fevers night after night.

Aurelia was frantic. 'What if he dies, *mamma*? How will I live? A year ago I was the most fortunate of women, with a wonderful husband and pregnant with our first child. Now the child has been taken away, and maybe Gerardo too. It is too cruel. To have had so much and lost it all. Oh please, please, *mamma*... make him well.'

Violetta, who had lost both her own husband and Lorenzo to the self-same malady, could not bring herself to make false promises to her daughter. But she nursed him devotedly, taking it in turns with Aurelia and Maria to sit with him, changing his sheets and his nightshirt every few hours as he lay bathed in sweat. The maids washed and scrubbed and dried the linen, heating water constantly on the open fire in the kitchen, sweat pouring down their own backs as they worked in the terrible summer heat. For weeks, Gerardo lay ill, hardly eating, drinking just enough to keep him alive. He grew gaunt and thin, his beard long and straggly, until he resembled one of the disciples that Aurelia had seen in paintings in the Duomo.

One afternoon, as Aurelia sat by his bedside, she nodded off, her head lolling on her chest. When she woke, she saw Gerardo smiling at her.

'Hello, little flower,' he said. He reached out for her hand and pulled her towards him. His straggly beard prickled her delicate skin, but she allowed him to hold her close, and gazed into his sea green eyes.

'Oh *caro*, thank God. I have been so worried that you would never come back.'

'Well I have; I am back and I will not go away again.'

In the weeks that followed, Gerardo grew stronger. A week after the fever subsided, he began to sit in a chair in their bed-

room. Maria cooked him little rice puddings, made with almonds and milk, to coax him to eat. Although he protested at
first, he allowed Aurelia to shave off the beard, and relished the
feel of his smooth skin beneath his hand. He was soon able to
leave his room, and go downstairs to read in the sitting room and
eat with the rest of the family. Within a month, he was taking
short walks to the Campo, and could see the progress that had
been made in his absence on the Tower.

Deotisalvi was pushing the men hard. 'I am glad to see you,
Gerardo; we have missed you here.'

Gerardo was touched by the old man's comments. 'Thank
you, *magister*. I hope to be back at work within another week or
so. I just need to get my strength back. It is fortunate that you
did not fall prey to the same fever as I did on our journey.'

'Oh, I have had the fever many times, on trips to the Holy
Land, so it affects me less. I remember a terrible fever that kept
me in Damascus for many months. So I know what it is, and
you have my sympathy. But we are strong, you and I, no? It will
take more than sickness to topple us.'

And the two men laughed. It was the first time, Gerardo realised, that he had ever seen the *magister* do so.

By the autumn, the Tower was completed up to the first storey, but the foundations, Gerardo was alarmed to notice, had
shifted slightly on the southern side, causing the Tower to lean
in that direction. He met with Deotisalvi to discuss a solution.

'Oh this often happens; you should know that,' Deotisalvi
said calmly. 'It's a problem with most tall buildings in Pisa. It's
the soil. But it will settle again, I am sure.'

'Are you? I'm worried that the building will be so tall, and
its base is so narrow. We may need to intervene. Could we not
weight it somehow, on the north side, to pull it back to the vertical?' Gerardo asked anxiously.

'Mmm, well we could, I suppose. We could add some weight to the cornice on that side. That should do the trick.'

And so the cornices of the first open gallery were duly ordered to be made heavier on the northern side.

By the spring of 1177, the second storey was complete. One day in early April, Aurelia came to see her husband and to check on the progress of his work. She brought him a picnic, much as her mistress had done all those years before when visiting Gerardo at the Duomo. Her basket was filled with with ham, cheese and bread and a little rice pudding made especially for him by Maria.

Delighted to see her, and grateful that she had emerged finally from her terrible sadness, Gerardo guided her carefully up the ladders and onto the scaffolding. He proudly showed her his work, walking her around the graceful gallery on the second floor, from where she could already get a view of the Duomo and Baptistery and the city beyond.

'It is beautiful, Gerardo, you must be so proud.'

'I am, *cara*. It is all that I could have wished for.'

'I have something else that might make you proud.'

'And what is that, little flower?'

'I am expecting another child.'

Gerardo picked her up in his arms and swung her round, until she begged to be put back down safely on the ground.

Their son was born in October of that year. He was named Gerardo after his father, and his father's father, and his father before him. Now, it seemed, Aurelia and Gerardo had everything they had ever desired.

CHAPTER 30

June 1999

Grey rain clouds glowered above the city early on Tuesday morning. The intense heat of previous days had given way during the night to torrential rain. Falling in sheets, the water poured onto roofs and out of gutters, and filled up the drains, causing them to overflow.

Sam woke early, momentarily confused by her surroundings. Her dreams, just before she woke, had been filled with such clear images of Michael playing with the children in their garden at home. He had been a jolly Michael, a fit Michael – running round the garden, giving the children piggybacks, rolling on the grass, laughing and shouting. As the grey dawn light filtered through her closed eyelids, the reality of her situation seeped into her brain, as she recognised the now familiar room in the pensione.

Sam had spent the previous day with Michael, trying to be as positive as possible. Carrie's unannounced appearance had had the surprising effect of creating a bond between her and her husband. His obvious distress at Carrie's visit was as clear a demonstration of his determination to finish the affair as she could have hoped for. And it brought out Sam's protective streak. She had spent the whole day with him, virtually camping out in his room, ready to defend him should the need arise.

Finally, at ten o'clock in the evening, he had woken from a nap and found Sam sleeping in a chair by his bed.

'Sam,' he'd said, 'Sam, go back to the hotel, darling. It's OK. I'm OK.'

She had left, but reluctantly.

Now, her first thought was whether Carrie had materialised overnight in her absence. She showered and dressed quickly, before hurrying over to the hospital.

She was relieved to find Michael sitting up in bed, sipping a bowl of coffee that the nurses had made for him. She put the now redundant cappuccino down on the bedside table.

'Any sign?' she asked him.

'None… I think she's gone,' he said with an almost palpable sense of relief.

'I've got to go out this morning, Michael. Professor Moretti is meeting me at Signor Visalberghi's shop this morning. He's got something rather exciting to show him.'

'Oh,' he said, 'and what's that?'

'Are you just being polite, or do you actually want to know?'

'I want to know,' he said.

And so, she filled him in on the details of Visalberghi's extraordinary image of the Tower, and of her theories about Berta.

He leant back on his pillow, stunned by her story. 'My God. I think you might have something rather interesting there – well done. Have you told Miracle Productions?'

'No, not yet – I'm waiting till after this meeting. I want to be sure.'

As she left his room half an hour later, he grasped her hand. 'Sam, if nothing else comes out of this bloody experience, you getting back to work, showing the world how clever you are, is worth every minute I've had to spend in this bed.'

'Oh Michael, don't be silly. But thank you.'

'I mean it... I'd forgotten what a talent you are. Go. Have fun.'

The meeting at Visalberghi's was scheduled for 11 o'clock. The Professor arrived at one minute before the hour. The bookseller welcomed him with considerable deference and turned the shop sign to '*chiuso*', pulling down the blinds.

With Dario acting as interpreter, Sam was able to follow the conversation.

'Professor, I have something that I think would be of interest to you,' said the old shopkeeper. He unrolled a large piece of parchment and placed it carefully on the table, setting a powerful magnifying glass next to it.

The Professor pulled on a pair of white cotton gloves, picked up the magnifying glass and studied the drawing with care. He rubbed his chin and made little clucking noises to himself. Finally he said: 'This is extraordinary. I am amazed that I have never seen this before. Where did you find it?'

As Visalberghi explained the remarkable hiding place of the drawing, Dario translated for Sam.

They all waited, silently, as he studied the image, touching the paper delicately, examining every square centimetre with the magnifying glass.

'The initials,' Sam blurted out impatiently, 'ask him about the initials.'

Dario nodded.

Professor Moretti studied them carefully. 'They look like BP?' he said.

'Bonanno Pisano?' asked Dario.

'Pah – no it cannot be. I know everyone has always thought the Tower was the work of Pisano, but I don't believe it. It has to be the work of Deotisalvi.'

'Might the initials be BB – for Berta di Bernardo?' asked Sam. 'What about that?'

Dario translated.

The Professor looked at her in astonishment. 'The widow!' he exclaimed. 'I don't think so. No, not the widow. Perhaps it is some sort of code. I don't know… we will have to investigate it further.'

The two elderly men then spoke together, with Dario attempting to keep up with the translation. 'The Professor would like to study the drawing further,' he said, 'he's asked my father if he it can take it to the university and show it to his colleagues.'

As they left, Sam shook the Professor warmly by the hand. 'Thank you so much, Professor,' she said. 'I am beginning to understand a little of what might have gone on all those years ago. I can't tell you how grateful I am to you.'

'And I to you,' he said, 'for letting me spend some time with charming Visalberghi here and for finding this extraordinary piece of evidence about the Tower.'

'*Amico mio, non tenere queste cose per te in futuro – a lui l'interessa sempre tutto cio che ha c che fare con la Torre!*' he said cradling his arm around Visalberghi's shoulder.

'He says to my father,' translated Dario, 'don't keep such things to yourself in future – he is always interested in anything to do with the Tower.'

As Sam and Dario walked back towards the hospital, she turned to him. 'Dario – thank you so much for everything. Really…'

'It's OK,' he said. 'It's been a pleasure. I don't really feel I've done much.'

'Oh, you have. Your father has been pivotal, you helped me get to Moretti, you introduced me to Gina. I simply couldn't have done it without you.'

'That's where you're wrong… you could have done those things. You'd already found my father through his book. You knew about Moretti – I just acted as translator – and as for Gina, well, you'd have got there without me quite easily. You're a good researcher, Sam. Have faith in yourself.'

Sam blushed. 'You're very kind. Well, let me thank you for something else then – for giving me my confidence back. The whole thing with my husband has been very hard to deal with, but if nothing else, it's shown me that I can't go back to the life I had before. I need my independence. Marriage can be great, having children is wonderful. But work is good too. You know, it's strange, but I feel such an affinity with this woman, Berta. There she is – a hugely important patron of the arts, who might even have been involved with the design of this amazing building here... who knows?'

They stopped and gazed up at the Tower.

'Either way, she was of vital importance, and it seems that she's almost been forgotten; she's just a footnote in history. That's how I have felt, if I'm honest. I used to be a reporter, working all over the world. I achieved things, I was respected, if you like. And then I had my children. And... don't get me wrong... they are the most important thing I've ever done; I adore them. But I am more than that – just as Berta, I believe, was more than a mere widow who left some money. Does that make sense?'

'Sure... but whereas we can never be sure about Berta, we can be quite clear about you... don't lose that confidence, Sam.'

CHAPTER 31

April 1178

The Tower progressed at a pace. By the spring of 1178, Gerardo and his team were well on with the third storey. But whatever they did to add or subtract weight, the tower kept on leaning. Deotisalvi began to mutter about who was to blame.

'This is all the fault of that Bonanno and his dreadful calculations,' he said. 'And I should never have listened to that woman. What did she know about building! A woman, for goodness' sake.'

'What woman – who are you talking about?' replied Gerardo innocently.

'Berta di Bernardo, of course. That witch! She bullied me and that idiot the *Operaio* into accepting this design. I always had my doubts about it; I was a fool to listen to them.'

'She bullied you... so who designed it then?'

'Well she had something to do with it – based on my original design, of course. That was a solid, sensible building, beautifully calculated, magnificent, strong. But that woman, or one of her acolytes, added these extra galleries, which created more weight and thus instability. I should never have allowed myself to be persuaded by them. It was a mistake all along.'

Gerardo, shocked at this revelation, thought back over Berta's last months of life. Of her determination to get the Tower built, for Gerardo to work on it. Why, he wondered, had she never told him of her involvement?

The next day, having set the masons to work carving the arches on the third gallery, Gerardo paid a visit to Bonanno Pisano.

'Thank you for seeing me, *signore*; I am grateful to you.'

'You are welcome, Gerardo. It is a great pleasure to meet you. I have heard much about you.'

'Really?' Gerardo was confused. 'From who?'

'From Berta di Bernardo of course. She spoke of you often; she was very proud of you.'

'She spoke to you of me?' Gerardo was genuinely surprised.

'She was very keen that you work on the Tower. And I am sure that she is looking down at us now, and delighted that you are doing so well. I hear the building is progressing well?'

Bonanno gestured to Gerardo to sit down.

'Thank you, yes, in many ways it is progressing very well indeed. But there are some problems. The tower is tilting very slightly to one side. We have tried to correct it by weighting it on the opposite elevation, but I see no sign of it working as yet.'

'Mmm,' said Bonanno, 'that must be worrying.'

'It is, and I came to see you because I understand that you were involved in the original calculations for the building. Is that correct?'

'No, well not really. Berta came to me and asked me to do the calculations, but I did not feel qualified to do it, so I took the designs and showed them to a colleague at the School of Architecture here in Pisa. He really prepared the calculations and Deotisalvi approved them, I believe. So I do not think I can be blamed for the fault.'

'No, no, *signore*,' Gerardo said, hurriedly, 'I do not seek to lay blame at your door; merely to try to work out what is happening and what we might to do to rectify matters.'

'Well,' Pisano said, rising from his chair and beginning to pace the room, 'let's think about that. It is a round building, which will spread the load, but of course it is quite a load. The galleries, the staircase, the sheer weight of the building, must take its toll – and the ground there, as we all know, is so silty and soft.'

'But we put in huge foundations,' argued Gerardo, 'more than enough to take the weight of the tower. And look at the Baptistery: the same soil, also a round building, and no sign of subsidence there. It is a mystery.'

'Well, the Baptistery's got a lower point load, so it's almost floating on the ground, but in general I agree. Your beautiful tower seems to have struck unlucky with the soil. I am very sorry.' Bonanno indicated the meeting was at an end.

'There is nothing more I can add. I bear no responsibility for the faults of the tower, and I wish you well.'

Gerardo left Bonanno's house and walked desultorily back to the Piazza. The problems on the tower were causing him to have sleepless nights. He had calculated that, at the present rate of lean, the tower would, by the time they reached the seventh storey, be unsustainable. There was even the possibility that it might fall down.

Aurelia tried to lift his spirits when he returned home that evening. 'Gerardo, darling, come and see the baby. He is so clever, Gerardo; he has said some words, come and listen.'

Baby Gerardo was sitting on the floor with his grandmother Violetta, clutching the wooden camel that Carlo had carved for Gerardo all those years before.

Aurelia knelt down on the floor by his side, and pointed to the camel.

'Gerardo... baby... what's that?'

The baby laughed and blew bubbles at his mother.

She laughed back, but asked again, pointing at the camel, 'What's that? Tell Mamma.'

'Camel,' said the baby, throwing it on the floor.

Gerardo swept his baby son in his arms and kissed him. 'Clever boy, clever boy. Well done.'

The child buried his head in his father's neck and said very softly, '*Papa.*'

Later that evening, as Aurelia lay contentedly in Gerardo's arms, she asked, 'Is he not clever, our darling little boy?'

'He is, *cara*, very clever.'

'Does he make you proud?'

'Of course, Aurelia, of course he does.'

'And would it make you happy to know that I am carrying another child?'

'When? How soon?' he asked excitedly.

'A while yet, I think; before Christmas.'

That summer, the weather was very hot. Aurelia's belly grew, along with the tower. By the autumn, the third storey was complete. Gerardo, who agonised about the instability of the tower, had concluded, after much thought, that the staircase was the cause of the problem. He tried to discuss this with Deotisalvi.

'*Magister*, forgive me for troubling you, but I am concerned about the tower. I fear that the wide staircase is the problem: it's adding too much weight to the structure and is causing the instability.'

'You are the *lapicida*, Gerardo. You are not paid to design buildings, but to build them. Get on with your work and leave the design to me.'

Unhappy with this response, he took his concerns to Benetto Vernacci, the *Operaio*.

'I am sorry to disturb you, Signor Vernacci,' Gerardo said nervously, as he entered the *Operaio*'s offices on the Campo.

'Not at all, not at all,' Vernacci said, beckoning him to a chair. 'It is good to see you, Gerardo. What can I do for you?'

'I am concerned about the tower, s*ignore.*'

'Really? It all looks splendid to me,' the Operaio said airily. 'What can be so worrying that you have had to take time out of your day to see me?'

'The tower is unstable, *signore*. It has begun to sink into the ground on the southern elevation. We have tried to weight it on the opposite side to right it, but nothing we have done works.'

'Surely, this is something you should raise with the *Capo Magister* and not me.'

'I have tried, *signore* – believe me – but he will not listen.'

'I see,' said the *Operaio*. 'Well, Signor Deotisalvi can be a little stubborn at times, we all know that, but really I must insist that you raise any concerns you have about the building with him. I am sorry, Gerardo – there is nothing I can do to help you.'

'It is the staircase, *signore*. That is the problem,' Gerardo continued desperately, 'it is too wide, too heavy. It is making the building unstable. I believe we need to remove it. I know it's there so that visitors can easily climb up to the seven galleries, but if it is making the building unsafe. Could we not manage with something simpler, lighter – perhaps a ladder could suffice?'

The *Operaio*, irritated to be hectored in his own office by a mere *lapicida*, stood up, indicating that the meeting was at an end. 'This building is intended to reflect the glory of Pisa at the height of its powers, Gerardo. We chose the design – a design that was submitted by your patron Berta di Bernardo – precisely because it featured seven galleries. Galleries that will allow the great citizens of Pisa to stand and look out over their city, in particular to observe the procession of the citizens into the Duomo by the East Doors on the Feast of the Assumption. I do not think ladders will suffice, do you?'

Sensing that there was no purpose in continuing the argument, at least for that day, Gerardo withdrew. But his doubts and concerns grew, and as summer turned to autumn, and the birth of his second child drew near, he was unable to take pleasure in either his family or his work, so fearful had he become of a disaster looming on the Piazza del Duomo.

Aurelia fretted about Gerardo.

'*Mamma*,' she said one morning to Violetta, 'he has barely slept this week. I'm so concerned when he goes off each morning that something bad will happen. He is exhausted all the time, and it's risky working on such a high building.'

'I know,' said Violetta kindly, 'but Gerardo is strong, try not to worry. Think about the baby, Aurelia… that's all you need to do. Gerardo will sort out his problems; he's a very experienced *lapicida.*'

'But he says that no one will listen. Deotisalvi flies into a rage each time he mentions his concerns about the tower; Pisano won't help him, or can't. He went to see the *Operaio* a little while ago, and he just washed his hands of the whole affair. Why can't they see that he is just trying to save them from a potential disaster? He is worried the Tower could actually fall down. I can't believe they won't take his concerns more seriously.'

Aurelia paced the kitchen, ringing her hands. Little Gerardo sat in front of the fire, playing with his wooden camel and a kitten that the family had recently acquired. The kitten, tired of his game, scratched the little boy on the hand. He began to scream – a high-pitched, penetrating wail.

'Gerardo, stop it,' she snapped, 'stop crying.' She grabbed the kitten and almost threw it outside into the well-stocked garden at the back of the house.

Violetta picked the boy up and kissed his scratched hand. 'There, there Gerardo, *nonna* will make it better. I shall put a little poultice on the nasty scratch.' She carried the boy out into the garden and picked a few leaves of wild garlic, which she brought back into the kitchen. She mashed them up in the big stone pestle before laying the crushed leaves on the boy's hand.

'You should be ashamed of yourself, Aurelia,' Violetta said harshly. 'I suggest you occupy yourself with something practical and stop this worrying. Gerardo will be fine. Why don't you make him a nice picnic and take it over there this afternoon for his lunch. He would appreciate that far more than knowing you were fretting at home and failing in your duty as a mother.'

'I'm sorry, *mamma*,' Aurelia said, wounded by her mother's words. 'I know you're right. But I have been so worried about him; I keep dreaming terrible things – and I've got myself into a state about it all.'

'What things?' asked Violetta.

'I have recurring dreams of seeing Gerardo falling, *mamma*... off the tower, I think... or at least from a great height. I had the dream again last night. And when I woke myself up from it, because it was so frightening, I couldn't go back to sleep. Maybe I woke Gerardo too with my restlessness, because he was sitting in the chair in our room, working at the little table by the window, sitting so silently in the moonlight. I said, "Gerardo come back to bed, you will be so tired tomorrow," but he didn't hear me. He just went on writing. I don't know what exactly, but calculations I think they were. He looked so upset, so wretched, *mamma*, and I am at my wits' end.'

Violetta put the little boy down on the stone floor and hugged her daughter.

'*Cara*... all will be well, you will see. Now prepare that picnic; a little tart, perhaps, or a rice pudding... you know he likes that.'

For the next hour, Aurelia busied herself preparing Gerardo's lunch. While Maria packed it into a small basket, Aurelia went to her bedroom and changed into her pale blue gown. Taking her cloak from behind the door, she picked up the laden basket and set off for the Campo.

As she walked up the wide avenue leading to the Piazza, she could see the tower ahead of her. Now four storeys high, the building was covered in raffia scaffolding. Blocks of stone were being hauled up to the top storey on pulleys, and bowls of mortar winched into position. Dozens of men and boys hung off the scaffolding, laughing and joking. They brought back memories of Gerardo when she first saw him all those years before, hanging precariously on a piece of scaffolding on the Baptistery.

A young mason, a sixteen-year old boy named Guido, recognised her as she walked into the square.

'Hi Aurelia, good to see you,' he called down to her.

She waved her hand in greeting. 'Is Gerardo at the top?' she asked.

'Yes… up there with the *capo*,' said the young man.

She began the long climb to the top of the tower. The stairwell was dark, in spite of the bright light outside which spilled through the narrow windows on each level, illuminating the small landing leading to the open galleries. There was a rudimentary handrail made of rope that she hung on to as she climbed.

As she got to the third level, she heard raised voices coming from the top. She stopped to catch her breath and was suddenly startled by Guido jumping in through a narrow doorway in front of her.

'Oh!' she said, nearly dropping her basket. 'You frightened me.'

'Sorry, *signora*,' said Guido.

'What are they shouting about?' she asked.

'Oh they shout a lot. I wouldn't worry... we just let them get on with it. They'll calm down soon,' the boy said casually, 'they usually do. Shall I carry your basket for you?' he asked gently.

'Thank you, yes that would be kind. I am a bit tired,' said Aurelia. She patted her large stomach and smiled at the boy.

They carried on up to the fourth storey, the sounds of the argument raging overhead becoming more insistent. As she squeezed out through the narrow opening to the staircase, she was almost blinded by the bright sunlight that bathed the top of the Tower.

As her eyes adjusted to the light, she saw Gerardo and Deotisalvi standing a few feet away, Deotisalvi bellowing at his *lapicida*.

'Listen to me – you had no right going to see the *Operaio* or that man Pisano. How dare you go above my head. I am *Capo Magister* here, Gerardo, and don't you forget it. I gave you a chance when no one else would have looked at you. Perhaps that was a mistake; I see now that it was. You have always had ideas above your station, ideas put there by that meddling woman di Bernardo. I wouldn't have looked at you if it hadn't been for her.'

'Leave her out of this,' Gerardo shouted back, 'if it hadn't been for her, there would be no tower.'

'Pah!' exclaimed Deotisalvi, 'what are you implying? Women have no business getting involved in architecture. What did she know of anything?'

'She was an accomplished artist,' shouted Gerardo, 'and a generous patron – an extraordinary woman. But that is not the issue now, *signore*. We have a problem with the building and you surely must see that. The Tower is perilously close to falling down. I do not believe it is sustainable. We have to make some changes here; we cannot just ignore it and hope it will go away.'

The old man roared suddenly, unable to contain his rage any longer; he swung his hand and slapped his *lapicida*a across the face.

Aurelia gasped in alarm. Gerardo instinctively hit back, striking the older man on the jaw, causing him to stumble and lose his footing.

Steadying himself, Deotisalvi punched Gerardo squarely on the chin, knocking him backwards and down onto the half-laid stone floor. Guido dropped the basket and moved towards them to intervene.

'No,' said Aurelia, 'leave them... Gerardo will be all right.'

The boy hung back helplessly.

Gerardo clambered back up and raised his hands in front of his chest, in a gesture of conciliation. 'Signor Deotisalvi – please.'

But the old man saw his chance and punched him hard on the side of his face.

Gerardo, caught unawares, took the full force of the blow and stumbled, lurching clumsily towards the edge of the building Tripping on a pile of stones that had been left ready for laying that afternoon, the makeshift rope barrier gave way as he stumbled, and he disappeared over the edge of the tower.

It seemed to Gerardo that he was floating. His hands, he noticed, caught the sunlight, and the almost imperceptible webs between his widely spread fingers glowed bright red shot through by the sun, revealing the complex pattern of veins moving blood around his body. Keeping him alive. The blood pumped harder now, pressing into his skull, restricting the brain until it hurt. Then nothing. A thud. And the birds free-wheeling high in the sky looked down on the body spread-eagled and lifeless in the shadow of the tower.

CHAPTER 32

June 2001

It was in early June, almost exactly two years after they had first arrived in Pisa, that Sam and Michael finally returned to the city to finish the film.

Back home in England, Michael had made a good recovery and, although not completely back to his old self, was much improved. Speech therapy and physiotherapy had all played their part, and Miracle had agreed to let him oversee the project, with Sam as reporter/director.

Their relationship had gone through something of a transformation too. Sam had finally come to terms with Michael's indiscretion with Carrie, due in part, she now realised, to her own attraction to Dario; how could she in all honesty be angry with Michael for doing something that she had herself toyed with? But more importantly, she saw how very determined Michael was to recover both his health and her good opinion of him when he returned to England. He seemed so grateful that she had not abandoned him, so delighted with his children, and ultimately, so proud of his wife and her strength of character and professional ability. He had seen, when they were in Pisa, just how much she enjoyed and relished the film-making process, and understood, for the first time, how much she had given up to try to conform to his ideal of motherhood. Ultimately, she was a professional woman who also happened to be a mother, and they resolved over the months during which he recovered from his stroke, to get more help and make it possible for Sam to go back to work. Her instinct too, about the history of the Tower, proved to him that she had remarkable depth and insight, and he was delighted that Miracle agreed with her hypothesis and interpretation.

And so, over the following months, Sam travelled to Pisa on four occasions, shooting sequences with academics at the university, filming all the pieces of 'evidence' she had unearthed. By now, the remarkable drawing of the Tower had now been verified by carbon-dating as originating in the middle of the twelfth century.

Michael, meanwhile, remained at home, caring for the children and, over time, their roles of parent and worker merged, and they arrived at a place of mutual respect.

Just one final sequence remained to be shot: the official opening ceremony of the Tower of Pisa on June 16th.

'Come with me, Michael?' she had asked.

'You don't need me there,' he'd argued.

'Yes I do. I've got an important piece to camera I want to write – and I could do with your editorial judgement. Come... please – for me.'

Sam and Michael arrived in Pisa the day before the official ceremony. They were staying in a large hotel on Via Santa Maria, and met the crew that evening to plan how they would shoot the grand opening.

Sam was decisive: 'We'll need one crew at the bottom of the Tower to cover the official opening sequence and shoot wide shots of the Tower. Michael... will you take charge of that? And the rest of us will wait at the top, ready to shoot the guests as they make their way up and shoot the speeches that take place up there. I'll do one piece to camera there, and then I think the final piece down on the Campo.'

Michael smiled in agreement.

The following day, the crews in position, the guests assembled at the foot of the Tower of Pisa for the grand celebratory opening. Soldiers dressed in medieval Pisan costume, with daggers, swords, muskets and pikes, stood guard around the Tower and the Duomo. Attended by the world's press, there were prayers, music, tributes and speeches – most memorably by Professor Moretti who thanked the team of engineers led by the British engineer, John Burland, for his 'invaluable contribution to the saving of the Tower'. The crowd cheered as Professor Burland then returned the key of the campanile to the *Operario*, in a symbolic gesture. A ribbon was cut, and guests were duly invited to cross the threshold and climb to the top of the Tower, for the first time in eleven years.

As the visitors made their way up, slowly climbing the 296 stairs, they were able to admire the city, looking out through the narrow windows set into the thick walls – at the terracotta roofs, the cupola of a distant church, and the waves of apricot buildings. Once at the top, the group admired the view and then stood respectfully as Moretti addressed them once more, this time pointing out some of the restored features of the bell chamber. He was coming to the end of his speech, and Sam tapped the cameraman on his shoulder delicately, indicating that he should zoom in a little.

'I am more grateful than I can ever say,' he said, his voice slightly cracking with emotion, 'for the help and dedication of Professor Burland. Without his hard work and inspirational leadership, this Tower might not have had the happy outcome that it now enjoys. A few years ago we were very concerned that this beautiful monument to the glorious past of the city of Pisa might very well collapse… a tragedy of incalculable proportions.

But now, thanks to him and his team, we are proud to be able to open this, the most popular and most recognised building in the world, to the visiting public again.'

The Professor wiped his eyes with a tatty handkerchief as the audience applauded loudly. Sam looked around at the assembled guests. Professor Burland, a diminutive, almost humble figure, in a simple grey suit, stood surrounded by the other thirteen members of the Commission set up to oversee this latest rescue of the Tower, and by senior dignitaries representing the city of Pisa, resplendent in their formal robes of office – the mayor, the president of the Opera Primaziale Pisana… even the archbishop and his entourage were all there.

'Finally, I would like to thank one other person. Many of you living in Pisa will know him well, but he is not a man who has sought an international reputation. Signor Lino Visalberghi has made it his life's work to research and collect images of our beautiful city. He has one of the most splendid collections it is possible to imagine. Just two years ago, he unearthed a remarkable new image of the Tower, dating, we now know, from the middle of the twelfth century. It is remarkable, because there are virtually no plans or drawings of buildings at that time; architects worked from models. The drawing is signed too. We believe it says BB. We are uncertain who that was. Might it have been a misnomer for Bonanno Pisano, or perhaps a pseudonym for the man I believe to have been the designer – Deotisalvi? I think we will never know. But I am indebted to Signor Visalberghi nevertheless.'

The audience applauded loudly. Sam looked around and smiled at Dario who stood near to his father.

The cameraman zoomed in on Moretti as he grasped Visalberghi's hand.

As the guests then began to make their way down the winding staircase, Sam rushed over to Dario and his father. 'I'm so delighted you could be here,' she said. 'How are you, Signor Visalberghi?'

Dario translated, as always. 'He is well thank you – and delighted to be here today.'

'And you… how are you, Dario?' .

'I'm well. Busy as always, but well. And you?'

'I'm good – thanks.'

'And your husband?'

'Much better and… we're much better too,' she smiled and a faint blush spread almost imperceptibly up her neck. It did not go unnoticed. The older man moved off to speak to Professor Moretti.

'Look Dario, I'd like to credit you on the film – as an assistant producer or something,' she said

'Don't do that; I'm not sure my employers would be very understanding about me moonlighting on my holiday. No… seeing you here and happy again is thanks enough.'

At that she leant up and kissed him lightly on the cheek, inhaling once again the lemony scent of his aftershave.

'And if you ever change your mind… about your husband,' he whispered into her ear, 'you know where I am.'

She smiled. 'I won't, but thank you.' She squeezed his arm, before going over to Signor Visalberghi and the Professor and shaking them both warmly by the hand.

Dario indicated it was time to leave, and taking his father's arm, together they began the long descent to the Campo.

'OK,' said Sam briskly, 'let's get set up for the final pieces to camera.' She brushed her hair, adjusting her appearance reflected in the camera's big lens, before taking up her position near the edge of the Tower.

'OK, Fabio?' she said to the cameraman.

'*Si*, we're good… cue.'

'And so this remarkable and unique building has, at last, been rescued. For the first time in over a thousand years the Tower dominating the Campo dei Miracoli is safe.'

The cameraman panned round to a stunning wide shot of the Piazza.

The crew then moved their equipment down to the square and Sam set up for her final remarks, with the Tower, in all its glory, behind her.

'Fabio – I'm going to do the first bit of the piece to cam in a tight shot, then can you zoom out to reveal the whole Tower behind me?'

'No problem... OK, cue'

'But what of the other mystery that hangs over this Tower: the question of who designed it? Why does that remain un-solved? Could it be that the shadowy figure of the widow, Berta di Bernardo, holds the key to that mystery? Could the drawing of the Tower that has recently been discovered, signed with the enigmatic initials BP or BB, provide the answer? The academ-ics find it hard to accept our theory about Berta's possible role... because she was a woman, and women in medieval times had little or no status. The question of Berta's involvement with the design of the Tower will now be up to the academics to decide. But whether they accept our new evidence or not, I have a gut feeling that she was much more than merely a footnote in the history of architecture. To me, she was a heroine, a woman who not only wanted to give a lasting legacy to her beloved city, but more importantly, with her dying breath, yearned to be a key player in the creation of this extraordinary edifice.'

The cameraman zoomed out to reveal the Tower glistening in the evening sunlight.

'So here it stands, in all its flawed glory, still leaning, but no longer in danger of collapse. A testament to the vision of its designer and the many people involved in its construction over 200 years. A unique masterpiece, whose imperfection has made it the most famous building in the world.'

'OK,' said Sam, 'do we have it?'

Michael, who had been watching his wife on a monitor, gave her a thumbs up.

'Perfect, darling – couldn't be better.'

'Fabio... good for you?'

'*Si* – all good.'

'Well, it's a wrap then. Thanks everyone. Drinks in the Bar Duomo on us in half an hour?'

The crew packed up their gear and went to load it into their cars.

Michael wandered across to Sam and put his arms round her. 'Well done, darling. You're going to create quite a stir with this, you know.'

'I don't know... I somehow doubt it. The establishment will close ranks, and it's just a theory after all. But if it makes people think a bit... and wonder about the people, and most especially the women, who history forgot, then I'll be pleased'.

The two of them turned round to face the Tower. The sun had begun its slow descent, and cast a warm apricot glow on the Tower. It shimmered in the evening light.

'Michael, this Tower was Berta's artistic vision, her opportunity to do something extraordinary. And in some very tiny and humble way, I feel this beautiful campanile has provided me with a creative opportunity too.'

'It helped you and me too, didn't it?' said Michael. 'To bring us back together, I mean.'

Sam smiled, nodding gently.

'I'm a very lucky man, aren't I,' said Michael, taking her hand and kissing it.

'I think, perhaps, that you are... yes,' said Sam.

CHAPTER 33

Siena 1203

The little boy ran through a field of barley, his hand brushing across the prickly surface of the crop, tickling his palm. At the edge of the field, he grasped a stalk and pulled upwards, stripping it bare. He sat down and played with the creamy ears, pouring them from one hand to the other.

'Pico, Pico...'

He heard his name, but ignored it. The sun was hot on his back and he felt safe, surrounded by the tall barley crop. His grandmother would not find him here.

Moments later, she stood over him, blocking out the sun. 'Pico, what are you doing here? I've been calling you for hours. I need your help with the milking. Come...'

Reluctantly, he let the ears of barley fall to the ground, keeping back one or two and putting them carefully into the pocket of his trousers. He followed his grandmother to the cow shed. His grandfather was already there.

'Gerardo, I told you Pico and I would do that – go back inside and rest.'

'No, *cara*, I want to do it. I've had a siesta and feel fine. I'll do it with little Pico – you go back inside and organise Angela. She's such a terrible cook.'

'All right, if you're sure. Pico, look after *nonno* will you?'

The little boy nodded earnestly and sat obediently at the side of his grandfather, pushing the wooden bucket under the udders of the cow as he milked.

Later that evening, after supper, as they sat around the wood fire, Pico nestled at his grandmother's feet as she sewed.

'Tell me, *nonna*... about the Tower?'

'You've heard all our stories, Pico.'

'Please, Nonna, please tell me. I want to know about *nonno* and how he fell.'

'You ghoul... I don't like to talk about that. You know very well... he broke both his legs and arms. It was a miracle he survived.'

'He floated like a bird... he's magic,' said the child.

'He's not magic, silly boy. He was just lucky. We were lucky.'

'And is the Tower finished now?' asked the boy, knowing the answer.

'You know it is not. It is just as your grandfather left it – four storeys high. But maybe one day, someone will finish it. But it won't be grandpa, he's much happier living here in the country-side.'

Gerardo, who had been dozing by the fire, listening to the familiar conversation, thought back, as he often did, to the days when he was young and fit. He opened his eyes and looked lovingly at Aurelia... her fair hair greying, her hands a little rough from farm work, but her eyes still the colour of the Madonna's dress.

Sleepily, he fingered the ruby ring he wore round his neck and a vision of the beautiful Berta floated into his mind. He thought of her as she lay dying, her hair fanned out around her like a halo of fire, and a tear rolled down his weathered cheek.

LETTER FROM DEBBIE

Thanks for choosing *The Girl with Emerald Eyes* - I hope you enjoyed it!

It was both a huge pleasure and a major commitment writing this book. I'm the daughter of two architects so it was especially important that I got the architectural detail right. I was also determined to get the historical backdrop as accurate as possible; there's nothing worse than finding anachronistic anomalies in a historical novel. But the major issues with this book were the same as for any novel: does the story grab you, and did you love the characters?

Berta di Bernardo was a real person but very little is known about her, so I had carte blanche to create a character from scratch. Funnily enough, her personality took shape in my imagination very quickly. A woman who had the money and the determination to see such an historic building created was bound to be quite a strong personality. That she was beautiful - in a very Tuscan way - was a given. The other elements of her character, such as her enormous pragmatism, also seemed very clear to me. Maybe I secretly wish I could be like her! My modern character Sam was harder to find - which is odd because I had experienced much of her 'journey' myself - when my dear husband also had a stroke in Pisa whilst making a documentary about the Tower. The rest of Sam's story however is just that - a story!

I'd be really delighted if you could find the time to write a review of the book in order that others coming after you have some idea what it's about. I'm a debut novelist so it's important that readers give me feedback! I'm already hard at work on my next novel and I hope you might take a moment to look at that and read it when it comes out.

Thanks again and if you want to keep up to date on future projects, or take a look at some of the inspirational images I used whilst I was writing *The Girl with Emerald Eyes* then go to my website: www.debbierix.com, or follow me on twitter @debbierix.

POSTSCRIPT

It may be helpful to the reader to understand how much of this story is based on fact. Historical novels are always rooted in real events and often feature real people, but the novelist is at liberty to mix the real with the fantasy, and it can be frustrating to find yourself wondering what is fact and what is fiction.

All of the modern characters are, of course, fiction, except one. I occasionally refer to Professor John Burland of Imperial College in London. He is one of Britain's leading civil engineers, and in the 1990s was widely credited as having stabilised the Leaning Tower, 'saving it for the next 300 years'.

Of the medieval figures, Berta di Bernardo was a real historical figure. We know nothing about her beyond what is contained in her will, dated 5th June, 1172. In it, she is described as a 'widow' and a faithful servant ('*devota*') of the *Opera della Primaziale di Pisa,* the organisation in charge of the three magnificent ecclesiastical buildings whose construction began in the eleventh century in the *Campo* ('large field') just inside Pisa's city walls. Written almost entirely in ecclesiastical Latin, the will says that she wishes to bequeath *solidos sexaginta* ('60 coins') specifically 'for the stones of the *campanile*', the building now known as the Leaning Tower. The will also tells us that, at the time of its drafting, she was living in premises owned by the Opera, and thus overlooking the Piazza del Duomo. She would presumably have ended her days there.

That her legacy was not only substantial, but also that she was a substantial figure in her own right, can be inferred from the fact that the chief witness to the will was no less than the notary of the Emperor Frederico himself, a man called Ugoni Belacto (sometimes referred to as Ugo). The will also contains signatures of four other witnesses, including that of Gerardo di Gerardo.

Who was Gerardo? Documents deep in the Opera's archives list Gerardo as a *lapicida*, a master mason. He is also recorded as being Deotisalvi's assistant. A *lapicida* is today's equivalent of a Clerk of Works, thus ranking significantly below an architect.

So there's something odd here. Why was Gerardo asked to be a witness at the will-signing ceremony of such a distinguished figure as Berta di Bernardo? This was the starting point for the novel.

All the other individuals I have described as connected with Berta are fictitious. She did have a husband called Calvo, but it is mere guesswork that he was a maritime trader – although that was how most wealthy Pisans made their money.

The rest of the medieval characters, however, are real historical figures, with known occupations: chief among these are Benetto Vernacci, the *Operaio,* or Rector of the Opera; Deotisalvi, the architect; and Bonanno Pisano, the architect/sculptor.

It was Deotisalvi who designed the splendid rotund Baptistery (the second building to be constructed on the Campo after the Duomo, the cathedral) as well as the church of San Sepulcro and the Tower of San Nicola – making him a major architectural VIP of the day. Almost as famous was Bonanno Pisano, who designed the magnificent bronze doors of the Duomo. These authorships are well established, partly through contemporary documents, but also because it as was customary for architects and sculptors to sign their work *in situ.* You can still see the names of Deotisalvi and Bonanno engraved on their creations today.

However, there is no signature on the Leaning Tower; what's more, the Tower's designer is not named in any original documents. So who was the architect of this immensely celebrated building?

Over the centuries, scholars have debated about his (obviously 'his'!) identity. A number of candidates have been suggested, including Gerardo, Bonanno Pisano and Deotisalvi. The latter is the current favourite, but the question remains: why did such a great man choose not to put his name to the Tower?

Although there are theories, nobody has come up with a satisfactory explanation.

So the Leaning Tower of Pisa is an enigma. Here stands a remarkable construction, whose unique imperfection has made it the world's most recognisable building, whose grace and elegance has few equals, and which attracts over a million awed visitors a year. But nobody really knows who designed it.

TIMELINE

1063 – Pisa raided Palermo, the capital of Saracen Sicily, and made off with galley-loads of precious cargo which funds the building of the Duomo.

1064 – Building work on the Duomo was started by architect Buscheto di Giovanni Guidice.

1081 – Holy Roman Emperor Henry IV grants Pisa full independence as a commune– the Pisan Republic is born.

1095 – Pisa participated in the First Crusade, with a Pisan the first to scale the walls of Jerusalem.

1111 – Pisa concludes a treaty with Byzantium, gaining free transit for Pisan trade in the Holy Land.

1118 – The Duomo was consecrated by Pope Gelasius II.

1153 – Work began on the Baptistery; designed by architect Deotisalvi.

1171 - Work ceases on the Baptistery due to lack of funds

1172 – On January 5, Berta di Bernardo, a widow and resident of the house of *dell'Opera di Santa Maria*, bequeathed *solidos sexaginta* or 'sixty coins' to the *Opera Campani-*

lis petrarum Sancte Marie. This money was to be used toward the purchase of a few stones which still form the base of the bell tower today. The legacy is witnessed by builder Gerardo di Gerardo.

1173 – August 9th: The first stones are laid on the Campanile. Records are unclear as to the architect's identity, but possible contenders include Deotisalvi, who also designed the Baptistery, or Bonanno Pisano who was a well-known sculptor. However, modern scholars believe Deotisalvi the likeliest contender.

1178 – Work stops on the tower when it reaches only four storeys. It has already begun to lean.

1250 – Work starts again on the Baptistery.

1272 – Work on the tower begins, now led by Giovanni di Simone and Andrea di Pisano

1278 – Work comes to a halt once again, with the tower at seven storeys.

1350 – The Baptistery is completed.

1370 – The tower is officially completed – leaning 1.6 degrees from the vertical. Over the years the Leaning Tower becomes a worldwide tourist attraction.

1589 – Galileo, a young professor at University of Pisa, conducts experiments on falling objects, using the tower.

1838 – The Leaning Tower has become an international tourist attraction; work is done to clear the base for visitors, but this opens up an underground spring, causing the Tower to lean further.

1934 – The Tower, now tilting at the rate of about half an inch every ten years, has concrete injected into its foundations... but the lean continues.

1990 – After a medieval bell tower at Pavia collapses, the more famous Tower ofPisa is closed to the public and the bells silenced. British Professor of Soil Mechanics, John Burland, offers his 'soil extraction' technique to correct the lean.

1995 – One summer night, subsequently dubbed 'Black September', the tower nearly collapses while stabilising cables are installed.

1987 – The Piazza del Duomo, including the Tower, is declared a World Heritage site.

1999 – After years of bureaucratic delay, English Professor of Engineering John Burland is allowed to proceed with his 'soil extraction' technique. The Tower slowly starts to tilt backwards, the lean being halted at 3.9 metres from the vertical - a position which will remain stable "for the next 300 years."

2001 – June 16th: Official ceremonial opening. - December 15 Public opening.

Printed in Great Britain
by Amazon